Christian Jacq is one of France's leading Egyptologists. He is the author of the internationally bestselling *Ramses* series, which has been translated into twenty-four languages and sold more than six million copies worldwide. He is also the author of the stand-alone novel *The Black Pharaoh.*

Also by Christian Jacq:

*Ramses: The Son of the Light*
*Ramses: The Temple of a Million Years*
*Ramses: The Battle of Kadesh*
*Ramses: The Lady of Abu Simbel*
*Ramses: Under the Western Acacia*
*The Black Pharaoh*
*The Living Wisdom of Ancient Egypt*

***About the translator***

Sue Dyson is a prolific author of both fiction and non-fiction, including over thirty novels, both contemporary and historical. She has also translated a wide variety of French fiction.

# The Stone of Light

## Nefer the Silent

Christian Jacq

Translated by Sue Dyson

SIMON & SCHUSTER
A VIACOM COMPANY

First published in Great Britain by Simon & Schuster UK Ltd, 2000
A Viacom company



1 3 5 7 9 10 8 6 4 2

Simon & Schuster UK Ltd
Africa House
64-78 Kingsway
London WC2B 6AH

Simon & Schuster Australia
Sydney

A CIP catalogue record for this book is available from the British Library

HB ISBN 0-684-86627-7
TPB ISBN 0-684-86628-5



Printed and bound in Great Britain by
The Bath Press, Bath

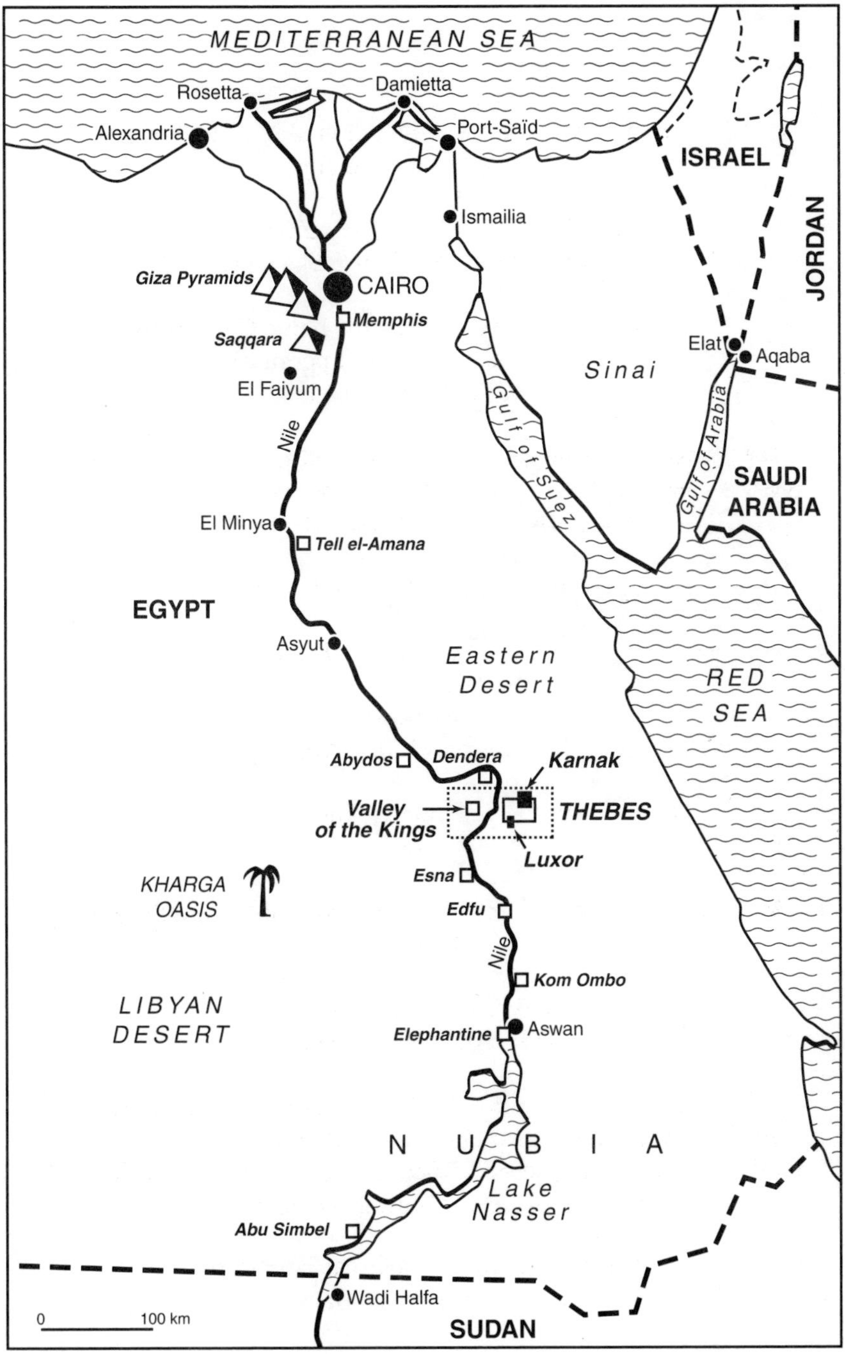
MEDITERRANEAN SEA
Rosetta
Damietta
Alexandria
Port-Saïd
Ismailia
ISRAEL
JORDAN
Giza Pyramids
CAIRO
Memphis
Saqqara
Elat
Aqaba
Sinai
El Faiyum
Gulf of Suez
Gulf of Arabia
Nile
SAUDI ARABIA
El Minya
Tell el-Amana
EGYPT
Asyut
Eastern Desert
RED SEA
Abydos
Dendera
Karnak
Valley of the Kings
THEBES
Luxor
KHARGA OASIS
Esna
Edfu
Nile
Kom Ombo
LIBYAN DESERT
Elephantine
Aswan
N U B I A
Lake Nasser
Abu Simbel
Wadi Halfa
0
100 km
SUDAN

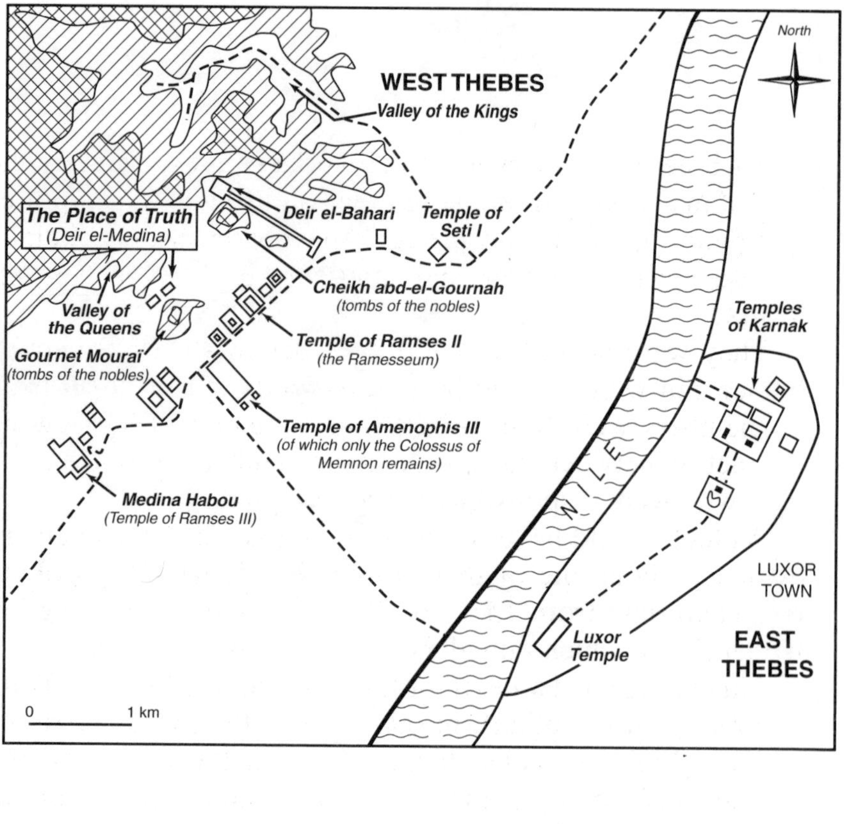

North
WEST THEBES
Valley of the Kings
The Place of Truth
(Deir el-Medina)
Deir el-Bahari
Temple of
Seti I
Cheikh abd-el-Gournah
(tombs of the nobles)
Valley of
the Queens
Gournet Mouraï
(tombs of the nobles)
Temple of Ramses II
(the Ramesseum)
Temple of Amenophis III
(of which only the Colossus of
Memnon remains)
Medina Habou
(Temple of Ramses III)
NILE
Temples
of Karnak
LUXOR
TOWN
Luxor
Temple
EAST
THEBES
0
1 km

# Foreword

The whole world marvels at the works of art created by the Egyptians, from pyramids, temples and tombs to sculptures and paintings. But who brought these wonders into being? Whose spiritual power and magic is it that touches our hearts?

They were never the work of hordes of slaves or captive labour, but were created by brotherhoods whose select band of members were both priests and craftsmen. They saw no distinction between the spirit and the hand, and formed a true elite who were responsible directly to Pharaoh.

As luck would have it, we possess abundant documentary evidence about one of these brotherhoods which, for about five centuries (from 1550 to 1070 BC), lived in a village in Upper Egypt which outsiders were forbidden to enter.

This village had an extraordinary name, the Place of Truth (*set Ma'at* in Egyptian), in other words the place where the goddess Ma'at revealed herself through the righteousness, justice and harmony of the work carried out by generations of 'Servants of the Place of Truth'.

Situated in the desert, not far from the cultivated area alongside the Nile, the village was enclosed by high walls, had its own court, its own temple and its own burial ground; the craftsmen and their families lived there and enjoyed special status, owing to the importance of their primary mission: to create Houses of Eternity for the pharaohs in the Valley of the Kings.

Even today, it is still possible to see the remains of the Place of Truth by visiting the site of Deir el-Medina, on the western bank of Thebes; the foundations of the houses are intact, and you can explore the narrow streets that the master-builders, painters, sculptors and priestesses of the goddess Hathor walked along. Shrines, premises belonging to the brotherhood and wonderfully decorated tombs emphasised the sacred nature of the place, which was also provided with reserves of water, granaries, workshops and even a school.

I have tried to bring these exceptional people to life, along with their adventures, their daily lives, and their quest for beauty and spirituality, in a world which sometimes proved hostile and envious. Safeguarding the very existence of the Place of Truth was not always easy, and there were many dangers of all kinds, notably during the unsettled period in which this story takes place.

I should like to dedicate this novel to all the craftsmen of the Place of Truth, who were guardians of the secrets of the 'House of Gold', and succeeded in passing them on in their work.

# Prologue

Around midnight, in the light of the full moon, nine craftsmen left the Place of Truth and began to climb up a narrow path, guided by their overseer.

A hill overlooked the Place of Truth, the desert village where Pharaoh's builders lived, encircled by walls which guarded their secrets from prying eyes. Hidden on the summit, behind a block of limestone, Mehy stifled a cry of delight.

For several months, the charioteer officer had been trying to glean information about this brotherhood, whose task was to excavate and decorate the tombs in the Valley of the Kings and the Valley of the Queens. But nobody knew anything, with the exception of Ramses the Great, protector of the Place of Truth, where masterbuilders, stone-cutters, sculptors and painters were initiated into trades which were essential for Egypt's survival. The artisans' village had its own government, its own legal system, and was responsible directly to the king and his most senior minister, the tjaty.

Mehy should have concentrated solely on his military career, which promised to be brilliant. But he could never forget that he had applied to join the brotherhood and had been rejected – a noble of his high birth should not have been scorned like that. In his disappointment, Mehy had directed his ambitions towards the elite corps of charioteers. There his talent had been recognised immediately, and as a result he had risen swiftly to an important place in the military hierarchy.

Hatred had blossomed in his heart, a hatred which grew with every day that passed, every time he encountered that accursed brotherhood which had humiliated him and whose very existence prevented him from knowing perfect happiness.

So Mehy had taken a decision: either he would discover all the secrets of the Place of Truth and use them to his advantage, or he would destroy this apparently inaccessible settlement, which was so proud of its privileges.

To achieve this, he must make no mistakes and arouse no suspicions. In recent days, he had experienced twinges of doubt. But 'the Servants of the Place of Truth', to give them their official title, were nothing but contemptible braggarts, whose pretended powers were no more than mirages and illusions. And as for the closely guarded Valley of the Kings, surely all it preserved was the corpses of monarchs, frozen in the immobility of death.

By hiding himself in the hills which overlooked the forbidden village, Mehy had hoped to spy upon the rites which no one spoke of; his disappointment had been in proportion to the effort he had expended.

But tonight, at last, it had happened! The event he had been waiting for for so long.

One behind the other, the craftsmen climbed up to the crest of the western hill and walked slowly along the cliff until they reached the pass, where stone huts had been built to house them at certain times of the year. From there, all they had to do was follow the path that led down into the Valley of the Kings.

Despite his feverish excitement, Mehy took care not to dislodge any loose stones which might roll down and betray his presence. He knew the locations of all the observation posts, but nevertheless he was risking his life. The posts were manned by armed guards whose duty was to ensure the security of the forbidden valley, and the archers had orders to shoot on sight and without warning.

At the entrance to this most sacred of places, where the pharaohs' mummified bodies had been interred since the beginning of the New Empire, the guards stepped aside to allow the ten Servants of the Place of Truth to pass.

Mehy's heart was pounding as he climbed the steep slope. If he lay on his belly on a flat rock, so that he could see without being seen, he would not miss a single detail of the incredible spectacle.

The overseer stepped away from the group. Turning his attention to the burden he had carried since they left the village, he laid it on the ground, before the entrance to the tomb of Ramses the Great, and removed the white cloth that covered it.

A stone.

A simple stone, hewn into the shape of a cube. Light sprang forth from it, a light so powerful that it lit up the monumental gateway to Pharaoh's House of Eternity. The sun shone in the night, darkness was driven away.

For a long time the ten craftsmen paid homage to the stone, then the overseer picked it up again and held it while two of his subordinates opened the door to the tomb. He entered first, the other craftsmen followed, and the procession vanished from sight, the dark depths lit up by the stone.

Mehy remained utterly dumbstruck for several minutes. No, he had not been dreaming. The brotherhood did indeed possess fabulous treasures. They knew the secret of the light: he had seen the stone from which it came, a stone which was neither an illusion nor a legend. Human beings, and not gods, had fashioned it and knew how to use it. And what about the persistent rumours that they were producing piles of gold in their workshops?

Undreamt-of horizons were opening up before him. He now knew that the origin of Ramses the Great's prodigious fortune was right here, in the Place of Truth. That was why the brotherhood lived apart from the world, hidden behind the walls of their village.

'What are you doing here, fellow?'

Mehy turned round slowly and saw a Nubian guard armed with a cudgel and a dagger.

'I . . . I'm lost.'

'This area is forbidden,' said the guard. 'Who are you?'

'I belong to the king's personal guard and I'm on a special mission,' declared Mehy with a flourish.

'No one told me anything about this.'

'They wouldn't have. No one was to know about it.'

'Why not?'

'Because I have to check that the security measures are being applied with the necessary rigour and that no intruder can get into the Valley of the Kings. Well done, guard. You've just demonstrated that the current system is effective.'

The Nubian looked puzzled. 'All the same, my commander should have warned me.'

'Can't you see that that was impossible?'

'We'll go and see him. I can't just let you go.'

'You are doing your job perfectly.'

Under the light of the full moon, Mehy's conciliatory smile reassured the Nubian and he slipped his cudgel through his belt.

As swiftly as a sand-viper, Mehy charged head-first and struck the guard full in the chest. The unfortunate man staggered backwards and tumbled down the slope, coming to rest on a ledge overlooking the Valley.

At the risk of breaking his neck, Mehy climbed down after him and saw that, in spite of a deep wound on his forehead, the man was still alive. Mehy paid no heed to his victim's pleading gaze; he picked up a pointed stone and finished him off with a crushing blow to the skull.

The cold-hearted assassin waited for a few long moments. When he was certain he had not been spotted, he climbed back to the top of the hill, taking great care to find secure hand-holds. Taking even greater precautions than before, he walked away from the forbidden place.

Thanks to this wonderful night, he now had only one idea in his head: to decipher the mystery of the Place of Truth. But how could he achieve that on his own? Since he could not enter the village, he would have to find a means of obtaining reliable information.

The murderer foresaw a splendid future. The secrets and riches of the brotherhood would belong to him, and him alone!

# 1

Life was so monotonous. Ploughing immediately after the annual Nile flood, sowing, reaping and harvesting, stocking up the granaries, watching out for locusts, rodents and hippos which might lay waste the fields. Then there was irrigation, looking after your tools, plaiting ropes at night instead of sleeping, watching over the flocks and the teams, not to mention forever worrying about your piece of land and never thinking of anything beyond the quality of the wheat and the state of your cows' health . . . Yes, it was utterly monotonous, and Ardent could stand it no longer.

The young man was sitting under a sycamore tree, where the fields met the desert. It offered him plenty of shade, but he was unable to get off to sleep and enjoy a well-deserved rest before heading to the family pastures to tend the oxen. At sixteen, Ardent was over three and a half cubits tall and built like a giant; and he had no desire to settle for the life of a peasant, as his father, grandfather and great-grandfather had done.

Just as he did every day, he had come to this quiet spot and, using a little piece of wood he had whittled, had drawn animals in the sand. Drawing. He would have loved to draw for hours on end, then add colour and recreate a donkey, a dog and a thousand other creatures.

Ardent had great powers of observation. What he saw

entered his heart, which then gave orders to his hand – though his hand was completely free to trace the contours of an image which seemed more alive than everyday reality. What the young boy really needed were papyrus, styli and pigments. But his father was a farmer, and had laughed in his face when the young lad told him what he wanted.

There was only one place where Ardent could find everything he desired: the Place of Truth. Nobody knew what went on inside the walled village, but those walls enclosed the greatest painters and illustrators in the kingdom, those who were authorised to decorate Pharaoh's tomb.

A peasant's son had no chance of entering that fabled brotherhood. Yet the young man could not help dreaming of the happiness of those who could devote themselves wholly to their vocation, forgetting the meanness of daily life.

'Well, Ardent, having a rest, are we?'

The voice, heavy with irony, belonged to a lad of about twenty named Hayseed. He was tall and muscular, and dressed only in a short kilt of plaited rushes. By his side stood his younger brother, Fat-Legs, a stupid smile on his face. At fifteen, Fat-Legs was much heavier than Hayseed, because of all the cakes he gobbled every day.

'Leave me alone, you two,' said Ardent.

'This place doesn't belong to you,' said Hayseed. 'We've a right to come here.'

'I don't want to see you.'

'Ah, but we want to see you. And you've got some explaining to do.'

'What about?'

'As if you didn't know!' said Hayseed. 'Where were you last night?'

'Who do you think you are, a policeman?'

'Does the name Nati mean anything to you?' demanded Hayseed.

Ardent smiled. 'It certainly does.'

Hayseed took a step towards him. 'You filthy swine! She's betrothed to me, and last night, you . . . you *dared*—'

'It wasn't my idea. Nati came looking for me.'

'You're lying!'

Ardent got to his feet. 'I don't let anyone call me a liar.'

'Because of you, my bride won't be a virgin.'

'So what? If she has any sense, Nati won't marry you at all.'

Hayseed and Fat-Legs produced a leather whip. It was a rough and ready weapon, but a formidable one.

'Let's leave it there,' suggested Ardent. 'Nati and I spent a pleasant moment together, it's true, but that's just nature, isn't it? As a gesture of goodwill, I agree not to see her again – to be frank, I shan't miss her.'

'We're going to spoil your looks,' announced Hayseed. 'With your new face, you won't be seducing any more girls.'

'I'd quite enjoy correcting two imbeciles, but it's hot, and I'd rather finish my siesta.'

Raising his right arm, Fat-Legs threw himself at Ardent. Suddenly, his target disappeared from in front of him and he was lifted up and flung into the air; he fell back down again head first, and crumpled against the trunk of the sycamore, unconscious and unmoving.

Hayseed was rooted to the spot for a moment; then he reacted. He lashed the whip through the air, intending to slice Ardent's face open, but the young giant parried the blow with his arm. An ugly cracking noise put an end to the short struggle. Hayseed dropped the whip and fled, howling with the pain of a dislocated shoulder.

There was not even a drop of sweat on Ardent's brow. Since the age of five he had been used to fighting, and he had taken some real drubbings before learning the winning moves. He never provoked a fight but, confident in his strength, he never walked away from one, either. Life did not hand out gifts, and neither did he.

The thought of spending the afternoon in the pasture and then returning home like a good boy, bearing milk and firewood, made Ardent feel sick.

Tomorrow would be even worse than today, even duller, even more boring, and the young man would continue to lose heart, as if his blood was slowly draining away. What did his family's little farm mean to him? His father dreamt of ripe corn and milch cows, the neighbours envied him his success, the girls already saw Ardent as his father's lucky heir who, thanks to his great strength, would double production and become rich. They dreamt of marrying a wealthy peasant and having lots of children, thus ensuring a happy old age.

Thousands were content with that destiny, but not Ardent. On the contrary, to him it seemed more oppressive than the walls of a prison. Abandoning the cattle, which would be perfectly all right without him, the young man set off into the desert, his gaze fixed on the Peak of the West. It loomed over Thebes, the fantastically rich city of the god Amon, where the sacred precinct of Karnak had been built to house numerous temples.

On the west bank were the valleys of the kings, queens and nobles, which had welcomed the tombs of these illustrious people, and also the pharaohs' houses of eternity, including the Temple of a Million Years built by Ramses. The craftsmen of the Place of Truth had created wonders – people said they had worked hand in hand with the gods, and under their protection.

In the secret heart of Karnak, as in the humblest shrine, the gods and goddesses spoke, but who truly understood their message? As for Ardent, he deciphered the world by drawing in the sand, but he lacked the knowledge to progress further.

He could not accept this injustice. Why did the goddess hidden in the Peak of the West speak to the craftsmen of the Place of Truth, yet remain silent when he begged her to answer his call? The sun-beaten mountain abandoned him to his loneliness, and his young, pleasure-hungry mistresses could never understand his aspirations.

As a kind of revenge, he drew the mountain in the sand as accurately as he could, then angrily kicked the drawing apart, as if in one fell swoop he was wiping out both the silent goddess and his own frustration.

But the Peak of the West remained intact, imposing and impenetrable. And, despite his physical power, Ardent felt laughably insignificant. No, things could not go on like this.

This time, his father must listen to him.

# 2

Sobek had left his far-off native Nubia at the age of seventeen, and enlisted in the Egyptian police. He was tall, athletic and skilled with the cudgel, and the black man with the confident bearing had made a deep impression on his superiors. A period of training in the desert police had allowed him to prove his abilities: he had arrested no fewer than twenty Bedouin looters, three of them particularly dangerous men who specialised in attacking caravans.

Sobek's promotion had been rapid: at twenty-three, he had just been appointed head of the forces that guarded the Place of Truth. In fact, the post was hardly sought-after, because of the responsibilities it entailed; the incumbent could not afford to make mistakes. No outsider was permitted to enter the Valley of the Kings, no curious person allowed to disturb the serenity of the craftsmen's village. It was Sobek's job to prevent any incidents, on pain of immediate punishment by the tjaty.

The Nubian occupied a small office in one of the small forts that controlled access to the Place of Truth. Although he could read and write, he had no taste for paperwork and filing reports, which he left to his subordinates. A low table and three stools made up the essential furnishings provided by the government, which also took responsibility for the upkeep of the place and whitewashing the walls.

Sobek spent most of his time out in the field, even when the sun was at its fiercest, patrolling the hills that overlooked the forbidden sites. He knew every path, every crest, every slope, and never stopped exploring them. Anyone discovered where he should not be was arrested and interrogated ruthlessly, then transferred to the west bank where the tjaty's court sentenced him to a severe punishment.

At seven in the morning, the Nubian began receiving reports from the watchmen who had been on guard during the night. Usually, when asked, 'Anything to report?' they replied, 'Nothing, sir,' and went off to bed. But on this particular morning, the first watchman could not conceal his unease.

'There is a small problem, sir.'

'What do you mean?'

'One of our men was killed during the night.'

Sobek was worried. 'Was he attacked?'

'No, sir,' said the watchman, 'nothing like that. If he had been, we'd have caught the guilty party. Do you want to see the body?'

Sobek left his office and went to examine the remains of the unfortunate man.

'Crushed skull, and an injury to the forehead,' he observed.

'Hardly surprising, after a fall like that,' opined the guard. 'It was his first night on watch, and he didn't know that area well. He must have slipped on the scree and fallen down the slope. It's not the first time it's happened and it won't be the last.'

Sobek questioned the other sentries: none had seen an intruder. On the basis of the evidence, this looked like just a nasty accident.

Ardent's father was sitting on a mat on the floor of their house, weaving papyrus fibre into a rope. 'What are you doing here?' he demanded. 'You should be out in the fields.'

'I've finished with all that, father.'

'What do you mean?'

'I don't want to inherit the farm.'

The farmer put down his papyrus rope and raised disbelieving eyes to his son. 'Have you gone mad?'

'Farming bores me.'

'So you've said a hundred times. Well, we can't all spend our time having fun. I never had peculiar ideas like yours. I've been content to work hard to feed my family. I've made your mother happy, I've brought up you and your three sisters, and I've become the owner of this farm and a large piece of land. Doesn't that count as success? When I die, you'll be well off, and you'll thank me for that for the rest of your life. This year has been an excellent one and the gods have been kind. The harvest will be huge, but we shan't have to pay high taxes, because the authorities have given me permission to pay in instalments. Surely you don't want to destroy all that?'

'I want to build my own life,' said Ardent resolutely.

'That sounds very grand, but cows can't eat fine phrases.'

'The cows will graze perfectly all right without me, and you'll have no difficulty finding a replacement.'

Ardent's father was so upset that his voice shook. 'What's happening to you, my son?'

'I want to draw and paint.'

'But that's impossible – you're a peasant and the son of a peasant. Why set your heart on what you can't have?'

'Because it is my destiny.'

'Be careful,' said his father. 'There's a dangerous fire burning in you. If you don't put it out, it'll destroy you.'

Ardent smiled sadly. 'You're wrong, father.'

The farmer seized an onion and bit into it. 'What do you really want?'

'To join the brotherhood of the Place of Truth.'

'You're mad!' said his father with conviction.

'Do you think I can't do it?'

'Can, can't – what do I know? But it's madness anyway. And you have no idea what a miserable life those craftsmen lead! They're sworn to secrecy, deprived of their liberty, forced to obey pitiless masters . . . The stone-cutters' arms get so tired they feel broken, their legs and backs ache, they almost die of exhaustion! And what about the sculptors? Handling a chisel is far more backbreaking than jabbing at the soil with a hoe. At night, they have to keep on working by lamplight and they never have a rest day.'

'You seem to know an awful lot about the Place of Truth,' said Ardent.

'It's what people say. Why shouldn't I believe it?'

'Because rumours are usually lies.'

'Don't you try to teach me morality, my lad! If you follow my advice, you'll do all right. But how could a headstrong boy like you put up with all those rules and regulations? Two seconds' discipline, and you'd be up in arms. Be a peasant, like me, like your ancestors, and you'll be happy in the end. You'll calm down as you get older, and laugh about this childish rebelliousness.'

'It's no good, father, you'll never understand. It's pointless talking about it any more.'

The farmer flung his onion away. 'Right, that's enough. You're my son and you'll obey me – or else!'

'Goodbye.' Ardent turned to leave.

His father seized the wooden handle of a gardening-tool and hit him on the back.

The young man slowly turned round.

What the farmer saw in Ardent's eyes frightened him, and he backed away towards the wall.

A little woman with a lined face sprang out of the store-room where she had been hiding, and clutched her son's right arm. 'Don't hit your father, I beg of you!'

Ardent planted a kiss on her forehead. 'You don't understand me either, mother, but I don't blame you for it. Don't worry, I shan't hurt him. I'm going away and I'm not coming back.'

'If you leave this house,' his father warned him, 'I'll disinherit you.'

'That is your right.'

'You'll end up with nothing.'

'I don't care.'

Ardent stepped out through the front door of the family home; he knew he would never return.

As he set off down the track, which ran along the edge of a wheatfield, the young man breathed in deeply. A new world was opening up before him.

# 3

Ardent left the farming area and headed towards the Place of Truth. Neither the sun's scorching rays nor the waterless desert frightened him. And the young man wanted to clear his mind of what had happened: if he knocked at the village gate, it just might open.

This late in the afternoon, there was no one on the track, which had been trodden down by the hooves of the donkeys that passed to and fro each day, taking the brothers water, food and everything else they needed to work 'far from the eyes and ears of the world'.

Ardent loved the desert. He relished its implacable power, felt its spirit vibrate in unison with his own, and could walk across it for whole days without feeling tired, revelling in the contact between his bare feet and the burning sand.

But this time he did not get very far. The first of the five forts which guarded the Place of Truth barred his way. As Ardent had spotted sentries, who were following his every movement, he walked straight up to the fort. He might as well confront the guards and find out what he could expect.

Two archers came out of the watchtower. Ardent kept going, his arms hanging down by his sides to show that he was not armed.

'Halt!'

The young man stopped in his tracks.

The elder of the two archers, a Nubian, came towards him. The other took up position to one side, drew his bow and took aim.

'Who are you?' asked the Nubian.

'My name is Ardent, and I wish to knock at the door of the brotherhood of the Place of Truth.'

'Have you got a permit?'

'No.'

'Who recommended you?'

'Nobody.'

The Nubian frowned. 'Are you making fun of me, boy?'

'I can draw and I want to work in the Place of Truth.'

'This area is forbidden, you ought to know that.'

'I want to meet a master craftsman and show him what I can do.'

'I've got my orders. Off you go – *now* – or I'll arrest you for disturbing the peace.'

'I don't mean any harm. Please, just give me a chance.'

'Clear off!'

Ardent glanced towards the surrounding hills.

'And don't even think about trying to sneak in that way,' the Nubian warned him. 'You'd be shot on sight.'

Ardent could have knocked the man out with one punch, thrown himself to the ground to avoid the second guard's arrow, then tried to force his way through. But he didn't know how many other archers he'd have to fight to reach the village gate.

Dejectedly, he retraced his steps.

As soon as he was out of sight of the sentries, he sat down on a rock. He decided to watch everything that happened on the path. By doing so, he was sure, he'd find a way of succeeding.

Ardent's mother wept for hours, and her daughters were unable to console her. His father had had to take on three young peasant boys to replace the young giant. Still furious with his son – his anger had not abated even a little – he had gone to see the public scribe and dictated a letter to the tjaty's office. Announcing his decision in implacable, unambiguous terms, the farmer decreed – as the law permitted – that he was disinheriting Ardent and that all his possessions were to go to his wife, who would dispose of them as she saw fit. If she died before he did, their three daughters would inherit equal shares.

But settling the provisions of his will was not enough for the scorned and humiliated farmer. Ardent had gone mad, and must be brought back to sanity. The best way of doing that was through force, exerted by an unassailable authority.

So the farmer went to see the man responsible for compulsory work, a pernickety scribe who was ill-tempered and increasingly bitter. He held a difficult, unsatisfying post, and had schemed in vain to obtain promotion and work in the town, on the east bank. Here, during the months preceding the Nile flood, he had the task of taking on labourers to clean out the canals and repair the dykes, while paying the lowest wage possible. As volunteers were few and far between, it had been necessary to decree that the work was compulsory and convince the landowners to allow him a certain number of agricultural workers, whose brief absence would be compensated for by a lowering of taxes. The discussions had been long, difficult and tiring.

When the scribe saw Ardent's father come into his office, he expected another string of moans and complaints, which he would reject in their entirety, as usual.

'I don't want to bother you,' began the farmer. 'I've come to ask for your help.'

'Out of the question,' retorted the official. 'The law is the law, and I cannot give you any privileges, even though we have known each other for many a long year. If one single landowner gets away with challenging the compulsory-work decree, the benefits of the flood will be lost and Egypt will be ruined.'

'I'm not challenging anything. I just want to talk to you about my son, Ardent.'

'Ardent? But he's exempt from compulsory work.'

'He has just left the farm.'

'Where has he gone?'

'I've no idea. He thinks he's an artist – the poor boy has lost his mind.'

'Do you mean he's no longer taking care of the farm and the pastureland?'

'Unfortunately, yes.'

'That certainly is madness!'

'His mother and I were distraught, but we couldn't stop him leaving.'

'You should have given him a good thrashing. That would soon have sorted things out.'

The farmer hung his head. 'I tried, but Ardent is so big – almost a giant. And the young ruffian threatened me – I thought he was going to hit me.'

'A son hitting his father!' exclaimed the scribe. 'He must be dragged before a court and sentenced.'

'I have a better idea.'

'I'm listening.'

'Since he is no longer really my son, and since he has left my house, why should he go on being exempt from compulsory work?'

The scribe smiled. 'I'll conscript him. You can count on me.'

'We could do even more.'

'I don't understand.'

The farmer lowered his voice to a whisper. 'The villain needs a good lesson, don't you think? If we punish him severely, it'll be a warning to him not to do anything seriously wrong or stupid. If we don't act now, you and I might be held responsible in future . . .'

The scribe did not take the argument lightly. 'What do you suggest?'

'Suppose you conscript Ardent for obligatory work and he refuses to come? He'd then be classed as a deserter. You could imprison him with a few rough lads who would mete out a suitable punishment.'

'Yes, I could do that. But what are you offering me in exchange?'

'A milch cow.'

The scribe's mouth watered with satisfaction. A small fortune in exchange for a simple task.

'Agreed,' he said.

'I'll throw in a few sacks of grain, of course. Don't damage Ardent too much. He has to come back to work on the farm.'

# 4

A moist snout touched Ardent's forehead and his eyes shot open.

A bitch with a coat the colour of ochre was sniffing the intruder, but with no trace of hostility. The sun had not yet risen, and a cool breeze was blowing across the western bank of Thebes and the track leading to the Place of Truth.

The young man stroked the dog until she ran off, alerted by the sound of hooves. Led by a grey with a measured step, a hundred or so donkeys laden with food were coming along the track towards the craftsmen's village. The lead donkey knew the track perfectly, and led the way with confidence.

Longingly, Ardent watched them pass. Like him, they knew where they were going, but they would get past the obstacle of the forts.

A little way behind the donkeys came fifty or so water-carriers. In their right hands, they carried sticks to beat out a rhythm and to drive off snakes; on each man's left shoulder was balanced a long, solid log, on the end of which hung a fat goatskin of water.

The yellow-coated bitch left Ardent to walk beside her master, an old man who was struggling under his load.

The young man joined him. 'May I help you?'

'This is my work, boy. I don't earn much, just enough to

live on until I go back home to the Delta. If you help me, I can't pay you.'

'That doesn't matter.'

On Ardent's shoulder, the burden seemed as light as a feather from the god Amon's sacred goose.

'Do you do this every day?' he asked.

'Yes, boy. The craftsmen who live in the Place of Truth must lack for nothing, especially not water. After the first delivery of the morning, which is the largest and most important, there are several others, all through the day. If the need increases for one reason or another, we increase the number of carriers. We aren't the only people who supply the needs of the Place of Truth. There are washermen, bakers, brewers, butchers, metal-workers, wood-cutters, weavers, tanners and all sorts of others, too. Pharaoh demands that the craftsmen enjoy the most comfortable life possible.'

'Have you ever been inside the village?'

'No. As an approved water-carrier, I am allowed to go and empty the contents of my goatskin into the great pit, in front of the northern entrance; there is a second pit close to the southern wall. The inhabitants of the Place of Truth go there to fill their water-jars. I'm not allowed inside the walls.'

'Who is?'

'Only the members of the brotherhood. We suppliers and workers must stay outside. But why are you asking all these questions?'

'Because I want to enter the brotherhood and become an artist.'

'Well you won't do it by carrying water!' said the old man.

'I must knock at the main gate, meet a craftsman, explain to him that—'

'Don't count on it. Those people are neither talkative nor welcoming, and if you behave the way you are at the moment, they won't like it at all. The best you could hope for would be a few months in prison. And don't forget that the guards know every one of us water-carriers.'

'Have you ever talked to a member of the brotherhood?'

'Oh, just a word here and there, about the weather, or family matters.'

'They've never spoken to you about their work?'

'Those people are sworn to secrecy, boy, and they never break their oath. Anyone who couldn't hold his tongue would be expelled immediately.'

'All the same, they do take on new recruits.'

'Yes, but not very often. You'd best listen to me and forget your dreams. There are many better things to do than lock yourself away in the Place of Truth and work day and night for the glory of Pharaoh. If you think about it, it's not a very enviable life. With looks like yours, the girls must like you. Enjoy yourself for a few years, marry young, make fine children and find a good job, something less arduous than being a water-carrier.'

'Aren't there any women in the village?' asked Ardent.

'Yes, there are, and they have children, but they're bound by the rule of the Place of Truth, like the men. The most surprising thing is that they don't gossip more.'

'Have you seen them?'

'A few.'

'Are they pretty?'

'There are all sorts. But why do you ask?'

'If you've seen them, they must be allowed to leave the village,' said Ardent thoughtfully.

'All the inhabitants are. They move freely between the Place of Truth and the first of the forts. It's even said that they sometimes go to the eastern bank, but that's none of my business.

'So I might be able to meet a craftsman.'

'If you do, you'd better make sure he really does belong to the brotherhood – there are plenty of tricksters around. Anyway, he'd never agree to speak to you.'

'How many forts are there?'

'Five. They're also called the "Five Walls" – that's how many guard-posts there are. The guards watch anyone who approaches the village, and the system is effective, believe me. Even the hills are closely watched, especially since Sobek was appointed.'

'Who's Sobek?'

'The new commander. He's a pretty ruthless Nubian, who's determined to prove how good he is. Most of the guards belong to his tribe and obey him without question. In other words, it would be no use trying to bribe them. They're so afraid of him that they'd denounce you on the spot.'

Ardent had made up his mind: at all costs, he must get past the first of the forts and speak to someone from inside the village.

'If you say you're ill,' he suggested, 'and I'm a cousin who's come to help you carry the water, will the guards believe you?'

'We can try, but it won't get you far.'

When Ardent saw the guards at the first fort, he knew fate was on his side: the guard had just been changed, these weren't the same archers, and there was no risk of his being recognised.

'You don't look well,' said the black guard to the old water-carrier, who was leaning heavily on the young giant's arm.

'I'm worn out. That's why I've brought this lad along to help me.'

'Is he a relation?'

'One of my cousins.'

'Do you answer for him?'

'Soon I shall give up work, and he has offered to take my place.'

'You may go on to the second guard-post.'

A first victory! Ardent had been right to persevere. If luck continued to favour him, he was going to see the village at close hand and meet a craftsman who would understand his vocation.

The checks at the second fort were more meticulous than at the first, and at the third they were even more so, but the guards decided that the water-carrier was genuinely unwell. As the water had to be delivered, and no guard could leave his post to carry out this arduous task, the two men were allowed to pass.

The fourth check was a formality, but there was intense activity in front of the fifth and final watchtower. Labourers from the supply workforce were unloading their donkeys and sorting through baskets and jars of vegetables, dried fish, meat, fruit, oil and unguents. People were shouting at each other, telling each other off for moving too slowly, laughing, joking.

A guard signed to the water-carriers to come forward and empty the contents of their goatskins into an enormous jar. Ardent was filled with admiration when he saw it. What potter had been skilful enough to create such a gigantic vessel?

For the young man, this was the first visible miracle of the Place of Truth.

# 5

A thickset man called out to Ardent, 'You look amazed, my boy.'

'Who made that giant water-jar?'

'A potter who works at the Place of Truth.'

'How did he go about it?'

'You're very curious.'

Ardent's face lit up. Without a doubt, he was talking to one of the village craftsmen.

'No, it's not curiosity,' he said earnestly. 'I want to be an artist and enter the brotherhood.'

'Oh, I see. Come and tell me all about it.'

The thickset man led Ardent beyond the fifth and last fort, towards a row of workshops where sandal-makers, weavers and smiths were working. He invited him to sit down on a block of stone, at the foot of a rocky hillside.

'What do you know about the Place of Truth, my boy?'

'Nothing – or almost nothing. But I'm certain that that's where I belong.'

'Why?'

'My only passion is drawing. Shall I show you?'

'Can you draw my face in the sand?'

Looking keenly at his model, Ardent took a pointed flint and, very quickly, made an accurate sketch.

'There,' he said when he had finished. 'What do you think of it?'

'You seem gifted. Where did you learn?'

'Nowhere. I'm a farmer's son and I've always spent hours drawing what I saw. But I lack secret knowledge which is taught here, I'm sure of it. And I want to paint, to use colour to make my drawings live.'

'You're not short of ambition as well as talent,' said the man. 'But that may not be enough to get you into the Place of Truth.'

'What else do I need?'

'I'll take you to someone who should be able to solve all your problems.'

Ardent couldn't believe his ears. How right he had been to be audacious! In a few hours, he had passed from one world to another, and his dream was going to come true.

As they walked along the workshops outside the village, Ardent saw that the high village walls, though they looked impenetrable, were in fact very lightweight wooden constructions, which were easy to put up and take down.

His companion noticed his interest. 'Some of the lay-workers aren't here every day. They come only when they're needed.'

'Are you one of them?'

'I'm a laundryman. It's a dirty job, believe me! I even have to take care of the women's soiled linen. Whether they live in this village or another one, it makes no difference.'

The thickset man headed straight for the fifth fort.

Ardent froze. 'But . . . where are you taking me?'

'You didn't think you were going to walk into the Place of Truth without answering a lot of questions, did you? Come along. You won't regret it.'

The young man stepped through the doorway of the guard-post, under the mocking gaze of a Nubian archer, and walked along a dark passageway which opened out into an office presided over by a tall black man as athletically built as Ardent.

'Good day, Sobek,' said the laundryman. 'I've brought you a spy who succeeded in getting through the Five Walls with the help of a water-carrier. I hope the reward will match the service I've done you.'

Ardent spun round and tried to run away.

Two Nubian archers seized him. He elbowed the first man in the face and kneed the other in the testicles. He could have escaped, but he preferred to seize the laundryman under the arms and lift him off his feet.

'You betrayed me,' growled Ardent, 'and you're going to regret it!'

'Don't kill me! I was only obeying orders!'

Ardent felt the point of a dagger jab into his back.

'That's enough,' ordered Sobek. 'Let him go and calm down, or I'll kill you.'

Ardent could tell that the Nubian was not joking, so he set the laundryman back on the ground – the man promptly made himself scarce, without waiting for his reward.

'Put the wooden manacles on him,' ordered Sobek.

Manacled, and with his legs bound, Ardent was flung into a corner of the office. His head hit the wall hard, but he did not utter a sound.

'You're a tough one,' commented Sobek. 'Who sent you?'

'No one. I want to become an artist and enter the brotherhood.'

'Very amusing. Is that the best you can think of?'

'It's the truth!'

'Ah, the truth,' said Sobek drily. 'So many people think they're telling it. But here, in this office, a lot of them have changed their minds and admitted they were lying. I think that's sensible. What do you think?'

'I'm not lying.'

'You've shown that you're more skilful than most, I agree,

and my men have proved inadequate, for which they'll be punished. As for you, you're going to tell me who's paying you, where you come from and why you're here.'

'I'm a farmer's son and I want to speak to a craftsman from the Place of Truth.'

'Why?'

'To tell him I want to be an artist.'

'You're a stubborn one,' said Sobek with a grim smile. 'It's not an unattractive quality, but don't try my patience too far.'

'I can't tell you anything different, because it's the truth!'

Sobek rubbed his chin. 'Understand this, my lad: my job is to ensure the absolute security of the Place of Truth by any and every means. People in high places think I'm competent and conscientious, and I value my reputation highly.'

'Why won't you let me talk to a craftsman?' asked Ardent.

'Because I don't believe your story, lad. It's touching, I agree, but completely implausible. I've never known a candidate just turn up at the village gates like this, and ask to be let in.'

'I've no family, no protector, no one to recommend me, and I don't care about any of that because all I know is what I want. Let me meet an artist, and I'll convince him.'

For a moment, Sobek seemed to waver. Then he said, 'You've plenty of cheek, I grant you, but that won't wash with me. There are a lot of nosy people who'd love to know the secrets of the craftsmen of the Place of Truth, and who'd pay any price to achieve their aim. I know you've been sent by one of those nosy people – and you're going to tell me his name.'

Furious, Ardent tried to get to his feet, but his bonds held him tight. 'You're wrong! I swear to you, you're wrong!'

'For now, I'm not even going to ask your name – you'd only lie. You really are a cool customer, and your mission must be a very important one. Up to now, I've caught only small fry. With you, it's a serious matter. If you talked right now, you'd save yourself a lot of unpleasantness.'

'Drawing, painting, meeting the masters – that's all I want.'

'Congratulations, friend, you don't look afraid. People don't usually hold out so long, but in the end you'll talk, even if your skin is tougher than leather. I could take care of you immediately, but I think it's better to soften you up a little so as to make my job easier. After a fortnight in prison, you'll be much less stubborn and much more talkative.'

# 6

Silent was returning from a long journey into Nubia. He had visited the gold mines and quarries, and the many temples built by Ramses the Great; the two at Abu Simbel celebrated the Divine Light, the goddess of the stars and Ramses' eternal love for Nefertari, the Great Royal Wife, who had died young. Silent had stayed in oases and spent weeks alone in the desert, unafraid of the company of wild beasts.

Silent was the eldest son of a family who had long lived in the Place of Truth, and his destiny as a sculptor seemed mapped out for him. He would carve statues of the gods, of leading citizens and of craftsmen of his brotherhood, in order to continue the tradition which had been faithfully passed on since the time of the pyramids. As he grew older, he would be given more and more responsibility and, in his turn, he would pass on his knowledge to his successor.

But one condition was still unfulfilled: he had not yet heard the call. For the door of the brotherhood to open to him, it was not enough to have a father who was a craftsman, or to be highly skilled. Each member of the brotherhood bore the title 'He who has Heard the Call',* and each knew what it meant without ever having to put it into words.

The young man was well aware that only if he lived a truly

**Sedjem âsh* in Egyptian.

good life would he become one of his craft's 'beloved', and he could not tell a lie: the call was vital, and he had not heard it. He, who was nicknamed 'Silent' because he so rarely spoke, suffered from a silence which no echo had broken.

His father and the elders of the brotherhood had agreed that Silent's approach was the only acceptable one: he should explore the world outside, and if the gods looked favourably upon him he would at last hear the call.

The young man could not bear to live far from the Place of Truth, the unique place where he had been born, had grown up and been educated with a thoroughness for which he was grateful; but going back was impossible. He had the painful feeling that with each day he lost a little more of himself and that he was becoming no more than a solitary shadow.

Silent had hoped that this journey and the powerful Nubian landscapes would create the conditions necessary to make the mysterious voice ring out; but nothing had happened, and now there was nothing left for him to do but wander from one small job to another.

In Nubia, he had tried to forget the Place of Truth and the masters he held in such esteem; but his efforts had all been in vain. So he had come back to Thebes to join a team of workmen who were building houses not far from the precinct of Karnak.

The owner of the building business was a widower with one daughter. He was over fifty and walked with a limp, the result of a fall from a high roof. He disliked both pretentious people and those who talked too much, so he thoroughly approved of Silent, who was never ostentatious, and set an excellent example to his fellow workers. They, however, took a dim view of him: he was too conscientious, worked too hard, and kept himself too much to himself. Just by being there, and without ever wishing to do so, he made their faults stand out.

Thanks to his new workman, the builder had finished a two-storey house a good month earlier than expected. More than satisfied, the buyer had heaped praise on him and had obtained two new sites for him.

His colleagues had gone home, but Silent was cleaning his tools as he had been taught to do by a sculptor in the Place of Truth.

'I've just been given a jar of cool beer,' his employer said. 'Come and have a drink.'

'I don't want to put you to any trouble.'

'I'd like you to come.'

The builder and Silent sat down on mats in the hut that sheltered the workers from the sun during their midday break. The beer was excellent.

'You're not like the others,' said the builder. 'Where do you come from?'

'Oh, nowhere in particular.'

'Have you any family?'

'Yes.'

'And you don't want to talk about them . . . Very well, as you wish. How old are you?'

'Twenty-six.'

'It's high time you settled down, don't you think? I know how to judge men: you work remarkably well and you are improving all the time. There's a rare quality in you: you love your work. It makes you forget everything else, and that's not so sensible. You have to think about your future. I'm getting on, my joints hurt, and my leg is dragging more and more. Before I took you on, I had decided to employ an overseer who would gradually take over from me on the building-sites, but there is nothing more difficult than finding someone trustworthy. Do you want to be that person?'

Silent was astonished. 'No, sir,' he said. 'I wasn't born to lead men.'

'You're wrong, you know. You'd make a good overseer, I'm sure of it. But I've sprung the proposition on you. At least say you'll think about it.'

Silent nodded.

The builder changed the subject. 'I have a small favour to ask you. My daughter, Ubekhet, tends a small garden, an hour's walk from here, on the banks of the Nile, and she needs some pots to protect the young shoots. Would you mind loading up a donkey and taking them to her?'

'Of course.'

'There'll be a bonus for you.'

'Do you want me to go straight away?'

'If you don't mind.'

The builder described the route in detail; Silent could not possibly go wrong.

The donkey moved off, plodding along with a calm assurance. Silent, having checked that the load was not too heavy, walked alongside. At first he took the narrow streets, then a beaten-earth track which ran alongside little white houses separated by vegetable gardens.

The gentle north wind had just begun to blow, promising a peaceful evening when families would once more gather together and go over the small events of the day, or listen to a story-teller who would make them laugh and dream.

Silent thought over his employer's proposition, already knowing that he would not accept. There was only one place where he wanted to settle down, and that was impossible unless he heard the call. In a few weeks, he would leave for the North and continue his nomadic existence.

From time to time, he felt tempted to lie, to run to the village and tell everyone that he had at last received the call. But the Place of Truth did not bear that name by chance. Ma'at reigned over it, her rule was the daily food of hearts and minds, and cheats were always unmasked in the end. 'You must hate falsehood in all circumstances, for it destroys the Word,' he had been taught. 'It is abhorrent to God. When falsehood sets out, it becomes lost, it cannot cross by the ferry and its journey fails. He who sails with falsehood will not find a safe mooring, and his ship will not return to its home port.'

No, Silent would not be dishonourable. Even if he could not be admitted to the Place of Truth, he would at least respect the promise made to him. It was poor consolation, true, but one which might perhaps allow him to survive.

The waters of the Nile were as blue as the sky, their surface stirred up by a strong, fast current. It was said that people who drowned in the river were cleansed of their sins by the court of Osiris and were brought back to life in the paradise of the world beyond.

Rush down the slope, dive in, refuse to swim and thank death for coming quickly, allowing you to forget a life shorn of all hope . . . That was the only call that Silent heard. But one small thing prevented him from offering himself up to the Nile: he had been entrusted with a task, and he must not betray that trust. Once his mission was fulfilled, he could at last free himself from his chains, thanks to the generosity of the river, which would carry his soul away to the world of the dead.

The donkey left the main track, passed to the left of a well and headed straight for a garden enclosed by low walls. The animal had obviously come here before, and remembered the way.

A pomegranate tree, a carob tree and another which Silent did not know spread their benevolent shade over the garden, where centauries, narcissi and marigolds grew in profusion. But the beauty of the flowers was as nothing compared to that of the young woman, who, dressed in a robe of immaculate white, knelt there, planting out seedlings.

Her hair tended towards the fair; she wore it loose and it fell in soft curls over her shoulders. Her profile was as perfect as that of the goddess Hathor, as Silent had seen it carved by a craftsman from the Place of Truth, and her body was as supple as a palm-tree bending in the wind.

The donkey munched a few thistles. Silent thought he was about to faint when the young woman turned round and looked at him with eyes as blue as a summer sky.

# 7

'I recognise the donkey,' Ubekhet said with a smile, 'but I haven't seen you before.'

'I . . . I've brought you some pots from your father.'

Silent was a slim, well-built man, of average height. His chestnut hair emphasised a wide forehead, and his grey-green eyes enlivened a face which was at once open and serious.

'Thank you for your kindness,' she went on. 'But . . . you seem to have something on your mind?'

The young man rushed to the donkey, which was still feasting, and took the pots out of the baskets with feverish hands.

He would never dare to look at her again. What magic could make a woman so beautiful? Her features were so perfect, her skin so lightly bronzed, her limbs so slender and supple, and the light that radiated from her transformed her into a vision, a dream too enchanting to last. If he touched her, she would dissolve away.

'Is anything broken?' she asked.

How magical her voice was, and so was she! Honey-sweet, smooth and melodious yet with a hint of firmness, clear and bright and lively like the waters of a freshwater spring.

'I think so.'

'Let me help you.'

'No, no – I'll bring the pots in to you.'

When Silent walked into the garden, a black dog barked, reared up on its hind legs and put its front paws on the newcomer's shoulders, then gave his eyes and ears a thorough licking.The young man's arms were full, and all he could do was stand there and submit.

'Ebony has adopted you,' commented Ubekhet delightedly. 'And yet he's rather wary as a rule, and only grants such privileges to long-standing friends.'

'I'm flattered.'

'What is your name?'

'Silent.'

'That's a strange name.'

He shrugged. 'It isn't a very interesting story.'

'Tell me, anyway.'

'I'm afraid you'll be bored.'

Ubekhet shook her head. 'Come and sit at the other end of the garden.'

Ebony consented to put his front paws back on the ground, and Silent was able to accept the invitation. The dog, which had a big, powerful head, a short, silky pelt, a long, tufted tail and alert hazel eyes, trotted alongside its guest.

'With him near me,' said Ubekhet, 'I'm not afraid of anything. He's as swift as he is brave.'

Silent put the pots down on the grass and sat down beside a bank of tall, daisy-like flowers the colour of gold.

'I've never seen flowers like these before,' he said.

'They're a special kind of daisy, and this is the only place they like. Quite apart from their elegance, these flowers are also very useful; the substances they contain are used to treat inflammation, circulatory problems and back pain.'

'Are you a doctor?'

'No, but I had the good fortune to be cared for by Neferet, a remarkable doctor. After my mother's death, Neferet took me under her wing, despite her heavy responsibilities. Before retiring to Karnak with her husband, Pazair, the former tjaty, she passed on a great deal of her art to me. Today, I use it to relieve suffering among those around me. Here, in this garden, I like to meditate and talk to the trees. You may think I'm mad, but I believe plants have a language. We must show them humility in order to hear it.'

'The sorcerers of Nubia think that, too.'

'Have you been to Nubia?'

'Yes, I spent a few months there.' Silent looked round the garden. 'What is the name of this tree with the greyish-brown bark and the green and white oval leaves?'

'The styrax. It gives a fleshy fruit and in particular a precious balm which trickles out in the form of a yellowish gum when you cut into the trunk.'

'I prefer the carob tree, with its dense foliage and its honey-flavoured fruits. It tolerates droughts and hot winds so well; I think it embodies all the sweetness of life.'

Ebony had lain down at the feet of the young man, who could not move without disturbing him.

'You still haven't explained,' said Ubekhet, 'why you're called Silent.'

'To live up to it, I ought not to tell you.'

'Is it such a big secret?' She sank another upside-down pot into the loose earth to protect a young plant. As the roots grew, the pot would shatter and its fragments become mixed into the earth.

The young man had never before felt the urge to confide in someone, he couldn't help telling Ubekhet.

'I was brought up in a craftsmen's village, the Place of Truth, where my father was a sculptor. When I was born, he and my mother gave me a secret name which will be revealed to me when I, too, become a sculptor. Until that moment, I must remain silent, watching, listening and learning to understand.'

'When will that moment come?'

'Never.'

'But . . . why not?'

'Because I shall not be a sculptor,' said Silent. 'Fate has decided otherwise.'

'What will you do instead?'

'I don't know.'

Ubekhet was building up a bank of damp earth round the carob tree, to retain the water when it was next watered.

'Are you planning to work in my father's business for long?' she asked.

'He's asked me to become his overseer.'

'Have you talked to him about the Place of Truth?'

'No. You're the only person who knows about my past. At this moment, it is well and truly dead. I don't know any of the craftsmen's secrets and I'm just a workman like the others.'

'That hurts you, doesn't it?'

'It isn't that I'm ambitious. I just wanted to . . . But that's not important. Rebelling against life is pointless. We must learn to accept what it brings.'

'Aren't you rather young to be talking like that?'

'I . . . I don't want to bore you.'

'What about the overseer's job?'

'It's truly generous of your father to offer it to me, but I couldn't carry out such responsibilities well, and I wouldn't want to disappoint him.'

'I'm sure you underestimate yourself,' said Ubekhet. 'Why not try? In the meantime, you can help me.'

She looked down at her dog: immediately, he opened his eyes and got to his feet. Ebony could sense what she wanted, and most of the time she did not even need to speak to him.

Free now, Silent also stood up. He stroked the dog's neck and head for a while, then Ebony went and lay down again in the shade.

Silent set about helping Ubekhet with the garden chores, imitating what she did. It was a long time since he had experienced such peace, far from all anguish. Looking at the young woman made him so happy that he forgot his doubts and his suffering.

'Each night, said Ubekhet, 'the darkness tries to devour the light. Because it fights valiantly, the light manages to drive it away. Anyone who watches the sun rising over the Peak of the East will see a turquoise acacia tree which marks the triumph of light reborn. That tree is given to us all. In order to perceive its beauty, we simply need to know how to look at it. That thought has guided me whenever I have undergone hard trials. The beauty of life does not depend on us; it dwells also in our capacity to grasp it.'

Silent marvelled at the way Ubekhet worked, unhurriedly yet with movements that were authoritative, precise and graceful. Alas, the planting would soon be finished, and he would have to set off back to town.

'Let's go and wash our hands in the little canal,' she suggested.

The surveyors, irrigation specialists and men doing compulsory labour on the land had done well; between the fields and gardens ran veins and arteries which carried the water of life.

Kneeling beside Ubekhet, Silent breathed in her perfume, a blend of jasmine and lotus-flower. And, as he could not lie to himself, he knew that he had fallen hopelessly in love.

# 8

Sobek hated social occasions, but he was obliged to attend the annual festival organised by the security forces on the west bank of Thebes, during which promotions, postings and retirements were announced. A few pigs were killed for the occasion, and the tjaty provided red wine for everyone to drink.

The Nubian's size made him far from unobtrusive, and he was the object of much attention. His colleagues might be security guards, but they were no less curious for that, and a number of them asked if he had discovered any of the secrets of the Place of Truth. Inevitably, people joked about the affairs he had presumably had with the village women, who surely could not resist the charms of the magnificent black man.

Sobek concentrated on eating and drinking, and let them rattle on.

'It seems you like your new job,' whispered the scribe in charge of compulsory labour, an embittered man whom Sobek detested.

'I have no complaints.'

'People are saying there's been a death, one of your men . . . ?'

'A new recruit who fell in the hills, at night. The inquiry is closed.'

'Poor devil,' said the scribe. 'He won't benefit from the pleasures of Thebes. Still, everyone has their problems. Mine is that I can't lay my hands on Ardent, a farmer's son who's trying to avoid doing his compulsory work.'

'That must happen a great deal.'

'No, it doesn't,' said the scribe. 'It's a duty which everyone accepts, and the penalties are heavy for anyone who doesn't. What's more, bearing in mind the size of the lad – even though he's only sixteen – arresting him is liable to be an eventful business.'

The scribe launched into a description which corresponded perfectly to that of the spy Sobek had imprisoned.

'Has this boy committed any other crimes?' asked the Nubian.

'He's fallen out with his father, who wants to teach him a proper lesson so that he'll come back to the farm. The problem is the offence of desertion. The court will probably pronounce a heavy penalty.'

'Haven't his brothers told you anything useful?'

'Ardent has no brothers, only sisters.'

'It's strange, though. As an only son, shouldn't he be exempt from compulsory work?'

'You're right, I had to . . . adjust the procedures a little to satisfy his father, who's an old friend of mine.' The scribe smiled. 'We've all done that from time to time, haven't we?'

A few days in prison had not diminished Ardent's pride, and he stood ramrod-straight before Sobek.

'So, my lad, have you decided to tell the truth?'

'It hasn't changed.

'When it comes to obstinacy, you take the prize. Normally, I'd have interrogated you in my usual way, but you've been lucky – very lucky.'

'You mean you believe me at last?'

'I've found out the truth. Your name is Ardent and you're

a fugitive trying to avoid compulsory work.'

'But that's impossible! My father's a farmer, and I'm his only son.'

'I know that too. You have problems, lad, serious problems. But it just so happens that the scribe in charge of compulsory work is no friend of mine, and your case doesn't fall under my jurisdiction. I've just one piece of advice for you: leave the area as quickly as possible and let people forget about you.'

On the construction site, the workers were taking their break after the midday meal. As usual Silent had chosen to be alone, leaving the hut to his four workmates, a Syrian and three Egyptians.

'Have you heard the latest news?' asked the Syrian.

'We're going to get a pay-rise,' suggested the oldest of the Egyptians, a fifty-year-old with a belly swollen by too much strong beer.

'The new man delivered pots to the master's daughter.'

'You're joking! The master always takes care of that himself. No one's allowed near his daughter– she's a real beauty. She's twenty-three, and still not married. People say she's a bit of an enchantress and that she knows the secret language of plants.'

'I'm not joking,' said the Syrian. 'It really was the new man who delivered the pots.'

'Which means the master likes him a lot.'

'That fellow never opens his mouth, he works faster and better than we do, and he's got the master under his thumb. He's going to be made overseer, I'm telling you.'

The pot-bellied Egyptian pulled a face. 'I ought to get that job, I'm the most senior man.'

'At last you understand! That schemer is going to steal it from under your nose and then we'll have him ordering us about.'

'We'd have to keep up with him – and he'd wear us out, that's for sure! We can't let it happen. What do you suggest, Syrian?'

'Let's get rid of him.'

'How?' asked the Egyptian.

'We'll talk to him in a language he understands. Tomorrow, when he leaves the market with his purchases.'

Silent was moulding the last of a hundred unbaked bricks which he would place above the stone course that formed the base of a house intended for a soldier's family. For the son of a sculptor from the Place of Truth, it was simplicity itself. As a boy, Silent had amused himself by making bricks of all sizes, and in the end he had even made the moulds himself.

'You're exceptionally good at that,' commented his master.

'I have the knack and I take my time.'

'You know a lot more than you show, don't you?'

'No, not really.'

'It doesn't matter to me.' The builder coughed. 'Have you thought about my proposition?'

'Let me have a little more time.'

'Very well, my boy. I hope some other businessman isn't trying to tempt you away . . . ?'

Silent smiled. 'Don't worry.'

'I trust you.'

Silent understood the builder's plan. He had introduced Silent to Ubekhet so that he would fall for her, ask for her hand in marriage, accept the post of overseer and set up home. He would thus be forced to take up the family business.

The master was a good man, and thought he was acting in his daughter's best interests. Silent felt no resentment towards him. The manoeuvre could have ended in a fiasco, but the young man had fallen madly in love with Ubekhet. Even if the future that his prospective father-in-law mapped out for him looked like a cage which he did not want to enter, he could no longer envisage life without her.

It was thanks to her, her face and her radiance, that he had not thrown himself into the Nile to put an end to his wanderings. But there was no sign she shared his feelings, and he would not have her marry him just to please her father.

How could he go to Ubekhet and confess a love so intense that it would frighten her? Silent had imagined a thousand and one ways of approaching the subject, but each seemed more ridiculous than the last. He must be realistic. It was better to hide his passion deep inside himself and leave for the North, as he had planned to do, dreaming of an impossible happiness.

In the little room his master had provided for him, Silent found himself unable to sleep. He believed he had made the right decision, but it brought him no peace at all. The village, the never-ending roads, Ubekhet's blue eyes, the river . . . everything was mixed up in his head, as though he were drunk.

To live for her, become her servant, remain by her side for ever, and never ask for more . . . perhaps that was the solution. But she would tire of that, and in the end she would marry. And then the pain of separation would be even more unbearable.

Silent had no choice. Tomorrow morning, he would finish the work he had started, go to the market to buy food, and leave Thebes for ever.

# 9

Ardent headed for the ferry, judging it advisable to leave the west bank for a while, but he did not lose sight of his goal: to persuade a craftsman from the Place of Truth to become his sponsor. He intended, after spending a week on the east bank, to swim back across the Nile and try to approach the village through the highest hills.

The ferry's berth was next to the market, which was situated on the riverbank. There you could buy meat, wine, oil, vegetables, bread, cakes, fruit, spices, fish, clothing and sandals. The majority of the vendors were women, experts in the art of handling scales. Seated comfortably on folding stools, they haggled fiercely, and drank sweet beer through a straw when their throats became too dry.

At the sight of so much food, Ardent suddenly felt hungry. The daily prison fare had not nearly satisfied his appetite, and he longed to munch fresh onions, a piece of dried beef and a soft cake. But what would he exchange for them? He had nothing to barter with.

His only option was to steal a long loaf without being caught by the baker and while avoiding the guards' watchful baboon, which rushed at thieves and bit their legs to stop them running away.

A widow tried to barter a piece of fabric against a sack of wheat, but the vendor considered the quality of the material too poor; a lively discussion began, and it looked likely to go on for some time. A pretty brunette who was holding her child tightly to her breast wanted a little jug in exchange for some fresh fish, and a leek-seller was proudly displaying his magnificent produce.

Ardent slipped into the crowd, hoping to approach the stalls from behind and take advantage of a moment's inattention on the part of a cake-seller; but there was a second guard-baboon sitting on the ground, watching the passers-by.

'Well, perfume-seller, you're happy and so am I!' exclaimed a nobleman's steward who had just acquired a conical vase filled with myrrh.

Ardent moved away from the baboon; it had impressive jaws, and was too alert to be fooled. Still ravenous, he left the market, following a young man who was older and less athletic than he was. The man was carrying a bag filled with vegetables and fruit, and set off along a narrow street covered by palm-trees.

Ardent saw three men suddenly move towards the man with the bag. Intrigued, he followed them.

At the far end of the street, the three thugs rushed their prey. The Syrian hit Silent in the back, the two others seized his arms and forced him to lie face-down on the ground.

The Syrian set his foot on his victim's neck. 'We're going to teach you a lesson, my lad, and then you're leaving town. We don't need you here.'

Silent tried to turn on to his side, but a kick in the flank made him cry out in pain.

'If you struggle, we'll hit you harder.'

'How'd you like to try that with me, you bunch of cowards?' shouted Ardent.

He leapt at the Syrian, grabbed him by the neck and hurled him against a wall. The other two thugs tried to drive Ardent off, but he hit the first man in the face, then parried the second and elbowed him hard in the belly.

Silent tried to get up but he saw stars* and fell back on to his knees, while Ardent knocked the Syrian out with a single two-fisted blow. The Syrian's accomplices fled, but they were intercepted by guards with a baboon which displayed sharp teeth.

'No one move!' ordered one of the guards. 'You're all under arrest.'

When Silent came to, the sun had been up for a long time. He found himself lying on his belly, his arms hanging down on either side of a narrow bed.

He felt a delicious warmth in the small of his back. A very gentle hand was smoothing a balm on to his painful flesh. Suddenly, he realised that he was naked and that Ubekhet was massaging him.

'Keep still,' she commanded. 'If it's to work, this balm must soak into the bruises properly.'

'Where am I?' asked Silent.

'At my father's house. You were attacked and beaten by three of my father's workmen, and you passed out. Those ruffians have been arrested, and you were brought here. You slept for the rest of the day and all through the night, for I made you drink sedative potions. As for the balm, it is made of henbane, hemlock and myrrh; it will help your injuries to heal rapidly.'

'Someone came to my aid.'

'A young man. He was arrested, too.'

'That's unjust! He risked his life for me, he—'

'According to the guards, there are "irregularities in his circumstances".'

'I must get up,' said Silent resolutely, 'and go and speak on his behalf.'

Literally, 'the lights of the thirty-six decans'; this ancient popular expression is of Egyptian origin.

'The case will be heard tomorrow, at the tjaty's court. My father has made a complaint, and it's to be heard immediately, because of the seriousness of the matter. The most pressing thing is to get you back on your feet, which means you must let yourself be looked after. Please be kind enough to lie on your back.'

'But I'm . . .'

'We're both too old for false modesty.'

Silent closed his eyes. Ubekhet smoothed balm across his forehead, his left shoulder and right knee.

He said, 'My attackers wanted me to leave town.'

'Don't worry: they will be sentenced to a heavy penalty, and my father will take on other workers. More than ever, he hopes that you will accept the post of overseer.'

'I'm afraid I wouldn't be very popular.'

'My father is amazed by your skill. He doesn't realise you were brought up in the Place of Truth, and I've kept your secret.'

'Thank you.'

'I have a favour to ask,' said Ubekhet. 'When you have made your decision, I'd like to be the first to know it.'

She covered the injured man with a linen sheet which smelt of the good, scented air of the Theban countryside.

Silent sat up. 'Ubekhet, I'd like to tell you . . .'

The luminous blue eyes looked at him with infinite gentleness, but he dared not take the young woman's hand or tell her how he felt.

'I have always worked under the supervision of someone more qualified than myself, and I'm sure I'd be no good at directing other people's work. Please understand.'

'Does that mean you're turning down the job?'

'All I can think of is helping the boy who saved me. If it hadn't been for him, I might be dead.'

'You're right,' she admitted, in a voice tinged with sadness. 'He's the one you must think of.'

'Ubekhet . . .'

'Excuse me, I have a lot of work to do.' Radiant and inaccessible, she walked out of the room.

Silent would have loved to hold her back, explain to her that he was stupid, unable to open his heart to her. The door that had just closed would probably never open again. He should have taken her in his arms and covered her with kisses, but he was too much in awe of her.

The balm was effective; little by little, the pain faded. But the young man wished his attackers had finished their sinister task. What point was there in living, when he hadn't heard the call and couldn't marry the woman he loved?

As soon as his rescuer had been acquitted, Silent would vanish for ever.

# 10

The judge appointed by the tjaty for the day's trial was a mature man with years of experience. He was dressed in a loose tunic held up by two broad straps which knotted behind his neck. At his throat he wore a golden collar, from which hung a figurine representing the goddess Ma'at.

Ma'at was depicted as a seated woman holding the key of life. On her head was the rectrix, the tail feather which allowed birds to direct their flight without error. At once truth, justice and righteousness, she was the true patroness of the court.

At the judge's feet was a piece of red cloth, on which had been laid forty batons of command, the symbol of a true state of law.

'Under the protection of Ma'at and in the name of Pharaoh,' declared the judge, 'this trial now begins. May truth be the breath of life in the nostrils of men, and may she drive away evil from their bodies. I will judge the lowly in the same way as the powerful, I will protect the weak from the strong, and I will turn aside the rage of the evil being from each and every one. Bring in those who were involved in the brawl in the street leading to the market.'

The Syrian and his two henchmen admitted the facts and begged the court for mercy. The jury, which was made up of four scribes, a businesswoman, a weaving-woman, a reserve officer and an interpreter, sentenced them to five years' labour in the public service. If they offended again, the punishment would be tripled.

When Ardent appeared before the judge, he did not hang his head. Neither the austere atmosphere of the court nor the jurors' closed expressions seemed to daunt him.

'Your name is Ardent and you claim to have helped the victim,' said the judge.

'That is true.'

The guards confirmed what Ardent had said, then Silent gave his evidence.

'I was struck on the back, the attackers made me lie face-down on the ground. I could offer only feeble resistance and I might have been killed if this boy had not rushed to help me. It was one against three, and he showed exceptional courage.'

The judge nodded. 'The court agrees that this is true,' he said, 'but the scribe in charge of compulsory work, whom you see here before you, has lodged a complaint against Ardent for desertion.'

The scribe, who was sitting in the front row, gave a satisfied smile.

'Surely Ardent's bravery merits the jury's indulgence?' pleaded Silent. 'Can we not forgive him this youthful mistake?'

'The law is the law,' said the judge, 'and the obligation to carry out work for the public good is essential to the general well-being.'

Sobek came forward. 'As commander of the guard for the area around the Place of Truth, I support Silent's view.'

The judge frowned. 'What justification have you for saying this?'

'Respect for the law of Ma'at, to which we all hold. As the only son of a farmer, Ardent is legally exempt from compulsory work.'

'The scribe's report does not mention this vital point,' commented the judge.

'Then the text lies, and its author should be severely punished.'

The scribe was no longer smiling.

Ardent gazed at the Nubian in astonishment. He would never have thought that a guard officer would come to his aid.

'Arrest the dishonest scribe,' ordered the judge, 'and free Ardent immediately.'

Silent scarcely heard the decision, for he had been staring fixedly for several seconds at the figurine of Ma'at that hung on the judge's chest.

The Place of Truth, the place of Ma'at, the most privileged place of all, where justice was expressed, where its secrets were taught through the work of the craftsmen who had been initiated into the House of Gold . . . Silent had not realised it until now.

As he gazed at the goddess, his heart opened. The figurine grew larger, became immense, filled the courtroom and rose through the ceiling to reach the heavens. Ma'at was vaster than humanity. She stretched beyond the stars and lived on light.

Silent saw the village houses once more, the workshops and the temple. And he heard the call: the voice of Ma'at asking him to come back to the Place of Truth and accomplish the work he was destined to do.

'I am not going to repeat myself,' said the judge irritably. 'I asked you if you are satisfied, Silent. Did you hear?'

'Yes. Oh yes, I heard!'

Silent walked slowly out of the courtroom, gazing towards the Peak of the West, the protector of the Place of Truth.

'I should like to speak to you,' said Ardent, 'but you really do look very strange.'

Silent was still haunted by the call which had filled his soul, and at first he barely recognised his saviour. He pulled himself together and said, 'Forgive me. I very much want to thank you. If I am alive, it's thanks to you.'

'Rubbish! I enjoyed myself.'

'Do you like fighting, Ardent?'

'In the country, you have to know how to defend yourself. Sometimes situations blow up quickly, and people will happily squabble over nothing.'

'Where do you live?'

'On the west bank, but I've left the family farm once and for all.' Ardent cleared his throat. 'I'm dying of thirst, aren't you?'

'The least I can do is offer you a cool beer.'

Silent bought a jar, and the two friends sat down on the riverbank, in the shade of a palm tree.

'Why did you leave your family?' asked Silent.

'Because I don't want to become a farmer and take over from my father.'

'What *do* you want to do, then?'

'I have only one passion: drawing. And there's only one place where I can prove that I'm gifted, and acquire the knowledge I lack, and that's the Place of Truth. I tried to get close to it, in the hope of getting inside, but it seems impossible. But I shan't give up my aim. It's my only reason for living.'

'You're very young, Ardent. You might change your mind.'

'I never shall, you can be certain of that! Ever since I was a child, I've observed nature, animals, peasants, scribes – and drawn them, too. Shall I show you?'

'Please do.'

Breaking off the end of a dried palm-frond, in the earth Ardent traced a picture of the judge, drawing his face, his collar and the figurine of Ma'at, all with remarkable precision.

For the first time in his life, he was anxious. He had always been so sure of his own talent and scorned the criticism of others, but now he was in torment waiting for this calm, thoughtful, older man to pass judgement.

Silent took his time.

'It's quite good,' he pronounced eventually. 'You have an innate sense of proportion and your hand is very steady.'

'So . . . you think I really am gifted?'

'Yes, I do.'

'That's wonderful! I'm a free man and I can draw!'

'But you still have a great deal to learn.'

'I don't need anyone else!' shouted Ardent. 'I've managed on my own so far, and I'll carry on that way.'

'In that case, why do you want to join the brotherhood of the Servants of the Place of Truth?'

The contradiction hit the budding artist like a slap in the face.

'Because . . . because I'll be able to draw and paint all day and not have to bother about anything else.'

'Do you think the brotherhood needs you?'

'I'll prove to them that I am the best.'

'Vanity is probably not the best way to force open the door,' said Silent drily.

'It isn't vanity, it's a desire that burns hotter than fire. I know I must go there and I will, whatever the obstacles may be.'

'Fervour may not be enough.'

Ardent raised his eyes to the heavens. 'It isn't just fervour, it's a kind of call I heard, a call that was so strong and imperious that I can't help responding to it all the time. The Place of Truth is my true homeland – I must live there, and nowhere else . . . But you can't possibly understand.'

'I think I can.'

Ardent's eyes widened in astonishment. 'You're saying that out of sympathy, but you're too much in control of yourself and your emotions to share my passion.'

'I come from the Place of Truth,' revealed Silent.

# 11

Ardent seized Silent by the shoulders, so fiercely that Silent thought he'd be broken in two.

'That's not true!' said Ardent. 'It's impossible! You're mocking me.'

'When you know me better,' said Silent, 'you'll know that that isn't in my nature.'

'But in that case . . . you know how to get into the Place of Truth!'

'It is even more difficult than you think. For a new craftsman to be engaged, all the members of the brotherhood, plus the pharaoh and the tjaty, must be in agreement. And it is preferable to belong to a long line of sculptors or artists.'

'Don't they ever recruit anyone from outside?'

'Only people who have been observed for a long time, working in the sites which serve the temples, like Karnak.'

'You're trying to make me think it's hopeless. But I won't give up,' declared Ardent.

'And that's not all. Before you can present yourself before the court of admissions, you must have paid all your debts, and you must own a leather bag, a folding chair and enough wood to make a chair with arms.'

'But that would cost a small fortune!'

'About seven months' wages for a beginner. That is the proof that you know how to work.'

'I'm an artist, not a carpenter,' protested Ardent.

'The Place of Truth has its special conditions for entry, and you won't change them.

'What else do I need to know?'

'I've told you everything.'

Ardent looked at Silent curiously. 'What about you?' he asked. 'Why did you leave?'

'Everyone is free to leave whenever they want to. I never really entered.'

'What do you mean?'

'I was brought up there, I've met some outstanding artists, and my family hoped I'd become a sculptor.'

'Surely you didn't refuse?'

'No, it wasn't that,' replied Silent. 'It was because I couldn't cheat. I'd fulfilled the necessary conditions, and I wanted to go on living there, but one vital thing was lacking: I hadn't heard the call. So I decided to travel, in the hope that my ears would eventually be opened.'

'And . . . have they been?'

'This very day, in the courtroom, after years of wandering. I owe you a great deal, Ardent, and I don't know how to thank you. If you hadn't come to my rescue when I was attacked, I wouldn't have been called to appear before that judge and I wouldn't have heard the call. But, unfortunately, I can't help you in return. Each candidate must succeed entirely alone. If he's had any help at all, his application to join the brotherhood is refused.'

'And you? Are you certain to be accepted?'

'By no means. People who know me may speak on my behalf, but their opinion won't weigh heavily in the balance.'

'Tell me everything you know about the Place of Truth,' demanded Ardent.

'To me, it was just a village like any other. I wasn't initiated into any of the secrets.'

'When are you going back there?'

'First thing tomorrow.'

'But what about the bag, the folding chair, the wood?'

'I left my savings with a guardian.'

'You won't need a pass,' said Ardent wistfully.

'That's true. I'll be allowed to pass through the five forts and present myself before the court of admissions. But I may not get any further than that.'

'You're already a grown man, and you seem as patient as stone and as calm as a mountain. The brotherhood must look favourably on candidates like you, with temperaments like yours.'

'The vital thing is to have heard the call – and then to convince the craftsmen chosen to judge your application.'

'In that case,' declared Ardent, 'I shall succeed.'

Silent laid his hands on the young man's shoulders. 'I hope so, with all my heart. Even if our destinies lie far apart, I shall never forget what I owe you.'

Thanks to the donkey which carried the pots, Silent found his way back to Ubekhet's garden. The south wind had blown up, and angry waves disturbed the surface of the Nile. Sand was flying around, attacking animals, people and houses.

Silent put the donkey into the shelter of a stable, alongside two milch cows, then continued along the path. He felt both calm and tormented. Calm, because hearing the call had liberated unsuspected powers inside him; like Ardent, he had made up his mind to try to enter the brotherhood of the Place of Truth and learn its secrets. Tormented, because if he succeeded he would lose the woman he loved.

Furious gusts of wind swept through the garden; it was empty. Silent felt a lurch of emotion as he saw the seedlings he had helped Ubekhet plant. He would have liked to watch them grow with her, care for them day after day, grow old to the rhythm of their growth. But the call of Ma'at and the Place of Truth was so pressing that he had no choice: he had to rediscover his lost home and unveil its secrets.

The empty years were wiped away, the doubts forgotten . . . Silent felt as though he had emerged from a pitch-dark night which he had thought would never end. But he must still not fail on the threshold of an adventure which he sensed would be breathtaking.

'Were you looking for me?' Ubekhet appeared, her shoulders covered by a woollen shawl, an expression of concern on her face. 'I was sheltering in a hut,' she explained. 'I hoped you'd come.'

'You wanted to be the first to know my answer to your father, and I'm keeping my promise.'

'You're turning down the post of overseer, aren't you?'

'Yes, but for such a special reason that I want to tell you about it.'

Her blue eyes were sad. 'There's no need.'

'Listen to me, I beg you!'

He stepped closer to her. She did not move away.

He said shyly, 'Will you let me put my arms round you?'

Ubekhet did not reply, and made no move. Silent put his arms round her tenderly, as though she were so fragile that she might break. He felt her heart beating as hard as his own.

'I love you with all my heart,' he said. 'You are the first woman in my life, and there will never be another. And because I love you so much, I couldn't bear to make you unhappy.'

She laid her head on his shoulder, savouring this moment of happiness. 'What has happened? Why should you make me unhappy?'

'I've heard the call of the Place of Truth and I must answer it. If I'm refused admittance, I'll be a broken man, unbearable. If I'm accepted, my life will be played out inside the craftsmen's village, far from this world.'

'And you won't go back on your decision?'

Silent shook his head. 'I've heard the call, and it's as

strong as my love for you. If it were possible to forget it, I would. But I don't want to lie, either to you or to myself.'

Ubekhet was quiet for a moment. Then she asked, 'Will you marry a woman from the village?'

'I shall never marry. I shall live alone, thinking of you every day.'

'Will you have to stay inside the village all the time?'

'I could leave it from time to time to meet you, but that would only be torture for us both.'

'Kiss me,' said Ubekhet.

Their bodies melted together hungrily, tenderly. Entwined, they lay down underneath the carob tree, whose dense foliage protected them from the south wind.

Ebony stood guard as they made love, bathed in the rays of the setting sun.

# 12

There were three simple ways for Ardent to acquire the folding stool, the wood and the leather bag. The first was to buy them or barter for them, but he had no money and nothing to exchange for them. The second was to ask his father for them, but Ardent would never willingly set eyes on him again – a man for whom he felt no affection at all. The third was to steal them, but there was the risk of being caught, and a prison sentence would definitely prevent him entering the Place of Truth. What was more, when the craftsmen questioned him, they would probably ask him where he had acquired his things, and he would have to lie – and if the truth should come out, the village would be barred to him for ever.

The conclusion was inevitable: Ardent would have to find work so that he could obtain what he needed. Seven months of hard work – much too long! He would go without sleep to shorten this period and present himself before the brotherhood at the earliest possible moment.

Ardent espied an old man dozing on a stool, and went up to him.

'Excuse me for waking you, grandfather. Could you tell me the way to the area where the tanners live?'

'What takes you there, youngster?'

'I'm looking for work.'

'It's not a very pleasant profession. Haven't you got any

better ideas?'

'That's my business,' said Ardent stiffly.

'As you like, young fellow. Head north until you're out of the town, leave the little palm-grove on your left-hand side, then keep straight on and follow the smell.'

With the aid of the old man's directions, Ardent had no trouble in finding the tanners' district. His nose was assailed by an appalling smell, which came from large vats of urine, manure and tannin, used to soften the hides. There were stacks and stacks of skins from sheep, goats, cattle, gazelles and other desert animals. On stalls were laid out belts, straps, sandals and goatskin bags destined for the market.

Ardent's eye was caught by a superb leather bag.

'Are you looking for something?' demanded a badly shaven man of around fifty.

'Work.'

'Have you any experience?'

'I was a farmer.'

'Why did you leave the fields?'

'That's my business.'

'You're not very polite, are you?'

'Are you the owner?'

'I might be. And I definitely don't like the way you're eyeing my leather bag. I reckon you're not looking for work, you just want to steal a few nice pieces.'

Ardent smiled. 'You're wrong. Unfortunately, I have to ask you for work.'

'I'm going to give you something else which will do you the world of good.'

The tanner snapped his fingers. Two workmen came out of the workshop where they were softening skins with salt and oil. They were low-browed and broad-chested.

'Right, lads,' said the tanner, 'teach this little whipper-snapper a lesson. I don't think he'll complain to anyone, and he won't try to steal from us again.'

An unpleasant grin of satisfaction lit up each workman's coarse face. But in the time it took them to exchange glances, gloating over the fun their master was giving them, Ardent leapt on the first man, kicked him hard in the throat and sent him off to dream of a better world. His astounded comrade tried to react, but he was too slow and his fist met empty air. Ardent's, on the other hand, landed smack on the back of his adversary's neck and he collapsed in a heap, unconscious.

Pale as a ghost, the master retreated until his back was against the stall. 'Take what you want and go away,' he quavered.

'All I want is to work, so I can earn a fine leather bag. When I've done that, I'll go away.'

'The one you like is a very good one. I'd suggest something less expensive.'

'I want a very good one. But there's a condition, master: no rest days for me, and no limit on the hours I work. I've no time to lose – I need that bag as soon as possible. Where do I start?'

'Follow me.'

The tanner was astonished by the sheer energy with which Ardent worked. He was tireless. He rose at dawn, never complained about anything, and easily did the work of several apprentices. He learnt new tasks quickly, and proved extremely clever at stretching and softening the leather by laying it out on a three-legged wooden trestle. Given the ease with which the young man was learning the trade, the tanner even showed him how to grease and oil a top-quality skin, in such a way as to prevent it drying out and being ruined.

One evening, when the other workers had left the workshop, the tanner came over to Ardent. 'You don't have much to do with your fellow workers,' he said.

'Each man to his own. I've no intention of settling down here, so there's no point making friends.'

'Perhaps you're wrong. This trade isn't as inferior as you think. Look at these.'

'They're acacia pods.'

'They have a high tannin content, as does acacia bark, and this product enables us to practise true tanning, which is vital for exceptional items. A fine leather bag, for example, or even better—'

'I'm only interested in the bag,' interrupted Ardent.

'I've had an order for a case in which a ritualist at the temple at Karnak will keep papyrus scrolls. It will be a little marvel, and I shall make it myself. If you like, I could make a replica and give it to you as your wages.'

'As well as the bag?'

'Of course.'

Ardent looked at him closely. 'Why are you doing me this favour?'

'If you want the bag that much, it's to impress somebody. With the case as well, you'll be sure to succeed. And also, you amaze me – I've never met anyone like you before. You could have a fine future if I made you my right-hand man. I've only got daughters, and I need a successor.'

'The bag is all I want. I wouldn't say no to the case as well, but as for the rest I'm not going to stay here and rot.'

'You'll change your mind.'

'Don't count on it.'

'We'll see, my boy, we'll see.'

Ardent needed only three or four hours' sleep a night to recover his strength; he was always the first to arrive at the tannery and the last to leave. He lived in a hut which he had built himself out of reeds. It was a crude affair but, as the hot season was approaching. and the tanner had allocated him a blanket of coarse linen, the young man could put up with the discomfort.

Darkness had long since fallen when he entered his little retreat.

Suddenly, he had a feeling he wasn't alone. 'Who's there?' he demanded.

Something stirred under the blanket.

Ardent lifted it up and discovered a naked girl, who was clumsily attempting to cover her modesty with her hands. She was neither pretty nor ugly, and must have been about twenty years old.

'Who are you?' he asked, astonished.

'Your master's cousin. I noticed you, at the workshop. I like you a lot, and I didn't have the patience to wait any longer.'

'You were right not to wait, my beauty,' he said, hastily shedding his kilt.

She stretched out on her back and held out her arms to him.

'I was starting to miss this,' he confessed. 'You've turned up at exactly the right moment.'

She welcomed his athletic body with a she-cat's growl.

A good trade, a future, a master who was well-disposed to him, a mistress who was considerate and not at all shy . . . what more could Ardent wish for?

# 13

When Silent announced that he was leaving, the builder flew into a rage and threatened to drag Silent before a court of law if he did not finish the house he was working on.

Mindful of his duty, Silent agreed not to leave Thebes without meeting all his obligations.

The builder grew calmer and asked him to sit down. 'I lost my temper. Forgive me.'

'You were right,' said Silent, 'but don't worry. Even if I have to do everything myself, I'll see that the job is finished.'

The builder sighed. 'Why won't you become my overseer and marry Ubekhet?'

'Has she spoken to you about it?'

'No, but I can tell she's unhappy. And there's no one except you who could make her unhappy.'

'That's true,' said Silent. 'And I do love her – very much.'

'Then I don't understand. If she's refused you, I'll persuade her to change her mind.'

'Do you really think she's that biddable?'

'She'll have to be.'

'Don't upset her. I shan't go back on my decision.'

'Why are you so stubborn?'

'Because I intend to enter the brotherhood of the Place of Truth.'

'But that's impossible! Who'd support your application?'

'I was brought up there.'

'So that's it – that's why you don't work like other men! I suppose there's no argument in the world that could dent your resolve?'

'No, none.'

'Well, I'm sorry. We could have lived happily together, we three. Finish that house, Silent, and then you can go.'

In less than a fortnight, Ardent had done three months' ordinary work. No workman tanned skins better than he did, and it was his which sold most quickly and for the best prices. He was conscientious, carrying out every procedure with care and scraping the skin as long as necessary before tanning. Rejecting oils which might be about to turn rancid, the young man had instinctively inclined towards quality, and he had just finished a pair of sandals which only a substantial landowner could afford.

Now he was working on a charioteer's shield. Using a leather-knife with a semi-circular blade, Ardent cut well-softened straps out of a goatskin. He would fix them to the shield, which would then be strengthened with a metal edging.

'Are you the new man?'

The voice was curt and authoritarian. Ardent did not turn round, but concentrated on his work.

'Chariot officer Mehy is talking to you, and he doesn't like it when people turn their backs on him.'

'I don't deal with customers,' said Ardent. 'See the master.'

'You're the one I'm interested in. It seems you're as strong as a wild bull and you knocked out two big lads who are no novices at fighting.'

'It didn't take much effort. They bumped into each other.'

Mehy seized Ardent by the arm and forced him to look at him. 'I don't like insolence, boy!'

'Let go of me – *now*!'

There was such menace in the young man's black eyes that Mehy loosened his grip and took a step back.

Ardent found himself looking at a short, round-faced man with black hair plastered to his scalp. His lips were thick, his hands and feet pudgy, his torso broad and powerful. The officer seemed sure of himself, and his chestnut-coloured eyes were full of arrogance.

'Are you daring to threaten me?' said Mehy.

'All I want is for you to treat me with respect.'

'Very well, boy.' Mehy turned towards Ardent's work-bench and asked, 'How is my shield coming along?'

'I'm working on it now.'

'Show me.'

Ardent did so.

'You must add nails and metal plates. I want a shield so solid that it will impress even the finest soldiers.'

'I'll do my best.'

Mehy surveyed him for a moment. 'Wouldn't you like to leave the tannery for the army? With a build like yours, you'd be taken on at once.'

'The military life doesn't appeal to me.'

'You are wrong. It offers many advantages.'

'For you perhaps, but very few for me.'

'You're young and much too hot-headed, my friend! If you served under me, you'd soon learn flexibility.'

'Flexibility is what I teach the leather.'

'If you decide to do the intelligent thing, come to the main barracks in Thebes and say Officer Mehy recommended you. In the meantime, finish my shield as quickly as possible. I'll send a soldier to collect it tomorrow morning.'

As soon as Mehy had left, the master-tanner appeared in the workshop. 'How did it go?' he asked.

'Well, we didn't exactly make friends.'

'That Mehy's an influential man. He's very ambitious, and

there's a rumour that he'll soon be promoted to an important position. Have you finished his shield?'

'If you want, I can finish it tonight.'

'It would be as well not to annoy Mehy.'

'Tomorrow evening,' said Ardent, 'I'll have finished the work you set as the price of the leather bag.'

'I know, I know. We'll talk about it again.'

When Ardent woke up, the tanner's cousin was sleeping on her belly. For a few moments he looked admiringly at the superb behind which had given him so much pleasure, but his gaze was drawn by the first rays of the sun. They filtered through the reed wall and lit up two objects placed on the ground: a leather bag and a leather case.

Ardent got up to touch them: they were of the finest quality.

'Do you like them?' asked the shrill voice of the girl, who was still only half awake.

'Two little marvels.'

'Like my breasts?'

'If you like.'

'They're a gift from the master.'

'Wrong, my pretty. I earned them with my work.'

'When are we going to get married?'

'Do you want to?'

'Of course, because the tannery will come to you.'

Ardent rewarded her with a slap on the backside. 'This is a good start to the day.'

'Quick, go and see the master,' she begged him languidly. 'Then hurry back to me.'

By dawn Silent had finished the house; it was for a confectioner, his second wife and their two children. His duty was done: he could leave for the Place of Truth. He headed for the ferry.

A hundred times, he had longed to rush to the garden to see

Ubekhet for the last time, but that would only have worsened the pain of being torn apart, the agony of separation. He had immersed himself in his work to stop himself thinking about her, but visions of her haunted him constantly; giving up speaking to her had been an almost unendurable ordeal. Now it was time to leave Thebes – a few days more, and he might not have the courage to do so.

The early-morning breeze was deliciously aromatic. The ferry, laden with goods, crossed the Nile diagonally to take advantage of the wind and the current. As it neared the riverbank, the dozing travellers began to wake up.

Silent was the first to jump ashore. He climbed up the short slope and stopped in his tracks.

Ubekhet was there, sitting under a palm tree.

He rushed to her and gave her his hand to help her to her feet.

'I'm coming with you,' she declared.

# 14

The tanner dropped his piece of bread and ran after Ardent. 'Where are you going?'

'I've worked well, you've paid me, and now I'm leaving.'

'That's crazy! Don't you like my cousin?'

'She has a splendid backside and the brain of a sparrow.'

'Don't you want to take over the tannery from me?'

'At your age, you shouldn't be deaf,' said Ardent. 'I've got what I came for and, as I warned you, I'm moving on.'

'Think, Ardent!'

'Goodbye, master.'

Instantly forgetting the tannery, the young man thought about how to acquire the wood to make a chair. He could barter the beautiful leather case, but he was reluctant to part with it. And it would be something else in his favour when he presented himself at the gates of the Place of Truth. Right now, he needed to find a carpenter who would employ him.

Around mid-morning, the young man introduced himself to the owner of a workshop which employed over twenty apprentices and as many seasoned professionals, and produced simple but solid furniture. The owner was about sixty, a solidly built man with a small moustache. He did not seem exactly easy-going.

'Name?'

'Ardent.'

'Work experience?'

'Farmer and tanner.'

'Were you dismissed?'

'No, I left of my own accord.'

'Why?'

'That's my business.'

'Mine too, boy. Unless you tell me, you can look elsewhere.'

Ardent liked the carpenter's aggressive tone, and he felt like a fight. 'My father is a spineless man of limited imagination, the tanner I worked for is a petty opportunist. I could have taken over from either of them, but I want a better master.'

The carpenter gaped at him in astonishment. 'How old are you?

'Sixteen, but people think I'm older because I'm so big. Are you going to take me on, or do I look elsewhere?'

'What exactly do you want?'

'To work the number of days needed to earn enough wood to make a chair with arms and buy a folding wooden stool. And to do it as quickly as possible.'

'You know the going rate?'

'For a lazy man,' said Ardent, 'five months' work without overexerting himself. For me, no more than a month.'

'Don't you ever sleep?'

'Not much when I've got a job to finish.'

'What happens when you've finished?'

'When I've got what I want, I shall leave.'

The carpenter stroked his moustache. 'Don't you want to learn the trade in depth?'

'I've nothing else to say. It's up to you to decide.'

'You're a strange one! Well, I give the orders here, and I don't like unruly lads. If you agree to do as I tell you, I'll take you on for a trial period.'

'Shall I start right away?'

'Since you need wood, you can go and cut it yourself. My woodcutter will teach you how to use the axe.'

Ubekhet and Silent made slow progress towards the Place of Truth. They skirted wheatfields interspersed with palm-groves and copses of sycamore trees.

'This isn't a village like other villages,' he explained. 'They won't let you in.'

'Unless we live under the same roof and so become husband and wife.'

He halted and took her in his arms. 'That . . . that's what you really want?'

'How can you doubt it?'

Never had the air been so invigorating, the sky so clear, the sun so radiant. But Silent knew this happiness would be short-lived.

'The other women will make your life impossible and drive you out. I'll try to make them accept you, try to convince them that you're more than just my wife and that you're no stranger to the work carried out by the Place of Truth, but—'

'That won't be necessary.'

So Ubekhet was giving up, thought Silent. She had understood that her desire was no more than a dream.

'It won't be necessary,' she went on, with tranquil determination, 'for I too have heard the call.'

'How?' asked Silent in amazement.

'I heard it when I looked up at the Peak of the West, where the goddess of silence dwells. She protects the forbidden valleys which house the immortal souls of the pharaohs and their wives, doesn't she? And she's the secret patroness of the craftsmen of the Place of Truth. Her voice was in the wind; it made my heart blossom and grow. Now I know I shall spend my life discovering, knowing and serving it. And there's only one place where I can do that.'

'I'll do everything in my power to help you,' said Silent, 'and I won't pass through the gates of the village without you.'

Hand in hand, gazing steadfastly at the Peak of the West, they continued on their way to the Place of Truth. Henceforth, the love that united them would make them inseparable. They wanted to live the same life, in all its dimensions, from the most worldly to the most spiritual. Whatever trials they might have to endure, they would never complain or lament; and if they had to confront the spectre of failure, they would not shy away from it.

Two paths gave access to the village. The first passed very close to Ramses' Temple of a Million Years, but the way was permanently barred by soldiers who refused to allow anyone to pass except craftsmen coming from the Place of Truth. The second was the only approved route for those who wished to try to reach the village.

To their right, Ubekhet and Silent left behind the temple of Amenhotep, son of Hapu, the great sage who had faithfully served Pharaoh Amenhotep III, whose huge shrine had been erected nearby. To their left was the mound of Djemeh, where the primordial gods were buried. Leaving the cultivated area, they entered the desert.

The first of the five forts marked the limit of the sacred domain which came under the jurisdiction of the 'great and noble Tomb of a million years to the West of Thebes'. Called 'the Tomb' for short, the institution brought together the craftsmen whose task was to excavate and decorate the houses of eternity of the pharaohs and their wives, and besides the Place of Truth itself, its territory comprised the Valleys of the Kings and Queens.

Ubekhet was conscious of venturing into another world, at once so close and so remote, a world where humans continued to love, suffer and struggle with daily cares but where their work consisted of shaping eternity as though it were a fabric.

Since she had heard the call, Ubekhet saw Silent differently. A creative desire which fascinated her poured forth from him, but it still remained to place the vital tools in his hands so that he could give that desire solid form.

The guards seemed no more friendly than usual. 'Your passes.'

'We haven't got passes,' said Silent.

'Then go back where you came from.'

'I am Silent, son of Neb the Accomplished, overseer in the Place of Truth. Please inform my father that my journey is done and I wish to return to the village with my wife.'

'Ah . . . I'll have to tell the senior officer. For the time being, stay where you are.'

The guard relayed the request to a colleague, who went to the second fort, and the same scene was played out from one fort to the next, until it reached Sobek's office. He authorised the couple to pass through the Five Walls in order to appear before him.

When they saw the aggression in his eyes, Ubekhet and Silent sensed that their case was far from won.

'Your story strikes me as highly suspicious,' declared Sobek haughtily. 'If you have lied to me, you will pay a heavy price.'

# 15

Sobek did not offer his guests a seat. He had slept badly, was suffering from indigestion after eating a dish of beans in sauce. He cursed the heat, and got angry when Silent contradicted him.

'You do know the overseer called Neb the Accomplished?' asked Silent calmly.

'Do you take me for a fool? You're the one who doesn't know him – Neb the Accomplished hasn't got a son.'

'In the secular sense of the word, that is true.'

'What is this nonsense?'

'My parents died, and Neb adopted me. In the eyes of the craftsmen of the Place of Truth, I became his son. I suppose you've been in your post for only a short while, so this is the first time you've heard of me.'

Sobek tapped his forehead. 'All these stories, all these mysteries . . . How am I going to check this? I'm not allowed to enter the village.'

'Let me speak to the guardian of the great gate. He'll tell my father I'm here.'

'Very well. Now, who is this woman?'

'Ubekhet, my wife.'

'And who is her father?'

'A masterbuilder from the east bank.'

'Ah, so she doesn't live in the village.'

'Not yet, but she'll live there with me.'

Sobek pointed an accusing finger at Silent. 'How do I know you're really married?'

'You know perfectly well that no official documents are required.'

'I also know that you must live under the same roof. And where is it, this roof?'

'If you authorise us to leave here and go into the quarter where the lay workers live, I'll show you.'

Sobek pushed back his chair and stood up. 'Let's go.'

Certain craftsmen who worked for the brotherhood in a secondary capacity had been allowed to build modest houses outside the village walls. One such householder was the blacksmith, Obed, a forty-year-old Syrian with enormous arms, short legs and a beard. He both made and repaired metal tools.

As soon as he spotted Silent, Obed came out of his forge, rushed forward, and embraced him so forcefully that he almost knocked the young man over.

'At last you're back! I knew you hadn't vanished for ever, but Ramose the scribe is ill, and your father was beginning to lose hope.'

Irritated, Sobek cut in. 'I'm not stupid, Silent. This house is Obed's, not yours.'

The blacksmith asked, 'What's the problem, sir?'

'This man claims to be married to this woman, but they have no house.'

Obed looked at Ubekhet. 'By all the gods of heaven and earth, she's beautiful! If she wanted me for a husband, I wouldn't hesitate for a second. You're wrong, sir. I've just donated my bedroom to this young couple, who will enter for all to see. They'll therefore be in their own home and will consummate their union there.'

Sobek was furious, and tried to argue. 'What if the girl hasn't consented? What if they're brother and sister, or—'

'Take me in your arms,' Ubekhet told Silent.

He picked her up.

'I congratulate you on your diligence, Sobek,' he said. 'Ubekhet and I love each other, we are husband and wife, and we are going to worship Hathor, goddess of love, to thank her for the happiness she has given us.' He carried his wife across the threshold of the house.

Obed grinned at Sobek and asked, 'Are you sure you don't want to attend the ceremony and draw up an indictment?'

Obed's guttural laughter ringing in his ears, Sobek went back to his office. He wanted to know everything about Silent. If he had committed even the smallest offence, Sobek would show him no mercy.

How sweet it had been, that night of love in a little room furnished with a rickety old bed! Their bodies were made for each other, and they had spontaneously expressed the magic of their mutual desire and tenderness.

'How happy this moment is,' said Silent when the sun rose. 'If only some goddess could make it last for ever.'

'I have slept by your side, my love, your hand resting upon me, and I have become your wife. Never leave me; let nothing and no one ever part us.'

Silent was embracing her when a sound made him start.

'If the young bride and groom are awake,' boomed the blacksmith, 'I'll bring them something to eat.'

Milk, warm pancakes, soft cheese, figs – it was a veritable feast!

Obed went on, 'Your wife is as beautiful as a goddess, Silent, and she must possess countless good qualities, but . . . are you sure you've warned her that you haven't brought her to paradise? The village is a closed world, and new faces aren't welcome – especially when they put all the others to shame.'

'My husband has told me everything,' replied Ubekhet.

'Ah. And you aren't afraid?'

'Like him, I have heard the call.'

'Well then, my warnings are a waste of time. In your position, I'd forget the Place of Truth, go and live on the east bank and enjoy life. At your age, shutting yourselves up in this village, with nothing to look forward to but some mysterious task . . .' Obed shrugged. 'Ah well, each to his own destiny.'

'My kilt's rather shabby,' said Silent ruefully. 'With your new dress, you'll make a much better impression.'

Ubekhet smiled. 'I hope the court of admissions doesn't base its judgements on appearances.'

'To be frank, I don't know how it decides, or even who belongs to it.'

'You aren't worried, are you?'

'I'm afraid of failing, disappointing you, being unworthy of my father . . .'

'I'm anxious, too,' she said. 'But we've no choice. We must be honest, and just be ourselves.'

'There's something else bothering me,' said Silent. 'I've fulfilled all the material conditions to present myself before the court, but what will they demand of you?'

'We shall see.'

The blacksmith came in again, and handed Silent a leather bag, enough good-quality wood to make a chair with arms, and a folding stool.

'Here's what you entrusted to me before you left,' he said. 'But I'd still like to know why you didn't go before the court when you'd fulfilled the conditions laid down. After all, you're the spiritual son of a famous craftsman.'

'Because I hadn't heard the call,' said Silent.

'And that's why you travelled for so long, to hear the call?'

'Yes. And then I realised that it was very close, so close that its power had made me deaf.'

The blacksmith sighed. 'Thank you for being so frank, but

really I don't understand anything. Good luck, anyway.'

The morning was fine, and the heat was intense. The couple went to the main guard-post, where a better-humoured Sobek was eating his breakfast.

'I can't find a reason to imprison you,' he said regretfully. 'Leave here and present yourselves at the north gate.'

Silent and Ubekhet obeyed.

The walls that encircled the village seemed impenetrable. To the left of the locked gate stood one of the two gate-keepers, holding a large staff. He had a square head, broad shoulders and was accustomed to all kinds of fighting. He was not authorised to cross the threshold, but had a hut in which he could shelter from the sun. Like his comrade, he lived in the farming area, far from the Place of Truth.

Each guard was on duty for twelve hours at a time, the shifts changing at four in the morning and four in the afternoon. For this he was paid a modest salary, supplemented by bonuses when he acted as a witness during business transactions.

'My name is Silent, and I am the son of Neb the Accomplished. My wife, Ubekhet, has heard the call, as have I, and we ask you to open the village gate.'

'You are not authorised to enter.'

# 16

The woodcutter's skin was tanned like leather and he chewed constantly on privet-leaves. In front of him and Ardent walked a dozen goats guided by the eldest nanny, who seemed to know where she was going.

'Are we cutting wood or tending the flocks?' asked Ardent.

'Don't be so impatient, my boy; I can see you don't know the trade. Thanks to my goats, I save time and energy.'

The old nanny-goat spotted an acacia tree growing at the edge of the desert, and started eating the most accessible leaves. Unable to resist such delicacies, the other goats threw themselves into the attack on the tree.

'Let's sit down in the shade of that palm-tree over there,' said the woodcutter, 'and let the goats do their work. I've brought bread, onions and a goatskin full of fresh water.'

'I don't want to rest. I want to cut wood, lots of wood.'

'What for?'

'To make a chair.'

'Why? Have you got a house to furnish?'

'I just need the wood.'

'Want to keep your secrets, do you? Well, you're right. The tighter shut you keep your mouth, the better off you are. I've divorced two wives because I trusted them too much. Between them they ruined me, and I shall end my days as a woodcutter in the service of a carpenter.'

'When do we start?' asked Ardent.

'Watch those fine beasts and be grateful to them.'

Standing up on their hind legs, the goats were assiduously stripping the tree. When they had eaten everything they could reach, the woodcutter came to their aid. He fixed ropes to the high branches and pulled them down to within reach of the animals, which were delighted to continue their feast.

'They've done their work well,' said the woodcutter when they had finished. 'The tree is stripped perfectly clean. Now it's up to us.'

Ardent was given a hatchet with a wooden handle and a curved bronze blade. He sliced off the branches with deft, well-aimed strokes, then, without pausing for breath, started chopping at the trunk with a strength that amazed the woodcutter. Not only did the young man seem tireless, but he worked like an experienced professional.

'You're going too fast for me,' grumbled the woodcutter. 'If you carry on at that pace, you'll ruin the trade.'

'Don't worry, I've no intention of making it my career. As soon as I've finished, ask your goats to choose another tree.'

'The master said—'

'I'm the one swinging the axe, not the master.'

The woodcutter decided not to force the issue. So the goats went off in search of another banquet, while he enjoyed a well-deserved rest and Ardent set about his second acacia tree.

Silent and Ubekhet waited for three days. Obed brought them frugal meals but never said one word, as though he had been ordered to observe an unbroken silence. Sobek walked past them without speaking.

They were present when the donkey-train arrived, laden with foodstuffs and raw materials, and when it was unloaded, watched by the gatekeeper. And they were there when the lay workers carried out their tasks, ensuring the continued comfort of those who lived in the Place of Truth.

'Is this what normally happens?' asked Ubekhet.

'I don't know. The people inside are doing as they see fit.'

She smiled. 'Waiting at your side is no trial, and this place is so magical that it makes the time flow like honey.'

Silent shared his companion's serenity. With her and thanks to her, he feared nothing that fate might bring. If the court of admissions thought it could make them bend under the weight of anxiety, it thought wrongly. They were here, in the desert, in the heart of the wild hills over which loomed the majestic Peak of the West. They were very close to the place where people had toiled since the beginning of time, learning the secrets of matter. That in itself was happiness.

Towards the end of the third day, as the sun was sinking towards the horizon, the gatekeeper came to meet them.

'Silent, do you still wish to be admitted to the Brotherhood of the Place of Truth?'

'My intentions have not changed.'

'And you, Ubekhet?'

'Neither have mine.'

'With my colleague, I run the postal service. Do you wish to send a letter to someone close to you, before you appear before the court of admissions?'

Silent shook his head, as did his wife, although she was thinking of her father, who would not understand her decision.

'Then follow me.'

Night was falling quickly. The lay workers had gone back to their homes on the plain, and an onlooker would have sworn that the darkened village had been abandoned.

Despite her determination, Ubekhet's heart was in her mouth. The sweet magic of this place had disappeared with the last rays of the setting sun, and all that remained was a diffuse, oppressive fear.

Following the gatekeeper, the couple came to within a pace

or two of the northern gate, the main entrance to the Place of Truth.

'Wait here,' said the gatekeeper.

Silent gripped his wife's hand tightly.

The gatekeeper crouched down, lit a torch and stepped away from the couple. Peregrine falcons danced in the sky, where the last orange-tinted gleams were fading away.

The gate opened a little way.

An old man stood on the threshold. He wore a heavy black wig and a long white kilt, and carried a gnarled stick in his right hand. Silent thought he recognised a pernickety stone-cutter, a man it was as well not to antagonise.

'Who are you,' asked the old man, 'you who dare to disturb the serenity of the Place of Truth?'

'Silent, son of Neb the Accomplished, and my wife, Ubekhet.'

'Are you known to the court of admissions?'

'We wish to present our request to it.'

'What is that request?'

'To be admitted to the brotherhood of craftsmen and to live in the Place of Truth.'

'Have you fulfilled the conditions laid down?'

Silent presented the leather bag, the folding stool and the wood for making a chair. The man examined them without comment.

'And you, Ubekhet?'

'I have heard the call of the Peak of the West.'

The old stone-cutter reflected for a long moment, as though weighing up the answer. Then he commanded, 'In the name of Pharaoh, swear that you will never, under any circumstances whatsoever, reveal to anyone what you are about to see and hear.'

The couple swore the oath.

'If you betray that oath, may the demons of hell torment you for all eternity! Follow in my steps.'

First Silent then Ubekhet slid through the chink in the gate. On the other side, they saw a narrow street lined with houses, but they had no time to let their gaze wander over this mysterious place, for they were directed towards the left, where there was a porch with two craftsmen standing before it; it was too dark to make out their faces.

One of them stepped forward and seized Ubekhet by the wrist.

Silent reacted immediately. 'Where are you taking her?'

'If you refuse to submit to our laws, leave the village immediately.'

'You must have trust,' said Ubekhet.

The artisan vanished with the young woman.

Silent felt the full force of solitude and feared what was to come. He had hoped that he and Ubekhet would not be separated, and that they would join forces before the judges, but he would have to face them without her.

'The time has come,' announced the stone-cutter.

# 17

Four acacia trees. Ardent had sawn up four whole trees in record time.

The woodcutter had looked on in alarm. He stammered a confused report to the carpenter, who had to believe him when he saw the pile of logs stacked in front of his workshop. The young man had learned to use a saw, which was vital for cutting the finest pieces lengthways, and had made planks which a seasoned professional would not have disowned.

Ignoring the discussion between the woodcutter and the carpenter, Ardent turned his attention to some objects which were ready to be delivered: fan-handles, combs, little dishes and small items of furniture, chests and stools.

The carpenter came over to him and said, 'I gave you precise instructions, and you have disregarded them. Do you know that the felling of a tree requires authorisation? I shall have to justify your zeal to the government!'

'That's your problem, master. I have given you stocks for the future and, what's more, you will save on wages. How many more trees must I chop up to obtain the quantity of wood I need?'

'Your time as a woodcutter is over.'

'Are you dismissing me?'

'That would undoubtedly be the best solution, but you have to learn to make a chair with arms, and also a folding stool, if I remember rightly.'

'Indeed you do.'

'You don't enter a workshop like a bull charging a fence. I employ meticulous craftsmen, who have worked here for many years, and the apprentices know that they must obey and behave in the correct manner. I'm afraid you may be incapable of that.'

'Let us try, anyway.'

'I warn you: at the slightest lapse, I shall sack you.'

The carpenter and his employee shook hands.

'Can I start now?' asked Ardent.

'Wait until tomorrow, you—'

'I've no time to lose.'

When the carpenter introduced Ardent to the others in the workshop, the atmosphere became icy. The faces turned towards the new arrival were closed: clearly, he was not welcome.

'I ask you to accept Ardent as an apprentice,' said the carpenter. 'He'll help you finish jobs which are running late and will be available to help anyone who needs him.'

'What can he do?' asked the oldest workman.

'Learn,' replied the young man. 'Who wants to start teaching me?'

'Take this.'

The workman handed Ardent an adze, a small tool with a wooden handle. One of its faces was flat and bent up almost at a right angle; a bronze blade was bound to it with a leather thong.

'Show us what you can do,' he ordered with irony.

Ardent examined the blade, ran his finger over the cutting edge then took a long, hard look at the workshop as if preparing to take possession of it. He lingered for a few moments over a block, before choosing a plank and smoothing the surface with the adze.

'Who taught you?' asked the worker in astonishment.

'A tool is necessarily adapted to the material it must work.

And this one is made for smoothing wood, isn't it?'

'You aren't a novice!'

'I haven't needed anyone up to now and I'm wondering if that's going to continue. Haven't you anything else to show me?'

The master signalled to the workmen to leave. 'Who are you really, my boy?' he asked.

'Someone who wants to learn how to make a folding stool.'

'Are you after my job?'

'Don't worry about that. As soon as I have what I want, I'll be off.'

'Good. Now, watch me.'

The carpenter sat down on a bench, and took a mallet in his right hand and a wooden chisel in his left. Clamping a narrow plank between his knees, he dug out remarkably regular mortises.

'Now you try,' he said.

Ardent took the master's place, and imitated him faultlessly.

The carpenter stared at him. 'I can't believe you've never worked with wood!'

'Believe what you like, but let's get on.'

In the workshop, there were several kinds of hatchets, saws, knives and chisels. Ardent tried them with a minimum of hesitation. His hand was steady, his movements precise.

Staggered, the carpenter showed him how join carefully cut planks with dovetail joints strengthened with dowels and clamps. He explained how to produce mitred corners and pegs, the art of marrying tenons and mortises. He showed him how to make catches for chests which would prevent their contents spilling out if they were dropped, and how to make boxes and chairs by means of perfect adjustments.

Ardent's hands understood everything and forgot nothing. Sometimes they proved more skilful than their teacher, who looked on in wonder.

'You were born to be a carpenter, my boy. There's nothing you can't do – you'll make your fortune.'

'How many stools must I make to earn my folding stool?'

'Ten will do. But I'm sure you'll develop a taste for it.'

'Show me how to put a rush seat on a chair.'

'We'll see to that tomorrow.'

'Are you tired?' asked Ardent.

Stung, the master used vegetable fibres plaited together to make a chair-seat strong enough to support a considerable weight.

The night passed very quickly, with the master testing his pupil's surprising abilities more and more rigorously; Ardent did not disappoint him once.

When the carpenter fell asleep, Ardent completed his first stool.

A few days later, there was a holiday. The workmen were resting, except for Ardent, who was working under a sycamore tree. It amused him to wield a mallet and chisel, and he took delight in the traps the wood set for him. With a polished stone, he made the surface of a stool perfectly smooth. With the benefit of experience, he would succeed in making a little piece of furniture which was as beautiful as it was sturdy.

'Are you Ardent?' asked a rangy young girl with short black hair.

'Yes.'

'Can I sit down?'

'If you like.'

She was wearing a short-sleeved blouse and a skirt which stopped above the knee. She was bronzed, and cast him alluring glances as she sucked a stalk of sweet papyrus.

'Do you know what people say abaout the sycamore tree, Ardent? They say the whispering of its leaves is like the scent of honey, that its foliage is like turquoise, its bark like earthenware, and its fruit redder than jasper. Its shade is cooling, but I am hot, so very hot . . . Will you help me take my blouse off?'

'I'm busy.'

She took off the scanty garment herself, baring breasts as delicious as love-apples, and snuggled against the young man's powerful thigh. 'Don't you like my description of the sycamore?'

'How closely are you related to my employer?'

The fresh young face drew back. 'I . . . I'm his niece.'

'I'm beginning to get tired of this. Every man I work for sends me a pretty girl to loosen my tongue and make me stay with him.'

'You're wrong, I—'

'Don't lie. You can tell your uncle that I told him the truth and I've no intention of becoming a carpenter. Thanks to him, I have made rapid progress, and I shall soon be the owner of a fine folding stool.'

'Won't you stay here?'

'I've got better things to do.'

'But what about your future?'

'Let me take care of that. And my immediate future is a fine young woman who wants to make love.'

# 18

The whole of Thebes was in uproar, for the rumours had been confirmed: Ramses had arrived from Pi-Ramses, his capital in the Delta, to spend a few weeks in his palace at Karnak. Some courtiers believed it was simply a holiday, or even a withdrawal into the seclusion of the temple; others were of the opinion that the aged king would announce important decisions.

Ramses had ruled Egypt for fifty-seven years, and he was nearly eighty. In the twenty-first year of his reign, he had signed a peace treaty with the Hittites, marking the beginning of an era of peace and prosperity which would remain engraved in mankind's memory. But misfortune had struck several times, when his father, Seti, his mother, Tuya and his adored wife, the Great Royal Wife Nefertari, had died. Close friends, too, had left the land of the living and two years earlier Kha, the wise, scholarly son who should have succeeded him, had also rejoined the paradise of the world beyond. It would fall to his other son, Meneptah, to take up this heavy burden.

Because of his great age and painful rheumatism, Ramses had already delegated to Meneptah the worries of governing the Two Lands, Upper and Lower Egypt; but it was Ramses who signed the royal decrees drawn up by the faithful scribe Ahmeni, who was becoming more and more grumpy with age, but still worked as hard as ever.

The Egyptian people were sure it was because of the pharaoh that truth had driven away falsehood, evil-doers were struck down, the Nile flooded punctually every year, and darkness yielded to light. They believed the king possessed millions of ears, allowing him to hear the words of all men – even if they were hidden deep within a cave – and that his eyes were brighter than the stars. Pharaoh was a canal, regulating the flow of the river, a vast hall where all could find rest, a rampart with walls of heavenly metal, cooling water in times of overpowering heat, a warm, dry shelter during the winter; he was crowned in everyone's heart, for he made Egypt more fertile and prosperous than the great Nile itself.

Carried on a throne, Ramses arrived at the palace of Karnak, where he was welcomed by the High Priest of Amon, the tjaty, the mayor of Thebes and a few other officials; some were paralysed with alarm at the thought of being so close to the illustrious monarch, whose fame had long since spread beyond the borders of Egypt. His safety was under the direction of Mehy, the charioteer officer, who had arranged everything so as to ensure that his own good and loyal services would be noticed.

Despite the effects of old age, Ramses was still as impressive as he had been on the day of his coronation. A long, slightly hooked nose, rounded, delicately formed ears, a commanding jaw and piercing eyes made up the face of a ruler whose authority was unquestionable.

The palace was a delight to behold. The floor and walls of the pillared reception hall were decorated with painted lotus flowers, papyrus reeds, fish and birds frolicking amid magnificent landscapes. Ramses' names had been painted in blue on a white background, enclosed within ovals symbolising the course of the sun. Friezes of cornflowers and poppies decorated the upper parts of the walls.

When the pharaoh took his place on a throne of gilded

wood, dressed in a white robe and a gold and white kilt, gold bracelets and white sandals, each person admitted to this exceptional audience sensed that Ramses still retained a firm grip on the helm of the ship of state.

'Majesty,' said the mayor of Thebes, 'the city of Amon rejoices in your presence. Thanks to your guidance its existence is a happy one, for you are the father and the mother of all beings. May your word continue to nourish our hearts. You are the master of joy, and he who rebels against Pharaoh will destroy himself.'

'During my journey,' replied Ramses, 'I have examined the reports concerning your government of my beloved city of Thebes. You are a good mayor, but you must pay more attention to the wellbeing of those who live in the new district. Some of the road-building projects are not as far advanced as they should be.'

'It will be done according to your will, Majesty, and we will make up the delay.' The mayor bowed low. 'May I suggest that you admit Charioteer Officer Mehy to the Order of the Golden Collar? He is in charge of your safety in Thebes, and has given complete satisfaction in running his elite detachment.'

Ramses acceded with a tired wave of his hand. For a long time now, he had been bored by handing out decorations or the childish game of honours to which so many dignitaries devoted all their energies.

For Mehy, this was the beginning of a magnificent career. When he received the thin gold collar from the tjaty's hands, his merits thus being recognised in Pharaoh's name, not only would he be raised to the rank of captain, but he would also become one of the senior administrators of the rich city of Thebes. His thick lips gleaming with satisfaction, Mehy was nevertheless a little disappointed that Ramses did not look at him for longer, and that the ceremony was so brief.

'I have received a letter from the governor of the west bank of Thebes,' the king revealed, 'and its contents are the real reason for my presence here. Let the author of this document set out his grievances.'

Abry, a portly senior scribe, approached the king and bowed. 'Majesty, I wished to warn you about an abnormal situation. The craftsmen of the Place of Truth have constituted a separate community since the reign of your glorious ancestor, Tuthmosis I. It has existed for over three centuries and creates houses of eternity in the Valley of the Kings . . . Would it not be opportune to reform this institution?'

'What are your criticisms of it?'

The question was too direct, and embarrassed Abry. 'Majesty, they are not exactly criticisms, but the brotherhood demand a certain quantity of foodstuffs every day, and a number of lay workers are involved in serving the Place of Truth, and this is a heavy expense. Moreover, as the brotherhood are sworn to secrecy, it is impossible to control their work and consequently to tax them. Many officials wonder about the exact role of this body, which enjoys privileges which some consider exorbitant.'

'What do you suggest?' asked Ramses.

Abry felt encouraged to continue. Clearly, the king had seen the force of his arguments. 'I suggest that we abolish the Place of Truth and disperse the craftsmen who live there. The village covers only a small area, and could be transformed into a storage-place. By doing so, we would make substantial savings – and then there would be the taxes levied on families and individuals who have been exempt until now. The abolition of this archaic institution would therefore be entirely beneficial to the state.'

All that remained was for Ramses to pronounce the decree which would transform this plan into reality.

'Do you know the mission of the Place of Truth?' asked the king.

Abry tensed. 'Yes, Majesty. As I said, it is to create houses of eternity for the reigning pharaoh, the great royal wife and those close to them.'

'My own tomb was begun in the second year of my reign, and no doubt you believe that the craftsmen of the brotherhood are idle because their task was finished long ago, since I have lived so long.'

'Oh no, Majesty!' said Abry hastily. 'I am well aware that they have other things to do, and I did not mean to say that—'

'Pharaoh builds the city of God on earth, in accordance with his duty, and he proves his beneficence by the works he undertakes for the gods, building their temples and fashioning their images. At Bubastis, Athribis, Pi-Ramses, Memphis, Iunu, Khmun, Abydos, Thebes, Edfu, Elephantine, in both Lower and Upper Egypt, the work is accomplished and continues in many forms. At the heart of this work is Pharaoh's House of Eternity, which is created by the craftsmen of the Place of Truth. That is why my father, Seti, decreed that the village should be extended, for the essential mystery from which everything proceeds is the birth of what limited minds like yours consider to be a tomb and which, in reality, is a dwelling-place of light. Each day the craftsmen toil to vanquish death; they build for the *ka*, that intangible energy which resides within all living things without being fixed within it or dying with it. And it is for the royal *ka*, which passes from pharaoh to pharaoh without ever belonging to any one of them, that they continue to perfect my final dwelling. But what can you understand of the nature of this secret? For you are a scribe with a closed heart and limited intelligence. Know that my stay in Thebes has one goal only: to improve and extend the brotherhood's village, to offer them better resources and to reinforce the community's stability. To this task I shall devote the last years of my earthly existence, for there is nothing more important than the Place of Truth.'

# 19

Ramses was resting in the palace garden, which was shaded by palms, jujube trees, tamarisks and a willow planted by the side of the lake. The sandy paths, bordered with buttercups, cornflowers and poppies, had been marked out with rope and were weeded constantly. Settled in a comfortable chair, his head resting on a cushion, the old king sat in a pavilion with slender wooden columns painted green. Cool, light beer, grapes, figs and apples were set out on a low table by his side. The king savoured the gentle north wind, which had just started to blow, and watched hoopoes and swallows playing in the light of the setting sun.

The arrival of a visitor jolted the king out of his reverie. The man who bowed before him was one of the most discreet but important dignitaries of his long reign: Ramose, a messenger's son, had been appointed Scribe of the Tomb and of the Place of Truth on the tenth day of the third month of the inundation, in the fifth year of Ramses' reign. The king himself had chosen Ramose for this difficult post, after a career which had already been full. He had been brought up in a House of Life, trained as a scribe's assistant, then took up a post as the scribe in charge of the cattle belonging to the Temple of Amon at Karnak. Later he had been promoted to supervisor of correspondence, the royal archives and Pharaoh's treasury, before taking the plunge and becoming an 'insider'.

Ramses had left this last decision to Ramose, since for the scribe it meant a radical change to his way of life. After working in the immensity of Karnak and the temples of Tuthmosis IV and Amenhotep, son of Hapu, Ramose would have to abandon a life of easy luxury to run the secret village of the artisans from the inside.

The scribe had not hesitated long: the challenge was exceptional enough to appeal to him. As soon as he was appointed, he had asked the Servants of the Place of Truth, in accordance with the king's wishes, to build Ramses a house in the private enclosure. They were also to enlarge the temple of Hathor, the community's protector, while continuing to work on the king's House of Eternity.

At the age of eighty-seven Ramose had retired, but he had remained in the village. He was loved by everyone there, and no important decision was taken without his advice being sought.

To meet his king, Ramose had dressed in the clothes he wore on festival days: a shirt with long, pleated sleeves, an apron with vertical pleats, and leather sandals. Thanks to Ramses, he had led an inspiring life, watching over the prosperity of the Place of Truth, and he was happy to be able to thank the king before dying.

After greeting his guest and offering him refreshments, Ramses said, 'Do you remember the text you loved to read to apprentice scribes: "Imitate your fathers who lived before you; success depends on your ability to learn. The sages passed on their teaching in their writings: consult them, study them, read and re-read them unceasingly"?'

'Despite the weakness of my eyes, Majesty, I continue to observe that precept myself.

'Do you also recall the great celebration in Year Seventeen, which you organised with Pazair, the best of my tjatys? We were young then, and our energy seemed inexhaustible. Today you are an old man, like me, but also the most venerated man in the Place of Truth and the only dignitary authorised to bear the title of "Scribe of Ma'at".'

'It is you who gave me the chance to serve Ma'at during my lifetime, at the heart of the brotherhood which lives by her rule every day. But now the time of the great journey is approaching.'

'Have you had three tombs prepared close to the village, as you planned?'

'Yes, Majesty. In the first, I pay homage to the gods and to your ancestors who have done so much for the brotherhood, Amenhotep I and his wife, Horemheb and Tuthmosis IV; it is there that I have placed the stele on which you appear. The second depicts my two cows, West and Beautiful Tide, and the cowherd who looked after them. In the third are the people who were dearest to me.*

'Is Silent one of them?' asked Ramses.

'He is the greatest joy of my last days, Majesty. You know that my wife, Mut, and I were unable to have children, despite the statues, steles and other offerings we made to Hathor, to Tawaret, the Great Mother, and even to foreign divinities. So I have prepared for the afterlife with care, not forgetting to train my successor, the scribe Kenhir. But the person for whom I have the most esteem and affection is Silent. When he left the village to undertake a long journey into the outside world, I feared I would die before he came back – though I never doubted that he would. Happily, the brotherhood's court of admissions has just admitted him into the ranks of those who have heard the call, so he is now a Servant of the Place of Truth. I am convinced that he will play a vital role there, and not only as a stone-cutter and sculptor.'

'What initiation name have you given him?'

'Nefer-hotep, Majesty.'

'"Nefer", accomplishment, beauty, goodness, and "hotep",

*Theban tombs 7, 212 and 250.

peace, plenitude, offerings . . . a daunting name to live up to!'

'The plenitude of inner peace, the "hotep", will not perhaps be given to him until the end of his life, and then only on condition that he is effectively "Nefer" as a craftsman. But I must tell you that he did not arrive alone at the village gates.'

'Who was with him?'

'His wife. Her name, Ubekhet, which the court retained as her initiation name, means "clarity and brilliance". She impressed the court with her determination and her radiance. She is beautiful, intelligent, free of ambition, and does not for a moment realise the extent of her abilities. The marriage is a solid one, the harsh tests in store will not destroy it. For me, these two young people represent the brotherhood's hope for the future.'

'Where does Ubekhet come from?'

'She is Theban, the spiritual daughter of the late Neferet, Your Majesty's head doctor.'

'Neferet . . . she took wonderful care of me. If Ubekhet has inherited some of her gifts, the brotherhood is extremely fortunate. But tell me frankly, Ramose: do you doubt the good qualities of your successor, Kenhir?'

'No, Majesty, although he does not have an easy personality and is sometimes a little heavy-handed in performing his duties. But I regret neither choosing him nor leaving my furniture, my library, my fields and my cows to him. Of course, he is only the Scribe of the Tomb – the overseers, stone-cutters, sculptors and painters count as highly as he does. Perhaps he has not yet realised that, but time will do its work.'

'In the last few years, several craftsmen have not been replaced,' recalled Ramses, who, as supreme head of the brotherhood, followed its development attentively. 'There used to be forty brothers, and now there are only thirty.'

'Thirty-one with Nefer, Majesty.'

'Is that enough to complete all the works in progress?'

'I have only one lesson to pass on: quality is more important than quantity. As you well know, the essential thing is the proper working of the House of Gold and its ability to create. In that respect, there are no worries. I am even convinced that Nefer's arrival portends a radiant future.'

'I am relieved to hear you say so, Ramose, because hostility towards the Place of Truth continues to grow. The senior scribes think of nothing but growing rich and they are forming a more and more pernicious class, concerned solely for its own future, not the country's. For them, the brotherhood is an administrative anomaly which they would like to get rid of.'

'But it is you who reign, Majesty!'

'For as long as I live, the Place of Truth will have nothing to fear from those who are envious or speak ill of it. I hope that my son, Meneptah, will walk in my footsteps and understand that, without the activity of this brotherhood, the great light of Egypt would be doomed to decline, then be extinguished. But who can predict how a man will behave when he has supreme power at his disposal?'

'I have faith in him, Majesty.'

Ramses knew that Ramose had always been generosity itself and that the brightness of his soul had lit up the brotherhood, but he knew also that the brotherhood was in danger. Although he had caused arms to be laid down all over the known world, the king had not wiped out hatred or ambition, and he was conscious that only the fragile goddess Ma'at, the incarnation of justice, could prevent the human race from following its natural tendency to corruption, injustice and destruction.

Since the time of the pyramids, the pharaohs had relied upon a brotherhood of craftsmen initiated into the mysteries of the House of Gold and capable of writing eternity in stone. After the Thebans had expelled the Hyksos invaders, three centuries before, and raised Thebes to the rank of capital, it was the community of the Place of Truth which took up the torch.

And that flame was vital for the survival of civilisation.

'I have an amusing anecdote, Majesty, about a completely unexpected application we have just received. But I hesitate to bother you with such an trivial incident.'

# 20

'Go on,' said Ramses. 'I'm listening.'

'Almost all the requests for admission are rejected, even though they come from experienced craftsmen who have proved their worth. In this case, the applicant is a sixteen-year-old giant with no proper references. He's a peasant's son, who has spent time in a tanner's workshop, then working for a carpenter. But he's so obstinate that Sobek, the head of security, has had to imprison him twice!'

'Has he fulfilled the conditions necessary to present himself before the court of admissions?'

'Yes, Majesty, but—'

'A number of those who today belong to the brotherhood came from outside – beginning with you, Ramose. Allow this boy to face the judges of the Place of Truth.' Ramses gazed into the distance.

The old Scribe of the Tomb sensed that he was sharing one of those privileged moments during which the king's vision exceeded that of other men. Often, during the course of his long life, Ramses had had premonitions which enabled him to see through the walls of the future and to walk outside the well-trodden paths.

'Majesty, do you think this boy . . . ?'

'Let him appear before the court, and make sure they do not take their decision lightly. If he succeeds in passing the tests, this young man may perhaps play a decisive role in the history of the Place of Truth.'

'I shall inform Sobek.' Ramose drank some beer, then asked, 'Are you planning to inspect your House of Eternity, Majesty?

'Of course. But something else has become clear to me: the shrine of the royal *ka* must be enlarged. You oversaw its construction; you shall decide when the work is to begin and how it should proceed.'

Ramose felt intense happiness. 'This is a great honour for the village! In consultation with the wise woman, we shall choose the right moment.'

In his youth, Ramses, too, had heard the call. He would have liked to share the life of these men, whose thoughts were transformed into a creation filled with light, but his father had chosen him as his successor, to keep Egypt on the path of Ma'at and to preserve the bonds between earth and heaven. Ramses had not been able to escape from his duties for a single day. And it was good that it had not been otherwise.

Sobek opened the cell door. 'Have you finished making a racket?'

'I intend to break through the walls of this prison – and I'll succeed,' replied Ardent.

With nothing but his bare fists, the young man had already seriously damaged the brick wall.

'If you don't stop immediately, I'll have you clapped in irons.'

'You had no right to lock me up. I brought with me the items needed to present myself at the village gates.'

'Oh, so you know the law better than I do?' said Sobek sarcastically.

'In this case, yes.'

Sobek scratched a scar under his left eye, a souvenir of a struggle to the death with a leopard in the Nubian grasslands.

'You're really starting to annoy me, my lad. I'm going to deal with you myself, and I promise you you won't want to talk back to a guard officer ever again.'

Ardent squared up to him. He was as powerfully built as Sobek, but the latter was a little taller and, most importantly, was brandishing a club in his right hand.

A guard ran up, panting. 'Sir, sir! I must speak to you immediately!'

'Not now,' snapped Sobek.

'It's about the prisoner.'

The man's panic-stricken manner convinced Sobek he should listen, so he went out and slammed the cell door shut.

Ardent thought of the ways the torturer might use his club. If he lifted it too high, Ardent would parry the blow, butt Sobek in the chest and break his ribs. But Sobek was a professional and would not fight like a novice. The young man would have no easy task, and might not come out on top. But the Nubian would not emerge unscathed, either, for Ardent would throw all his strength into the battle.

The door opened again. 'Get out of here,' Sobek ordered, the club still in his hand.

'Why? So you can hit me from behind?'

'I'd like to, believe me, but I've had orders. A guard will escort you to the main gate of the village.'

Ardent stuck his chest out. 'So there is justice in this country, after all.'

'Get out of here before I lose my temper.'

'If we happen to see each other again, Sobek, we'll settle our differences man to man.'

'Get out of my sight!'

'Not without my things.'

With clenched teeth, Sobek gave back to Ardent the leather bag, the papyrus-case, the lengths of wood, securely tied together, and the folding stool Ardent had made. Equipped with these precious items, Ardent walked out of the fort with his head held high, like a victorious general advancing into a conquered land.

The Nubian who accompanied him was a solidly built fellow, but next to Ardent he seemed almost puny. 'You shouldn't have made an enemy of Sobek,' he advised. 'He's inclined to bear grudges, and the first chance he gets he'll cut you down to size.'

'Well, if he tries he'd better succeed, otherwise I'll be the one doing the cutting.'

'But he's the commander of the local guards!'

'The important thing is a man's worth, not his titles. If Sobek comes looking for me, he'll find me.'

The guard gave up.

Ardent's excitement grew with every step he took towards his goal. This time, no gatekeeper was going to prevent him from crossing the threshold of the forbidden village. He did not know what was going to happen, but that mattered little. He would know how to convince the judges that he had heard the call and that therefore all doors should open to him.

The sun was shining generously, and its brightness gave even more energy to the young man, who had no fear of even the most pitiless summers. The fact that the craftsmen's village was situated in the desert was, for him, a bonus.

'This is where I stop,' said the guard. 'Go on alone.'

Ardent did not hesitate. Striding determinedly ahead, he crossed the space that separated the fifth and final watch-tower from the edges of the village.

At this time of day, in the late morning, the lay workers had deserted their workshops to eat their lunch in the shade of an awning. They watched the young man pass with curious eyes.

The gatekeeper stood up and barred his way. 'Where do you think you're going?'

'My name is Ardent. I wish to enter the Place of Truth and I have all the necessary items.'

'Are you sure?'

'Absolutely sure.'

'If you've made a mistake, you'll rue the day. In your place, I wouldn't take the risk. I'd go back where I came from.'

'Stay in your own place, gatekeeper, and don't bother yourself with mine.'

'Don't say I didn't warn you.'

'Stop chattering and open the gate.'

The man did so, very slowly.

For a few moments, realisation took Ardent's breath away: at last, his dream was coming true!

# 21

Two craftsmen came out of the village. One took up position behind Ardent, the other in front of him.

'Follow me,' ordered the man in front.

'But . . . aren't I going inside?'

'If you ask any more stupid questions, we shan't even take you before the court of admissions.'

Ardent was angered, but managed to control himself. In this mysterious place, he did not know the rules of the game and he must not make any false move which would condemn him to failure.

The trio walked away from the gate and headed towards the wall that surrounded the largest temple in the Place of Truth. Nearby there was a shrine to the goddess Hathor; high walls hid it from profane eyes.

In front of the closed temple door, nine men sat in a semicircle, on wooden chairs. They all wore simple kilts, except for one old man who was dressed in a long white robe.

'I am the scribe Ramose,' said the old man, 'and you are on the sacred territory of the great and noble Tomb of a Million Years. Here Ma'at reigns, in her land of light. Be sincere, tell the truth, and speak from your heart; if you do not, she will turn you away from the Place of Truth.'

The members of the court of admissions did not look very friendly, and Ardent preferred to keep looking at Ramose, whose face was imbued with goodness.

'Who are you, and what do you want?' asked the old scribe.

'My name is Ardent, and I want to spend my life drawing.'

'Is your father a craftsman?' asked one of the other judges.

'No, he's a farmer. I have broken off all connection with him.'

'What trades have you practised?'

'Tanning and carpentry, to satisfy your requirements.'

Without waiting for permission, Ardent set down his belongings. 'Here is the leather bag,' he declared proudly. 'To it I add a fine case for papyrus scrolls.'

The two objects were passed from hand to hand.

An ill-tempered-looking judge said, 'We require a leather bag, not this case.'

'Surely it isn't a fault to do more than is asked?'

'Yes, it is.'

'Not for me!' blazed Ardent. 'Only the lazy and mediocre keep strictly to the rules, because they're afraid of others and of themselves. If you're passive and never take the initiative, you end up being as lifeless as a stone.'

'Don't shout. Now, why have you presented us only with a folding stool, but not the chair that should accompany it? If you're so eager to do more than we require, why are you content to present us with pieces of wood instead of the finished chair?'

'You set a trap for me,' said Ardent, furious with himself as well as with the judges, 'and I fell into it. Do I have the right to a second chance?'

'Sit down on the stool,' ordered the ill-tempered judge.

As soon as his bottom touched the seat, Ardent heard sinister cracking noises. Without a shadow of doubt, the stool would not support his weight.

'I prefer to remain standing,' he said hastily.

'So, you did not even check the quality of this stool. To

your arrogance, you add carelessness and incompetence.'

'You asked for a stool, and you have it!'

'A poor answer, young man. You're nothing but a braggart and a coward.'

Ardent clenched his fists. 'You are wrong! I tried to satisfy your demands, but my goal is not to make furniture. I can draw and I can prove it.'

Another craftsman placed a brush, a piece of old papyrus and a pot of black ink in front of Ardent. 'Very well then, prove it.'

The young man knelt down. His gaze fixed on the old scribe Ramose, he drew his portrait. His hand did not shake, but he was unaccustomed to these materials, whose use seemed to require an extremely delicate touch.

'I can do much better,' he said. 'This is the first time I've ever used a brush and drawn on papyrus with ink – usually I make do with sand.'

Nervous and rushed, Ardent made a mess of the forehead and the ears. The portrait was dreadful. 'Let me try again,' he begged.

The drawing was passed round. No one commented on it.

'What do you know about the Place of Truth?' asked Ramose.

'It holds the secrets of drawing and I want to know them.'

'What will you do with them?'

'I will decipher life – and that quest is unending.'

'We don't need thinkers, we need craftsmen,' retorted a judge.

'Teach me to draw and paint,' insisted Ardent, 'and you'll see what I am capable of.'

'Are you betrothed?'

'No, but I have already known several girls. For me, they are one of the pleasures of life, nothing more.'

'You don't intend to marry?'

'Certainly not! I've no wish to burden myself with a wife

and a horde of noisy children. How many times must I tell you, my only goal is to draw creation and to paint life?'

'Would you find the demand for secrecy difficult?'

Ardent shrugged. 'It's too bad for those who can't break through it.'

'Do you realise that you will have to submit to a very demanding rule?

'If it doesn't stop me learning, I'll try to put up with it. But I won't obey stupid orders.'

'Are you intelligent enough to know when they're stupid?'

'If need be, I'll find out the hard way.'

The ill-tempered judge mounted another assault. 'With an attitude like that, do you think you're worthy of belonging to our brotherhood?'

'That's for you to decide – you told me to be honest, and I am.'

'Are you patient?'

'No, and I don't want to be.'

'Do you think you're so perfect that your character shouldn't be improved?'

'That's not a question I ask myself. It is desire which allows us to reach our ends, not our personality. It is normal to have enemies: either they'll beat me because I'm weak, or I'll beat them. Either way there'll be a fight, which why I'm always ready for one.'

The judge looked shocked. 'Don't you know that the Place of Truth is a haven of peace, where quarrels are forbidden?'

'Since there are men and women there, that's impossible. Peace doesn't exist anywhere on this earth.'

'Are you certain that you need us?'

'You are the only ones who have the knowledge I need – I can't acquire it on my own.'

'What else have you to say to convince us?' asked Ramose.

'Nothing.'

'Then we shall withdraw to our deliberations, and you will

await our verdict. There will be no appeal.'

The old scribe signalled to the two craftsmen who had brought Ardent to take him back to the northern gate of the village.

'Will it take long?' he asked.

They did not reply.

# 22

Ramose was still in a state of shock. He had often presided over the court of admissions, but this was the first time he had come up against a candidate like this. Ardent had made a profoundly bad impression on the judges, among whom was the ill-tempered Kenhir, Ramose's successor and the serving Scribe of the Tomb.

At least the deliberations would be over quickly and there would be nothing resembling the lively debate that had followed Silent's hearing. Kenhir had responded particularly aggressively, saying that, since Silent was gifted with numerous talents, many careers lay within his grasp and the Place of Truth would be too narrow a space for him. That had not been the opinion of the majority of the craftsmen, on whom the applicant's powerful personality had made a strong impression.

It had taken all Ramose's authority to prevent two craftsmen siding with Kenhir and thus rejecting Silent's application. As a unanimous decision was vital, the old scribe had waged a long and difficult fight until he succeeded in changing Kenhir's mind.

Over Ubekhet, the deliberations had been brief. When she described hearing the call of the Peak of the West, a flood of intense emotion had washed over the court, which was made up of the priestesses of Hathor who lived in the village. And the leader of the judges, the one they called the 'wise woman', had joyfully welcomed Ubekhet.

'Who wishes to speak?' asked Ramose.

A sculptor raised his hand. 'This Ardent is vain, aggressive and tactless, but I am convinced that he has indeed heard the call. It is on that point, and on that point alone, that we must pronounce a decision.'

A painter was the next to give his opinion. 'I don't agree. I don't dispute the fact that he has heard the call, but what about his character? What he wants is to perfect his own skills, not to become one of our brotherhood. We'd give him knowledge, and he'd give us nothing. Let this boy follow his own path, which is far removed from our own.'

Kenhir cut in vehemently. 'A strange fire burns within that boy, and it disturbs you, you who love only insipid people! It's quite true that he's no ordinary craftsman, subservient to his overseer, incapable of thinking and so dull that nobody notices him! If we admit him to our ranks, we run the risk of seeing a storm rage through the village and destroy many of our customs. Are the craftsmen of the Place of Truth so timid that they'll reject this remarkable talent? For he does indeed possess that talent, as you saw. The drawing was imprecise, I agree, but that's because of his inexperience. As a portrait, it was superb – name me one single artist who has shown talent like that before receiving any proper teaching.'

'All the same,' objected the sculptor, 'you can be certain that he'd refuse to obey orders and trample all over our rules of conduct.'

'If he does,' retorted Kenhir, 'he'll be expelled. But I'm sure he'll comply with our rules in order to achieve his aims.'

'Yes, let's talk about his aims,' said the sculptor. 'He's nothing but a nosy boy who wants to learn our secrets.'

'If he is, he wouldn't be the first. But you all know that the merely curious have no chance of staying here long.'

Ramose was astonished at Kenhir, who refuted, one by

one, all the objections to Ardent. It was unheard-of for the Scribe of the Tomb to take sides so passionately. The craftsmen who were most hostile towards Ardent began to waver.

'We need balanced, peaceful individuals like Nefer,' Kenhir went on, 'but also men with fevered hearts like this future painter. If he truly understands the meaning of the work done here, think what splendid figures he will create on the walls of the houses of eternity! Believe me, we must accept the risks.'

The overseer, Neb the Accomplished, cut in. 'Our vocation is not to take risks but to carry on the traditions of the House of Gold and to preserve the secrets of the Place of Truth. This boy won't share our beliefs. He'll behave like a plunderer.'

Ramose sensed that Neb's opposition would be implacable; so he no longer had the right to remain silent. He said, 'I had the honour to converse with His Majesty, and we discussed this boy's case. If I have read Pharaoh's thoughts correctly, he believes Ardent is imbued with a special power which we must not neglect, in the greater interests of the brotherhood.'

'You mean . . . the power of Set?' asked Neb.

'His Majesty did not say so.'

'But that's what it is, isn't it?'

The judges shivered. The murderer of Osiris, made flesh in a supernatural creature which some compared to a hound and others to an okapi, the god Set possessed the power of the skies, which humankind experienced as sometimes beneficent, sometimes destructive. Without it, it was impossible to struggle against darkness and to cause light to be reborn each morning. Only a pharaoh with the stature of Ramses' father would have dared bear the name of Seti. No monarch before him had borne such a symbolic burden; it had led him to build the most vast and splendid of all temples to Osiris at Abydos.

Usually, those imbued with Set's power were prey to excess and violence, which only a society solidly built on the foundation of Ma'at could channel. Surely someone like that should be barred from a community of craftsmen whose mission was to create beauty and harmony.

'Ramose, did His Majesty give you any orders about Ardent?' asked Neb.

'No, but he urges us to be clear-sighted.'

'What more need be said?' added Kenhir. 'We must obey the will of Pharaoh, who is the supreme master of the Place of Truth.'

Even the most sceptical members were convinced; except for Neb. He said, 'My appointment as overseer was approved by Pharaoh. He trusts me to judge the quality of those who wish to enter the brotherhood, so any weakness on my part would be irresponsible. Why should we ask less of this boy than of other applicants?'

'Our decision must be unanimous,' said Kenhir. 'You're the only judge who still opposes Ardent's admission – isn't that cause enough for you to reconsider?'

'Our brotherhood mustn't run any risks.'

'Risks are part of life, and refusing to take them would lead us to stagnation, then death.'

Neb, usually so calm, was on the brink of rage. 'This boy is already creating dissent among us! Isn't that good reason to distrust him?'

'Don't exaggerate!' said Kenhir. 'This isn't the first time we've argued heatedly about a candidate.'

'True, but we've always achieved unanimity before.'

Ramose decided he must intervene again. 'We must find a way out of this situation. Neb, is there no way we can change your mind?'

'No. I believe Ardent would disturb the harmony of the village and disrupt our work.'

'You're the overseer,' said Kenhir. 'Don't you know how to prevent that sort of thing?'

'I know my limitations.'

Ramose realised that further argument would never change Neb's mind. He said, 'Flat opposition isn't a constructive attitude, Neb. How do you suggest we resolve this impasse?'

'We must test Ardent in greater depth. If he has truly heard the call, and he has the strength to create his own path, the gate will open.'

Neb outlined his plan. All were won over, even Kenhir, though he grumbled that their precautions were a waste of time.

# 23

'Will this take much longer?' Ardent asked one of his escorts, who had sat down beside him outside the main village gate.

'I don't know.'

'But surely they're not going to deliberate for days on end!'

'It's been known.'

'When it goes on for a long time, is that a good or a bad sign?'

'That depends.'

'How many candidates do you accept each year?'

'It varies.'

'Is there a limit?'

'You don't need to know that.'

'How many of you are there at the moment?'

'Ask Pharaoh.'

'Are there many great artists among you?'

'Everyone does his work.'

Ardent realised it was pointless to question the craftsman; as for the other one, he said nothing at all. And yet, Ardent wasn't discouraged. If the judges were men of integrity, they'd understand the intensity of his desire.

Someone passed the western corner of the curtain wall. Ardent recognised him instantly, stood up and hailed him.

'Silent! Did they let you in?'

'I had that good fortune.'

'At least you'll tell me about the village!'

'I'm sorry, but I can't,' said Silent. 'I've sworn an oath of secrecy, and there's nothing more important than a solemn oath.'

'So you aren't my friend any more!'

'Of course I am, and I'm sure you'll succeed.'

'Can you speak to them in my favour?'

'Unfortunately not. It is the court of admissions alone which decides.'

'I was right,' said Ardent bitterly. 'You aren't really my friend any more – and I saved your life.'

'I'll never forget that.'

'You already have, now that you belong to another world. And you won't help me?'

'I can't. You have to face up to this test alone.'

'Thanks for the advice, Silent,' grumbled Ardent.

'The brotherhood has given me a new name: Nefer. And I must also tell you that I got married.'

'Oh. Is she pretty?'

'Ubekhet is sublimely beautiful. The court has admitted her to the Place of Truth.'

'You have all the luck! The seven spirits of Hathor must all have been present around your cradle, and they weren't mean with their gifts. What work have you been given?'

'I can't tell you about that, either.'

'Oh yes, I was forgetting – for you, I don't exist any more.'

'Ardent—'

'Go away, Nefer the Silent. I prefer to stay alone with my guards. They're no more talkative than you, but then they're not my friends.'

'Have faith. You've heard the call, so the judges won't send you away.' Nefer put a hand on Ardent's shoulder. 'I believe in you, my friend. I know the fire blazing inside you will burn away all obstacles.'

When Nefer went away, Ardent longed to follow him into the village; but he would have been driven away for ever.

A little before nightfall, one of the judges appeared. All Ardent's muscles burned, as if he was about to fight his final battle.

'We have made our decision,' announced the judge. 'We are admitting you to the outside workforce, and placing you under the supervision of the potter Beken, head of the lay workers. Go to him to learn what work you are to do.'

'The outside workforce? What does that mean?'

The judge ignored the question and went away, followed by the two craftsmen.

'Wait!' cried Ardent. 'I want to know—'

The gatekeeper stepped in front of him. 'Don't make a fuss! You've heard the decision and you must accept it or you'll have to go away for ever. The outside workforce isn't so bad. You'll find your place as a potter, a woodcutter, a laundryman, a water-carrier, a gardener, a fisherman, a baker, a butcher, brewer or shoemaker. Those people all work to ensure the wellbeing of the craftsmen of the Place of Truth, and they do well on it. I and the other gatekeeper are men of the outside.'

'You didn't mention artists or painters.'

'Those people know the secrets . . . But what good does it do them? They're no happier or richer for it, and they spend most of their lives toiling away. You're getting the best of all worlds, believe me. Try to get on with Beken, and you'll have a good life.'

'Where does he live?'

'At the edge of the farming area, in a little house with a stable. He's got nothing to complain of, but he's cantankerous, convinced that all the lay workers are after his job – and he may be right, at that. Watch out for his attacks. Beken's a sly one and he didn't get where he is by chance. If he doesn't like you, he'll break you.'

'If you belong to the outside workforce, can you still enter the brotherhood?'

'The outside is the outside. Don't seek to progress any further. Be content with what you've been given. For the time being, you can sleep in one of the lay workers' workshops. In a little while, you'll live in a house in the farming district, you'll marry a beautiful girl and you'll give her fine children. Don't be a laundryman – that's a nasty job. The best ones are fisherman and baker. If you're crafty, you can re-sell fish or loaves without declaring them to the scribe who keeps the tally.'

'I'm going to see Beken right now,' declared Ardent.

'I wouldn't advise that.'

'Why not?'

'After a day's hard work, he likes to be left alone. Having a stranger turn up out of nowhere would put him in a terrible mood, and he'd take against you. Go and get some sleep. You can see him tomorrow morning.'

Ardent felt like knocking out the gatekeeper, then demolishing the wall round the forbidden village. That milksop Silent had become Nefer, while he, whose call was so intense, had been dumped into the outside workforce, where he'd be left to rot like an idiot. He'd been humiliated. Well, he'd retaliate by destroying what he could never have.

The gatekeeper had sat down on his mat, his eyes lowered. Ardent heard children's laughter, women's voices, snatches of conversation. Life had started up again inside the village, a life of which he could see nothing.

Who were they, these people who'd been admitted to the Place of Truth? What were the qualities that had convinced the court to admit them? Ardent knew only Nefer the Silent, who couldn't have been more different from himself. He'd have to fight with his own weapons. No one would help him, and advice was nothing but poison. But he wouldn't give up.

He headed towards the lay workers' empty workshops,

knowing that the gatekeeper was watching him out of the corner of his eye. He pretended to go into one, but went round the side of it so as to escape the watcher's field of vision. Then he skirted the hill, taking care to tread as silently as a desert fox.

Since the brotherhood had relegated him to the outside workforce, he'd show them just what he was capable of.

# 24

Charioteer Captain Mehy sat in his private rooms in his fine new house in Thebes, and rubbed his Order of the Gold Collar between his pudgy fingers. It had transformed him into one of the most prominent figures in Theban society. Thanks to this decoration, he would now be invited to all the most select parties and would become a trusted confidant to the people who really counted. Little by little, Mehy was weaving a web that would make him secret master of the fabulously wealthy city of Amon.

He had made one important decision: he would allow the mayor of Thebes to retain his position. The man was a petty domestic tyrant, who was becoming entangled in a struggle between warring factions and had no long-term plan. While he was wearing himself out in a sterile battle and parading up and down at the front of the stage, Mehy would install his friends in various branches of the administration so that, little by little, they could take control.

Fine prospects, true, but they were not enough. The most important thing was the secret of the Place of Truth, that secret which he had been fortunate enough to witness and which he wished to possess. When the Stone of Light was in Mehy's hands, he would become more powerful than Pharaoh himself and he would be able to lay claim to the right to rule Egypt.

Mehy had long suspected that the craftsmen of the Place of Truth had made many important discoveries, but reserved them for the exclusive use of the king. Such privileges must disappear. Egypt would provide herself with new weapons, crush her adversaries and eventually undertake a political expansion which Ramses had shown he was incapable of.

Mehy would never have signed a peace treaty with the Hittites. Ramses should have taken advantage of their weakness, crushed them and then formed a modern army powerful enough to dominate the world. Instead of this magnificent policy of conquest, he had gradually dozed off in peace, and the senior army officers no longer thought of anything but their retirement, which they would live out on a little country estate given to them by the king. Such a terrible mess was enough to make you weep!

Mehy's cupbearer came in. 'Would you like something cool to drink, master?' he asked.

'Some white oasis wine.'

A servant fanned the captain while he sipped the costly wine. It was not easy to obtain the best vintage, but Mehy had bribed a winegrower who delivered his wares to the palace and raked off a little for his own benefit.

The supreme art was surely to build up compromising files on absolutely everybody, and then, when the time came to make use of them, to add a few plausible inventions. That was how Mehy had managed to oust some young officers who were better qualified than he, but much less skilful.

'Lady Serketa would like to see you, master,' announced the doorkeeper.

Serketa was the rather stupid girl he was obliged to marry because of her fortune and her father's position as treasurer of Thebes. She had opulent breasts, a mass of dyed yellow hair and washed-out blue eyes.

He had been expecting someone else, but nevertheless he went down to the reception hall. He was particularly proud of this room because of its tall windows with their yellow-painted frames and its luxurious ebony furniture.

'Mehy, my darling,' cooed Serketa. 'I was afraid you wouldn't be at home. How do you think I look?'

He felt like replying, 'Too fat,' but he was careful to hide his thoughts, for Serketa was obsessed with her weight, which her daily consumption of sweet pastries did nothing to diminish.

He said, 'More ravishing than ever, my darling. That green dress suits you delightfully.'

'I knew you'd like it,' she said, executing a little twirl to show it off.

'There is just one slight problem: I'm expecting a visitor, a leading citizen, and he's a rather difficult person. Would you mind waiting, then joining me for dinner?'

Her smile was idiotic, but full of promise. 'I hadn't hoped for so much, my darling.'

Roughly, he pulled her to him; Serketa did not protest.

She liked to simper and play at being a little girl; she dreamt of being a baby again, cossetted by her mother and her wet-nurse, protected from the outside world. Her real problem was boredom. Thanks to the wealth of her father, a widower with a taste for ever-younger girls, she could satisfy all her whims and buy anything she fancied. Over time, her life had become so wearisome that she had sought out any and every pleasure which might make her less unhappy. Wine had amused her for a while, but had not broken through her loneliness.

When she met Mehy for the first time, at a reception, she had thought him fat, vulgar and pretentious, but he had offered her an unexpected sensation: fear. There was a barely contained brutality in him which fascinated her and which she needed. As he scarcely concealed his ambitions and seemed ready to crush beneath his chariot-wheels anyone who got in his way, Serketa had decided to marry him. Perhaps he would provide her with other unexpected sensations which would cure her lassitude.

'How much longer,' Mehy asked, 'must we wait until we can be married?'

'That depends on you, darling. Now that you're a member of the Order of the Golden Collar, my father thinks you will become an important man in Thebes.'

'I shall try not to disappoint him.'

Serketa nibbled Mehy's right ear. 'And me, my treasure, you won't disappoint me either, will you?'

'You need have no fear of that.'

Unseen by them, the steward came to the open door. He was embarrassed when he saw the couple embracing, so hastily announced his presence by knocking on the door-frame.

'What is it?' demanded Mehy.

'Your visitor has arrived.'

'Ask him to wait, and close that door!'

Serketa devoured Mehy with her eyes. 'About our wedding . . .' she said.

'Let's have it as soon as possible. We'll wait just long enough to organise a grand reception where the whole Theban nobility will envy our happiness.'

'Do you want me to arrange it?'

'You will work wonders, my darling.'

He kneaded Serketa's breasts, and she moaned with pleasure.

'As to our marriage contract, my father is rather demanding.'

Mehy was astonished. 'What contract?'

'Father thinks it advisable, because of his wealth. He's sure we'll be very happy and have several children, but all the same he thinks we should have a contract keeping our money separate. What does it matter, my love? We shouldn't mix law and feelings. Caress me again.'

Mehy began again, but with less enthusiasm. This news

was a veritable disaster, for getting his hands on Serketa's father's wealth was one of the major stages on his road to power.

'You look vexed, my ferocious lion. Surely it's not because of this little legal detail?'

'No, of course not,' said Mehy. He kissed her again. 'You will come and live here, won't you?'

'Of course, when we're in Thebes. This house is superb and well-situated, and my father has decided to pay off what you owe on it, and so make you the owner immediately.'

'He is very generous. How can I thank him?'

'By making his daughter mad with love!' She kissed him full on the mouth. 'We shall also have a big house in the Theban countryside, another in Middle Egypt and a beautiful home in Memphis – they'll stay in my name, but that's just another detail.'

Mehy would gladly have raped her like a common soldier, but she wanted it too much and, besides, his visitor was waiting. He was already recovering from being hit where it hurt most. He had long since realised that hypocrisy and lies were formidable weapons, which enabled him to turn difficult situations to his own advantage. He would pretend to accept and be defeated, all the better to prepare a decisive counter-attack. Serketa's father was wrong to think that a man of Mehy's calibre could be brought to heel.

'Forgive me, delight of my heart,' he said, 'but this meeting is really important.'

'I understand. I shall go and begin the preparations for our wedding. We'll meet again this evening, at dinner.'

# 25

Mehy was proud of his big house. He had persuaded an old Theban noble, who was distracted with grief following his wife's death, to sell it to him cheaply. As the military authorities had advanced him a loan at an extremely advantageous rate, the captain had won on all counts. And thanks to his future father-in-law, he would become the owner sooner than expected. In reality, Serketa's father wanted to present to society a son-in-law who seemed rich, cushioned against any financial problems, without mentioning that it was he, the leading citizen, and he alone, who controlled the situation. Mehy would make him pay dearly for this humiliation.

The two upper storeys of the house had been built on a raised foundation to prevent dampness. On the ground floor were the rooms reserved for the servants, who were supervised by a steward; Mehy ate only bread made by his own baker and insisted that his clothes, which were washed and cleaned with great care by his laundryman, were absolutely spotless. On the steps which led to the upper floors were vases containing cut flowers, which were replaced as soon as they showed signs of losing their freshness.

On the first floor were the reception rooms; on the second, the master of the house's study, the bedrooms, the bathrooms and the conveniences. Mehy had had plumbing installed to carry away waste water, and enjoyed a level of comfort not far below that of Pharaoh's palace.

He loathed gardens and farming; there were plenty of peasants to take care of that. Men of his quality deserved better, and only the centre of a great city like Thebes could contain a residence worthy of the name.

When he entered the reception hall with its high ceiling, Mehy savoured the coolness of the room which, thanks to a clever ventilation system, was constant even in the summer. Nothing was more detestable than heat.

His visitor was sitting in an armchair upholstered in multi-coloured fabric. He had drawn scented water from a blue jar, to wash his hands and feet.

'Welcome, Daktair,' said Mehy. 'How do you like my house?'

'It's splendid, Captain. I know of none finer.'

Daktair was short, fat and bearded. Dark eyes enlivened his sly face, which was covered in a thick red beard and whiskers. His legs were too short and gave him a lumbering gait, but he could be swift as a snake when he had to strike down an adversary.

The son of a Greek mathematician and a Persian alchemist, Daktair had been born in Memphis where, while still very young, he had got himself noticed because of his pronounced taste for research. Lacking all moral sense, the student had quickly realised that stealing other people's ideas would enable him to take giant strides forward, with the minimum of effort. But that was only a strategy, for use in the service of his grand design: to make Egypt the chosen land of pure knowledge, free of all superstition, knowledge which would allow man to dominate nature.

Thanks to his gifts in the workshop and as an inventor, Daktair had made himself indispensable to the mayor of Memphis before becoming the protégé of the mayor of Thebes, in which position he had attempted to decipher the mysteries of ancient wisdom. His calculations predicting the levels of the Nile flood were remarkably accurate, and he had improved the method of observing the planets. However, these were still mere trifles; tomorrow, he would impose a new vision of the world which would drag Egypt out of her lethargy and her outdated traditions, and set her on the road to progress. Think what such a rich, powerful country would be capable of once it had renounced its old beliefs . . .

'Congratulations on your golden collar, Captain,' Daktair said. 'It's a well-deserved reward, which makes you an important and influential man.'

'Not as influential as you. I've heard it said that the mayor of Thebes could not get by without your advice.'

'That's rather overstating it, but he's a sensible man who, like me, is more interested in the future than the past.'

'I've also heard that your ideas offend certain important people.'

Daktair ran his fingers through his bushy beard. 'I can't deny it. The High Priest of Karnak and his ritualists disapprove of my investigations, but I'm not afraid of them.'

'You seem very sure of yourself,' said Mehy.

'My opponents will soon be swept away by a river more powerful than the Nile: the natural curiosity of humankind. We all have a need to acquire knowledge, and I'm helping satisfy that need. In a country like this, hidebound by tradition, the road threatens to be a long one. However, one could save time, a lot of time . . .'

'How?'

'By learning the secrets of the Place of Truth.'

Mehy swallowed a mouthful of white wine to mask his excitement. Was he about to gain a considerable ally? 'I don't quite follow you,' he said. 'They're just a company of builders, aren't they?'

Daktair wiped his forehead with a scented cloth. 'That's what I believed for a long time, but I was wrong. Not only does the village bring together craftsmen with exceptional skills, but it also harbours secrets of vital importance.'

'Secrets? What kind of secrets?'

'If I wasn't afraid of sounding pompous, I'd say they concern eternal life. After all, the brotherhood of the Place of Truth is in charge of preparing the pharaoh's House of Resurrection. I believe that some of its members know the alchemical process which allows barley to be turned into gold,* not to mention other wonders.'

'Have you tried to get to the bottom of these mysteries?'

'More than once, Captain, but without success. The Place of Truth answers only to Pharaoh and the tjaty. I have many friends in high government positions, but each time I've asked to visit the village my request has been refused.'

'Isn't your attitude rather . . . ill-advised?'

'I've had this conversation several times, and people have just laughed in my face.'

'Yes, so they tell me. But I wanted to hear it from your own lips. You see, I take you seriously.'

Daktair was astonished. 'I'm flattered that you do, Captain, but may I ask why that is?'

'Because the Place of Truth interests me, too. Like you, I tried to find out what is hidden its walls, but I failed. A secret that well guarded must be of the utmost importance.'

'An excellent deduction, Captain.'

Mehy looked his guest in the eye. 'It isn't a deduction.'

'What . . . what are you saying?'

'I have seen the secret of the Place of Truth.'

Daktair got to his feet, his hands trembling. 'What is it?'

'Don't be so impatient. I'm telling you that it really exists, and your help will be vital if we are to get our hands on it and make use of it. Are you prepared to strike a bargain?'

*'Turning barley into gold' is the oldest expression of the alchemists' ambition later known as 'turning lead into gold'.

# 26

Daktair's small, dark eyes became piercing, as if they could detect Mehy's ulterior motive.

'A bargain, you say. What kind of bargain?'

'You are brilliant, but your research has come up against unbreachable walls, the walls of the Place of Truth. For personal reasons, I have decided to set in motion the destruction of this archaic institution, but not before stripping it of its treasures and its secrets. Let us join forces to achieve that.'

Daktair seemed unconvinced.

'You have the intelligence and the ability,' Mehy went on, 'but you need material means. Soon, I shall have at my disposal one of the largest fortunes in Thebes, and I intend to use it to extend my influence.'

'You have your sights set on a senior post in the army, I suppose?'

'Of course, but that's only a stepping-stone. Egypt is old and sick. She has been ruled for too long by Ramses, who is now merely a senile despot incapable of seeing the future and taking good decisions. This over-long reign condemns the country to dangerous stagnation.'

Daktair went white. 'You . . . you can't mean that!'

'I am perfectly clear-headed, and that is an essential quality when one aspires to high office.'

'Ramses is a living monument! I've never heard a single

word of criticism of him – it's thanks to him that this is an era of peace.'

'It is only the prelude to new wars, for which Egypt is extremely ill-prepared. Ramses will die soon, and no one can replace him. With him, an outdated civilisation will be extinguished. I have come to realise this – and so have you. You must work on advancing your ideas; I shall take care of the institutions. There is the basis for our bargain. If our vision is to be realised, we must make ourselves masters of the most important elements of Egypt's power. Foremost among them is the Place of Truth.'

'You're forgetting the army, the police, the—'

'I'm taking care of those, I told you. Pharaoh's fortune depends not on his elite troops, which I shall succeed in controlling, but on the mysterious science of his craftsmen, who know both how to create a house of eternity and to obtain gold for it in profusion.'

Daktair's passions were roused. 'You know a great deal about the Place of Truth.'

'What I saw proved that you and I are right about the scope of its knowledge.'

'Is that all you're going to tell me?'

'Have we a bargain?'

'It's dangerous, Captain, very dangerous . . .'

'Yes, it is. We shall move with as much caution as determination. If you lack the courage, say so now.'

Daktair knew that, unless he joined the plot, Mehy would kill him: the captain could not leave alive a man who knew even part of his plan. But Daktair still hesitated. Mehy gave the impression of being able to make the most insane dreams come true, but his road was a perilous one. In looking towards a day when knowledge would rule supreme, Daktair had forgotten that the pharaonic state and its armed forces would take a keen interest in such an upheaval. Behind his smile and his good manners, Mehy had the soul of a killer. Basically, he was giving Daktair no option: either he collaborated without a second thought, or he would die a brutal death.

'I accept, Captain. Let us unite our strengths and our wills.'

A smile spread across Mehy's round face. 'This is a great moment, Daktair! Thanks to us, Egypt will have a future. Let us seal our pact by drinking some fine wine from Year Five of Ramses' reign.'

'I'm sorry, I drink only water.'

'Even on this special occasion?'

'I prefer to keep a clear head in all circumstances.'

'I like men with backbone. Starting tomorrow, I shall undertake a series of official visits to put forward a plan to improve the efficiency of the Theban armed forces. I shall have no difficulty getting it accepted, and it will mean promotion for me. After my marriage, many leading citizens will listen to my opinions, and little by little I shall worm my way into the administration until I have become indispensable.'

'For my part,' said Daktair, 'I'm optimistic that I shall be appointed deputy to the head of the central research workshops in Thebes.'

'A word from my future father-in-law, and you will be. We shall have to let a little time pass before you take sole control, though.'

'It'll be an important step. I'll be able to do research which so far I've been forbidden to do, and to make use of new skills and resources.'

Mehy thought immediately of the manufacture of new weapons which would make the troops under his command invincible.

'We shall have to learn more about the Place of Truth,' he said, 'to distinguish lies from truth. We know the village is run by Ramose, an experienced scribe appointed by Pharaoh. He has held office for many years, but no one has ever been able to get a word out of him about it. I know his successor's name, since he signs the official documents: he is called Kenhir. We must find out all we can about him. If he can be manipulated, we can strike at the leadership.'

'If he is indeed the real leader of the brotherhood,' pointed out Daktair.

'There must be a leader or even several, in charge of building projects, and a whole village administration. We must discover the names and exact roles of all the leaders.'

'The craftsmen certainly won't talk, but some of the outside workers might.'

'If I'm not mistaken, they don't enter the village.'

'That is true, but they are present at certain events.'

'Carrying water, food, clothes, I know. What use is that?'

Daktair gave a satisfied smile. 'A detailed examination of those things will tell us much about how the brotherhood lives and the approximate number of its members.'

'That might be useful,' conceded Mehy. 'Have you already got informants?'

'Only one, a laundryman to whom I gave a powder which enables him to clean soiled linen more quickly. That's only a beginning. If we're prepared to pay, we'll soon find other sources. The launderer told me that something interesting and unusual has happened recently.'

Daktair let Mehy salivate for a few seconds, then went on, 'It's a long time since any new craftsmen were admitted. Now, a young man call Nefer the Silent has been accepted. His progression is rather surprising, because he left the village – where he was brought up – and travelled for several years before coming back.'

'Yes, that is curious. Is there anything unsavoury in his past?'

'We'll have to find out. But there's more. Accepted with him was a young woman from outside the village, probably the daughter of a wealthy Theban.'

'Are they married?'

'That's something else we must find out.'

Mehy was already dreaming up several ways of disrupting the Place of Truth and forcing its leaders to emerge from their refuge. Once breached, the village walls would not remain standing for long.

'My dear Daktair, I didn't think our first meeting would bear so much fruit.'

'Neither did I, Captain.'

'Our task will be difficult, and patience isn't one of my greatest virtues. All the same, I must practise it. Now, to work.'

# 27

Beken the potter was pleased with himself. As leader of the outside workers at the Place of Truth, he skilfully cheated on the hours he worked and used his position to obtain advantages that made his life more agreeable. He had taken the shoemaker's daughter into his bed; for the shoemaker was more preoccupied with safeguarding his job than with the virtue of his first-born. She was neither beautiful nor intelligent, but was twenty-five years younger than Beken.

'Come to me, little bird,' he said. 'I won't eat you up.'

The girl stayed huddled by the front door.

'I'm a good and generous man. If you're nice to me, I'll give you a delicious meal and your father will carry on his trade without the slightest problem.'

Her heart in her mouth, the girl took a step forward.

'Just a little further, my fickle sparrow, and you won't regret it. Start by taking off your tunic.'

Very slowly, she did so.

Just as Beken was reaching out to seize his prey, the door of the house burst open, hit him hard on the shoulder and knocked him over.

The terror-stricken young woman saw a young giant appear, looking for all the world like a mad bull, and she made a clumsy attempt to hide her curves with her tunic.

'Get out of here,' he told her.

She fled, sobbing, while the giant picked up his victim by the hair.

'Are you Beken the potter, head of the outside workforce at the Place of Truth?'

'Yes, yes, but what do you want with me?'

'My name is Ardent, and I had to see you as quickly as possible so that you could give me a job to do.'

'Let go! You're hurting me!'

The young man threw the potter on to his bed. 'We're going to understand each other very well, Beken, but I warn you: patience is not my strong point.'

Furious, Beken sprang to his feet. 'Do you know who you're talking to? Without me, you won't get anything at all!'

Ardent pushed him up against the wall. 'If you give me any trouble, I shall get angry. And when I'm angry, I tend to forget myself.'

Beken saw the anger in Ardent's face, and believed him. 'All right, all right, but calm down!'

'It annoys me, having somebody like you giving me orders.'

The potter recovered some of his lost pride. 'All the same, you'll have to obey me. I'm the head of the lay workforce, and I like work to be done properly.'

'Then I shall be your right arm, and you won't be disappointed. If your work is backbreaking, you need an efficient assistant.'

'It's not as simple as that.'

'Don't tell me stories. Since that's all agreed, I'll settle in here. I like the place, and I'm sleepy.'

'But . . . but this is my house!'

'I hate repeating myself, Beken. Don't forget to bring me hot flatcakes, cheese and fresh milk, just before dawn. Our day is likely to be taxing.'

Ardent needed only three hours' sleep, and he awoke when he had planned to, long before the sun came up. He breakfasted on stale bread and dates, then left Beken's house and hid in the stable, where a fine fat cow watched him with calm eyes. Everyone knew that the gentle beast was one of the incarnations of Hathor, goddess of love, and that her eyes had unrivalled beauty.

What Ardent had foreseen duly happened: the potter approached, accompanied by two sturdy men, each holding a cudgel. Beken had no intention of giving in, and he thought that a serious punishment would dissuade the troublemaker from bothering him any more.

Ardent saw the trio disappear into the house. He left the stable and listened outside Beken's door. He heard cudgel-blows falling on the bed where he should have been lying. He went into the house just as Beken's accomplices were finishing their dirty work.

'Were you looking for me?' he inquired.

Terrified, the potter hid behind his acolytes. The first rushed at Ardent, who grabbed a stool and knocked him out. The second succeeded in hitting the young giant on the left shoulder, but received a punch so violent that his nose broke and he collapsed, his arms flung out sideways.

'That just leaves you, Beken,' said Ardent.

The potter collapsed in a heap.

'You disappoint me greatly. Not only are you a coward but you're stupid, too. If you start again, I shall break your arms – and then it'll be goodbye pottery. Now, do we understand each other?'

Beken nodded rapidly.

'Get rid of these two weaklings and bring me something to eat. I'm hungry.'

With obvious pride, Ardent walked past the five forts with Beken, who introduced him to the guards as his assistant. Kenhir had told them the young man had been taken on, but no one had expected such rapid promotion.

It was a long time since the potter had arrived so early at

the lay workers' site. Even Obed, a very early riser, was still asleep.

'Everybody up!' ordered Ardent, in a thunderous voice which awoke the few workers authorised to sleep near the village.

They got up, white-faced and anxious. What catastrophe had just befallen the Place of Truth?

'Beken has decided you're all lazy,' declared Ardent, 'and he's not going to tolerate it any longer. Everyone confines himself to his own trade, and takes no notice of anyone else. That has to change. From today, we are going to join in unloading the provisions, which takes too long and is too chaotic. Next, I shall come round to see each one of you to take stock of the work in progress and satisfy myself that there are no delays.'

The blacksmith, who was still drowsy, protested. 'What are you talking about? These aren't Beken's orders.'

'They're the orders he gave me, and I shall carry them out zealously.'

The potter's chest swelled. After all, Ardent's intervention would restore his authority, which faltered from time to time.

'I have noticed some slackness,' he agreed. 'So I've made new arrangements and taken on an assistant so that they will be applied rigorously.'

Ardent pointed to a fellow with muscular legs. 'You, you will run to the plain and fetch those who should already be here. We're not officials, paid to sleep in our offices, but workers for the Place of Truth. If we become slaves to routine, we shall swiftly be dismissed.'

That argument carried the day, and no one protested.

'Beken will set an example,' said Ardent. 'He's going to make more vases in one day than he's made in the last two months.'

'Yes, yes . . . I swear.'

'If we are aware of the importance of our work, it will be

done all the better. I shall begin by examining yours, blacksmith.'

'Do you think you are capable?' asked Obed.

'You will teach me.'

# 28

Mehy and Serketa's wedding was sumptuous. Five hundred guests, the cream of Theban society, all the senior nobles. The only one not there was Ramses the Great, but the old king never left his palace at Karnak, where he worked with his faithful Ahmeni, who kept the number of audiences to an absolute minimum.

Serketa was drunk and sprawled across a pile of cushions. Her father's immense house had emptied of its guests and Moseh, the treasurer of Thebes, was drinking vegetable broth to dispel his migraine while Mehy, who was strangely calm, was gazing into the lotus pool.

Moseh was a podgy but alert fifty-year-old, who always seemed worried. Premature baldness made him resemble the 'pure priests' of the temples, with whom, however, he had nothing in common. Since his childhood, Moseh had juggled with figures and been interested in management; leaving the service of the gods to others, he had spent all his time getting rich, and the death of his wife had increased his thirst for power even more. He had recognised that same thirst in Mehy, which was why he had allowed his daughter to marry him.

'Are you happy, Mehy?' asked Moseh.

'It was a wonderful reception. Serketa is a dazzling mistress of the house.'

'And now you have been admitted to the best society . . . Shall we talk about your future?'

'The army, of course. But it's in the doldrums.'

'That's only to be expected,' said Moseh. 'Thanks to Ramses, lasting peace has been established, and the senior officers are more interested in making careers in the government than in fighting non-existent enemies. Do you have a particular ambition?'

'I should like to reorganise the elite troops so that the safety of the city is perfectly assured.'

'That's a praiseworthy aim, but you must look further. What would you say to becoming assistant treasurer for the province of Thebes? You'd be assisted by a large number of scribes, who'd handle the tiresome problems, and I'd advise you on how to make the maximum profit from your administration – perfectly legally.'

'You're very generous,' said Mehy, 'but I'm not sure my skills—'

'No false modesty. You, like me, have a head for figures and you'll acquit yourself splendidly.'

'I don't want to leave the army.'

'No one's asking you to. You'll soon be promoted and you'll play on two stages, the civil and the military, like so many other senior officers. Ramses is very old, he is preparing his succession, but who can predict the behaviour of Meneptah, the son he would like to see on the throne?'

'How well do you know Meneptah?'

'Not well enough,' said Moseh. 'He is an upright man, almost inflexible, with a character that is just as difficult as his father's, and hostile to anything new. We should prepare ourselves for a conservative reign, without great distinction, during which our dear Thebes will retain a pre-eminent position. But Ramses' longevity may yet surprise us. If Meneptah died before him, whom would he choose to ascend the throne?'

'Have you, by any chance, got someone in mind?'

'Certainly not! I stick to finance, not dangerous power-games which might harm my son-in-law. My way, you will occupy a strategic position which will enable you to face up to any eventuality: you'll be needed either as a soldier or as an administrator. If troubles arise, neither my daughter nor her husband will run any risk.'

'I met a strange man, a foreign alchemist called Daktair.'

'The mayor of Thebes thinks the world of him – he's a sort of inventor, whose brain never stops working.'

'I rather liked him, and I'd like to do him a service. Could we help him to become one of the managers of the central workshop at Thebes?'

'Easily, and indeed it's an excellent idea. He'll shake up a few slumbering researchers and will be grateful to us for his promotion. One day, he may be useful to us. Surround yourself with people who owe you something, Mehy, and build up files on them. They will hate you but will be forced to obey you without question.'

'One detail upsets me, dear father-in-law.'

'What's that?'

'Why don't you trust me?'

'Your question surprises me, after so much talk of the future.'

'If you really trust me, why did you demand a contract separating my wife's possessions from mine?'

Moseh drained his bowl of broth. 'You don't know what it is to be rich, Mehy, and I don't know how you're going to behave towards my daughter. You might be unfaithful, you might even want to divorce her. One small slip, and you'll lose everything. That is how I intend to protect Serketa, and no one will make me change my mind. Now that this problem is resolved, I shall help you to become an important man, for my son-in-law cannot possibly be second-rate. You will enjoy all the pleasures of life, nobles will envy you – what more could you wish for? Make the most of your good fortune, Mehy, and don't demand more.'

'Those are wise words of advice, dear father-in-law.'

A pair of ibis unfurled their broad wings in the orange-tinted sunset sky. On the Nile, boats of all sizes sailed along thanks to the north wind, and the lively river currents. At the stern of a boat with six oarsmen and a new white sail, Mehy and Daktair were taking the cool air.

'The mayor has appointed me assistant to the director of the central workshop,' said Daktair. 'I suppose I owe this promotion to you?'

'Moseh appreciates your worth and he has not the slightest idea about your real personality. How did the director take the news?'

'Rather badly. He's an experienced man, educated at Karnak by scribes of the old school, and he's content with existing knowledge. He firmly requested that I restrict myself to authorised experiments and not do anything new. I'm being watched, and I shall have no room for manoeuvre.'

'Have patience, Daktair. He won't be there for ever.'

'He seems in excellent health.'

'Ah, but there is more than one way of removing an obstacle.'

'I don't understand.'

'Don't play the innocent,' said Mehy scornfully. 'For the moment, make no waves; be content to obey instructions. Why did you wish to see me so urgently?'

'Through my contacts at the palace, I found out that Ramses granted a long audience to Ramose. Ramose is not a suspicious man; he confided to a courtier, a long-standing acquaintance, that the king has great plans for the Place of Truth.'

'That's hardly a revelation! When he made his last official appearance in Thebes, Ramses sharply lectured the authorities of the west bank, who were asking for the village to be closed and the craftsmen dispersed.'

'I don't want to fight Ramses. The struggle would be too unequal.'

'He's only an old man,' sneered Mehy.

'Do I have to remind you that he is the pharaoh, and master of the Place of Truth? We are not of equal stature, Mehy; we should give up before it is too late.'

'Aren't you forgetting the vital secrets you want so much to know?'

'No, of course not, but they're out of reach.'

'You're wrong, Daktair, and I shall prove it. Remember that you have sworn to follow a path and you cannot go back. What else did you find out?'

'Ramose is delighted that Nefer the Silent has been admitted into the brotherhood, for he is sure Nefer will uphold its prestige.'

'In other words, he considers him one of its future leaders.'

'That's only Ramose's opinion,' the scientist objected, 'but he bears the title of "Scribe of Ma'at" and he is highly esteemed by all. There is another plausible rumour: Nefer has married Ubekhet, who was admitted to the brotherhood at the same time.'

Mehy gazed thoughtfully at the Nile. 'To weaken the Place of Truth,' he mused, 'we must first discredit it. When its reputation has been definitively harmed, even the king will no longer be able to defend it. And we have a good chance of succeeding.'

# 29

'You must yield, Ardent, you must yield!'

'Keep talking, Obed.'

The blacksmith and the potter's new assistant were arm-wrestling in the forge, screened from the gaze of the other lay workers.

'I'm the strongest man in the Place of Truth and I'm staying that way,' declared Obed.

'You're wasting energy.'

Ardent's arm was as hard as a block of stone, and Obed couldn't move it. Slowly, very slowly, the blacksmith's arm began to lean over. Calling on his final reserves, he managed for a few seconds to halt the inexorable descent. But the pressure was too great and, with a cry like that of a wounded beast, he conceded defeat.

Obed's forehead was bathed in sweat, and he wiped it away with the back of his left hand. There was not a single drop on the young giant's brow.

'Nobody has ever beaten me before,' said Obed. 'What kind of energy flows in your veins?'

'You weren't concentrating,' commented Ardent. 'I produce the strength I need according to necessity.'

'Sometimes, you frighten me!'

'As long as you're my friend, you have nothing to fear.'

Ardent spent a good part of the day in the forge, where

Obed had taught him how to make and repair metal tools. The blacksmith did not count his hours, unlike the majority of the lay workers, who were constantly goaded by the young man.

'You haven't got many friends,' remarked Obed. 'Usually, our leader manipulates the sensitivities of one person or another, and tries to reduce the work-rate to the minimum – Beken used to manage it beautifully. Since you were appointed, this place is like a beehive! But it seems that the Scribe of the Tomb, that grouch Kenhir, is rather pleased.'

'Then he will support me.'

'Not likely! He's a frightful man, cantankerous and authoritarian. Avoid him as much as you can.'

'Why was he appointed to the job?'

'I've no idea – it was the will of Pharaoh. But we all preferred Ramose: he was so human and so generous. He gave us all the benefit of his largesse without asking for anything in exchange, and unalloyed joy reigned when he was Scribe of the Tomb. With Kenhir, the atmosphere has really changed.'

'Why don't you ask to be admitted to the brotherhood?'

'I'm too old and I like my trade. Anyway, a blacksmith can only belong to the lay workforce.'

'That seems unjust.'

'It's the law of the Place of Truth, and I'm satisfied with my lot. If you were sensible, you would be, too.'

Ardent emerged from the forge to check that Beken's instructions were being followed. The routine had been the same for several weeks, and the young man was acquiring a taste for this unworthy task, which obliged him to check the quality of the water, fish, meat, vegetables, firewood, linens washed by the laundrymen, and pots.

In line with tradition, the various activities were carried on more or less intensively according to the quarters of the moon, and the 'outsiders', also called 'those who carry', had realised that the young man would show no mercy to bad workers or cheats. The women whose task it was to pick fruit wasted less time chatting, and the drovers stopped less frequently on the road to drink and talk. Ardent demanded more from the fishermen and the gardeners, who were inclined to be content with the minimum, and he tasted the baker's loaves himself. From the start, he had rejected products which were less than perfect, because of poor-quality flour; since then, the baker had made no more mistakes like that, and had even provided cakes filled with honey and almond paste, which were greatly appreciated by the craftsmen.

Ardent had accompanied the shepherds into the waterlogged strips of earth at the edge of the marshlands, where the grass grew thick and the animals loved to graze. In the company of these rough and ready men, he had slept in a reed hut, listened to their complaints, and understood their fear of crocodiles and mosquitoes. But he had been unyielding: despite their difficulties, they must not spend all day playing the flute and dozing alongside their dogs, but must provide food for the Place of Truth, in accordance with their contract. After the first, rather bitter, contacts, mutual liking had prevailed and Ardent had made himself understood.

Nevertheless, as he made his way towards the open-air butchery, the young man knew he might be heading for failure.

Bes, the head butcher, had short hair, and was dressed in a leather kilt on which hung a knife and a sharpening stone. He had apparently stopped work while his assistants plucked geese and ducks before gutting them, salting them and hanging them on a long pole or putting them into large jars for storage.

'Good morning, Bes,' said Ardent. 'Are you ill?'

'I'm resting. Is that a problem?'

'A gazelle and an ox were delivered to you this morning. The cooking-pots are ready. All they're waiting for is the meat you were supposed to cut up.'

'I've got sore hands.'

'Show them to me.'

'Are you a doctor?'

'Show me anyway.'

'If you want meat, cut it up yourself.'

Ardent picked up an assistant's flint knife and sliced off the front left hoof of the ox, in accordance with prescribed ritual. In this way, the sacrificed animal gave its full energy to those who ate it. Its blood, collected in a bowl, was healthy. Ardent inserted the knife into the animal's joints, sliced through the tendons, selected the best cuts and gave them to the cooks. The ox's liver would also be cooked and greatly enjoyed.

'I'm not as skilful as you, Bes, but the craftsmen's dinner-table will be well-laden.'

'That's fine for them.' The butcher chewed a chunk of raw meat.

'A question arises, though: what use are you?'

Hate-filled eyes turned on Ardent. 'Do you think you impress me, boy? I'm the head butcher and I'm staying that way. I don't give a damn about your orders, or Beken's.'

'Why should you have special treatment, Bes? You've been taking it easy for too long. Beken told me you're the leader of the lay workers. You will return to the ranks and serve the Place of Truth properly.'

The assistants and the cooks left. Knowing the butcher's character, they feared the worst and did not want to witness the inevitable drama. Afterwards, they would take up Bes's cause.

Bes stood up. He was shorter and less well built than Ardent, but his forearms and biceps were enough to terrify any adversary. He brandished his knife.

'Let's sort this out fairly, boy. I shall hamstring you, and then you won't be able to walk. Once you're powerless you won't cause us any more bother.'

Ardent threw his own knife away.

'You think you can defend yourself with your bare hands?' jeered Bes. 'You poor fool!'

Blade at the ready, the butcher charged at Ardent, who sidestepped at the last second. Encountering nothing but air, Bes was carried forward by the force of his charge. Before he could turn round, Ardent caught him in an armlock, forcing him to drop his weapon, and squeezed his throat so tightly that he could not breathe.

'You have a choice. Either you obey orders like the others, or I break your neck. A simple accident at work, for which you will be entirely responsible.'

'You . . . wouldn't . . . dare!' croaked Bes.

The stranglehold tightened.

'All right, all right!'

'Do I have your word?'

'Yes.'

Ardent freed the butcher, who fell to his knees, gulping air into his lungs.

'I'm hungry,' shouted Ardent, to the cooks. 'Bring me a nice joint of meat.'

# 30

Abry slapped his daughter, who began to howl and ran to hide in her mother's bedroom. Since being reprimanded by Ramses, Abry had felt his nerves getting worse every day. He could no longer tolerate either his staff or his servants – or even his own family. The smallest upset unleashed his anger, and he waited anxiously for the decree of revocation which would reduce him once again to the condition of a simple scribe, with no official residence, litter-bearers or zealous servants. And he would have to bear the ironic or vengeful looks of those he had pushed aside, often unceremoniously, to obtain his job. Furious at the reduction in her lifestyle, his wife would demand a divorce and obtain custody of their two children.

Abry did not have the courage to kill himself. The best solution would have been to run away and make a career abroad, but leaving Thebes was beyond his strength. The only thing left was to suffer his own inexorable decline.

'Master, Captain Mehy would like to see you,' his steward informed him.

'I am not receiving anyone.'

'He insists.'

Infuriated, Abry gave in. 'Tell him to join me in the reception hall.'

Abry had intended to have the room repainted, but he

would have to give up all thoughts of fresh expenditure. His eyelids twitching nervously, he paced back and forth.

Mehy made a grand entrance, dressed in the latest fashion, lavishly perfumed and with bracelets jangling at his wrists.

'Thank you for your welcome, Abry. Your house is remarkably comfortable.'

'Have you come, like a vulture, to feed on my carcass?'

'Confidentially, I did not approve of the king's criticisms.'

Abry was astounded. 'You don't mean to say . . . that you agree with me?'

'Yes I do, my dear fellow. Your arguments seemed very cogent.'

His initial surprise over, Abry felt a twinge of suspicion. The young man might be trying to make Abry incriminate himself. He said, 'The word of Ramses has the force of law. We must all submit to it.'

'Of course,' agreed Mehy, 'but no man is infallible, and today our beloved sovereign is a grand old man who is too attached to survivals from the past. Though we venerate his greatness, should we not exercise a minimum of critical judgement so that we can better prepare for the future?'

Abry stopped in his tracks. 'What you are saying is extremely serious, Captain.'

'As an officer, I owe it to myself to speak clearly. In case of war, our armed forces would not be ready to fight, and Egypt would risk being crushed. That is why I am proposing reforms – which my superiors are considering favourably. So you can see that I am not seeking to destroy.'

Somewhat reassured, Abry sat down on a stone bench. 'Do you like date wine with aniseed?'

'Indeed I do.'

Abry ordered his guest to be served with wine, and the captain sat down opposite him.

'Why should I trust you, Mehy?'

'Because I'm the only person supporting you through this

trial. You know that I have just married the city treasurer's daughter and that my influence is growing by the day. Why would I be interested in a man who has fallen from favour, if I did not share his opinions?'

Abry was in the habit of striking crushing blows at his opponents. Today, it was his turn to receive them.

'My days are numbered. I am no use to anyone any more.'

'You're wrong there. My father-in-law looks rather favourably upon you, and he has wisely disclosed to me messages recommending that you remain as governor of the west bank. The responses are quite encouraging.'

'It is Ramses, and he alone, who takes the decisions.'

'And he knows your opinions, so why would he replace you with a dignitary whose ideas he is uncertain of? Since the king is firmly opposed to your programme, you cannot put it into action and you'll have to be content with running your sector as you have in the past, without infringing on the craftsmen's privileges.'

'Are you serious?'

'Ramses is a very skilful man, and no one contests his authority. The order he has given will not be compromised and, because you fear for your job, you will be the first to ensure that it is strictly applied. At the moment, Abry, you are the most effective defender of the Place of Truth.'

In his heart of hearts, the governor had to admit that Mehy was right.

'You will remain in place,' promised the captain, 'and I'll help you to strengthen your position.'

'Nothing is given for free. What do you want in exchange?'

'The same thing as you: the destruction of the Place of Truth.'

'I don't understand. From my point of view, the whole population should be taxed, and no one should be exempt. But you, what are your grievances?'

'Faced with the necessary process of modernising the

country, this brotherhood is an anomaly which must disappear.'

Abry sensed that the captain was hiding his true motives, but in the end it mattered little. Was Mehy not a messenger of good omen? He had brought him hope and was offering him a future.

'I don't see how I can help you. You have just said that henceforth my role will be to safeguard the craftsmen's village.'

'To outward appearances, my dear fellow, only to outward appearances. No taxation or special levies for the moment. A show of benevolence, a declared adherence to the king's will: that is your official line of conduct.'

'And what will the other be?'

'Little by little, to undermine the foundations of the brotherhood.'

'That would mean taking considerable risks!'

'Fewer than you may think,' said Mehy. 'Don't worry: I'm a sensible man who knows how to operate in the shadows. You yourself have learnt that it's a good idea to hit your enemy from behind and not to confront him openly. My present demands are simple: do you agree to pass on to me what you know about the Place of Truth?'

'I know very little, but nonetheless it is confidential information. If I give it to you, I shall become your accomplice.'

'Not my accomplice, my ally.'

'How far are you planning to go, Mehy?'

'Do you really want to know?'

The sudden arrival of the governor's wife, a tall brunette, put a stop to the conversation.

She was in a state of great agitation. 'Why did you smack my baby?'

'May I introduce Captain Mehy? We mustn't involve him in our domestic affairs.'

'Have you told him that you've been making our lives

impossible, with your rages getting more and more frequent?'

'Control yourself, darling.'

'I've had enough of controlling myself! Why should I continue to put up with your outbursts of temper? Let Captain Mehy sign you on in his regiment and free us from your presence.'

'Things are going to improve, I promise.'

'Can an officer save you?'

'Why not?' asked Mehy.

Abry's wife gave their guest a suspicious stare. 'Who do you think you are? Go back to your barracks!'

The governor took his wife by the arm and led her to the door. 'Go and calm your daughter and don't disturb us again.'

Crossly, she went out.

'Because of Ramses,' confessed Abry, 'my life has become hell. I did not deserve that.'

'A man of your quality should not put up with such injustice without reacting,' said Mehy.

Abry started pacing the room again, in the grip of intense thoughts which the captain was careful not to interrupt.

'I don't wish to know your real aims, Mehy, and my only goal is to retain my job. Within the bounds of possibility, I agree to keep you informed. But don't ask more of me than that.'

# 31

Mehy was delighted. Abry had just taken the first step, and the others would follow.

'I am afraid you may be disappointed,' said Abry. 'Although I am the official who knows most about the Place of Truth, I can't tell you what really goes on there.'

'Who runs it?'

'As regards matters which concern me, it is Kenhir, the Scribe of the Tomb who succeeded Ramose.'

'Why do you say "matters which concern me"?'

'Because I am only involved with strictly administrative matters. Should the need arise, it is the Scribe of the Tomb with whom I correspond, and it is he who replies. But necessarily there exists a secret hierarchy which controls the craftsmen themselves, no doubt under the authority of an overall leader.'

'Do you know who he is?' asked Mehy eagerly.

'Only Pharaoh and the tjaty know. I have often tried to find out, but have never succeeded.'

'How many craftsmen are there in the brotherhood?'

'To discover that, you would have to enter the village or get a reliable answer from the Scribe of the Tomb.'

'Do you know exactly what it is they do in the Place of Truth?'

'Their official duty is to excavate and decorate the reigning pharaoh's house of eternity. On the pharaoh's command, one or more craftsmen will be assigned to different sites to carry out selected work.'

'Does that happen often?'

'Again, only the Scribe of the Tomb could tell you.'

'People claim that the Place of Truth can produce gold.'

'Indeed,' said Abry, 'that is an old legend, but don't give it any credence. In reality, this brotherhood enjoys unacceptable privileges. It occupies an entire village, it answers for its work only to the pharaoh and the tjaty, it has its own court and it is served by a veritable army of outside workers. This situation is intolerable. As I never cease to explain, good management means raising the taxes each year.'

Mehy was disappointed. Abry was timid. He was interested only in the privileges he had acquired and never took the initiative. But there remained one path to explore.

'What do you know about Kenhir?' he asked.

'Ramose was unable to have a child, despite his many offerings to the gods. When he had accepted his misfortune, he decided to adopt a son who would be his successor and to whom he would leave his possessions. His choice fell on Kenhir, whom Ramses designated Scribe of the Tomb in Year Thirty-eight of his reign. For many, this was a bad choice. Ramose is a generous, friendly man, a man of smiling firmness; Kenhir is an odious fellow, loud-mouthed and full of his own intellectual superiority. But he is also extremely able, and since his appointment, no serious criticisms have been levelled at him.'

'How old is he?'

'Fifty-two.'

'So, he's coming to the end of his career,' said Mehy thoughtfully. 'I suppose he wouldn't be averse to seeing his retirement made substantially more comfortable?'

'I doubt it! Like Ramose, he'll be content go on living peacefully in the village.'

'No man is like another, my dear Abry. Kenhir may have

hidden wishes which we could satisfy. Is he married?'

'Not to my knowledge.'

'Where did he work before he entered the Place of Truth?'

'In an obscure organisation on the west bank, where Ramose noticed him.'

'Could you approach him?'

'It isn't as easy as that. He seldom leaves the village.'

'Find a pretext to have a chat with him.'

'What should I say?'

'Win his friendship and suggest that he becomes associated with your administration in exchange for a substantial consideration – say, two milch cows, a few pieces of fine linen and ten jars of top-quality wine. Then come to an agreement to offer him more while extracting as much information as possible from him.'

'You ask a great deal!'

'You aren't running any risks, Abry. Either Kenhir is incorruptible or he will take the bait.'

The governor pulled a face. 'The generous gifts you suggest . . . It would be difficult for me to provide them from my own resources.'

'Don't worry, my dear fellow: I shall take care of that.'

Abry was relieved. 'In that case, I'll try to do what you want, but there is no guarantee of success.'

The captain felt a brief twinge of discouragement. With such second-rate allies, it would not be easy to uncover the secrets of the Place of Truth; but he was at the beginning of the road and, little by little, he would eliminate those who proved useless. At least Abry was easy to manipulate.

He asked, 'Do you control the work the craftsmen from the Place of Truth do outside the village?'

'No,' replied Abry with regret. 'I've protested about it several times, but the tjaty has taken no notice.'

'Do you know what sort of food is delivered to the village and how much?'

'The craftsmen lack for nothing. Plenty of water every day, meat, vegetables, oil, unguents, clothes, and goodness knows what else! And the Scribe of the Tomb complains if there is a delay, or if he thinks anything is of poor quality. Fortunately, he's been making fewer complaints recently.'

'Why is that?'

'The head of the outside workers has taken on a young giant as his second-in-command. His name is Ardent and he has shaken up the workforce, whose job is to ensure the brotherhood's well-being. The boy has a firm hand, it seems, and he knows how to make people obey him.'

'Didn't he work in a tannery?'

'Indeed he did. According to what I was told by Sobek, the head of security, this boy Ardent presented himself to the court of the Place of Truth, but was turned down. Nevertheless, he was engaged as a lay worker, and I get the impression he's taking revenge on his comrades.'

Mehy remembered the headstrong boy who had made him a sturdy shield, and who hadn't turned up at the barracks to enlist. Today, he must be bitter and disappointed.

'Who appoints the lay workers?' he asked.

'In theory, the Scribe of the Tomb, but he doesn't bother with every water-carrier. Commander Sobek and his men do, though. They allow only people they know to pass through.'

'This Sobek, what kind of man is he?'

'People criticise him for his propensity to violence and his lack of diplomacy, but he's been so efficient that he should stay in his post for a very long time.'

'Promotion would take him away from the Place of Truth . . .'

'The tjaty thinks very highly of him.'

'Get me a detailed dossier on this Sobek. He must have his weaknesses.'

'That is a very dangerous step, Captain!' protested Abry.

'You will benefit by it, my dear fellow. I'm sure some

expensive Cretan vases would look wonderful in your charming home.'

'I've long dreamt of owning some.'

'Well, this is one dream which is about to come true, and there will be others if you collaborate effectively. One more question: when they are not on an official mission, do the craftsmen have to remain in the village?'

'No, they can leave whenever they wish and go wherever they see fit. Some have family on the eastern bank and pay them visits.'

'As soon as one of them makes a move, tell me.'

'It won't be easy. When the members of the brotherhood travel, there are no administrative formalities. But I'll do my best.'

# 32

When the baker saw Ardent arrive, he hurried to give him a round, soft loaf with a golden crust.

'Excellent,' nodded the young man. 'You're improving. What have you made today?'

'Long loaves, triangular loaves, pastries and flatcakes.'

'Are you satisfied with the flour?'

'It's never been so fine.'

Satisfied, Ardent went off, leaving behind him a relieved man. Then he went into a brewery where half-cooked barley loaves were soaking in date liquor. The liquid obtained would be filtered through a sieve and would become a strong beer for festival days.

'Has the cauldron I ordered been delivered yet?' he asked.

The brewer looked uncomfortable. He hated having to speak ill of another worker, who would incur Ardent's wrath.

'Yes – at least, almost. There's only a slight delay. It's not serious.'

The young man walked angrily past the front of the workshop, where the shoemaker lowered his head as he passed. He took a narrow, rocky path and headed for the isolated valley hollow where the pot-mender worked, crouching in front of a hearth made up of little stones and fed with charcoal. His skin as hard as a crocodile's, stinking like a rotting fish, the man was working his goatskin bellows, whose metal nozzle he had inserted into the fire.

'Have you forgotten my order?' demanded Ardent.

'You aren't the master here,' said the pot-mender defiantly. 'I told Beken I've got two cauldrons that need the dents beaten out of them, and another to re-line. My assistant is sick. I can't do any more.'

'The fire looks as though you haven't lit it for a long time. You're taking advantage of your isolation to daydream.'

'Go and bother somebody else! I don't give a damn about your criticisms.'

Ardent picked up a cooking-pot with a hole in it and threw it into a pile of loose stones.

The pot-mender started up. 'You're out of your mind! It'll take me ages to mend that.'

'If you refuse to obey the rules, I shall leave not a single one of your cooking-pots intact, and you'll have to work like a dog day and night to repair them.'

The furious pot-mender attacked Ardent, brandishing his bellows, but the young man easily disarmed him and sent him sprawling in the sand.

He got up with difficulty.

'Are you going to obey me now?' demanded Ardent.

'All right, you win.'

'Congratulations, Ardent.' Sobek looked the young giant up and down. 'You're not very popular among the workforce, but they've learnt to respect you.'

'It's Beken who gives the orders.' Ardent took a mouthful of his meal of spiced beans.

'Save that for the others! He's putty in your hands. For your age, you show considerable promise. You'd make an excellent guard officer.'

'You're wrong, Sobek. The thought of being a prison guard fills me with horror.'

'Well, what do you think you are now? You give orders,

you exercise control, you mete out punishments. The workers have never endured such authority before! The Scribe of the Tomb is delighted, and so am I. I'm even willing to forget the little disagreement that set us at odds. A fine fellow like you shouldn't be damaged – you have become too valuable. It would have amused me to be the first person to give you a good hiding, but one must adapt to circumstances. You'll soon become leader of the lay workers, and then we'll have to work together. Sincere congratulations: you have chosen the right path.'

Sobek went away. Ardent gave the rest of his meal to the shoemaker.

'This . . . this is for me?'

'Eat it. I'm not hungry any more.'

'Have I done something wrong?'

'Nothing at all.'

'The two pairs of sandals I promised will be finished this evening.'

'I'm glad to hear it.'

Ardent went into the potter's workshop.

Beken woke up with a start. 'I suddenly felt tired,' he explained. 'I feel better now – I'll get on.'

'If you're exhausted, take a rest.'

'What do you mean?'

'You're the head of the workforce. It's for you to decide.'

Beken couldn't believe his ears. 'Are you laughing at me?'

'I'm simply telling the truth. Carry out the duties given to you, and all will go well. Above all, don't ask anything more of me.'

'Don't you want to take charge of the workers any more?'

'Each to his own role.'

'What are you going to do?'

Ardent left the workshop without replying. Sobek had forced him to face reality: in trying to prove his worth to the court of the Place of Truth, he had fallen into a trap. Since devoting himself to organising the lay workers, he had had no time to draw and had lost himself in secondary tasks which had satisfied only his vanity. In becoming a petty tyrant, he'd condemned himself to sterility. A few more weeks of this regime, and his hand would lose all its skill.

Beken ran up. 'Are you angry with someone?'

'Only with myself.'

'Don't get into a rage. I'll go and talk to the Scribe of the Tomb and suggest he should appoint you head of the workforce. That's what you want, isn't it?'

'Not any more.'

'I don't understand.'

'Go back to your workshop, Beken. You've nothing more to fear from me.'

'You . . . you're leaving me in peace?'

'Take up your privileges again.'

The potter was so happy that he did not pursue the argument.

Ardent headed feverishly towards the village gate. Since escaping from the prison of his family, he had made no progress. By bending to the demands of the Place of Truth, he had lost his way on a road with no way out and had not explored his own path. Having become an 'outsider', the most he could hope for was to rule over the workers and he would never discover the secrets of drawing and painting.

Ardent refused to accept this second-rate destiny.

When the keeper of the north gate saw him approaching, he brandished his club. Was the young man going to try to force his way into the village?

But Ardent sat down a few paces from the gate and meticulously cleared the ground to obtain a completely flat surface. With a flint, he drew in the sand the village walls and the surrounding countryside. When the sketch was finished, he refined the details with a piece of pointed wood, becoming wholly absorbed in his work.

Reassured, the gatekeeper sat down again, though he kept an eye on the artist. Ardent worked with supreme calm. When he was dissatisfied with a detail, he rubbed it out and began again. When the guard was relieved, at four o'clock in the afternoon, he was still drawing. And he was still drawing when the next change of guard took place, at four in the morning.

When the lay workers unloaded the donkeys, they glanced at the superb drawing, which was bigger than ever but filled with meticulous details worthy of a miniaturist. No one dared approach Ardent, who was completely oblivious of the outside world.

# 33

The court convened before the gates of the principal temple in the Place of Truth. An awning had been erected to protect the old scribe Ramose from the burning heat of the sun.

'The experiment has been completed,' declared Kenhir, as crusty as ever, 'and we can see the result. Neb the Accomplished thought that Ardent would never be just an obedient worker, dull and docile, and he was right. He predicted that Ardent would impose himself in one way or another, and he was right again, because this young battler has flushed out quite a few lazy people and given his colleagues back their will to work. But Neb was wrong to suppose that Ardent would forget the call and be content to exercise his authority over the "outsiders". For two days and two nights he has been drawing uninterruptedly, taking nothing but a little water the gatekeeper gave him. He might have reacted violently, but instead of that, he wishes to show us his gifts with the meagre means at his disposal. Is it not the duty of this assembly, this time, to hear his call?'

Ramose agreed, but Neb would not give in.

'On this last point,' he said, 'I admit I was wrong. Nevertheless, it is clear that it is indeed the power of Set which dwells within this boy and that he will not submit to any rule. I therefore still consider him a danger to the brotherhood and I would prefer him to go and exercise his talents elsewhere.'

'You drew up a plan, and we followed it,' objected Kenhir. 'Ardent did not fall into the trap laid for him, so you must give way. Don't forget that no admission is irrevocable, and that unworthy behaviour leads to demotion or even expulsion. In receiving this applicant into our brotherhood, we are taking only a small risk.'

'Before making my final pronouncement,' declared Neb, 'I ask that he should appear once again before this court.'

'Will you follow me?' the craftsman asked Ardent, who was drawing the village gate for the tenth time, each time seeking a more precise line.

Ardent got to his feet. He felt no tiredness, but he no longer knew which world he belonged in. He had lost interest in the world of the 'outsiders', and the Place of Truth was still inaccessible. Reduced to himself, he was becoming consumed by his own inner fire. What worse could he fear?

Without a word, he followed the craftsman, who led him to the court. Ardent sat down in the posture of a scribe and did not look at his judges.

'Is it true that you abused your power by mistreating the lay workers?' demanded Neb.

'There is no excuse for laziness.'

'No one suggested that you should make such radical changes.'

'You may tolerate hypocrisy, but I don't. I am not accustomed to acting in secrecy.'

'Did the potter tell you to behave like that?' asked Ramose.

'He's a spineless man who cares for nothing but his privileges and has no intention of shaking up his subordinates. I take sole responsibility for what I have done.'

'Do you want to become leader in Beken's place?'

'That would be the worst of all destinies! To be close to the Place of Truth, so close, and yet unable to enter . . .'

'But you developed a taste for your office.'

'That's true. I deluded myself, like any imbecile who exercises power. I was sinking into a state of deadly drunkenness, but I have just woken up.'

'Does that mean that you refuse to work as an "outsider" any more?' cut in Neb.

'I came here to learn how to draw. The rest is of no interest to me.'

'Don't you accept that the path begins with obedience?'

'The important thing is that the gate opens.'

'Do you think your behaviour means we should treat you leniently?'

Ardent smiled weakly. 'I don't hope for anything of the sort, but you have no right to leave me in uncertainty. Either reject me, or welcome me in.'

'What would your reaction be, were we to refuse you?'

The young man took a long time to reply. 'Whatever it might be, you would mock it.'

'Have you any new reasons why we should accept you?'

'There is only one: I have heard the call.'

A craftsman took Ardent back outside the main gate of the Place of Truth. With his foot, the young man rubbed out his drawing. This time, his destiny hung in the balance. If the brotherhood rejected him, he would have no more chances to realise his ideal. He was not afraid, but he cursed the fate that placed him at the mercy of a band of judges the majority of whom were undoubtedly narrow-minded. The fact that they were inflexible and inhuman did not bother him, but were they really capable of seeing his desire? Since he had escaped from the trap of the 'outsiders' Ardent felt the fire that had led him to the threshold of the village, once again burning inside him. It was here, and nowhere else, that his life would blossom. If he was refused any future, if he was prevented from passing through the wall behind which were the secrets he longed to learn, he would lose all hope.

It was pointless to burden his mind with this sombre perspective. Only reality was worthy to be confronted, and the reality was that he must simply wait. The wait would last long hours, perhaps several days, a wait which must not lessen his determination. Ardent was convinced that he must, even from a distance, impose his will on the court. If it remained intact and whole despite the test, the judges would necessarily perceive its intensity.

The discussions, set in motion by Kenhir, had been going on for two hours. Kenhir had demanded that the decision taken must be final and that each judge must take full responsibility in arguing the reasons behind his vote.

'This young man inspires no trust in me,' declared Neb.

'Surely his Setian fire doesn't frighten you?' inquired Kenhir ironically.

'Anyone who did not fear it would be totally irresponsible. As overseer, I have no right to endanger the harmony of the brotherhood. I maintain my position: Ardent should go and seek his fortune elsewhere.'

'The Place of Truth is the only place where he can follow his vocation, and you know that very well. How can you, whose name is Neb the Accomplished, refuse the possibility of achieving accomplishment to someone who has heard the call?'

Neb seemed shaken, but he did not yield. 'You're always so sour towards the members of our brotherhood. Why are you so concerned for Ardent?'

Kenhir's reaction was harsh. 'You have understood nothing, Neb! It is not a question of concern or benevolence. It is a question of the wider interests of the Place of Truth. I am only the Scribe of the Tomb. Is it up to me to tell you to accept a man who is gifted with such power? Are you incapable of transforming that power into creative strength and integrating it into your work?'

Neb's expression became closed. 'You go too far, Kenhir! The craftsmen recognise your administrative authority, but it is not your place to interfere in our work.'

'That is not my intention, Neb. My father and master, the scribe Ramose, has made me understand the nature and limits of my office. You are right that I have overstepped the limit. It is indeed for you and the other craftsmen who make up this court to take the final decision. If it must be negative, I shall go along with your opinion.'

Ramose, the Scribe of Ma'at, said quietly, 'My love for this brotherhood forbids me to influence it by citing my age and experience; but I must remind you that His Majesty recommended us to examine the case of Ardent with a clear head. Let each man put forward his thoughts calmly.'

The craftsmen proceeded to the vote.

Despite numerous reservations, each believed they must give Ardent the chance to become an artist, on condition that he scrupulously respected the brotherhood's rule and bent to the demands of apprenticeship.

It remained only to hear from Neb the Accomplished, who had listened carefully to his subordinates.

He said, 'This assembly has carried out its reflections wisely, and each judge has opened his heart without yielding to his feelings. I don't like Ardent's character, and I don't think he's capable of comprehending the importance of our work, but we must answer his call.'

# 34

Sobek drank three bowls of fresh milk and devoured a plateful of warm flatcakes. After a night spent patrolling the hills overlooking the Valley of the Kings he was exhausted, but he would not go to bed before he had heard his men's reports.

One after the other, they filed before him, and none reported anything suspicious. However, Sobek was still worried. His instinct rarely deceived him, and for several days it had been telling him that danger was in the offing. So he had increased the number of patrols, at the risk of annoying his men, who were not too pleased by this extra work.

Anxiety almost made him forget the major event for which the village was preparing: the initiation of a new member – and not just any member. Why had the court of admissions opened the door of the brotherhood to this fellow Ardent, who, on the available evidence, would only cause trouble? With that all-consuming energy of his, the fellow could only be a bandit or a guard. He would not stay long shut up in the village, and would refuse to obey the orders of his superiors, who would be forced to demote him to the ranks of the 'outsiders' or finally expel him. Ardent would turn out badly, and the only possible destinies for him were a brutal death in a brawl, or a long prison sentence.

As Sobek was preparing to lie down on his mat and take a well-deserved rest, a guard entered the office.

'It's the messenger, sir. He wishes to see you personally.'

The messenger came each day to the main guard post at the Place of Truth. He brought letters to the brotherhood and took away letters from the craftsmen and their families, who were thus able to communicate easily with the outside world; naturally he also delivered official reports from the Scribe of the Tomb to the tjaty. In times of necessity or emergency, a special service transported messages by the swiftest possible route.

'Can't you deal with it?' asked Sobek.

'It's you he wants to see, sir, and no one else.'

'Very well, send him in.'

Uputy, the messenger, was a lanky man of about thirty, with strong calves and shoulders. From his bag of papyrus scrolls in various degrees of wear, which were re-used for writing letters, he took out a limestone slate wrapped in a linen cloth, and he placed it on Sobek's desk.

'According to the text written in red ink on the cloth, this message is for you, Sobek.'

'Have you read it?'

'You know very well I'm not allowed to.'

Uputy was a well-thought-of and well-paid man, possessor of the Baton of Thoth, the embodiment of moral rectitude and meticulous work. His duty was to carry letters to their destination, in good condition and guaranteeing that only the recipient would know the contents. The profession was a hard one, for the palace and the tjaty's departments demanded that their orders be sent as quickly as possible, and there were many periods of intense activity. Uputy knew the importance of his work and felt honoured by the trust vested in him by the highest authorities.

'Am I to wait for a reply?' he asked.

'Just a moment.'

Sobek took off the linen cord and read the few lines, which were also written in red ink, on the small, carefully polished piece of limestone.

Stunned, he read the incredible message a second time. No, it wasn't possible!

'Well, Sobek?'

'You may go, Uputy. There is no reply.'

Sobek no longer felt tired. Once again, his instinct had been correct: a catastrophe had indeed just occurred, one so great that it threatened to sweep through the craftsmen's village with more violence than the most furious sandstorm.

Nefer the Silent was living such a happy life that he was almost in a daze. After hearing the call, he had been admitted to the brotherhood of the Place of Truth together with his beloved Ubekhet, and they had adapted to the customs of the enclosed village without too many difficulties, particularly because of the essentially sweet nature of the young woman, who had disarmed any hostility towards the new arrivals.

And then, in a few hours, Ardent was going to see his dream come true. The man who had saved his life, who had enabled him to encounter Ma'at and comprehend her greatness, would become a brother. Together, they would participate in the fabulous adventure whose full extent Nefer himself was just beginning to glimpse. With his feverish enthusiasm and his creative passion, Ardent would show he was equal to the mission which would be entrusted to him.

A life placed under the sign of the Great Work, a love filled with light, an exhilarating friendship . . . Nefer had been showered with gifts by the gods, whom he would never cease to thank. In exchange for so many good things, he must accomplish his duty with the most extreme thoroughness and not allow himself any delay in completing his tasks. Because he had heard the call and because he had replied, heaven and earth were heaping joys upon him; it was up to him to use them correctly, by showing he was worthy of the road he must travel.

As he was getting ready to leave for the sculptors'

workshop, Ubekhet showed him a letter which had just been brought to her. Nefer saw from the sadness in her eyes that it contained bad news.

'My father is very ill,' she revealed, 'and the doctor fears he may die. According to the message he has dictated, Father wishes to see both of us, as soon as possible.'

Nefer went immediately to the overseer to explain the reason for his absence, which would be recorded in the register kept by the Scribe of the Tomb. The couple took no luggage and left the village by the secondary gate, taking the path that ended near to Ramses the Great's Temple of a Million Years.

'You're worried, aren't you?' said Ubekhet. 'You're afraid you won't be back in time for Ardent's initiation.'

'Yes, I am.'

'As soon as you've seen my father, go back to the village and I'll stay with him for as long as necessary.'

'So shall I.'

'No. You must be present when your friend becomes a Servant of the Place of Truth.'

At the guard-post by the Temple of a Million Years, the guards asked their names, but allowed them to pass without further formalities. Nefer and Ubekhet were known to the authorities as members of the brotherhood, moved around freely within the precincts of the Place of Truth, and could leave whenever they chose.

The couple walked quickly to the cultivated area, crossed a field of grass, walked along the edge of a little market and headed for the bank, where a ferry was waiting to cross. Mingling with the other travellers, who were peasants going to Thebes to sell vegetables, they exchanged pleasantries on the stability of prices, the prosperity of the country and the generosity of the Nile. No one would have suspected that they had come from the most secret village in Egypt.

Despite her anxiety, Ubekhet managed to put on a brave

face and even managed to comfort a mother whose little girl had a fever.

As soon as the ferry arrived at the east bank, Nefer and his wife jumped down on to the quay and headed for the masterbuilder's house. When they were still some distance from it, Ebony ran towards them. Bounding from one to the other, he licked their faces, intense joy in his hazel eyes.

'Come quickly, Ebony,' said Ubekhet. 'We must hurry.'

Suddenly, the black dog growled and bared his teeth at a group of guards who were approaching the couple. At their head was Sobek.

'What is happening?' asked Ubekhet.

'Don't worry, your father's well. The letter you received was from me, not a doctor.'

'But . . . why?'

'I had no other way of making your husband leave the village. Several witnesses will testify that he came to the eastern bank of his own free will.'

'What is the reason for this trick, Sobek?'

'Justice.'

'Whatever do you mean?'

'Nefer is under arrest. He is accused of having killed one of my men, who was on night guard-duty in the Valley of the Kings.'

# 35

Mehy was fast becoming the darling of Thebes. There was no social function to which he was not invited, no official reception where he was not present, no major business meeting he did not participate in. A brilliant conversationalist, he was never short of an original observation, a compliment in good taste or a suggestion worthy of interest.

Everyone congratulated Moseh on having chosen such a remarkable son-in-law, whose career promised so much; all the more so since his plans for the reform of the Theban army were extremely well thought of in high places.

On the occasion of his birthday, the mayor of Thebes held a grand reception in the gardens of his house, where the leading citizens of the city of Amon rubbed shoulders with each other. Smiling broadly, talking arrogantly, he greeted his guests with the assurance of a tactician who had just snuffed out a dangerous faction.

'What elegance, my dear Mehy! That long-sleeved, pleated shirt, that immaculately white robe, those perfectly cut sandals. If you weren't married, a lot of young girls would try to seduce you.'

'I would resist the temptation.'

'Between ourselves, Serketa must know how to please a man, eh?'

'I couldn't possibly lie to the mayor of Thebes, whose

experience is universally recognised.'

'I like you, Mehy. I suppose that, for you, the army is just a stepping-stone?'

'When I've finished the reforms I've just begun, I'd like to be more closely associated with the running of our magnificent city.'

'A legitimate and laudable ambition,' nodded the mayor, 'but don't forget that Thebes is only the third city in the land, behind Memphis and our new capital, Pi-Ramses. Here, we value tranquillity and tradition.'

'The wisest of policies,' said Mehy smoothly.

'Excellent! With opinions like yours, you'll go far.'

'I owe a great deal to my dear father-in-law, who is my main worry.'

The mayor was astonished. 'Is something wrong?'

'Confidentially, his health is failing.'

'But he seems in excellent health.'

'His physical health seems intact, it's true, but his mind is affected. Recently I've begged him, tactfully, to rescind some nonsensical decisions. At the moment, he agrees, and recognises his inconsistencies, wondering what demon torments him; but what will tomorrow bring? His mental lapses are becoming more and more frequent . . . But I shouldn't have told you.'

'On the contrary, Mehy, on the contrary. Keep me regularly informed and go on intervening to prevent any mistakes. If the situation takes a serious turn, alert me immediately.' The mayor sighed. 'This evening has been a great success, but this is the second piece of bad news I've had today.'

'May I ask what the first one was?'

'A most vexing business. A young craftsman, Nefer, who has just entered the brotherhood of the Place of Truth, is accused of killing one of Sobek's guards. Sobek had thought the man's death was an accident, but new evidence has convinced him it was murder.'

'Will this Nefer be judged by the court of the Place of Truth?'

'No, because he was arrested on the eastern bank, where he was visiting his father-in-law. If he had stayed in the village, we would not have been able to arrest him. The court case is liable to cause a great deal of fuss.'

'Isn't there a risk that the craftsmen's reputation will be sullied?'

'The very survival of the village could be called into question! If this brotherhood shelters criminals, it must be dissolved. The authorities on the western bank will be delighted – Nefer's conviction will prove to Ramses that the Place of Truth is more dangerous than useful. It will defend itself tooth and claw, of course. And I shall no doubt be obliged to use the army – in other words, yourself – to conduct an orderly evacuation.'

'I am at your disposal.'

'I shall remember this. We'll see each other again soon. Enjoy yourself.'

The mayor engaged a rich landowner in conversation, leaving Mehy to savour his first great victory.

The anonymous letter he had sent Sobek to denounce Nefer was producing the effects he had hoped for. In this way, the murder he had committed was doing him incalculable services. Nefer would probably be sentenced to death, and the brotherhood would be dispersed. Mehy would occupy the village for as long as it took to search it from top to bottom and seize its treasures. Under cover of an official mission, he would therefore achieve his ends by perfectly legal means.

Ardent was sitting on the beaten-earth floor of a little room with whitewashed walls. There were no windows, and he did not know if it was day or night. Food and drink were brought to him, but not a word was said.

The door of the room was unlocked, and he could have

gone out. But he suspected that this false liberty hid a new trap and that the only solution was to await the court's verdict.

Although he was normally hot-blooded and impatient, he did not rebel against this test, for he sensed it was a vital one. It would allow him to exist for a while outside time, allow his soul and body to know a peace he had thought unattainable. His destiny no longer belonged to him; he detached himself from it and was nourished by this soothing emptiness where nothing happened. Until the verdict was announced, he would be neither dead nor alive. Here, in the secret precincts of the Place of Truth, he was no longer an 'outsider', but he might never be a member of the brotherhood. His past had disappeared; his future did not yet exist.

Already, and whatever the outcome of this fight without enemies might be, Ardent had discovered a world which surprised him. His usual points of reference had disappeared, the limits were fading away and another horizon was emerging. But this was only a shadow without consistency, like his own self, whose strength and desire had become useless.

The young man was convinced that all the members of the brotherhood had spent time here and that, like him, they had waited for a verdict with no appeal. None had obtained privileges, whatever his gifts or skills might be, and the fact of having experienced the same trial, in the same conditions, must unite them like brothers sharing the same ideal.

The door opened.

The craftsman carried neither bread nor water-jug. 'Come with me, Ardent.'

The young man would have liked to spend endless days in this peaceful place where nothing could harm him. He stood up very slowly, as though reluctant to follow his guide.

'Do you renounce your request for admission to the brotherhood?' asked the craftsman.

'Take me where I must go.'

They took the path to the temple, before which sat the court of admissions. The judges were impassive, with the exception of Ramose, who seemed to be smiling.

But Ardent, whose heart was thundering in his chest, preferred to ignore him and halted in front of Kenhir, Scribe of the Tomb. For the first time in his life, anguish constricted his breathing. He longed to run to the ends of the earth so as not to hear the words that were about to be pronounced.

'This court has reached its decision,' said Kenhir gravely, 'and it is irrevocable. His Majesty the king, supreme master of the Place of Truth, has approved it, and it will be registered at the tjaty's office. You, Ardent, have indeed heard the call and you will therefore be admitted to this brotherhood.'

Was the scribe really speaking to him? Suddenly, new fire flowed in his veins, and he would have loved to kiss grumpy old Kenhir.

'Unfortunately,' the scribe went on, 'we are obliged to defer your initiation. This is not because of you. The brotherhood as a whole has been struck by great misfortune.'

'What misfortune?' asked Ardent.

'The accusation of murder made against Nefer the Silent.'

'Silent a murderer? That's absurd!'

'That is our opinion, too, but we must devote all our energies to proving his innocence. When peace has returned among us, you will receive your new name and you will discover the first mysteries of the Place of Truth.'

# 36

At the end of an exhausting day's work, Mehy had made brutal love to Serketa, with his usual enjoyment. She could no longer do without him and from now on she would occupy the only position fitting for a woman: that of devoted and obedient servant. Since his childhood Mehy had despised women, and Serketa was not going to change his attitude. Like the others, she was looking for a lord and master with indisputable authority. She, at least, had had the good fortune to find one.

Since Nefer's arrest, Mehy had contacted dozens of people in order to deploy a strategy whose efficiency delighted him: the false rumour. Malicious people had seized upon it greedily and spread it like wildfire, imbeciles had repeated it without understanding, and blabbermouths had been only too happy to shine by broadcasting information which they claimed only they knew.

Thanks to these intermediaries, Mehy was succeeding in moulding other people's thoughts as he wished and was transforming rumour into reality. The public already saw Nefer the Silent as a fearsome criminal, perpetrator of several murders, and the Place of Truth as a den of brigands who enjoyed outrageous privileges.

Only Ramses the Great could have turned the situation round, with a single word. But Pharaoh was not above Ma'at, and he did not have the right to intervene in a legal process. This was the price of safeguarding Egypt's happiness and cohesion. Now that he had been accused, Nefer must be judged.

Because he had close links with the Place of Truth, the tjaty would not preside at the preliminary hearing designed to formulate the charge; the hearing would be headed by the senior member of the court of justice, an old man who was strictly wedded to procedure. Mehy did not need to buy him since, given the gravity of the facts, he would have to decide that Nefer must go before a jury.

When he did so, Mehy's behind-the-scenes plotting would be decisive. First, he must ensure that Abry was a juror, and make him spread new slanders about the brotherhood, in order to sully it further and make it even more hateful in the people's eyes. Next, he must ensure that a majority of the jury voted to sentence Nefer to death. Nefer would be presented as a cold-blooded murderer, a veritable wild beast devoid of all humanity, who had been brought up by artisans as cruel as himself. Thus, the trap would close on the village.

Mehy kneaded Serketa's backside. 'This filly belongs to me, doesn't she?'

She rubbed herself against him. 'Yes, I am yours. Make love to me again.'

'You're insatiable!'

'That's only natural, since I'm lucky enough to have a tireless husband.'

'Your father worries me, Serketa.'

'Why?

'His mind is failing.'

'I haven't noticed anything.'

'Because you don't work with him. The mayor of Thebes himself alerted me. During an important meeting, your father babbled incomprehensibly, he made mistakes in his accounts, then he suffered a temporary collapse. I myself have been present recently during similar, more serious incidents. Of course, I didn't say anything to the mayor and I tried to dispel his fears. Unfortunately, your father refuses to admit to reality. When he recovers from his attacks, he doesn't remember anything about them and refuses to admit to his blackouts.'

'What should I do?'

'Inform his doctor and ask him to prescribe a treatment, if one exists, without upsetting your father. If only this worrying illness was the only thing wrong . . .'

Serketa sat down on the edge of the bed. 'What's wrong?'

'I don't know if I should tell you.'

'I'm your wife, Mehy, and I want to know everything.'

'It's horrible.'

'Tell me!'

'You may be distressed and hurt, my darling,' said Mehy in a low voice, as though he were afraid of being heard. 'Your father visited an estate to revise its taxation, and he took me with him to teach me some details. Suddenly, he threw himself on a young girl and tried to rape her. Although I'm a good deal stronger than he is, I could barely stop him. Fortunately, I prevented the worst. Afterwards, when he returned to his senses, he didn't remember this appalling scene.'

'Did anyone else see what happened?'

'The girl's mother.'

'She'll lodge a complaint – she's bound to.'

'Don't worry, I persuaded her not to. I explained the situation and offered her a milch cow and four sacks of grain in return for her forgetting about it. But I shan't always be at your father's side, and I'm afraid he may do it again.'

Serketa was close to breaking down. 'We are going to lose our reputation, everything we have . . .'

'I love you for yourself, darling. Think only of your father's health.'

Serketa's course of action was clear: she must have the

family fortune transferred to herself and her husband, and not allow a mentally ill man to manage it. When the madness gained ground, her father might sign any old document and fritter away her inheritance. She could not bear the idea of poverty. Fortunately, she had married Mehy, whose clear-headedness would save her from this danger.

'Can you have my father constantly watched?'

'No, I—'

'Tell your soldiers to keep a discreet eye on his safety. If he does anything bad, tell them to intervene immediately and report back only to you.'

'That would be exceeding my authority, and—'

'Do it for us, Mehy! Our future hangs in the balance.'

The captain pretended to think, although he had already suggested this solution to the mayor, who had accepted it.

'If my superiors found out,' he said, 'I'd be punished severely for abusing my power, but I'll take the risk for you, my sweet.'

Serketa kissed her husband's chest. 'You won't regret it. And I shan't be idle, either.'

'Above all, talk to his doctor.'

'Of course, but I'll also consult our lawyers. As his only daughter, I owe it to myself to protect the family inheritance. And my real family is now you and our future children.'

He forced her down on her back and lay on top of her with all his weight. 'How many do you want?'

'Four or five.'

'Isn't that a lot for a woman of your quality?'

'I want several boys. They'll look like you, and I'll feel as though you're beside me all the time.'

'You really can't do without Mehy any more, can you, my beauty?'

Incapable of experiencing pleasure, Serketa really couldn't have cared less about her husband's sexual prowess, particularly since he was a second-rate lover. But he was nevertheless an ideal husband, ambitious and greedy for power. Thanks to him, she would preserve her fortune and would even manage to increase it, provided she could rid herself of a father who, having been an encumbrance, was now becoming dangerous.

To manipulate Mehy, all she had to do was flatter him and make him believe that he was her all-powerful master. By behaving like a bitch on heat and a delightful imbecile, good only for being shown off at receptions on the arm of her dazzling lord and master, Serketa would confirm his high opinion of himself while, in the shadows, she would busy herself with accumulating as much wealth as possible. Owning ever more possessions – that was the goal of life.

# 37

Daktair was enraged. 'You made sure I obtained the post I wanted, Mehy, but I'm reduced to the status of a menial! The director of the central workshop is a stupid old priest, incapable of understanding the prospects which knowledge offers. He opposes all innovation, all experimentation, and he has relegated me to sorting files!'

'Do have a little more roast goose, my dear fellow,' said Mehy. 'My cook is a true artist, don't you think?'

'Yes, but—'

'I'd have thought a scholar of your standing would be much more patient.'

'Don't you understand what I'm saying? I have hundreds of projects and I am reduced to helplessness!'

'Not for long, Daktair.'

The alchemist rubbed his beard. 'I see no sign at all that the situation is changing in my favour.'

'You're wrong,' said Mehy. 'My good relations with the mayor of Thebes are being consolidated all the time, and my influence grows from day to day. Your present director won't keep his post for much longer, and it is you who will succeed him.'

Daktair sank his teeth into a perfectly roasted goose-thigh. 'This court case involving the Place of Truth, is it really serious?'

'Absolutely, my dear fellow. Thanks to the abominable crime Nefer committed, we shall rid ourselves of this accursed brotherhood more quickly than I had envisaged. The craftsmen will be dispersed, and I'll be authorised to search the village from top to bottom. Of course, you will assist me in your capacity as an expert.'

Daktair's little eyes shone with excitement. 'But the sentence hasn't been passed yet.'

'Egyptian justice is very strict and it will pronounce heavy sentences, for both the murderer and those who have protected him. This brotherhood is, after all, an association of evildoers. Banning it will seem the best solution.'

When Obed the blacksmith next encountered Ardent, the young man was so overwrought that he had been working uninterruptedly for eight hours. Ardent had suggested to Kenhir that he should organise a raiding-party of two or three strong craftsmen, go and rescue Nefer and bring him back to the village to place him beyond the reach of the police, but Kenhir had refused point-blank. While waiting to be initiated, Ardent must return to the ranks of the 'outsiders' and make himself useful.

'So they accepted you, did they?' asked Obed, who was examining with approval some copper shears his companion of one day had made.

'I hope they won't go back on their word.'

'No, they'd never do that. But this case is a serious blow for the brotherhood.'

'Silent is innocent!'

'All the same, he'll be convicted of murder. Sobek is bound to have proof.'

'I ask myself only one question: who hates my brother enough to drag him through the mire like this and destroy his life?'

'You should forget this murky tale, Ardent, and work with

me. You like the forge, and you have a talent for it. Don't lock yourself away in a village whose days are numbered.'

'What do you mean?' demanded Ardent.

'If Nefer is found guilty, the brotherhood will be too. There'll be a detailed investigation into every single one of its members to establish possible complicity, the building projects will be interrupted, and the craftsmen will be split up and sent to different temples. It will be the end of the Place of Truth.'

'And what about my initiation?'

'It will never take place.'

The young man clenched his fists. 'All because some evil genius is lurking in the shadows!'

'Do you know Nefer well?' asked Obed.

'He's my friend.'

'That isn't enough to acquit him. When it comes down to it, you know almost nothing about him and his past. What kind of man has he become during his long travels? In Nubia, he must have faced violence and no doubt he learnt how to kill. Did he return to Thebes to get rich? In the village, he heard people talk of the treasures placed in the tombs of the pharaohs during their burial ceremonies. Perhaps he dreamt of seizing some for himself.'

'That would be monstrous!'

'He wouldn't be the first or the last to have had the idea. And he'd be better placed than most to carry it out. That must be why he was moving about, at night, in the hills overlooking the Valley of the Kings. But he didn't know that Sobek had become commander of the guards and had set up a new system of patrols. When a guard spotted him, Silent killed him. He could have found no better place to hide than the village itself, but he underestimated Sobek, who kept doggedly pursuing his inquiries and eventually identified him.'

'That's a stupid story,' snapped Ardent.

'It's what will be said at the trial, you'll see. The facts fit too well not to be believed.'

'That doesn't mean they're true.'

'This whole business stinks,' said Obed, 'and neither Nefer nor the brotherhood will come out of it unscathed. Follow my advice and keep your distance.'

'The craftsmen's hands are tied, but neither you nor I belong to the brotherhood. If I try to rescue him, will you help me?'

'Certainly not! We'd have no chance of success, and I want to keep my job. Nefer is in prison, and nobody is going to get him out.'

'Are Ubekhet's parents still alive?'

'Only her father.'

'Do you know his trade?'

'He owns a building company. He is a skilled man, with an excellent reputation.'

Thanks to Obed's directions, Ardent had no difficulty in finding the house belonging to Ubekhet's father. As far as he was concerned, there was no doubt that this man was the guilty party. Unable to bear his daughter's departure, he'd taken vengeance on Nefer by providing Sobek with false evidence so that her seducer would be accused. Feeling abandoned and betrayed, the builder had decided to destroy the couple who had escaped from him by withdrawing into the village. Either willingly or by force, Ardent would drag him before the court so that he could confess his misdeed and clear Nefer of all suspicion. That way, the business would be sorted out quickly.

It was late morning, and people were returning from the market. The young man plunged into the house, whose door opened out on to the street.

A black dog barred his way.

'Easy now, friend,' said Ardent. 'I don't mean you any harm.'

Determinedly standing its ground, the dog growled and bared its teeth. If Ardent ventured any closer, it would attack.

Ardent could have broken its neck, but he felt an affinity with the brave guardian and got down on his knees to look it straight in the eyes.

'Come and take a look at me. I'm not your enemy,' he said.

Doubtful, the black dog cocked its head as though it wanted to examine the intruder from a different angle.

'Come closer. I won't bite you.'

Ubekhet appeared at the top of the stairs to the first floor. 'Ardent! What are you doing here?'

He stood up. 'Can I stroke him?'

'He is a friend, Ebony. You can greet him without fear.'

The dog stopped growling and accepted a pat on the head.

'Ubekhet, I know everything. It was your father, wasn't it?'

'My father? I don't understand.'

'He resented your marriage and denounced Silent to Sobek. He must confess.'

She smiled sadly. 'You're wrong, Ardent. Our misfortune has made my father ill, very ill. Although he was hurt when I left, he took great pride in seeing me married to a Servant of the Place of Truth, the place where secrets of the trade are revealed: secrets to which he himself had no access. When I told him of Nefer's arrest, it weakened his heart.'

'Is he . . . ?'

'He's still alive, but I sense that death is very near.'

# 38

Ubekhet was right. An hour before the start of the preliminary hearing, her father died. She had comforted him by telling him that Nefer had nothing to be ashamed of and that justice would triumph in the end.

'I must make the funeral arrangements,' she told Ardent.

'No, go to the court. Your husband needs you there. I'll make the arrangements for you.'

'I can't accept, I—'

'Trust me, Ubekhet. Your place is at Nefer's side.'

'You don't know who to go and see, you—'

'Don't worry. It's at times of terrible trial like this that we find out who our real friends are. I wanted to save Silent by breaking down the walls of his prison, but that's impossible. You alone can support him and I must help you. If your father was a just man, he has nothing to fear from the court of Osiris, while your husband could go through hell because of the court of the living.'

The young man's words were rough and ready, but they restored Ubekhet's courage. She had no time for self-pity and there was no solution except to keep on fighting, even if the only weapons she possessed were pitifully weak.

'Be a juror? Me?'

'My dear Mehy, your appointment to the jury has been

approved by the tjaty,' said the mayor of Thebes. 'As an officer was required, I thought immediately of you.'

'It's a heavy responsibility.'

'I know, I know – and it isn't the last you'll exercise. When this irritating court case is over, I should like to entrust you with a few important tasks. My officials are getting old. I need some new blood.'

'As I told you, I am entirely at your disposal.'

'Perfect, Mehy. And . . . how is your father-in-law?'

'Getting worse.'

'That is extremely vexing. Are you having him watched?'

'Yes, as we agreed. By men of exemplary discretion who won't intervene unless it's absolutely necessary.'

'What does the doctor advise?'

'It's a sickness he knows little about, and which he can't cure.'

'Annoying, really annoying,' said the Mayor. 'Now, as regards the preliminary hearing, the tjaty has ordered it to be held on the west bank, before the gate of the Temple of a Million Years built by Seti. Here, on the eastern bank, he fears too many onlookers would turn up. A cordon of guards will keep curiosity-seekers at a distance and will guarantee that the court can convene in peace.'

This last-minute change annoyed Mehy, but it would not alter the outcome of the affair. Nefer the Silent would serve as a scapegoat and the brotherhood would be dragged down with him.

The delegation from the Place of Truth was made up of the old scribe Ramose, the Scribe of the Tomb, Kenhir, and the overseer, Neb the Accomplished. The whole village had hoped to process together to the court, but Ramose had advised them against this grand gesture, which ran the risk of displeasing the magistrates and so doing Nefer a disservice.

'Can you not request an audience with Ramses?' Neb asked Ramose.

'It would be pointless. Pharaoh must allow justice to take its course. As the Scribe of Ma'at, I stand as guarantor for the righteous behaviour of the brotherhood.'

'We could insist on seeing the tjaty.'

'That would be futile, too. At the moment, Nefer's fate is in the hands of the court.'

'What if it makes a mistake?'

'If there is no evidence, or if it is inconsistent, Kenhir and I will demand an acquittal.'

Neb did not share Ramose's optimism. He trusted only the court of the Place of Truth, where corruption had never gained a foothold.

'I'm convinced that Nefer is innocent and that someone is out to harm us,' said Kenhir.

'Ramses protects us,' retorted Ramose. 'The work of the Place of Truth is vital for Egypt's survival.'

'All the same, something diabolical is happening. It's as if a monster crouching in the darkness had decided to emerge and spread evil.'

'If so, we shall be able to resist him.'

'But we don't even know who he is yet. If he strikes from behind, we'll be dead before we've even begun to defend ourselves.'

The senior judge declared open the preliminary hearing of the case of Nefer, Servant of the Place of Truth. He was accused of murdering a guard belonging to the night detail charged with keeping watch over the Valley of the Kings.

'Under the protection of Ma'at and in her name,' declared the judge, 'I ask this assembly to consider the facts and only the facts.'

Present were the jurors who would have to pronounce a verdict at the trial, the deputation from the Place of Truth, and Ubekhet, wife of the accused, who took up a position to the left of the senior judge. On either side of Nefer stood a soldier armed with cudgel and dagger.

Nefer seemed calm, almost indifferent. When his eyes met his wife's, he felt that he was ready to face any test. Through her mere presence, she supplied him with a magic which strengthened his calm resolution.

'Are you Nefer the Silent?' asked the senior judge.

'I am.'

'Do you admit to being a murderer?'

'I am innocent of the crime of which I am accused.'

'Dare you swear that?'

'On the name of Pharaoh, I swear it.'

A long silence followed this oath, whose importance everyone knew well. Mehy was delighted: after such a declaration Nefer, once he was recognised as a liar, could not escape the death penalty.

'The prosecution may speak,' said the judge.

Sobek came forward and summarised the facts. He regretted the swiftness of his own investigation and his hasty conclusions, and handed the court the anonymous but extremely well informed letter accusing Nefer. After receiving it, Sobek said, he had given the matter a great deal of thought, and concluded that Nefer was indeed a likely culprit, particularly as he had no alibi for the night of the crime. Brought up in the craftsmen's village, he was bound to have heard talk of the riches of the Valley of the Kings and had dreamt up this insane plan for seizing them. Challenged by a guard while trying to check the details of a way into the forbidden area, he had had no choice but to kill him. With his characteristically calculating mind, Nefer had then taken refuge in the village which the guards were not allowed to enter.

'This grave accusation rests only on an anonymous document,' pointed out the judge.

'From the evidence,' replied Sobek, 'it was written by a remorseful craftsman who wishes the truth to be brought to light. What is more, the facts hang together extremely consistently.'

The judge turned to Nefer. 'Where were you on the night of the crime?'

'I can't remember.'

'Why did you come back to the village?'

'Because I had heard the call.'

Abry asked permission to speak. 'Nefer's defence is laughable! The boy is an adventurer, fearsomely cool-headed and capable of the worst. Let him be brought before a jury, which will convict him of murder and perjury.'

'There is no decisive proof,' opined the judge.

'Perhaps there is,' objected Sobek. 'One of my men, who was patrolling the scene of the crime that night, remembers seeing someone roaming around.'

The guard was called to give evidence. Overawed by the judge and jury, he had the greatest difficulty in expressing himself, but in the end he admitted that he thought he recognised the accused.

The judge no longer had any choice. 'I therefore decide—'

'One moment.'

'Who dares interrupt me?'

A thin old woman, with a magnificent head of white hair, came before the court.

'Nefer the Silent is innocent,' she said.

'Who are you?'

'The wise woman of the Place of Truth.'

# 39

Murmurs ran round the assembled throng. Everyone was stunned by the appearance of this strange woman, who had the bearing of a queen. For many, the wise woman of the Place of Truth was a legendary figure, gifted with supernatural powers. As she never left the village, her very existence had been cast into doubt.

The senior judge had difficulty in finding the right words. 'How . . . how can you be so sure?'

'Since Nefer the Silent has been living in the village, I have been watching him. He is not a criminal.'

'Your opinion is not without weight,' said the judge wisely, 'but only firm proof—'

'If it is established that Nefer could not have been on the western bank on the night of the murder, would he not be irrefutably proved innocent?'

'Certainly – but he himself cannot remember where he was.'

The wise woman approached Nefer, who marvelled at the depth and beauty of her gaze.

'Give me your left hand,' she said.

She held it tightly between her own hands. A gentle yet intense heat penetrated into Nefer's palm, rose up the length of his arm and entered his head.

'Close your eyes and remember,' she told him.

Nefer's soul-bird took off on a superb flight, soaring above the Nile and the boats pushed along by the wind. Then it was irresistibly drawn to a palm-grove and, nestling within it, a little village close to Swenet, called Happy Bank, where children were playing with a little green monkey.

'Yes,' he whispered. 'That night I slept at the edge of that village, rolled up in my mat. I was tired and depressed, a prisoner of my wanderings, with no taste for the outside world. But I was definitely there, at Happy Bank. The full moon was shining . . .'

He opened his eyes. The wise woman stepped away and turned back to the judge.

'Ask Commander Sobek to go immediately to this place and question the inhabitants,' she said.

Locked up in a cell in the fifth fort, Nefer waited patiently. Because of the wise woman's intervention, the guards were being particularly considerate to him, for fear of having a spell put on them. He was properly fed, allowed to walk outside for a while every morning and evening, and saw Ubekhet every day.

To reassure him, she had told him that everything was going well in the village, but he was convinced that some people, still doubting his innocence, must be making her life difficult.

At last, at the end of two weeks of travelling and investigation, Sobek opened the cell door.

'You are free and cleared of all suspicion,' he said. 'Several witnesses saw you at Happy Bank on the night of the crime, so it cannot have been you who killed the guard. As compensation for the harm you have suffered, the court awards you a wooden storage chest, two new kilts and a scroll of good-quality papyrus. As for me, I offer you my apologies.'

'You were only doing your job,' said Nefer.

'But you'll never be able to forgive me.'

'Why did you believe I was guilty?'

'I acted twice without thinking: first, in supposing that the guard's death was an accident, and then in thinking that the author of that anonymous letter was revealing the murderer's identity and enabling me to make good my mistake. If you ask it, I shall request my own dismissal.'

'I do not ask it,' said Nefer firmly.

The Nubian stiffened. 'I am not accustomed to people pitying me.'

'It isn't pity. You did indeed make two serious mistakes, but they have no doubt taught you much more than all your successes. You'll now be all the more alert and will watch over the village's safety with sharper eyes.'

Sobek had the feeling that Nefer was carved from a different wood from most of the craftsmen in the brotherhood. At no time had he ever raised his voice and there seemed not a trace of resentment in him.

'I still have one serious problem,' Sobek reminded him. 'Who wrote that letter?'

'Have you any ideas?'

'None, but I've been made to look a fool, and I bear grudges. There has been a crime, that is certain, and the murderer is probably the letter-writer. But why did he try to destroy you?'

'I haven't the slightest idea.'

'No matter how long it takes,' promised Sobek, 'I shan't leave this mystery unsolved.'

'May I re-enter the village and return to my wife?'

'You are free, as I told you, but listen a moment longer. You must realise that you're in danger.'

'But you'll see that I'm protected, won't you?'

'Yes, but I'm not permitted to enter the village.'

'What have I to fear there?' asked Nefer.

'Suppose the author of the anonymous letter is a member of the brotherhood? He won't stop trying to harm you – or even to kill you. And it is in the village itself that you will be in most danger.'

'Carry on with your investigation, and identify the demon lurking in the shadows.'

The Nubian sensed that Nefer had not taken his warning seriously, but he did not hold him back. Sobek was too relieved that he was not lodging a complaint against him, which might have put an end to his career.

Nefer had scarcely stepped outside the fort when a black dog bounded up to him with such enthusiasm that it almost knocked him over. After putting his paws on Nefer's shoulders and licking his cheeks, Ebony began running in wild circles round his master then, with his tongue hanging out, finally came to a halt and allowed himself to be stroked.

Ubekhet walked towards her husband, who took her in his arms.

'Ebony wanted to be the first to celebrate your release,' she said. 'What happiness to see you again!'

'During my ordeal, I thought of nothing but you. I saw your face, and it wiped away the anguish and dissolved the cell walls. If you hadn't been there at the hearing, I'd have broken down.'

'It was the wise woman who saved you.'

'No, it was you. As soon as I saw you, I knew the lies could not touch me.'

'My father is dead,' she said sadly, 'and Ardent took charge of the funeral arrangements so that I could be at the hearing. That boy has a heart of gold.'

'Have you seen the wise woman again?' asked Nefer.

'No, and I was advised not to bother her. It is high time you came back.'

'You kept yourself to yourself, didn't you?'

'I don't remember anything. Our life in the village begins today.'

Ubekhet was right. Now Nefer knew that happiness was at

once as fragile as the wings of a butterfly and sturdy as granite, as long as you savoured each second as though it were a miracle.

Accompanied by Ebony, the pair headed for the main gate.

'I am sorry I was not at your father's funeral ceremony,' said Nefer.

'He admired you a great deal, and I hope I calmed him before the great departure. I promised him that justice would be done, and it has been.'

'You have remarkable powers, haven't you?'

'No. It was your love which enabled me not to lose heart.'

The gatekeeper greeted them warmly. 'Happy to see you again, Nefer! My colleague and I, we always knew you were innocent. Seems they're getting ready for a celebration in the village. Enjoy yourselves.'

The gate opened, and Nefer and Ubekhet went back into their new homeland. With the two overseers at their head, all the craftsmen had gathered at the top of the main street to welcome the couple and cheer them home. The reunions were joyful, and several jars of sweet beer were emptied as the wise woman's praises were sung.

'Now that Nefer has returned,' said Neb the Accomplished, 'it is time to proceed with Ardent's initiation.'

# 40

'Wake up,' Obed told Ardent.

'What's happening?'

'Your friend Nefer has been freed, and two craftsmen are coming to fetch you.'

Although Ardent had been asleep for only two hours, after a day of heavy work at the forge, he leapt up in a single bound.

'Have you thought about what I said?' asked Obed.

'The moment of my initiation has arrived!'

The blacksmith did not press the point. And yet he was convinced that the young giant was heading for disaster.

'Where are we going?' Ardent asked his guides.

Their faces were not friendly.

'The first and foremost of the virtues is silence,' replied one of them. 'If you wish, follow us.'

Night had fallen, and no light shone either in the village or in the surrounding area. Sure-footedly, as though they knew every small irregularity of the ground, the two artisans guided Ardent to the threshold of a funerary shrine hollowed into the hillside bordering the western flank of the village.

Ardent flinched. It was not death he was in search of, but a new life! Although he would have liked to ask a dozen questions, he managed to hold his tongue.

The two craftsmen walked away and disappeared into the

shadows, leaving Ardent alone, facing a gilded wooden door framed with limestone and surmounted by a small pyramid.

How much longer must he wait? If the brotherhood thought they could wear out his patience, they were much mistaken. Now that he was standing before the first door, he would not slacken his grip.

He was ready to fight any adversary, but the one who emerged from the darkness sent shivers down his spine: there, on a man's body, was a jackal's head with a long, aggressive snout and pointed ears. In its left hand, the monster held a sceptre whose upper end was shaped like the head of a snapping dog.

The man with the jackal's head came to a halt less than a pace from Ardent and held out his right hand.

No monster, however terrifying, was going to stand in his way, so Ardent did not hesitate to take it, although he remembered the tales which said that the jackal of the night appeared only to the dead.

'If you follow Anubis,' said the strange creature, 'he will lead you to the secret. But if you are afraid, go no further.'

'Whoever you are, do your work.'

'This door will open only if you speak the words of power.'

The man with the jackal's head let go of Ardent's hand. He wondered what he ought to do. He did not know the words of power. Was he going to have to beat down the door with his bare fists to find out what was on the other side?

Before he could take a radical decision, Anubis reappeared, carrying a bull's foot carved from alabaster.

'Present this to the door,' he ordered Ardent. 'It alone holds the word of power, the word of offering.'

The young man raised the sculpted foot.

Slowly, the door opened. A man with a falcon's head appeared, dressed in a gold corslet and carrying a red wooden statuette representing a decapitated man, with his feet pointing towards the sky.

'Be careful not to walk upside-down, Ardent, or you will lose your head. Only honesty will save you from that sad fate. Now cross the threshold.'

Ardent found himself in a small shrine decorated with scenes showing the brotherhood making offerings to the gods. From the centre of the room, a flight of stairs led down into the bowels of the hill.

'Go to the centre of the Earth,' ordered the man with the falcon's head. 'Open the great vase you will find there, and drink its pure water so that you will not be consumed by the fire. It will enable you to discover the energy of creation.'

Ardent descended the staircase, step by step, gradually becoming accustomed to the darkness. He came eventually to a chamber where he found a large vase, which he lifted up by its handles. The water it contained was cool and tasted of aniseed. He felt reinvigorated, as in the blessed time of the Nile flood, when people were authorised to drink the floodwater.

The man with the jackal's head and his falcon-headed companion also came down into the chamber, their torches casting light on a block of silver and on a bowl of the same metal, filled with water. They used it to wash Ardent's feet, before taking up position on either side of him and emptying the purifying liquid over his head, shoulders and hands.

'You are born to a new life,' they told him, 'and you will sail upon the ocean of power.'

At the far end of the chamber, a passage led to a vault occupied by a sarcophagus in the shape of a fish, the very one which had swallowed Osiris's penis when the body parts of the murdered god were cast separately into the Nile. The two ritualists took off the lid and signalled to Ardent to lie down inside the enormous fish, which was richly decorated with lapis-lazuli.

There, he experienced his first metamorphosis, and came to see that he was not merely a man but belonged to the whole of creation and was thus linked to all forms of life. Thanks to the Fish of Light, for a moment he believed he had the power to swim back to the well-spring of life.

But the jackal and the falcon tore him from his meditation and made him return to the surface, leave the shrine, and enter another, which was much larger and contained four torches set in a rectangle. At their feet were four basins made from clay mixed with incense, and filled with the milk from a white heifer.

Several of the craftsmen were there. Overseer Neb the Accomplished began to speak.

'It is the eye of Horus which allows us to see these mysteries and to be in communion with the blessed ones who dwell in heaven. If you truly wish to become our brother, you must toil far from eyes and ears, and respect our rule, which is our bread and our beer. It is called *Tep-red*, "the Head and the Leg", for it both inspires our thoughts and our deeds and acts as the rudder of our community's ship. The rule is the expression of Ma'at, daughter of the Divine Light, the principle of all harmony and the creative word. Do you still ask to be admitted among us and do you wish to know the extent of your duties?'

'I do,' replied Ardent.

'Be vigilant so that you may accomplish the tasks entrusted to you,' said Neb the Accomplished. 'Never be negligent. Seek what is just, be consistent, pass on what you have received by embodying it in matter without betraying the spirit. May the mystery of the work remain hidden even though it is revealed; be silent and preserve the secret. Sit in the temple if you are called there, make offerings to the gods, to the pharaoh and to the ancestors, take part in processions, festivals and your brothers' funeral rites, contribute to our solidarity fund, submit to the decisions of our court, tolerate no ill-will. Do not go to the temple if you have acted against Ma'at, if you are in a state of impurity or lies. Do not falsify the weight or the measure, do not wrong the eye of the Light, do not be greedy. Are you ready to swear on the stone that you will respect our rule?'

'I am ready.'

Nefer the Silent came forward and unveiled a stone hewn in the shape of a cube, from which a soft light seemed to emanate.

'On your life and on that of Pharaoh, do you promise to respect the duties of which I have spoken?'

'I promise,' agreed Ardent.

'Today,' declared Neb, 'you become a Servant of the Place of Truth, a native of the Tomb, and you receive your new name: Paneb. May it endure like the stars of heaven, never to be forgotten for all eternity, and may it preserve your power day and night. May the gods make it as stable as truth itself.'

Holding in his left hand a cane topped with the head of a ram, the incarnation of Amon, Nefer inscribed Ardent's new name on his right shoulder with a fine brush dipped in red ink.

'You who are becoming a craftsman,' went on the overseer, 'learn to respond always to the call, work to have access to Thoth's incantations, resolve their difficulties and become an expert in their secrets. Thus will you reach the land of the Light.'

Paneb the Ardent was anointed with perfumed oils and ointments, then dressed in a white robe and white sandals. Nefer symbolically traced the image of Ma'at on his tongue, so that it might speak no more crooked words.

The overseer covered the stone again and extinguished the four torches by plunging them into the bowls of milk. Then the craftsmen went out of the shrine to gaze up at the stars.

# 41

When dawn came, Paneb the Ardent and Nefer the Silent were still sitting in front of the door of the shrine where Paneb had been initiated. They had watched the stars, eternal home of the souls of the pharaohs and wise men who had contributed to the building of Egyptian civilisation since its very origins.

'Did you go through the same rites?' Paneb asked his friend.

'Exactly the same.'

'And your wife?'

'She too, like the other women in the village. They all belong to the sisterhood of the priestesses of Hathor, but most of them advance no further than the first level.'

'Are there several?'

'Probably.'

'And is it the same with the craftsmen?'

'Of course,' said Nefer, 'but the important thing is that we are a team. Whatever our job, we are all sailing along in the same ship and everyone on board has a particular role.'

'What will mine be?'

'First, to make yourself useful.'

'To others?'

'To the work, and also to the brotherhood.'

'What is this work really, Nefer?'

'The construction of the royal tomb and all that implies. Thanks to it, the Invisible is present on Earth and the process of resurrection is carried out. But we still have a lot to learn before we can take part fully in the work.'

'At last I'm going to draw and paint!'

'The most urgent thing for you is to learn to read and write with the village children.'

'I'm not a child any more,' protested Paneb.

'Writing is the basis of your art, and you have no time to lose. Kenhir is a stern teacher, and sometimes pernickety, but his pupils are well-trained.'

'Well, if there's no alternative . . . Do you know what my new name means?'

'Paneb means "the master". Neb the Accomplished gave it to you, to give you an impossible goal to attain. He's sure you'll keep trying to be a master and that your energy will burn away in direct proportion to your failures. One day, you will be at peace.'

'He's going to be disappointed,' declared Paneb. 'Yes, I shall become a master of my trade and I shall deserve my name. He thought he was weighing me with a heavy burden, but he's giving me a fire which will go out only when I die.'

Outside the encircling wall, the lay workers were getting down to work. The donkeys were being unloaded, and water was being delivered for morning ablutions. The sun was coming up over the Place of Truth, where Paneb the Ardent was going to live out the adventure he had dreamt of for so long.

At last he was able to explore the village, which was so well sheltered behind its high walls. Other, lower walls were built with a foundation of large blocks to form an obstacle to the torrents of mud and loose stones produced by storms, which were as violent as they were rare.

Situated some five hundred paces beyond the limit of the strongest floods, which did not therefore threaten it, the village occupied the whole of the little desert valley, an old river-bed with hills all around, barring the view and protecting the sacred settlement from the eyes of the curious. At an equal distance from Ramses' Temple of a Million Years and the sacred mound of Djemeh where the primeval gods slumbered, 'the town', as the artisans sometimes called it, had the appearance of a place outside the world, isolated from the Nile valley. To the west was the 'Libyan' cliff; to the south a rocky spur against which the back of the main temple rested; towards the north, the way out of the valley and the gentle slope towards the fields.

Two cemeteries had been laid out, one either side of the village. The one on the east had been designed in three stages: the lower one for children, the middle one for adolescents, and the highest for adults. The one to the west, which was also set out in tiers, faced the sun and contained the most beautiful shrines.

Here, life, death and eternity were closely united in a harmony which was at once natural and supernatural. On the village land, there were also shrines, temples belonging to the brotherhood, water-tanks, granaries and other sacred or worldly buildings.

'Come,' Nefer said to Paneb, 'I'm taking you to your home.'

'You mean to say I have a house now?'

'A little bachelor's house. Just don't expect a miracle!'

'Have you got one, too?'

'I was luckier than you, for it is in better condition. No one chooses: it is the Scribe of the Tomb who allocates our homes, and the overseer allocates us our place in the brotherhood's shrine, where we meet.'

'Who really runs it?'

'The Scribe of the Tomb, Kenhir, and the two overseers of the teams – I should say crews, since our brotherhood is comparable to a ship. Neb the Accomplished reigns to starboard, the right-hand side, and Kaha to port, the left-hand side. You and I have been taken into the starboard crew as apprentices. We owe respect to the companions and experts who have spent long years here and have had access to the sources of knowledge.'

'How many of us are there?'

'Today, thirty-two, sixteen in the starboard crew and sixteen in the port. In earlier times there were more, up to fifty, but some died and some left for other horizons, and the pharaoh prefers a crew which is tight-knit and coherent. Your admission, like mine, is little short of a miracle. As apprentices, we are kept silent so that we may try to become truly "those who have heard the call".'

'What kind of work will you be doing?' asked Paneb.

'I shall be a stone-cutter, learning how to use the great chisel, which can split the hardest rock, but also to sculpt finely with the little adze.'

'Were you given a choice?'

'I haven't your gift for drawing,' replied Nefer, 'and I've always loved working closely with stone.'

'For me, it'll be drawing and nothing else!'

'Suppose the overseer assigns you to other work?' said Nefer, smiling.

Paneb masked his discontent badly. 'I have a specific goal, and no one's going to divert me from it.'

'Neb the Accomplished is not an easygoing man, and he doesn't like people questioning his orders. As you're the most junior apprentice, you must obey.'

'You're my friend, you know I can't do that! He may be the overseer, but he doesn't frighten me and he must explain what he expects of me. In Egypt, there are no slaves, and I'm not going to be the first.'

Nefer did not press the point, for fear of fanning the flames. Paneb's first steps promised to be difficult.

Paneb explored the village itself with curiosity. It was

crossed by a main street running north to south and a second, smaller street, running perpendicular to it. Within the encircling wall were seventy white houses, where the members of the brotherhood and their families lived, together with the Scribe of the Tomb. The northern part was the earliest inhabited area, dating from the time of Tuthmosis I.

The two friends walked past the beautiful house of Ramose, who had welcomed in his successor and spiritual son, Kenhir. Kenhir had the use of a pillared hall, where he could receive the craftsmen, and a perfectly equipped study.

Paneb felt eyes fix on him. They belonged to his colleagues in the starboard crew, who were resting. A dozen or so children, aged from four to twelve, fell into step with him, chattering and laughing.

The main street ended in a crossroads, and the two men headed off to the right, then took the main thoroughfare leading to the most southerly part of the village, where they found the house allocated to Paneb the Ardent.

Paneb gazed at it for a long time. 'But it's a ruin!'

# 42

The walls looked on the point of collapse, the woodwork was rotting away and the paint was peeling.

'This house certainly isn't in good repair,' agreed Nefer, 'but it does have the inestimable advantage of being in the village.'

The argument did not mollify Paneb. 'I'm going to see the Scribe of the Tomb.'

Without bothering about the consequences of doing so, he strode swiftly back along the street and into Kenhir's audience chamber, where the scribe was sitting on a mat, unrolling a papyrus scroll of accounts.

'Was it you who allocated me that tumbledown hovel?' demanded Paneb.

Kenhir ignored him and continued reading. After a while he said, 'Are you Paneb the apprentice?'

'Yes I am, and I insist on being given a habitable house.'

'Here, lad, an apprentice does not "insist on" anything. He listens and he obeys. With a character like yours, you're going to find that very difficult, and if you fail your overseer will soon "insist on" your expulsion. I'll be the first to support him.'

'Why aren't I being treated like the other artisans? They're housed decently.'

'For the moment, you are nothing at all. The brotherhood

has initiated you into your basic duties, but what did you understand of the ceremony? You have not spent one single day in the village and already you want to be housed like a leading citizen. Who do you think you are? Perhaps you think people will take one look at your pretty face and hand you a fine house, luxuriously furnished, with a cellar full of vintage wines. You should realise that all your colleagues built or repaired their houses, without whining and without protesting. To have the benefit of a site and a few walls, even rickety ones, is in itself an extraordinary piece of good fortune which hundreds of unlucky candidates dream of. And you dare complain about your lot! You add stupidity to your vanity.' Kenhir continued to unroll the papyrus carefully, all the time scanning the figures written on it.

Paneb seethed, but didn't dare grab the scribe, throw him out of his lair and wreck his equipment.

'Are you still there, apprentice? You would do better to make your hovel habitable, for no one will help you. In a brotherhood like ours, there is no place for people who are not self-sufficient.'

Paneb turned on his heel and went out. Kenhir breathed more easily: if the young man had given in to his anger, the scribe would have been no match for him.

The stone steps leading from the street to the doorway of the main living-room were worn. Apart from the lower stone foundations, which had survived the ravages of time, the whole structure was made of dried bricks and would have to be rebuilt. As for the beams, they had suffered so badly that Paneb would have to replace them. Obviously the hovel had not been lived in for many years, and the first task was to clean it from top to bottom.

But Kenhir's speech had pleased Paneb: he had just realised that this ruin was his first house. Suddenly, it seemed to him more beautiful than a palace.

'I'll help you,' said Nefer.

'Kenhir says that's forbidden.'

'There is custom, but there is also friendship.'

'I shall respect custom, and will do the restoration on my own.'

'You might make mistakes over some of the more skilled things,' said Nefer doubtfully.

'Yes, I probably will, but I want to do it all myself. On the other hand, if you were to invite me to dinner, I wouldn't say no.'

'Did you think for one moment that Ubekhet wouldn't?'

The front of Nefer's house looked very different from the interior. He had just had enough time to set up a little kitchen, where Ubekhet was preparing boiled beef and lentils with cumin. The smoke escaped through a round hole in the roof.

Once again, Paneb was struck by the extraordinary beauty of the young woman, whose luminous smile induced even the sourest people to be friendly.

'We may not have any chairs yet,' she said, 'but you are welcome to our home. I'm sure your own magnificent property has filled you with enthusiasm.'

Paneb burst out laughing. 'How well you know me, Ubekhet. Last night I slept under the stars; tonight I'll probably be squashed flat by old bricks falling on me. But at last I'm here, with you – and I'm starving!'

He ate the best meal of his young life. The bread was crusty, the meat tasty, the lentils soft and the beer smooth. The feast was finished off with goat's cheese.

'Tomorrow morning,' said Ubekhet, 'you'll have to go and fetch your rations.'

'Do people eat like this every day?'

'Much better, on festival days.'

'Now I know why it's so difficult to enter the brotherhood! Free housing, ample food, a wonderful profession . . . I've found paradise on earth.'

'All the same, be careful,' warned Nefer. 'It's very difficult to get in, it's true, but it's very easy to leave. If your overseer isn't satisfied with you, Kenhir won't support you. Those two can get you expelled on the spot.'

'How do you get on with Neb?' asked Paneb.

'He's a rough, authoritarian man, who doesn't tolerate the slightest imperfection in anyone's work. To be frank, he doesn't like you very much and he won't let you deviate from your orders by so much as a fraction of a cubit.'

'Could I transfer to the other crew?'

'I wouldn't advise it. It would severely displease the two overseers, and Kaha would be even stricter than Neb.'

'Understood. I'll do battle.'

'Why do you see these relationships as a war?' asked Ubekhet.

The question surprised Paneb. 'I must always struggle, here as elsewhere. Neb will try to break me, but he'll fail.'

'What if he intends to train you so that you can undertake major works?'

'I'm young, Ubekhet, but I have no illusions. Among human beings, the only relationships that exist are those based on strength.'

'Aren't you forgetting love?'

Paneb stared at his spoon. 'You and Nefer are an exceptional couple, but you cannot serve as my model. You're a priestess of Hathor, aren't you?'

'Yes. Since my initiation I go to her temple each day and I prepare the offerings which must be placed on the altars, in the temple and funerary shrines and in each house. In the village, life is different. There are couples, bachelors, children, but our houses are also shrines and there are no priests and priestesses except the craftsmen and their wives. In our respective functions, daily life is not kept separate from the sacred, and that is why I have felt as though I can sense the beating of one of Egypt's secret hearts, kept safe within the walls of this village. We are asked to experience the mystery, to taste its flavour, to listen to its music, and that destiny belongs to us.'

'As long as the overseers wish it.'

'I haven't lived here long,' added Ubekhet, 'but already I know that perseverence is an essential virtue if we are to perceive the invisible Law of the Place of Truth. She is a generous mother, who gives unstintingly, but our heart must be open to welcome her.'

Her words moved Paneb deeply. They tore away a veil which had clouded his sight and which the initiation itself had left intact. Although he had heard the call, he had never imagined that this modest village might be such a vast world and that it might contain so many treasures whose true nature still escaped him.

'Would you like to sleep here tonight?' asked Nefer.

'No, I must get on with my house, or Ubekhet and you will be ashamed of me.'

'As I said, you have my help if you want it.'

'If I don't do it on my own, I'm the one who'll be ashamed. I know I'm an idiot sometimes, but all the same I've realised that refurbishing this hovel is my first test.'

# 43

Mehy's secret work was producing the expected results. It had taken him a mere three months to reach the rank of commander-in-chief of the Theban troops, whose administrative and military reorganisation had been entrusted to him. Little by little, he was managing to oust the other high-ranking senior officers by means of his favourite weapon, denunciation. To this, he added a string of promises which were music to the soldiers' ears: higher pay, the chance of early retirement, better food, modernisation of the barracks. When these promises were not kept, Mehy accused the senior officers of negligence and hypocrisy, and expressed sympathy for the unfortunate soldiers who had been abused; he said he would defend them tirelessly before the responsible authorities. In reality, when he dealt with the authorities, he called the soldiers scum, and accused them of leading an easy, pampered life.

His appointment had been welcomed as warmly by the leaders as by the rank and file, and he maintained his excellent reputation by inviting a leading citizen of Thebes to dine at his house every evening, having first studied the individual's file carefully so as to be able to flatter him with the maximum efficiency. Each guest went away in the certain knowledge that he himself was an exceptional human being and the commander a dedicated man, worthy of great praise.

Moreover, Serketa excelled at playing the perfect mistress of the house, charming and light-hearted, sufficiently frivolous not to be annoying, and capable of playing the little girl to soften the hearts of tough senior officials, who were titillated by her smiles. But to the army of servants she ruled over, Serketa showed a very different face: that of a harsh, ruthless employer.

Mehy and Serketa had become the most fashionable couple in Thebes, and everyone who was anyone waited impatiently to be invited to their table. Nevertheless, the commander took care not to outshine the mayor, who was still powerful and wily enough to ruin him; when they met, Mehy affected modesty and displayed only reasonable, limited ambitions. Moreover, he had no intention of replacing the mayor, who was too embroiled in the quarrels between clans. It was better to manipulate him, leaving him to parade up and down, centre-stage. One did not conquer lasting power without shadowy dealings, or attributing the blame for failures to the imbeciles who thought they held that power.

As usual, tonight's banquet had been a great success. The principal scribe of the granaries and his wife, a rich, ugly, pretentious Theban woman, had stuffed themselves with meat and pastries, not to mention cool oasis wine which, as it went to their heads, had loosened their tongues. In this way, Mehy had obtained a few snippets of confidential information on the management of the grain stocks which he could use when the opportunity arose.

'At last they've gone!' Mehy said to Serketa, as he held her in a brutal embrace. 'Those were the most unbearable of the whole week, but they'll be our staunch allies from now on.'

'Darling, I have great news for you.'

'You're expecting a child?'

'You guessed!'

'A son! I'm going to have a son! Have you done the urine tests?'

'Not yet. If it's a girl, will you be disappointed?'

'Very. But you'll give me a son, I'm sure of it.'

Suddenly Mehy's enthusiasm collapsed, and his face darkened. 'I would so have liked your father to share our joy. Alas, he's getting worse and worse. His last reports contained so many aberrations that I had to alter them. Has his doctor prescribed a treatment?'

'On my recommendation, he dares not speak to my father about his illness, which he can't treat, anyway. He is content to care for his heart, which he says is weak. My father mustn't get excited or upset.'

'I'm worried,' said Mehy. 'He might do something monstrous and ruin all our efforts – and just when we're going to have an heir. We must think of the future, my love.'

'Don't worry. I've contacted a lawyer and explained our problem – in the strictest confidence, of course.'

'What does he think?'

'We have already made some legal arrangements which will prevent my father ruining my fortune if he loses his mind completely. But that isn't enough. Only if he is certified mad will I be able to take sole charge of our wealth.'

'Would you keep the contract separating our money?'

'As long as we had no heir, that was the best solution. Now, it's different. We make an excellent couple, I am expecting your child, and you are a remarkable manager. As soon as my father dies, or if he is certified mad, I'll annul the contract and we'll share everything.'

Mehy kissed her greedily. 'You're wonderful! And I shan't be content with just one son.'

Serketa had spent a lot of time thinking about the situation. Her father was getting old, he used outdated methods and he no longer had the energy necessary to increase his fortune. The new master of the game was Mehy. Deceitful, lying, cruel and skilful, he made constant progress and gained ground all the time. Whether she had children with him or some other man, what did it matter? It wasn't as if Serketa would bring them up herself, and Mehy would have the living proof of the virility to which he attached such great importance.

If there should be a divorce, Serketa would keep at least a third of the fortune and she knew how to attack her ex-husband in a court of law to get back the rest. Annulling the contract which separated their wealth would convince him of the blind trust of a woman in love, and he would lower his guard. Seeing Mehy grow greater and greater, harvesting the fruits of his scheming, then devouring him like a praying mantis . . . With the prospect of such an exciting future, there was no chance of Serketa lapsing into boredom.

'Every day,' said Mehy, 'I pray to the gods for Moseh to recover. If something unfortunate happened to him, I'd be devastated.'

'I don't doubt it for a moment, my love; but I'd be at your side to support you through the ordeal.'

Commander Mehy had invited his close subordinates and a few leading citizens to a hunt in the papyrus marshes to the north of Thebes. Abry was scared half to death. He knew the place could be dangerous and that his chances of survival would be slim. An enraged hippopotamus could easily overturn a boat, a crocodile charged its prey at a fearful speed, and there were plenty of water-snakes, too!

Abry had taken his place beside Mehy, who, with a throwing-stick, had already smashed the skull of a mallard. Killing birds gave him keen pleasure, and he liked to boast of his almost unrivalled skill.

'Can't we talk somewhere else?' asked Abry.

'I don't trust your colleagues or your wife,' retorted Mehy. 'Since Nefer's acquittal, the Place of Truth has re-established its glorious reputation. Attacking it is likely to be dangerous.'

'I couldn't agree more! So I suggest we give up and

confine ourselves to our official activities.'

'That's out of the question, my dear fellow.'

'But it isn't worth going on, is it?'

'Look at this place, Abry, and marvel. Here, nature is expressed in all its savagery, and there is but one law: kill or be killed. Only the strongest win.'

'The practice of Ma'at consists precisely of striving against that law.'

'Ma'at isn't eternal!' exclaimed Mehy, throwing a stick at a kingfisher and narrowly missing it. 'I missed because I wasn't concentrating,' he lamented. 'When you're hunting, a cool head is the best weapon. Do you want to try?'

'No, I'm hopeless at it.'

'We're going to press on, Abry, and you're going to help me. This little legal setback hasn't dented my determination, and I've many reasons to believe we'll succeed.'

'The Place of Truth is more impregnable than a Nubian fortress!'

'No fortress is impregnable. All you have to do is put the right plan into action. Today, the brotherhood thinks it is sheltered from all harm and it carries out its work in perfect peace. And therein lies its weak point.'

A genet leapt from one parasol-shaped papyrus flower to another to escape the hunters, while the ducks sounded the alarm with cries of fear.

'Patience,' said Mehy. 'A systematic sweep of the area, and we'll kill the lot.'

'Is that your plan for the Place of Truth, too?'

'In part, dear fellow, though I shall add a few other ingredients. Have you learnt anything new?'

'Not since Nefer the Silent and Paneb the Ardent entered the brotherhood.'

'Paneb, "the master".' Mehy laughed sarcastically. 'His colleagues have mapped out a fine future for him!'

'I don't think that kind of name has any real importance.'

'You don't know craftsmen very well. I'm certain they leave nothing to chance and that we must take account of the slightest sign. Have you set up a system of watchers who will alert you as soon as a member of the brotherhood leaves the village?'

'It's done, but there are no results so far.'

'As soon as it happens, let me know immediately.'

'Time is getting on. Shouldn't we be getting back to town?'

'I haven't killed enough birds yet.'

# 44

'"Listening is the best thing of all": those are the words of the sage Ptah-hotep, who lived in the time of the pyramids. You all know how to run, swim and talk, but your last writing exercises were pitiful because you don't listen to me.'

Kenhir was in a foul mood, as he was every morning. Often he delegated the work of instructor to the brotherhood's finest illustrator, who thus assumed the title of "scribe", but since Paneb's arrival, Kenhir had been taking the class himself, to the despair of the boys and girls, who were overwhelmed with work and reprimands.

'You hardly know the alphabet and you draw very badly. As for the hieroglyphics which represent two sounds, every single one must be done again. And then there's the way you've drawn your birds, in particular the owl and the fledgling which sticks its tongue out as it flaps its wings! How can I teach people who don't want to listen? It would take hundreds of strokes of the stick to open up the ear on your backs.'

Paneb cut in. 'I'm the eldest pupil, so I'm responsible for the mistakes made by the whole class. My back is broad enough to take all the strokes of the stick.'

'Good, good, we'll see about that later. Sit down in the writing position, dip your reed-tips into your diluted black ink, and write the mother-signs on your slates.'

These slates were slivers of limestone, which lay all

around the village. More precious ones came from the tomb excavations. They were used for writing practice by the schoolchildren and apprentice illustrators who were not judged worthy of using papyrus, even if it was second-hand and of inferior quality.

Paneb was amazed and delighted by this rudimentary material. At last he had a proper writing-surface and a tool with which to practise his art. He enjoyed tracing the hieroglyphs, and did so with a precision and elegance that surprised Kenhir. The young man learnt very quickly; one would have thought his hand had always known the signs.

Kenhir examined the slates and decided that the girls were markedly more gifted than the boys. 'You're like twisted sticks which people throw to the ground, where the light and shade strike them. The sages say that, if a carpenter passes by, he can attend to these miserable sticks, straighten them out and use them to make walking-sticks for leading citizens. I am that carpenter. Whatever your destiny may be, you will leave this school knowing how to read and write.'

And the exercise began again, and went on until it was time for lunch.

'Tomorrow,' announced Kenhir, 'we shall draw the fish. Now go and eat, and mind your table manners. The path of wisdom begins with politeness and respect for others. You, Paneb, stay here.'

The pupils dispersed, chattering excitedly.

'Are you hungry?' asked Kenhir.

'Yes.'

'So am I, but there are more urgent things.'

Kenhir handed Paneb a large, lightly polished shard of limestone and a real scribe's brush. At his feet, he laid a pot filled with very black ink.

The young man was filled with excitement. 'It's . . . it's magnificent! I'll never dare draw on it!'

'Afraid, are you?

The taunt made Paneb's blood boil, but he managed to hide his anger.

'Draw the signs that make up your name: "pa", the duck taking flight, and "neb", the crow, which is worthy to receive offerings and which is therefore mistress of what it contains.'

Paneb did so, without hurrying. His hand was steady and two well-formed signs appeared. 'That's right, isn't it?'

'That isn't for you to judge. Do you understand why you were given this name?'

'Because I must stop trying to fly towards heaven, and because the degree of my mastery will depend on what I have seen and learnt.'

'Mastery? You're still a long way from that!' grumbled Kenhir. 'Draw an eye, a face viewed from the front, another in profile, a head of hair, a jackal and a boat.'

Paneb took plenty of time, as if experiencing each sign within himself before tracing it with a sureness of touch that was astonishing for an apprentice.

'Now scratch the limestone and rub all that away,' said Kenhir. How could a spirit fired by the power of Set show such patience and meticulousness? he wondered. This lad was a true mystery.

'There.'

'Copy the text from this papyrus.' Kenhir unrolled a fine document whose small, pointed writing was not easy to reproduce.

'Am I to make an identical copy or interpret it in my own way?'

'As you wish.'

Paneb chose the second solution.

The work he produced contained not one mistake, and the text was markedly more legible. Without any doubt, the young man possessed a scribe's hand, combining speed with clarity. As Kenhir's writing had grown almost illegible from tracing signs all day long, he felt a certain irritation.

'Read this text to me.'

'"If the act of ceaseless listening enters him who listens, he who listens becomes he who hears. When the listening is good, the word is good. He whom God loves is he who hears; he who does not hear is hated by God. It is he who loves to hear who accomplishes what is said. As for the ignorant man who does not listen, he will accomplish nothing. He considers knowledge to be ignorance, the useful to be harmful, he does all that is hateful, he lives on what causes death. Do not put one thing in the place of another, be aware of the shackles breaking within you, be aware of that which is spoken by him who knows the rites."'

'You can read, Paneb, and you don't stumble over any of the words. But do you understand what you read?'

'I don't suppose you chose that text at random. Do you mean I don't listen closely enough to your teaching?'

'We shall see later. Go and eat now. And don't take the limestone; it doesn't belong to you.'

Paneb went away, and Kenhir went back to Ramose's house, where he had taken up residence. The village woman he had engaged as a cook had prepared a salad, asparagus and veal kidneys.

'Forgive my lateness,' said Kenhir. 'My class lasted longer than expected.'

'My wife is ill,' confided Ramose. 'She won't be having lunch with us.'

'Nothing serious, I trust?'

'I'm waiting for the wise woman to tell me what's wrong. Are you managing to tame Paneb?'

'He's a remarkable boy, and I'd love to make a scribe of him.'

'You know his vocation lies elsewhere,' said Ramose.

'If he bends to the demands of the lore of Thoth, Paneb will become an exceptional painter. But will he have the patience to learn and to take one step at a time?'

'You have a soft spot for him, haven't you?'

'His soul is quickened by a force the brotherhood needs. Who knows what works he carries within him?'

'I trust you, Kenhir; you and Neb will know how to bring him to maturity.'

'We must be prepared for many setbacks, and even failure. Paneb is demanding, fanatical and violent, a real rebel. The fire of Set within him is so powerful that we may not be able to control it.'

'Can he read and write?'

'As well as you and I. In less than a year, he has learnt what most people take ten years to learn.'

'How does he behave with the children?'

'Like a perfect grandfather. He protects them, reassures them and never refuses to play with them. His authority is natural, and he does not need to raise his voice to be obeyed. The worst thing is that he helps the dunces to do their homework without heeding my warnings. I ought to punish him, threaten him with expulsion, the—'

'Remember the rule for a teacher, for him who instructs future scribes: "to be to his pupils a patient teacher speaking gentle words, to earn their respect by awakening their sensitivity, to educate by inspiring love". Continue training this young man, Kenhir; fight his flaws without weakening, don't tolerate any misbehaviour, and little by little reveal to him what is admirable and everlasting.'

# 45

Moseh rubbed his scalp with a lotion containing moringa oil, to cure his baldness. A discourteous remark by his last mistress had made him realise he was getting old and that his powers of seduction were wearing thin. Moseh had had a violent tantrum and made himself ill. Called in urgently, his doctor had advised him to rest and to take care of his weak heart.

How could he listen to such advice when he was bent under the weight of responsibilities? Thebes was only the country's third city, but it was bursting with wealth, and the tjaty demanded unequivocal, efficient government. From time to time, Moseh wished he could retire to the country with his daughter, and indulge in the pleasures of gardening, for which he no longer had time.

And now she had just announced that she was expecting a child! What marvellous news, and what a fine couple she and Mehy made! Moseh would have a happy old age, surrounded by several grandchildren whom he would teach about accounting and management, hoping that they would be as gifted as their father, who was completely at home with figures. Mehy's mental agility was so acute that it worried Moseh; after all, there was a risk it would make him indifferent to everything but his career.

On reflection, Moseh thought he should be wary of his son-in-law. If Mehy sometimes played at being modest, notably when he was with the mayor, it was a calculated move. There were many men like that; but Mehy added cruelty to ambition, and he knew nothing of pity. Although Mehy wore a plausible mask, Moseh saw through it and feared he discerned a man of ruthless ambition who had married sweet, fragile Serketa only in order to get his hands on her money. It was up to him, her father, to protect her by persuading her above all not to change the contract separating her wealth from her husband's, and also to think about protecting her children.

His last conversation with the mayor of Thebes, a long-standing friend, had troubled Moseh. The mayor had seemed distant, almost suspicious, and had talked about his current projects only vaguely, as though speaking to a stranger. Moseh suspected that Mehy had subtly undermined his position as treasurer and had presented himself as Moseh's natural successor. If that was true, Mehy was becoming a formidable rival and a schemer of the worst kind, and Moseh must at all costs avoid antagonising him.

Moseh's steward announced the arrival of the couple, whom he had invited to lunch. Serketa was looking smart, Mehy sure of himself.

'How are you feeling, my darling daughter?'

'I'm very well. And how are you, my dearest father?'

'I have hardly any time to bother about it. The tjaty wants the financial returns for the province of Thebes by next week and, just as every year, I haven't had the reports yet.'

'Perhaps I can help . . . ?' suggested Mehy.

'That won't be necessary. My scribes will work extra time.'

For the first time, Mehy detected suspicion, even hostility, in his father-in-law's attitude. Was Moseh more perceptive than he'd thought?

'At last a moment of peace,' said Serketa appreciatively. 'This evening we're dining with the scribe in charge of the flocks of Amon, a dreadfully dull person who talks about nothing but cows and oxen. Couldn't you get him replaced by someone less boring?'

Moseh had been so busy watching his son-in-law that he hadn't been listening to his daughter. Serketa was instantly convinced that her father had fallen victim to one of the frightful blackouts described by Mehy.

'Father, are you listening to me?'

'Yes – I mean no. What's wrong?'

'It's not important.'

'Everyone says how efficent your staff are,' said Mehy condescendingly. 'But if need be, you can count on me.'

'I shall go and see what your cook has prepared,' announced Serketa; she was troubled.

'An excellent idea. Mehy and I will drink a glass of wine under the vine while we wait for you.'

The place was charming and would easily have lent itself to lazy meditation, but Mehy could not afford to lose any more time.

'My dear father-in-law, I have some confidential information to pass on to you.'

'Does it concern me directly?'

'Very directly. You undoubtedly know that several Syrian traders set themselves up in Thebes, at the start of the year.'

'Indeed, they were authorised to do so. No one has complained about them, and they pay the correct taxes, which are duly entered into the receipts of the province.'

'That's only how it looks. The reality is very different.'

'What have you found out?'

'While on watch, one of my men became intrigued by a closed warehouse. He made some discreet inquiries and I'm bringing you the results: the Syrians have organised a traffic in grain with the peasants who live on the west bank.'

'Have you any proof?'

'The most tangible possible: their secret accounts, which were hidden in this warehouse.'

'Have you arrested the men?'

'I was hoping to reserve that privilege for you.'

Lunch had been short. Serketa went home to prepare for the evening's banquet, and Mehy and Moseh set off for the warehouse district. Moseh was more and more keyed-up at the thought of putting an end to an illegal trade as big as this one.

Mehy seemed to hesitate.

'Don't you recognise the place?' asked Moseh.

'Yes, that's definitely the building, facing the alleyway, but I'm suspicious. These Syrians might be dangerous.'

'Are they likely to be on the premises?'

'I'll go and find out.'

'Don't be foolhardy, Mehy. Don't forget, you're my daughter's husband and the father of her child. Go and fetch some soldiers.'

'All right, but stay here and wait for me.'

Moseh watched the warehouse Mehy had pointed out. The taxation of grain was exceptionally rigorous, and he could not understand how the Syrians had succeeded in getting round it. The examination of their secret accounts would no doubt prove collusion, and the punishment would be severe.

The place was deserted, and the warehouse seemed abandoned. A perfect hiding-place for compromising documents. Curiosity and impatience seized Moseh. Mehy was taking a long time returning, so he decided to explore the area. There was nobody around.

His heart beating faster, he pushed open the door of the warehouse, which was not even locked. A ray of light filtered in through a high window, lighting up a chest filled with papyrus scrolls. Just as he was unrolling the first of them, Moseh had a shock.

A very young girl came towards him.

'Who are you?' he asked.

She shook her hair loose, tore her clothes and scratched her chest and arms with her nails.

'What . . . ? You're mad!'

'Help!' she screamed. 'I'm being raped!

Moseh took her by the shoulders. 'Shut up, you little liar!'

Her screams became even louder.

The door burst open, and two soldiers appeared, swords in hand. 'Let go of that child, you swine!'

Panicked, Moseh turned towards them. 'It's a mistake . . . I . . . She—' A savage pain in his chest silenced him. He put his hands to his heart, his mouth gaping wide to suck in the air he lacked, then collapsed.

The girl had dressed herself hastily and fled through a hidden opening in the far wall.

Mehy appeared. 'What's going on here?'

'The treasurer tried to rape a little girl, Commander. She ran away and he . . . I think he's dead.'

Mehy bent over Moseh. As he had hoped, his father-in-law's heart had given up the fight.

'He is indeed. Did you actually see the attempted rape?'

'No, but from the little girl's screams it couldn't have been anything else. And you ordered us to act if anything untoward happened.'

'You did right, but we must forget this tragedy. I want my father-in-law to have a fine funeral, and his reputation to remain spotless. There will be no report; you saw nothing and heard nothing. In exchange for your obedience, you shall receive cloth and wine.'

The two soldiers nodded their agreement.

The little Syrian girl Mehy had paid to play-act left for her homeland that same day, with a nice little nest-egg. Thanks to Moseh's death, the commander had just become one of the richest men in Thebes.

# 46

Nefer the Silent soon grew accustomed to the rhythm of the Place of Truth: eight days' work followed by two rest days, plus numerous state or local festivals, afternoons off granted by the overseer and leave for personal reasons authorised by the Scribe of the Tomb. The craftsmen started work at eight o'clock, ate lunch between noon and two, and then worked again until six. Several of them used their free time to execute outside commissions, for which they got good prices.

Work on official projects took up only half the year, and the brotherhood did not resent it as a tedious obligation; the two crews were fully aware that they were taking part in an exceptional adventure, work which Pharaoh himself considered a priority.

Nefer shared this feeling but he had some difficult moments. Joining the starboard crew had brought him up against the clannishness of his colleagues, who watched him suspiciously. As a stone-cutter, he was in daily contact with his counterparts: Fened, who was known as "the Nose" because he always had an instinct for the right thing to do, Casa the Rope, a specialist in moving and hauling materials, Nakht the Powerful and Karo the Impatient. As for the three sculptors, the painter, three artists, the carpenter and the goldsmith, they rarely spoke to him and even then only to exchange small-talk.

As the port crew left for work when the starboard were resting and vice-versa, they seldom spent time together. Their two leaders, Neb the Accomplished and Kaha, each had their own methods and their own way of running things, and never came into conflict.

Every evening, Nefer cleaned the tools, counted them and took them back to the Scribe of the Tomb, who locked them in the village strongroom before redistributing them the following morning. In fact, all the tools belonged to Pharaoh, and no craftsman might take any for himself. In exchange, the Servants of the Place of Truth were invited to make their own tools, which they used when making objects for the outside world.

Nefer had wielded the stone pick, which was as heavy as a dog, was sharpened to a point and was powerful enough to tackle the hardest rocks. He was often the last to leave the site in the Valley of the Nobles, where the starboard crew was preparing a house of eternity for a royal scribe.

By watching his colleagues, he had learnt how to use the mallet and the bevel-edged chisel, which he made more effective with the aid of a bow which made the tool turn rapidly in order to bore holes. With his left hand, he held the chisel in place with a kind of cap which had a notch into which the wooden handle slotted. After many unsatisfactory attempts, he succeeded in playing the two tools like musical instruments; he felt their vibrations like a melody and wasted no energy.

Learning to master the knife with the blade sharpened on three sides, the short-handled awl with the square point, and the copper adze for finishing had not been easy, and it had taken great patience to bring them to life in his hands.

Karo the Impatient called out to him. 'Check if the block I have just levelled will fit exactly into the wall we're putting up.'

The task was an arduous one, and only an experienced

stone-cutter could do it. Karo should not have entrusted it to an apprentice, but Nefer did not protest and tried to remember how the overseer had done it, the day before. So he used three adjustment sticks pierced with a hole at one end like a whistle. After checking that they were the same length, he placed them vertically on the surface to be checked and stretched a string between two of them, using the third as a point of reference. Not satisfied with the result, he used a limestone rasp to smooth away a few bumps.

'What are you fooling about with?' demanded Karo, visibly angry.

'You gave me a job, and I'm doing it.'

'I just asked you to check, and you're doing more than that.'

'More than checking was needed. I found flaws and I'm trying to remove them. This block is going to be absolutely level.'

'It is my block, not yours!'

Nefer laid down his tools and faced up to Karo, a thickset man with short, muscular arms. Thick eyebrows and a square nose made him look aggressive.

'You're more experienced than I am, Karo, but that doesn't mean you can spoil our work. This block belongs neither to you nor to me, but to the House of Eternity for which it is destined.'

'Right, that's enough! Get off the site and leave my block to me.'

'It certainly is enough,' retorted Nefer. 'I'm a member of this team and I shan't put up with this kind of annoyance much longer.'

'If you don't like our attitude, go back outside.'

'I don't give a damn about your attitude. The only thing I'm interested in is this stone. I proved to you that I know how to level it and integrate it into the wall. What more do you want?'

Karo seized a chisel and became threatening. 'We don't need you in the village.'

'The village is my life.'

'You should be afraid, Nefer. Believe me, you won't last long.'

'Put down that chisel. No threats of yours will stop me respecting my oath.'

The two men stared at each other for a long time. Karo put the chisel down on the stone.

'So, nothing frightens you?'

'I love my trade and I shall show I am worthy of the brotherhood's trust, whatever the circumstances and the provocations.'

'I'm leaving this block to you. Finish it.'

Karo walked off. Nefer rid the stone of its last imperfections without worrying about the time, though it was getting late. The regular movements of his hands were as gentle as the rays of the setting sun.

'Isn't it time you went home?' asked Neb.

'I've almost finished.'

'Trouble with Karo?'

'No. He has his ways, I have mine. If we make an effort, we'll get on better. But whatever happens, the work won't suffer.'

'Come with me,' said Neb. He led Nefer to a shed where different sorts of stone were kept. 'What do you make of that one?'

'A medium sandstone, soft enough to be worked with bronze chisels but too porous. It doesn't come from the best quarry, at Kheny, and isn't good enough to be used in a royal monument.'

'Yes, Nefer, the right quarry is essential: Swenet for pink granite, Hatnub for alabaster, Tura for limestone, Gebel el-Ahmar for quartzite. The Place of Truth demands the highest-quality stone, and accepts nothing but that. You shall visit each of these quarries and you will engrave their level of operation into your memory. Have you thought about the origins of stones?'

'I think they're conceived in the world below and grow in the belly of the mountains, but they're also born in light-filled space, because sometimes they fall from the sky. A block seems immobile, yet the stone-mason's hand knows that it lives and carries within it the trace of changes our eyes cannot see, because for stone time is not the same as it is for man. Stone witnesses changes which go beyond our existence; in perceiving them, perhaps we, in turn, are witnesses of eternity.'

'Do you like this granite?'

'It's wonderful. It will allow itself to be polished to perfection and will endure for centuries.'

'Would you like to become a sculptor?'

'Learning to hew stone can take an entire lifetime, but sculpture appeals to me.'

'The head sculptor, Userhat the Lion, thinks he needs no one else, and you'll have the greatest difficulty in persuading him to teach you. But if the stone speaks to you, it may perhaps open the way for you.'

'It is the stone I listen to, and only the stone.'

Neb the Accomplished made as if to leave the site, but from a hillock he watched the young man. First thing tomorrow, he would speak to his colleague Kaha about the need to promote Nefer the Silent.

# 47

Ubekhet could not have wished for more. She was experiencing profound, radiant love in a unique village whose customs and little secrets she was discovering by degrees, and each day she served Hathor by preparing the flowers that were laid on the altars and in the shrines.

The women initiates were not divided into two crews like the men. Although she was at the lowest level, Ubekhet was perfectly content and did her work happily. However, the village women of the Place of Truth exchanged no more than a few inconsequential words with her, and made her feel that she was still a stranger whom no one trusted.

In the evening, Nefer and Ubekhet talked of their respective experiences, and they agreed that the attitude of the craftsmen and their wives was normal. This village was unlike any other, and they would have to fight for a long time to be admitted without restrictions.

Hathor was the goddess of the stars; she caused the power of love to flow round the universe, and only she could unite all the elements of life. In celebrating her, the priestesses of the Place of Truth were helping to maintain the invisible harmony without which no visible creation, according to celestial laws, was possible. It fell to the brotherhood as a whole, as well as to the ritualists in all the temples of Egypt, beginning with Pharaoh himself, to uphold this subtle energy each day, thus ensuring that the people had the protection of the gods and that Ma'at was present on earth.

Ubekhet was happy to take a modest part in this essential work, which was all the more evident since the village had devoted its existence to it.

The door of Casa the Rope's house was closed. Ordinarily, each morning his wife cleaned her doorstep and living-room, and took the bunch of flowers from Ubekhet's hands herself.

Anxious, the young woman knocked.

A small brunette opened the door. 'My husband's ill,' she said aggressively, as though Ubekhet were responsible. 'The wise woman is looking after Ramose's wife, so I don't know when she'll come.'

'I might be able to help.'

'You know about medicine, do you?'

'A little.'

Casa's wife hesitated. 'I warn you, if it doesn't work, I shall tell everybody that you're nothing but a pretentious idiot!'

'And you'd be right.'

Ubekhet's calm disarmed the little brunette, who allowed her in.

Casa lay on a stone bench, a pillow under the nape of his neck. He was of medium height, with very black hair, a square face, chestnut-coloured eyes and enormous calves.

'What's wrong?' asked Ubekhet.

'It's my belly. It's burning.'

Ubekhet examined the patient as Neferet had taught her, taking note of his complexion, the smell of his body and his breathing, but above all feeling his abdomen and taking his pulse to hear the voice of his heart.

'Is it serious?' asked Casa anxiously.

'I don't think so; you aren't threatened by any demons. You've got stomach ache because you've eaten too much. For a few days, you are to eat honey, stale, toasted bread, celery and figs, and drink small but regular quantities of very mild beer. The pain will gradually fade.'

Casa felt better already. 'Prepare all that for me,' he told his wife, 'and don't forget to tell the Scribe of the Tomb that I won't be going to work today.'

The little brunette looked at Ubekhet suspiciously.

'Would you like me to arrange the flowers on your altar?' asked Ubekhet.

'I'll do it myself. Go away. I've got a lot to do.'

'May Hathor protect you and cure your husband.'

Ubekhet meant to carry on distributing her flowers, but she stopped in her tracks. A pace away from her, in the middle of the main street, stood the wise woman, with her impressive fleece of white hair and penetrating eyes.

'Who taught you medicine?' asked the wise woman.

'Pharaoh's doctor, Neferet.'

A faint smile lit up the wise woman's stern face. 'Neferet . . . So you knew her.'

'She brought me up.'

'Why didn't you become a doctor?'

'Because Neferet predicted that another destiny awaited me, and I listened to her.'

'Do you know how to treat the most serious illnesses?'

'A few.'

'Come with me.'

The wise woman's house, which was surrounded by hollyhocks, stood next to Ramose's. The local women were astounded to see Ubekhet follow the owner inside, for the wise woman had not opened her door to anyone in more than twenty years.

Ubekhet found herself in a large room filled with the good smell of honeysuckle. On the shelves stood pots and vases containing medicinal substances. Along the walls were chests filled with papyrus scrolls.

'I worked for a long time with Doctor Pahery, the author of

a treatise on problems of the rectum and anus,' said the wise woman. 'He made the villagers practise strict cleanliness, which is essential in preventing the majority of illnesses. We have available all the necessary water, which is our most important remedy. Be unbending on that point and combat uncleanliness rigorously; the most active remedies will be useless wihout cleanliness. Are you afraid of scorpions?'

'I'm wary of them, but Neferet taught me that their venom contains substances useful in treating many problems.'

'It's the same with snakes, and I shall take you into the desert to capture the most fearsome species and manufacture our own medicines. A good doctor is "one who masters scorpions", for that creature can drive away evil spirits and attract positive energies which the practitioner fixes into amulets. Treating the subtle body is as important as curing the apparent body. Do you know the first words of healing?'

'"I am the pure priestess of Sekhmet the lioness, an expert in her duties, she who places her hand on the sick person, a hand which is wise in the art of knowing sickness."'

'Show me how you would do that.'

Ubekhet placed her hand on the wise woman's head, on the back of her skull, her hands, her arms, her heart and her legs. By doing so, she heard the words of the heart in each energy channel.

'You suffer only from harmless ailments,' she concluded.

It was then the wise woman's turn to lay her hands on Ubekhet, who immediately felt an intense heat.

'I have more energy than you and I am going to wipe away all traces of tiredness from your body. Whenever you feel weak, come to see me and I shall give you back your strength.'

The session lasted more than half an hour. Ubekhet felt as though regenerated blood was flowing in her veins.

'Neferet must have taught you how to use medicinal plants and poisons.'

'I spent many days in her workshop, and her teachings are engraved in my memory.'

'You shall have access to my chests, which contain herbs; for the rest, here are the filtering-pots I use.'

The wise woman showed Ubekhet vessels separated into two by a filter; the upper part held solid drugs, and liquids were in the lower part.

'By heating them,' she explained, 'you produce steam which dissolves the solids, which then become mixed into the liquids. In some cases, you must not heat but must crush the solids in the water, with a mortar, and pour the resulting solution into a jar. Do you want me to teach you what I know?'

Ubekhet's face lit up. 'How can I thank you?'

'By working hard and placing yourself at the service of the brotherhood. You should know that the overseers, quite rightly, don't let a sick workman work, and he is free to seek treatment either in the village or outside. If he chooses to go outside, he will ask the doctor for a note detailing his fees, and the Scribe of the Tomb will reimburse his expenses. Never force yourself on anyone, and allow each person to be responsible for his own choice.'

'Do you mean that I'm to be your assistant?'

'Only the elders of the brotherhood know my age, but today, Ubekhet, I entrust this little secret to you: next week, I shall be one hundred years old. According to the sages, I have a few more years in which to meditate and devote myself to Ma'at. With you as my assistant, I may perhaps do so.'

'A hundred? That's incredible!'

'This village contains priceless treasures. One of them is the knowledge that the spirit is not irrevocably condemned to decline. One can combat its ageing by practising a means of regeneration. Prove yourself, and perhaps we shall speak of it again.'

# 48

Paneb continued his apprenticeship under the implacable direction of Kenhir, who was extremely sparing with his compliments. The Scribe of the Tomb felt that a future artist of the Place of Truth should be a complete master of hieroglyphics and never hesitate over which sign to trace. As soon as his pupil seemed too pleased with himself, his teacher set him a more difficult exercise.

Kenhir was still surprised by the striking contrast between the young man's physical strength and his delicately executed drawings. With an infinite patience, which contrasted markedly with his quick-tempered, violent nature, he displayed the talent of a miniaturist. As the boy never got tired, and would never give up until he had satisfied his instructor completely, Kenhir had asked the wise woman for a fortifying drink so that his strength would not fail in front of his pupil.

That morning, Kenhir had set no new tests for Paneb, who contented himself with swiftly tracing more than six hundred hieroglyphs, from the simplest to the most complex.

'Are you happy in the village?' asked Kenhir.

'I'm here to learn and I'm learning.'

'You don't seem to have much to do with the other members of your crew.'

'I spend my days at school, my evenings preparing exercises for the next day, and my free time rebuilding my house. For amusement, I draw portraits on pieces of limestone I collect in the desert. So I haven't time for idle chatter.'

'Portraits? Portraits of whom?'

'Of you, and of the other pupils. I think they're quite amusing, but I destroy them as soon as they're finished.'

'So much the better. The first phase of your education is finished, Paneb. The overseer is demanding your return, and I cannot lie to him by pretending that you aren't ready. It is time to make your choice.'

'What choice?'

'Whether to become a scribe in Thebes or an artist in the Place of Truth. If you choose the first, I'll recommend you to colleagues and you'll be employed in the government. I know you'll find it difficult to bend to the rules, but this slight inconvenience is as nothing compared to the brilliant career which would await you. You'd have an official house and every year you'd grow richer. Servants would make your life easy, and people would bow before you. With your capacity for work and your extraordinary memory, you would soon occupy a post of high responsibility. On the other hand, your future as an artist would probably be grim, because your brethren don't want to help you – quite the reverse. They have known each other for a long time and take a dim view of the arrival of a new member who keeps them working late.'

'We belong to the same community, don't we?'

'Indeed, but these are seasoned professionals and rough men whom it will be very difficult to soften. In my opinion, whatever your efforts and your gifts, they will reject you and you will remain a simple workman, disappointed that you missed out on a fine career as a scribe.'

'Would my brethren be so cruel?'

'To them, you are a threat,' said Kenhir. 'They'll defend themselves.'

'That isn't a very brotherly attitude.'

'The Servants of the Place of Truth are only men.'

'To hear you talk, you'd think my future was all mapped out for me.'

'If you follow the way of reason, you won't regret it.'

'One detail intrigues me, teacher. Why did a learned man of your talent accept the post of Scribe of the Tomb instead of becoming a high official in Thebes? The Place of Truth must have some charms if it attracted you.'

Kenhir was silent.

'Don't worry about me,' Paneb went on. 'I shall confront the artists and prove to them that I have my place among them.'

As agreed with Neb the Accomplished, Kenhir had tried to discourage the young man. He was happy to have failed.

As he walked along the village main street, Paneb felt as though he were awaking from a long sleep. Since his admission to the brotherhood, he had had only two objectives: to learn to draw hieroglyphs and to make his house habitable. The first had been achieved beyond all his hopes, to the point of often overshadowing the second.

Knowing how to read and write gave the young man a formidable impression of power. Each time he drew a panther, a falcon or a bull, he had the feeling that he was acquiring a little of the animal's qualities. Writing made abstract things live; reading gave access to the teachings of the sages.

Two years had flowed by like a dream. Paneb had made friends with no one but Nefer and Ubekhet, with whom he talked of nothing but hieroglyphs, and he had spent most of his time with Kenhir, either at school with the other pupils, or in private lessons. Now his teacher's strategy was obvious: the Scribe of the Tomb had tried to train another scribe and send him out into the world.

Paneb knew what lesson to draw from this quiet combat, which had been fought not with fists but with the mind. Kenhir had tried to cast a spell on him, to play on his vocation by diverting it and tempting him with the many dazzling advantages a scribe enjoyed.

Kenhir had failed. Without deviating from his path, Paneb had grasped his knowledge and he was now master of the signs of power which were essential for an artist in the Place of Truth. Their magic was so intense that it had absorbed his energy and attention to the point where he had forgotten the gods' most beautiful creation: women.

Since starting work, Paneb had not looked at them once! Ubekhet did not count, for she was different from the others, and anyway she was Nefer's wife. He viewed her as an elder sister who calmed him down and only ever gave him good advice.

How had he managed to do without women for so long? Sly old Kenhir's magic really must be effective! In future, he'd be cautious of that crafty character, one of the three leaders of the brotherhood. In drawing Paneb into his nets, Kenhir had deprived him of love.

It was a rest day for the starboard crew. Some of them were sleeping, others were improving their houses or making furniture to sell to buyers on the outside. Up to now, they had all ignored Paneb, who had ignored them in return. Soon he would confront them, but this morning he would allow himself an incomparable pleasure: looking at the village women and seducing them.

Instead of hurrying home to work on his house, he walked slowly along the main street and feasted his eyes on every member of the fair sex.

Before entering the village, Paneb had believed that the Place of Truth was an austere place, where the craftsmen's wives remained shut away in their houses or in shrines. But, as in other Egyptian villages, most of the women worked or walked about bare-breasted, and Paneb's gaze lingered enthusiastically on their young breasts. Unfortunately, the women did not enjoy this little game at all; some gave him black looks, others stormed back into their houses.

The hunt was not going to be easy, but the young man was sure he would succeed. After this abominable period of abstinence, he would not be choosy, it could be an experienced old woman or a naive young girl.

He thought he had found his prey when a slender fair-haired girl, good enough to eat, made eyes at him. But he walked towards her too quickly; frightened, she slammed her door in his face.

'Anyone would think you frighten girls,' murmured a sultry voice.

Paneb turned and saw a superb redhead, aged about twenty, wearing a green dress with shoulder-straps which left her breasts bare. She had a sumptuous bosom, and her curves inflamed him with desire.

'My name is Paneb.'

'I'm Turquoise, and I'm unmarried.'

He did not care whether she was married. The main thing was that she was a woman.

'Would you like to talk for a while?' she asked.

'Not at all. What I'd like would be to make love with you, right now.'

Turquoise smiled. 'You're a big lad, aren't you?'

'And you're a fine figure of a woman. We should suit each other wonderfully and enjoy ourselves a lot.'

'Is that how you think people talk to women?'

'That's enough talk of any kind.'

He climbed the few steps to the door of Turquoise's little house, took her in his arms and treated her to a fiery kiss. She did not resist, so he led her inside, into the soft twilight, and took off her fragile robe.

The young woman's heady perfume, her white skin and her way of rubbing herself against him were driving him mad with desire. She responded to each caress, and they set off on a wonderful journey together, to discover each other's bodies.

# 49

Sated with pleasure, the lovers rested at last.

'You certainly deserve your name, Paneb the Ardent,' purred Turquoise.

'I've never known such an exciting woman.'

'So you've made a lot of conquests, have you?'

'In the country, girls don't make a fuss about it.'

'Feelings don't seem to interest you.'

'Feelings are all right for old people,' said Paneb. 'A woman needs a man, a man needs a woman – why complicate everything?'

'Is that what your friend Nefer thinks?'

'Do you know him?'

'I've seen him with Ubekhet.'

'It's different for them. Their love is a miracle which will unite them until death, but I don't envy them. He won't know any other woman, you realise! In fact, if you think about it, it's a kind of curse.' Paneb propped himself up on his elbows. 'You really are magnificent. Why aren't you married?'

'Because, like you, I prefer my freedom.'

'That must make tongues wag in the village.'

'Yes and no. I'm the daughter of a stone-cutter in the port crew. My mother died when I was a baby, so I was brought up by all sorts of people until my father died, three years ago. I decided to stay here, in my village, and to become a priestess of Hathor – and she is the goddess of love, of all loves.'

'Have you had a lot of lovers?'

'That's none of your business.'

'You're right, it isn't. At the moment, your only lover is me.'

'You're wrong, Paneb. I'm a free woman and I won't submit to any man. I may never sleep with you again.'

'You're mad!'

He tried to lie on top of her, but Turquoise dodged out of the way.

'Get out of my house,' she ordered.

'I could take you by force.'

'If you did, you'd would be expelled from the village this very evening and sentenced to a long time in prison. Go, Paneb. Go now.'

The young giant went off sheepishly. How complicated women were, especially when they refused to submit. He'd lost Turquoise, but he'd find others. His sexual fire had been quenched for a while, and he'd busy himself with finishing his house.

It rested on a base of stones up to a height of about six cubits, above which were built walls of unbaked brick. In most houses, the brick was covered with rendering and numerous coats of whitewash, but Paneb's house lacked these finishing touches. It was nowhere near as solid as the older houses in the village, which were built directly on to the rock.

Nefer respected his friend's determination to do all the work himself, but had given him some advice on how to avoid serious mistakes. So Paneb made a great effort to make the external walls very thick and had separated the rooms by thinner interior walls, which were made from brick held together with a simple earthen mortar, and which supported the roof and the terrace. The roof structure was made from palm-trunks roughly squared off and pushed together, one against the other; placing them correctly had not been easy, but thanks to his strength and Nefer's precise directions Paneb had succeeded.

The arrangement of the windows had required all his attention, for it had to permit good ventilation while ensuring warmth in winter and coolness in summer. After an initial failure, which meant he had to rebuild part of the superstructure and make the exterior walls even thicker, Paneb had obtained a satisfactory result.

Like most of the villagers, he had three main rooms at his disposal, built on three levels, plus a kitchen, two cellars, conveniences and a terrace. But the whole was empty and bare, and there were no wall decorations to enliven it. Furniture was confined to a simple mat, and there were no paintings and other ornaments which would have given a soul to this lodging.

Paneb had a thousand ideas but he did not know how to realise them, and only perfection would do. For the time being, he made do with the flowers delivered daily to the priestesses of Hathor, which Ubekhet distributed to the villagers for use on altars, in homage to the goddess.

The moment had come to learn new skills which would allow Paneb to decorate his house and make it the most beautiful in the Place of Truth.

A man came up to him. Although a little shorter than Paneb, he was almost as well-built and his feet struck the ground heavily as he walked, as though he had difficulty in moving his mass of muscle around.

'Do you want to see me?' asked Paneb.

'Yes, if you're Paneb the Ardent.'

'What is your name?'

'Nakht the Powerful, stone-cutter.'

'That's a fine nickname. How did you earn it?'

'Even if you started lifting blocks of stone today, and didn't stop for a second until you were a hundred, you'd never handle as many as me.'

'I have no intention of becoming a stone-cutter. I want to draw and paint.'

'The brotherhood already has an exceptional painter and three brothers experienced in drawing. It is they who decorate Ramses' house of eternity, and those of the royal family and the nobility. What use is a tearaway like you to them?'

'I have been initiated, like them, and I belong to the same brotherhood.'

'You're confusing theory and practice, my boy,' said Nakht. 'Oh yes, you were lucky enough to be admitted, but how long will you stay?'

'As long as I like.'

'Do you think that's in your hands?'

'Along our road, there are gates. Some look at them, others knock in the hope that someone will open. I batter them down.'

'In the meantime, you are going to obey me.'

'What are your orders, Nakht?'

'A wall of my house needs restoring, and I've no wish to wear myself out. Since you've had some experience, you are to do it.'

'It is your house, not mine. Sort the problem out yourself.'

'You were hired to serve, boy.'

'To serve the work, yes, but not exploiters like you.'

'You insolent young puppy! You need a good lesson to set you straight.'

The two men were much of a size, but Nakht did not frighten Paneb, who was sure that he would be as swift in dodging as he was in attacking.

'Take care, Nakht. You might take a beating.'

'Come on, pup, come on.'

'Have you really thought about this? In your place, I'd go home and get my wife to fuss over me. If she finds you covered in wounds, she'll abandon you.'

This was too much for Nakht the Powerful, and he tried to

punch Paneb in the stomach. But Paneb leapt aside and struck his adversary on the left side, breaking one of his ribs and making him roar with pain.

Nefer came running up. He had come to bring his friend a fig-cake made by Ubekhet, and he was horrified at what he saw.

'Stop it!' he ordered.

Paneb obeyed and lowered his guard. Nakht did not. He rushed at his adversary, head-first.

# 50

Led by Karo the Impatient, who beat out the marching rhythm with a long, gnarled stick, the starboard crew headed for the area set aside for them at the foot of the northern hill, bordering the cemetery.

Nefer saw a small temple, which was entered via a porch. Carrying out the duties of gatekeeper, Neb asked each craftsman to identify himself.

Once this rite was over, each member of the crew walked through into a little open-air courtyard and knelt before a rectangular purification pool. A painter, Ched the Saviour, dipped a cup into it and poured water on to the outstretched hands of his brethren, their palms raised to heaven.

Ched was purified in turn, then the craftsmen entered the meeting-hall, whose ceiling, which was supported by two columns, was painted in yellow ochre. Stalls equipped with stone benches were set into the walls. Three high windows allowed in a gentle light during the daytime; as night was now falling, torches had been lit.

Low walls separated the meeting-hall from a raised shrine which only the overseer could enter. It was made up of an innermost shrine, holding a statuette of Ma'at, and two small side-rooms where vases of ointments, portable altars and other ritual objects were kept.

Neb took up position to the east, on a wooden chair which

had been occupied before him by previous overseers of the crew.

'Let us pay homage to the ancestors,' he ordered, 'and pray that they will enlighten us. May the stone stall nearest to me always remain free of all human presence so that it may be reserved for the *ka* of my predecessor, who dwells among the stars and is always present among us. May his example preserve our unity.'

The artisans fell silent. All felt that Neb the Accomplished's words were not empty and that the bonds uniting them were stronger than death.

'Two of us are in conflict,' declared the overseer. 'I must consult you to know if it is possible to settle this affair here and now, or if we must take it before the court of the Place of Truth.'

His head wrapped in a myrrh-soaked cloth which lessened the pain, Nakht asked permission to speak. He said, 'I was attacked by the apprentice Paneb the Ardent. He almost broke my skull and I must take several rest days, which will delay the crew's work. He must be severely punished by the court.'

'There is no other solution,' agreed Karo.

Paneb was about to protest vigorously, but Nefer put a hand on his shoulder to prevent him standing up.

'I saw the fight,' said Nefer calmly. 'It was obvious that they were going to come to blows and I intervened to stop them. Whereas Paneb listened to me, Nakht charged head-first. He tried to take Paneb by surprise, and in knocking him out Paneb was only defending himself.'

'Are you saying this because Paneb is your friend?' asked Neb.

'If he had done wrong, I wouldn't attempt to justify his behaviour. For me, there remains only one point which needs to be clarified: the cause of the fight.'

'That's not so,' objected Nakht. 'My wounds prove I wasn't the aggressor.'

'A specious argument,' opined Nefer. 'If you had listened to me, you wouldn't have been hurt. But what were you saying to Paneb?'

'I simply wished to talk to him, but he insulted me. It is an attitude unworthy of an apprentice.'

'Does a stone-cutter have the right to order an apprentice to leave the path of righteousness and betray his oath?'

Nakht turned pale. 'That question is meaningless! You were too far away, you couldn't have heard anything – and anyway I didn't order him to do anything.'

'It is true that I did not hear anything, but this is the only way your behaviour can be explained. We live in the Place of Truth, and Ma'at is our ruler. How can you go on lying?'

Nefer's voice held no anger. It was like that of a father trying to make his son see that he was making a grave mistake but that nothing was yet irremediable.

Nefer's arguments spun round and round inside Nakht's head, to a devilish rhythm. His colleagues' looks seemed heavier to him than the baskets of stones he had so often lifted, and the words of his first oath, so far off now, came back to him.

'I withdraw my complaint against Paneb,' he declared, hanging his head. 'A little squabble like this won't bring our brotherhood into question. Among ourselves, we can sometimes get a bit lively, but it's nothing serious. We had a scuffle because we wanted to measure our strength. It would be better to meet in a wrestling-contest.'

'Whenever you like,' said Paneb.

'The incident is closed,' judged Neb. 'Any other subjects to raise?'

'I am not satisfied with the quality of the last ointments I was given,' complained Karo the Impatient. 'I have delicate skin, and these are making it turn red. If we are treated like less than nothing, it will not be long before we hit back.'

'I'll tell the Scribe of the Tomb,' promised Neb, 'and the

quality of the ointments will be more strictly controlled.'

'We shall soon run out of fine brushes,' moaned Ched. 'I have been sending out warnings for several months, but they've gone unheeded.'

'I'll see to it. Is that all?'

No one asked to speak.

'We have a very heavy programme of work,' announced Neb. 'While the port crew is completing the immense house of eternity for Ramses' Royal Sons in the Valley of the Kings, we are to restore several tombs in the Valley of the Queens. If additional hours are necessary, you will receive best-quality sandals and fine pieces of fabric as compensation.'

'We also have a festival to prepare for,' complained Karo. 'When are we going to have the time to sleep? In the hot season, work will be more and more difficult. Above all, we must have plenty of fresh water.'

'Don't forget the beer,' added Nakht the Powerful. 'Without it, our strength will fail.'

'As an artist, and bearing in mind the scale of this project,' added Gau the Precise, 'I ask that the central workshop be particularly vigilant over the quality of colours it delivers to us. We must respect the original lines and shades.'

His two colleagues, Unesh the Jackal and Pai the Good Bread, concurred.

As no one else wished to speak, Neb got to his feet, extinguished the torches and addressed a last invocation to the ancestors.

Although the area was plunged into darkness, Paneb noticed a strange gleam coming from the innermost shrine. He could have sworn that a lamp was lit inside the little shrine and that its light was shining through the gilded wooden door. Thinking he was hallucinating, the young man stared at the weird light, but he had no time to dwell on it for he had to follow the craftsmen, who were leaving the meeting-hall.

'Did you see that strange brightness?' he asked Ched.

'Leave in silence.'

The night was mild; the village was asleep. As soon as they were out in the fresh air, Paneb repeated his question. 'Well, did you see that brightness?'

'There was nothing but the glow from the dying torches.'

'There was a light coming from the innermost shrine.'

'You're mistaken, Paneb.'

'I'm sure I'm not.'

'Go to sleep. That will stop you seeing things.'

Paneb questioned Pai the Good Bread, who also had seen nothing abnormal. Then he looked for Nefer but could not find him. His friend, who had succeeded in proving him innocent and sparing him punishment, must have gone home. No, that couldn't be. Nefer would want to talk to him.

The team had gone their separate ways, and Paneb stayed alone, facing the closed door of the meeting-hall.

What had become of Nefer?

# 51

Paneb waited until dawn, hoping to see his friend reappear. When the priestesses of Hathor arrived, heading for the temple to waken the divine power, he went home, disappointed.

Suddenly, the apparently peaceful village seemed disturbing and hostile. Just when he thought he had worked out its laws, he found himself abruptly plunged into the unknown. Had his one and only friend been the victim of a plot by powerful people determined to kill all those who were not of the same mould? Paneb had defied Nakht the Powerful. Nefer had defended Paneb. The two intractable friends must disappear.

But Paneb would not let them slit his throat like a butchered animal. Even alone, he was capable of putting this accursed village to fire and the sword! He was just getting ready to declare war when someone knocked at his door.

Instantly suspicious, he armed himself with a stick, ready to break the head of any craftsman who tried to grab him.

His right arm raised, he opened the door and found two women, Ubekhet and a small, shy girl with fair hair. Ubekhet was carrying a plaster bust, the other girl a bouquet of lotus stems, narcissi and cornflowers.

'Protection upon your face,' said Ubekhet, using the traditional form of words for wishing someone a good day. 'Uabet wanted to help me begin to bring your house to life.'

'Have you any news of Nefer?'

'You're not worried, are you?'

'He's disappeared!'

'Don't worry. He has gone to visit a dockyard to study the carpenters' methods.'

'Alone?'

'No, with the overseer and a few craftsmen.'

'Are you sure?'

Intrigued, Ubekhet stared at him. 'You look devastated.'

'I thought he'd been kidnapped, mistreated, I—'

'Everything's fine, don't worry. It's just a short working trip. Whatever did you imagine?'

Paneb laid down his stick. 'I was afraid for him. I feared that the entire brotherhood might be hostile to him.'

'Calm yourself,' urged Ubekhet. 'Here is the bust of an ancestor which you must venerate each day while thinking of the Servants of the Place of Truth who came before you.'

'Am I to put it in the living-room, like in your house?'

'That is the custom.'

Timidly, Uabet the Pure gave the flowers to Paneb.

'Their scent is sweet to the ancestors' *ka*,' commented Ubekhet. 'If we were not linked to them, if they did not offer us their strength, we could not survive.'

'The ancestors don't interest me,' said Paneb. 'Only the future matters.'

'You can't build without a foundation. Our predecessors fashioned the spirit of this village and they nourished its soul with their creations. We must pass on, in our turn, the things they passed on to us. If you neglect the ancestors, you will become deaf and blind.'

Paneb was so busy mulling over Ubekhet's words that he did not notice Uabet the Pure gazing lovingly at him.

With the bust of the ancestor carelessly placed in a corner of the first room in his house, Paneb ate quickly, then headed for the house of Ched the painter, whom he considered the best of the three artists. He would ask him for a detailed programme of work and would not be put off by vague promises.

Equipped with an impressive range of materials, Ched was preparing to set off for the Valley of the Queens. Endowed with a natural elegance, well-groomed hair and a small moustache, light grey eyes and a straight nose, and thin lips, he seemed to look disdainfully at what surrounded him.

'Wait for me!' cried Paneb.

'Wait for you? Why?'

'I'm coming with you to the Valley of the Queens, aren't I?'

Ched's smile was sharper than a blade. 'You're losing your mind, my boy. I'm going to do restoration work of the greatest intricacy, and I have no need of a useless idiot.'

'I can read and write, and I can draw the hieroglyphs perfectly!'

'So can everyone in the village. But what do you know of the art of the Line, the rules of proportion and the secret nature of colours? You want to become a draughtsman, it seems, and even a painter. Don't you know that it is not for you to dictate the demands of the brotherhood? You should learn to make plaster – that will probably be your highest occupation for the rest of your life.'

Ched's words were knives which sank into Paneb's flesh.

'Another vital thing you have not understood,' continued the painter, 'is that the house which was allocated to you is not the house of a peasant or a petty scribe, but a shrine. You have thought only of your material comfort. You know nothing of the symbolic significance of each room. And where are the paintings and the objects that give it meaning? You are still only a man of the outside, my poor Paneb, and I am not sure that you have the necessary intelligence and talents to be a true Servant of the Place of Truth. At least follow the example of your friend Nefer, who has already made a lot of progress. And don't forget that the village gate opens very easily on to the outside world, where you will soon find work fit for you.'

Stunned and unable to think of a single retort, Paneb watched the painter walk away. He was so angry that he almost rushed at Ched to snatch away his materials and trample them underfoot. But the painter's reproaches continued to sting like whiplashes, with all the more force because they were justified.

Ched was right: he was nothing but a peasant, crossed with a petty scribe. But why hadn't Nefer, his only friend, helped him realise that? And what 'progress' had Ched meant? To be clear in his own mind about it, Paneb decided to ask Ubekhet.

In the main street, he met two of the three draughtsmen, Unesh the Jackal and Gau the Precise, who were leaving for the Valley of the Queens. He barely greeted them, feeling the weight of their ironic looks.

The door to Ubekhet and Nefer's house was shut.

He knocked. 'Ubekhet! May I come in?'

'Just a moment,' she replied.

That was odd. She was usually so welcoming. Was she going to reject Paneb by treating him with scorn, as the painter had? He had no time to let these gloomy thoughts proliferate, for the door soon opened.

'Is Nefer back?' he asked.

'Not yet.'

'I want to see him.'

'He's working on a site.'

'Why is it that he's chosen the right path and I haven't? You must know.'

'Come in. I have some work to finish.'

Paneb was amazed to see the third illustrator, Pai the Good Bread, a round man with a cheerful face and plump cheeks. His right wrist was bandaged.

'A slight sprain,' he explained. 'Thanks to Ubekhet's care,

I shall be able to get back to work in a few days.'

The young woman checked that the bandage was not too tight. 'For now, Pai, complete rest. Don't worry, there won't be any after-effects.'

Paneb looked round the living-room with fresh eyes: a bizarre construction in one corner, an ancestor's bust on an altar, another altar covered in flowers . . . Nefer really had turned his home into a shrine.

'Ched the painter has just treated me like an idiot, my only friend disappears, and I don't understand anything any more. What's going on, Ubekhet?'

'You must simply pass through another stage, and it is for you to decide on the route.'

'The only advice Ched gave me was to become a plasterer.'

'It's good advice, too,' commented Pai.

Paneb seethed. 'You're laughing at me, too!'

'Do you still want to become an illustrator?'

'More than ever.'

'Then understand that the first site where you must prove yourself is your own house. You have shown us that you can do building work and basic repairs, but that isn't enough. You must learn everything about the trade, so that you will make no mistakes when you are working on the wall of a house of eternity.'

'You were never a plasterer!'

'Of course I was. How can you create a successful drawing without a good base? Making it is the first secret.'

'Will you teach me?' asked Paneb anxiously.

Pai contemplated his wrist. 'I don't much like enforced rest. We could try.'

# 52

Pregnant for the second time, Serketa waited anxiously for the results of the tests. When she had given birth to a daughter, her husband flew into a violent rage and refused to see the child, who would be brought up by wet-nurses and never appear before her father. Officially, the first-born must be a boy. Mehy sometimes wished he was a Greek or a Hittite; in their countries, the law permitted the killing of unwanted baby girls.

Since she benefited from a perfect circulation of blood and air around her body, Serketa was assured of a tranquil pregnancy and straightforward birth; but the only thing that mattered was the child's sex. For two weeks, she had been urinating every day on two bags, one containing wheat, dates and sand, and the other sand, dates and barley. If the wheat germinated first, Serketa would have a daughter; if the barley did, the baby would be a boy.

'We have a conclusive result,' announced her doctor.

'You look wonderful, my dear Mehy!' exclaimed the mayor of Thebes. 'The soldiers are devoted to you, and the manoeuvres you organised were greatly appreciated by the population. They feel protected from all danger.'

'The credit should go to the officers and troops, whose discipline is exemplary.'

'Ah, but you gave the orders.'

'Inspired by your recommendations,' recalled Mehy.

The mayor bowed his appreciation of this accuracy, then asked, 'Have you recovered from your father-in-law's death?'

'Will I ever recover from it? He had such personality and such skills that his absence leaves an immense void. I and my wife remember him every evening. We shall never quite get over his death.'

'Of course, of course. But you must think of the future, and there's no better remedy for pain than hard work. You are competent, conscientious and methodical; this combination of qualities will make you an excellent treasurer of our good city of Thebes.'

Mehy feigned surprise. 'That is a vitally important post. I don't know if—'

'That's for me to decide, and I know I'm not making a mistake. In becoming my right arm, you will be responsible for the prosperity of our dear city. For my part, I shall take a slightly less active role.'

Mehy knew it took all the mayor's time to break up the factions trying to weaken him, and to struggle against the many candidates ready to take his place.

'You are offering me an exciting challenge, but there's a a major reason why I can't accept.'

'What is it?'

'I couldn't succeed my dear father-in-law. The shock would be too cruel for my wife.'

'Don't worry, I'll make her see reason. Mehy, Thebes needs you. In certain circumstances, we must sacrifice our own feelings to the general interest.'

Mehy felt like dancing for joy. After gaining control of the armed forces, he was taking the public purse in hand. From now on, he would be the right hand of the mayor, who, as a good strategist, had clearly marked out their respective territories. It was up to Mehy to run a government which was financially sound and above reproach, while the mayor acted as the figurehead. The mayor had probably not believed that Mehy cherished an eternal affection for his father-in-law, but he could not suspect the truth. The fact that a murderer should go unpunished and even take his victim's place proved to the new treasurer that the law of Ma'at was nothing but a fable invented by false sages cloistered in temples, far from reality. The old world of the pharaohs would soon disappear, to be replaced by an all-conquering state with an unswerving faith in progress, and capable of imposing its will on decadent civilisations.

In order to become its leader, Mehy would use the talents of his friend Daktair, who was unhindered by moral scruples. Thanks to an entirely new class of men with no attachment to tradition, Egypt would be rapidly transformed into a modern country ruled over by the only law Mehy respected: that of the strongest. A skilful legal whitewash and a few well-chosen public declarations would soothe the delicate consciences of certain senior dignitaries, who would be swiftly won over by personal gain derived from the new order. As for the common people, they were made to be submissive, and no one would rebel for long when faced with a well-organised security force and army.

There was only one sizeable obstacle left: Ramses the Great. But he was very old, and his health was increasingly fragile. Despite his robust constitution, death would eventually get the better of him. The idea of murder hastening Ramses' death was not to be excluded, but it entailed countless precautions if Mehy was to escape investigation. It was better to corrupt the entourage of the new pharaoh, Meneptah, in the hope of cutting short his reign and replacing him with a puppet ruler whom Mehy could control.

Time was on his side. Above all, he must not give in to

impatience, or he might make a fatal mistake. And the major objective remained the conquest of the Place of Truth. Thanks to the secrets it held, Mehy would become sole Lord of the Two Lands. But attacking it meant a head-on clash with Ramses: until the balance of power tipped in his favour, Mehy would confine himself to indirect attacks, and sapping the building's foundations.

Bare-breasted, perfumed with frankincense, her hair loose and with bracelets of cornelian and turquoise at her wrists and ankles, Serketa threw her arms about her husband's neck.

'You're home very late! I couldn't bear waiting for you any longer.'

'The mayor kept me late.'

'He's a deceitful, heartless man. Don't trust him.'

'He has just appointed me treasurer of Thebes.'

Serketa took a step back to look at him. 'My father's post. That's splendid! How right I was to marry you, Mehy. You really are a remarkable man.'

'Of course, I was only moderately enthusiastic and went on about how wonderful your venerated father was, while saying that you would no doubt be dreadfully sad to see me take his place. The mayor will come to speak to you, to make you admit that one cannot live in the past and that I must accept this appointment.'

'Count on me, darling! I shall play the grief-stricken daughter and finally accept the hard reality of life, while every day laying flowers at the tomb of my untimely deceased father. But tell me, will we become even richer?'

'You can be sure of that. But I must take no chances, so that nobody can accuse me of diverting funds for my own use.'

'Father considered you an extraordinary manipulator of figures, didn't he?'

'The Theban government is unwieldy and complicated. It

will take me several years to become master of it, but I shall succeed.'

'And then?'

'What do you mean, Serketa?'

'Have you no higher ambitions?'

'It seems to me that such career prospects are by no means mundane.'

Serketa put her arms round him. 'I expect even better of you, my darling.'

Mehy made love to his wife with his usual brutality, but he did not reveal his real plans to her. Neither she nor any other woman was intelligent enough to understand their scope, but she would be a faithful and useful ally.

Her head resting on Mehy's chest, Serketa spoke in a voice filled with emotion. 'I went to the doctor and did the pregnancy tests.'

'Well?'

'The wheat germinated first.'

'Which means that . . .'

'Unfortunately, yes. It will be another girl.'

Mehy slapped his wife several times. 'You've betrayed me, Serketa! I must have a son, not daughters. This one shall share the fate of the first. Send her where you like, I shall never see her.'

'Forgive me, Mehy, forgive me!'

'I don't give a damn for your excuses. What I want is a son. And I demand that first thing tomorrow, you sign a deed in my favour, giving up all your possessions, which will be managed solely by me. Who would be stupid enough to trust a woman who bears only girls? I shall give you one more chance, but don't disappoint me again. If you fail once more, I shall cast you off.'

Her face burning red, forced down into a pile of cushions, Serketa wife tried to fight back. 'The law forbids it. And what if I refuse to give up my fortune?'

Smiling, Mehy seized her by the chin. 'I thought I had proved to you that no one resists me, my darling. Either you obey me without question, or you will become my enemy.'

'You wouldn't dare—'

'Bear this damned daughter, get rid of her, become an attractive wife again quickly and give me a boy. If you manage that, you will have everything you could ever wish for. While we're waiting, obey my orders.'

# 53

The heat was unbearable. In the hills surrounding the Place of Truth, life seemed to have stopped in its tracks. Even the scorpions were motionless, and not a breath of wind blew across the stony, sun-scorched valleys.

Paneb the Ardent was the only man alive capable of moving around in this furnace and working in perfect tranquillity. Bare-headed, he drank little, and was satisfied with the tepid water from a small goatskin. He had only one idea in his head: to collect as much gypsum as he could in the distant valley whose location Pai the Good Bread had told him. Because the directions were vague, Paneb had lost his way twice, but he had got back on to the right path.

Ordinarily, it took at least three strong men to do this work, but no one else was available. Paneb had not waited either for the heat to die down, or for the overseer to give him orders.

Once the baskets were full, he hoisted them on to his shoulders and returned to the village. He emptied them in front of the workshop where plaster was made, then set off again for the valley. And he toiled away like this until the sun went down.

Nefer greeted him at the entrance to the village.

'You, at last!' exclaimed Paneb. 'Where on earth did you go?'

'The overseer took me to work in some quarries, then to a dockyard to learn new ship-building methods. That's quite a load you have there.'

'It seems that my path takes me by way of plastering. And for plaster you need gypsum, so off I go to find some. As nobody told me exactly how much, I shall empty the valley if necessary.'

'Would you like a hand?'

'I've got used to managing on my own.'

The two friends walked to the workshop together. Paneb emptied out the contents of his baskets and contemplated the pile of gypsum.

'Tomorrow, I shall do even better. This morning, I wasted time trying to find the right place. Now I'm thirsty.'

'I'm sure Ubekhet will have kept a little cool beer for you.'

Paneb emptied a large jar and devoured a succulent meal whose highlight was stuffed pigeon.

'You took a lot of risks,' commented Ubekhet. 'The place you went to is infested with snakes and scorpions.'

'They were too hot. Those bugs only come out at night.'

'I can give you an antidote.'

'No need, I'm not afraid of them. When I have a job to do, nobody stops me doing it.' His eyes filled with fire, Paneb turned to Nefer. 'You saw that strange light that shone through the door of the shrine in our meeting-hall, didn't you?'

'Yes, I saw it.'

'Why won't the others talk about it?'

'I've no idea,' said Nefer.

'And you don't want to know.'

'The overseer has just entrusted me with such important work that it occupies my mind day and night.'

'Is it a secret?'

'Not for a craftsman of the Place of Truth,' replied Nefer, smiling. 'The pharaoh is asking us to rebuild and enlarge the shrine he built in our village, at the start of his reign. Neb has chosen me to implement the plan drawn up by himself and Ramose.'

'That's a great honour.'

'A heavy responsibility, too.'

'Be honest with me, Nefer. You've climbed several levels in the brotherhood, haven't you?'

'That is true.'

'And you can't tell me about it?'

'Like all of us, I'm sworn to secrecy.'

'And I'm lagging behind.'

'You are following another path, with other doors to get through, and you are doing so according to the rhythm that's right for you. There's no rivalry between us, and there never will be.'

The day promised to be as hot as the previous one. Paneb was getting ready to head back to the valley of the gypsum when the overseer barred his way.

'Where are you going?' asked Neb.

'To get gypsum.'

'Who told you to do that?'

'I must learn how to make plaster that gives a surface fit for drawing on. So I need gypsum.'

For the first time since his admission to the brotherhood, Paneb looked closely at his overseer. He was a serious, powerful man, slow of speech and stern of expression, the only man in the Place of Truth whom Paneb would not have liked to face in single combat.

'You don't understand yet, do you? Here, no one acts on a whim.'

'It's not a whim, it's necessary.'

Neb folded his arms. 'I'm the one who decides what's necessary, and I'll give you an example. Go and fetch gypsum, Paneb, and learn how to make plaster, then busy yourself making the fronts of all the houses in the village as good as new. When you've finished, we shall talk again about your career in drawing.'

Some past workmen were still renowned in the village for having been able to produce an incredible number of sacks of plaster per day: one hundred and forty for Sun's Ray of Morning, and two hundred and five for Man of the God Amon. But as soon as he had assimilated the methods taught by Pai the Good Bread, Paneb succeeded each day in producing two hundred and fifty at the open-air workshop where he toiled all day long.

The community's need for plaster varied according to the nature of the construction projects; but since he must make the fronts of the houses dazzling white again, Paneb must first produce an enormous quantity of raw material before attacking an arduous task which would take him several months and for which he had no enthusiasm. But disobeying an overseer would meant immediate exclusion from the village. So Paneb forgot his grievances and burnt the raw gypsum he had extracted from the ground. After calcination he mixed it with water to obtain the builders' plaster which was applied to a wall to even out its irregularities and obtain a flat surface.

'Your plaster's better than mine,' confessed Pai. 'You've mastered the firing incredibly well.'

'I've begun by putting several coats of whitewash on a wall and plastering the most badly damaged house-front. What do you think of it?'

'Good work, Paneb! Carry on like that. Did you know that one of our men was a plasterer all his life and provided the artists with perfectly smooth surfaces?'

'Good for him, but I want to do more than that. This plaster's only a stepping-stone.'

'You don't yet know all the secrets,' said Pai. 'It's also used to bind the pigments you may be allowed to use if the overseer judges you worthy. Don't forget that one can also use plaster as a lubricant when large blocks are being positioned.'

Paneb listened attentively.

'Above all, Paneb, be careful to check the quality of the plaster.'

'How do I do that?'

Pai showed him a limestone cone. 'This is a sample which will allow you to test your plaster and judge if its consistency is right for your purpose. If you let yourself hurry, you'll make bad mistakes and will have to begin all over again.'

Paneb did not take the warning lightly. He thought only of getting through the forced labour imposed on him and at last entering the world of the artists.

'When you were an apprentice,' he asked, 'were you ordered to replaster all the houses in the village?'

'Only my own, but I haven't got your capacity for work. We're given the tests that fit us.'

Suddenly, it struck Paneb that Pai might be less friendly than he seemed. Was his help spontaneous, or was he acting on Neb's orders?

'Ask the right questions,' Pai advised him. 'The wrong ones are sterile. And remember the maxim that has guided all our master craftsmen: "act for him who acts".'

# 54

The astonished villagers watched Paneb make such steady progress that even the most cynical could not help but admire him. He tackled each house-front with the determination of a warrior fighting for his life and did not stop for breath until he had obtained a smooth, beautiful, shining-white surface, made even more brilliant by the sun. Thanks to him, the houses were coming back to life.

Beautiful Turquoise stared at the young giant. An ironic glint in her eye, her hands on her hips, she leant casually against the frame of her front door.

'So you've reached my house, at last,' she said. 'I was afraid you would go on avoiding me.'

'I must attend to all the houses, but yours is in excellent condition.'

'That's just an illusion. Only a new coat of plaster will make it attractive again. You don't want me to complain to the overseer, do you?'

Paneb pounced on her, wrapped his left arm tightly round her waist, picked her up and carried her inside.

'Are you trying to blackmail me?' he asked.

'There's a crack in the bedroom, caused by too much tension when the plaster was drying. To make sure it doesn't get any bigger, you'll have to add straw to the rendering.'

'I only do house-fronts.'

'Ah, but you'll make an exception for me.'

She wrapped her long, slender legs round Ardent's waist and kissed him with such fervour that he could resist her no longer. Lifting his delicious burden, he climbed the three little steps which led to a brick bed built into the corner of the living-room. It was plastered and decorated with paintings of a naked woman beautifying herself and a girl flute-player half-hidden in morning glory, wearing nothing but a necklace. Enclosed and raised up, this couch was made comfortable with thick sheets and cushions on which the lovers lay down.

'You've got the wrong place, Paneb.'

'Isn't this a bed?'

'A ritual bed, placed under Hathor's protection and designed to bring the young Horus back to life each morning so he can fight the forces of evil and preserve our community from destruction.'

'Bring some new pleasures to life for me,' said Paneb.

Turquoise abandoned theology and allowed herself to be undressed by her lover, whose enthusiasm delighted her. Paneb was so busy caressing her perfect body, that he did not notice the face painted at the head of the bed: Bes, a bearded, laughing dwarf whose function was to cause a Servant of the Place of Truth to be born into his new universe.

Abry was getting fatter and fatter. His wife was becoming increasingly excitable and was making the atmosphere at home unbearable. She criticised him for his lack of enthusiasm at work, the way he dressed, his haircut, his taste for full-bodied wines – in other words, there was no longer any common ground between them, and at night she pretended to have painful migraines so that she could sleep in a different room. To forget his conjugal misfortunes, Abry stuffed himself with cakes.

He had often thought about divorce, but since the major

share of the family wealth was his wife's, he might find himself out on the street. As she was not being unfaithful to him and was managing the finances and the house very well, Abry had no cause for complaint against her.

It was impossible to spend long, lazy hours beside the lake, as he used to do, impossible to treat himself to long midday naps in the shade of the palm-trees and savour the hours as they passed by, because that harpy gave him not a moment's peace. She should have been satisfied. As Mehy had told him, Abry had been kept on in his post and had lost none of his privileges, but this was not enough for his wife, whose demands he no longer understood.

It would not have been so bad if that madwoman were the only problem. Mehy was a hundred times more formidable, despite his friendly manner and warm words. For several years now, Abry had watched Mehy's meteoric rise with astonishment tinged with fear. At first he had thought this ambitious officer would be rapidly broken by his superiors or by suspicious dignitaries, but Mehy had succeeded in avoiding all the traps and had proved himself more cunning than his opponents.

Today, the Theban troops were devoted to him, because of the numerous benefits they had been awarded, which he had consolidated since taking over management of the public purse. Mehy was the strong man of Thebes. He spun his web day after day, without causing any alarm, as though his conquest of power were inevitable. The mayor had abandoned the running of the great city to him, and Mehy was acquitting himself with a competence which had found great favour with the tjaty.

Because of his privileged relationship with the new treasurer, Abry should have been rejoicing, but it was precisely this relationship which worried him.

When he promised to collaborate, he had hoped that Mehy would be killed, so that he himself would have benefited from the commander's support without having to do anything in return. But the situation had not developed as he had hoped, and Mehy would soon ask him to settle his debt. As his alarming ally's powers had burgeoned, Abry could no longer claim that, despite his constant efforts, he had produced no result.

So, after more than two years of sleight-of-hand, Abry had decided to satisfy his formidable protector by attacking the Place of Truth as Mehy had demanded.

Abry had risen early, in the hope of eating his breakfast in peace. But hardly had he tasted his morning fermented milk when the fury turned up to scold him for the inadequate yield from their wheatfields. So he had gluttonously devoured several round cakes before fleeing his house and heading for the craftsmen's village.

How could the workmen bear to live in such a setting? No luxuriant gardens, no restful palm-groves, only the desert and arid hills where the sun reigned as absolute master. And what of this mysterious work whose secret the initiates of the Place of Truth had kept since its foundation? Abry did not envy their austere existence, at once so close and so far from the banks of the Nile and the pleasures of the town.

When the governor's litter arrived at the first fort, the Nubian guard on duty followed Sobek's orders to the letter. He asked Abry to disclose his identity and commanded him to wait for his superior officer to be told of his presence before he could be authorised to continue on his way. Abry's protests changed nothing.

This attitude confirmed his fears. Sobek had indeed toughened up the security measures and abolished preferential treatment. Abry had studied his file, from his first days in the guards up to his appointment to the Place of Truth, and had come to a worrying conclusion. Sobek seemed to be an honest man, whose only concern was his work. No trace of corruption in a spotless career. So Abry had no suggestions to offer Mehy on how to get rid of the Nubian, whose efficiency was a difficult obstacle. Nevertheless, Abry had come here in the hope of uncovering a flaw.

Sobek came up to meet Abry. 'Is there a problem?' he asked.

'I am here in my official capacity. I simply wish to check that all is well with the lay workforce.'

'Then come with me.'

Abry was not authorised to enter the village and he could not go beyond the forts unless accompanied by the commander of the guards.

'Are you satisfied with your post,' asked Abry.

'It's hard work, but interesting. If it weren't for that inexplicable murder . . .'

'Still no leads?'

'None.'

'It's years ago now, and no one blames you. In the end it'll be forgotten.'

'Not by me. It was one of my men who was killed, and one day I shall find out what really happened.'

'What if the guilty party was . . . someone from the village?'

'I don't exclude that possibility, but I have not a shred of proof.'

Abry pretended to be interested in the lay workers' work and visited their modest houses outside the village, before being invited to drink cool beer with Sobek.

'You aren't married, are you, Sobek?'

'No, and I've neither the intention nor the opportunity. Ensuring the complete safety of the brotherhood takes all my time.'

'In the long run, you may get tired of this life,' predicted Abry. 'Here, you've shown how able you are. Wouldn't you like another post, something more satisfying and less restricting?'

'That's up to the tjaty, not me.'

'When I have a private audience with him, I could speak on your behalf. He ought to understand that you deserve better than this exhausting work.'

Sobek seemed interested. Had Abry just found a flaw?

'What kind of promotion could I hope for?' asked the Nubian.

'Command of river security in the Theban region, for example. You could become assistant to the current commander, who'll be retiring soon, and then you could succeed him.'

'What do you want in return?'

'Nothing for the moment, my dear Sobek. This small favour will make us inseparable friends, of course. And friends exchange information and do each other favours, don't they?'

The Nubian nodded.

At last Abry had some excellent news for Commander Mehy.

# 55

Paneb the Ardent was in the throes of an all-consuming passion for Turquoise, who was introducing him to all the games of love, from the wildest to the most subtle. At the end of his day's work, when the sun was sinking towards the Peak of the West, the young giant went to his mistress's house to sample the intoxicating delights of inexhaustible pleasure.

Time passed, and Paneb continued to make the village house-fronts dazzlingly white, but all he drew were indifferent sketches on pieces of limestone and he abandoned his own house to its own devices. Since he spent every night with Turquoise, he rarely saw Nefer, who worked in the planning office under Neb's direction.

Turquoise's beauty changed with the seasons, like the beauty of the sky or the Nile. Full-blossomed in the summer, tender and yielding in the autumn, wild in winter, piquant and sharp in the spring, it revealed endless pathways of desire to Paneb.

Soon, the whole village was decked in resplendent white. Paneb had finished the work assigned to him, and he could ask to be admitted to the company of artists at last. As he entered Turquoise's house that day, he was planning to celebrate this success by making love to her with all the vigour of a ram, but he found her dressed in a long red dress, with necklaces and bracelets of malachite. A ceremonial wig made her magnificent features look almost stern.

'I am taking part in a ritual with the other priestesses of Hathor and I must go to the temple,' she explained.

'Are you leaving me all on my own?'

'I think you'll survive the ordeal,' she said with a smile.

'But usually you are only busy at the temple early in the morning and late in the afternoon—'

'Rest now, and tomorrow evening, you'll be more ardent than ever.'

Turquoise walked to the door so gracefully that the young man felt like throwing himself upon her and covering her in kisses. But she walked like a priestess, steeped in dignity, and he decided against it.

'Turquoise,' he blurted out, 'will you marry me?'

'I've already told you: I shall never marry.'

She was gone, and Paneb was alone again, stupid and useless. With a heavy step, he set off for home.

A few paces from his own doorstep, he noticed delicious smells, as if the air was filled with enchanting perfumes. The door was open, and he heard a woman humming a sweet song.

Paneb entered and saw slender, frail Uabet the Pure sprinkling the ground with scented water after fumigating the rooms with a combustible powder made up of frankincense, calamus root, camphor, melon seeds and hazelnuts. The smoke rising from the brazier would kill any insects.

'What are you doing in my house?' he asked.

Startled, the young woman paused in her work. 'Oh, it's you! Don't come in right now, or you'll make everything dirty.'

Hastily she brought a copper basin filled with water so that Paneb could wash his feet and hands.

'You have nothing more to fear from the demons of the night,' she added. 'In each corner of each room, I have spread ground garlic, reduced to a powder with beer. And the oriole fat I used to swab the walls will drive away the flies. Would you mind waiting a moment? I haven't finished cleaning the bedroom.'

Uabet picked up a broom,whose long, rigid palm fibres were folded and gathered into hanks, and ran off to finish her task.

Arms hanging uselessly at his sides, Paneb did not recognise the inside of his house. In the first two rooms, which only yesterday had been furnished with a single mat, there were now stools, folding chairs, solid little tables, lamps on stands, earthenware vessels, several storage-chests with flat or curved lids, different kinds of baskets, and storage-bags. Uabet had fitted wooden hooks all over the place, on which she had hung baskets.

Paneb found the bedroom cleaned and perfumed, with two good-quality beds, both with sturdy crosspieces to support a slatted base of plaited rushes, on which mats and new sheets had been laid. Using a brush made from reeds held together by a ring, Uabet was polishing the floor.

'You can take a look at the kitchen – it's almost done. I took some jars of oil and beer down into the first cellar, and put the preserved meat in the second. You'll have to put up some shelves in the little bathroom for my cosmetics and buy one or two large cooking-pots. Then we shall have time to see . . . If you could make me a little wooden cupboard quite quickly, to hold my mirror, combs, wigs and hairpins, I'd be the happiest of women. Oh, and we mustn't forget the lavatories. I've cleansed them, but the little bricks that hold the wooden seat are a fraction too low. You should take the time to raise them and check the outlet on the waste-water pipe.'

Paneb sat down heavily on a sturdy, three-legged stool as if he had just completed a long and exhausting run.

'What are you doing here?' he asked again.

'You can see what I'm doing: I'm imposing a little order.'

'All this furniture . . .'

'It's my dowry. It belongs to me and I can use it as I see fit. And you really couldn't go on living with just one mat, which is in a dreadful state into the bargain. And I get the impression you don't feed yourself properly. I don't want to upset you, but you've lost a little weight. That's not a criticism, because you work harder than anyone else and you've restored every house in the village. No one will praise you, but the inhabitants are well satisfied and most of them think you're an exceptionally good plasterer. If you listen to them, you won't change your trade.'

Uabet was a curious mixture of timidity and confidence. Her voice was thin, her gestures awkward, but she was in no doubt that what she was doing was for the best.

Her words made Paneb realise that he had fallen into a new trap. In doing the plastering and defying the whole village – to whom he had, certainly, shown his strength and perseverance – he had once again neglected his ideal.

'Because of the housework,' lamented Uabet, 'I've prepared only a second-rate dinner: toasted bread, mashed beans and dried fish. Tomorrow, I'll cook something better.'

'I didn't ask you for anything!' exclaimed Paneb.

'I know that, but what does it matter?'

'Listen, Uabet, I'm in love with Turquoise and—'

'Everyone knows that. That's your business.'

'Then you'll understand that I'm not free.'

'What do you mean, "not free"? She has always told everyone she'll never marry and you're content to make love with her without living under her roof. So you are free.'

'I'll persuade her to marry me one day.'

'You won't, you know.'

'Oh yes I will!'

'What you don't know is that Turquoise made a vow to Hathor. By consecrating to Hathor the thoughts that have awakened her heart, she'll enjoy the beauty the goddess had granted her all her life, so long as she doesn't marry. A priestess of Hathor will never break her vow.'

Paneb was crushed. But Uabet did not gloat.

'You love Turquoise, she likes you, and she'll play with you for as long as she enjoys it. With me, it's different: I love you and I offer you everything I have. Since we are going to live under the same roof, we shall be husband and wife without any other form of ceremony. I have to confess that my family are formally opposed to this union and have even refused to organise a small celebration.'

'You mustn't ignore their opinion.'

'Of course I must. I shall marry the man of my choice, and that man is you.'

'First thing tomorrow, I shall be unfaithful to you.'

'Physical pleasure doesn't interest me very much. On the other hand, I would like to give you a son – but that's up to you.'

'You can't just impose yourself—'

'Think about it. I promise to be a good housekeeper, to make your daily life pleasant and not to deprive you of your freedom. You have everything to gain and nothing to lose. Shall we drink some strong beer to set the seal on our union?'

'Isn't that rather rushing things?' said Paneb.

'It's the best thing for both of us. Whatever your destiny may be, you must live in a clean, well-kept house. I'll be like a servant – you won't even notice me.'

Overtaken by events, Paneb agreed to eat and drink. The beer did not clear his head, but he ate heartily, and he had to admit that the bed prepared by Uabet was much more comfortable than his old mat.

Here he was, married to a woman he didn't love and in love with another whom he could never marry. His head was spinning. If he didn't drive Uabet out of this bedroom and this house immediately, the next day she would introduce herself as his legitimate wife, while he didn't even know if he would remain in a brotherhood which had relegated him to the status of a plasterer.

Hoping it was all just a nightmare, but well aware of his momentary cowardice, Paneb fell asleep.

# 56

When Paneb awoke, Uabet had disappeared. She had folded the sheets and rolled up her mat. Relieved, he climbed the staircase to the terrace, where it was good to sleep on hot summer nights.

So he was free. The young man greedily drank in the rays of the rising sun before checking the wide opening which faced north and was sheltered by a triangular canopy. It was an air-shaft, ensuring good ventilation in the house; several of the walls included little bays which were easy to screen when the sun blazed in.

In the end, he had come out of this rather well. Uabet had realised that their marriage was impossible but she had left him an admirably clean house, together with some fine furniture. Had he the right to keep it? No, he would give it all back to her. It was her dowry, and he could not take it for himself.

The babbling of children caught his attention. Looking down, Paneb saw a dozen or so children arriving at his door with fragile little cages of freshly cut reeds, bound together with the pith from papyrus stems. Inside were the large stones of the doum-palm.

He went down to let them in. 'What do you want?'

'We've brought you a wedding present,' said a little girl knowingly. She gave a peal of laughter.

'A wedding present? But . . .'

'Uabet's nice, and the whole village knows you're living under the same roof.'

'You're wrong. She left this morning and—'

Uabet appeared, carrying on her head a basket of provisions. She looked radiant, and moved with fluid grace despite her burden.

'Are you awake already, my dear husband? I went to get some vegetables and fresh fruit. Isn't these children's kindness touching?'

Shattered, Paneb thought of the plaster and the last house-fronts awaiting him.

Abry had crossed to Thebes on the ferry reserved for senior officials. An official chariot was permanently at his disposal at the landing-stage, and it took him to the sumptuous house where Mehy and Serketa had recently taken up residence.

Abry introduced himself to the gate-keeper, who ordered a servant to go and inform his master. The cup-bearer invited the visitor to wash his feet and hands with perfumed water before entering a reception room whose ceiling was supported by two porphyry columns and which was decorated with red and blue traceries of flowers and plants.

Abry had time to take in the lotus pool, the garden planted with palm-trees, sycamores, figs, carobs and acacias, the pergola and its lake, and the great courtyard, which was bordered by granaries and stables and with a well at its centre. The vast and luxurious house must have had at least twenty rooms, not counting the servants' quarters.

Mehy's success had been dazzling and his rise was far from over. In the face of so much wealth, Abry took fright. He realised that his ally was a formidable character whose stature was continuing to grow.

'The treasurer will see you in the massage room,' announced the cup-bearer.

Abry breathed more easily. At least Mehy was not turning him away. This time, he would not disappoint him but, on the contrary, would give proof of his frank and wholehearted collaboration.

Led by the cup-bearer, he crossed a splendid hall with four columns, decorated with scenes depicting fishing and hunting in the marshes, then he was ushered into the massage room, where a stone bench ran round the room, covered in best-quality, many-coloured mats. Shelves were laden with row upon row of vials and ointment jars made from ivory, glass and alabaster. Some were shaped like lotus flowers or papyrus stems, pomegranates, bunches of grapes; one showed naked swimming girls, pushing before them a duck with jointed wings, its body serving as the container.

Mehy was stretched out on his belly. A masseur was kneading his back while a maid was cleaning his nails with a brush made from "date hair", the name given to the fibre at the base of the leaves.

'Do sit down, my dear Abry. Forgive me for greeting you like this, but I have such demands on my time, and I didn't wish to postpone this conversation. Have you got good news?'

'Excellent, but it's confidential.'

'My hands are done, and my masseur is deaf and dumb.'

The maid left; the masseur continued.

'It's a long time since we had the opportunity to take stock,' remarked Mehy. 'We're both busy leading our respective careers, which are at once different and convergent.'

'I agree. And I do congratulate you on the way you're running our dear city's finances. Your father-in-law would be proud of you.'

'That compliment goes straight to my heart, Abry. I often think of that dear man and his premature end.'

'Your responsibilities are increasingly heavy and numerous. Perhaps they lead you to neglect, or even forget, the plans we mentioned?'

'Not in the least,' replied Mehy cuttingly.

'So you still want to destroy the Place of Truth?'

'My intentions have not altered and neither has our bargain. But I am not sure that you have abided by it.'

Mehy's brutal familiarity made Abry tremble.

'I've done everything in my power, believe me, but my efforts have not met with success. The brotherhood's secrets are much better guarded than I realised. And one false move will unleash the fury of the tjaty or of Pharaoh himself.'

'There is only one opinion which counts in Thebes, and it's mine. I promised you you'd keep your job, and I kept my word. Unless you produce results soon, I might change my mind and inform the highest authorities that the governor of the west bank of Thebes is incompetent.'

Abry paled and stammered, 'You know that isn't true. I do my job properly, nobody complains, and I—'

'I need allies worth having. Didn't you say you had excellent news?'

In his fluster, Abry had almost forgotten that he had finally come up with some convincing arguments. 'It concerns Commander Sobek. I've studied his file closely.'

'And have you found something interesting?'

'Unfortunately not. I confess I was discouraged, for it seemed that he was incorruptible. So I went to the village on the pretext of inspecting the lay workers' camp. My only goal was to find out more about this man Sobek.'

'Excellent, my dear Abry. And the results?'

'He is a very conscientious officer, who does his work extremely thoroughly.'

'We knew that already. Have you nothing new to tell me?'

'Sobek says he's satisfied with his lot, but that's only a front. Actually, he is beginning to tire of a difficult job which takes up all his time and means he cannot start a family.'

Mehy sat up straight and dismissed his masseur with a curt wave of the hand. 'That could be interesting,' he said, looking at himself in a copper mirror whose handle was in the form of a naked young girl. 'Did you take things any further?'

'Much further. I offered him a more rewarding post directing river security at Thebes, knowing you'd have no difficulty obtaining it for him.'

'True. But did you give him to understand that such generosity requires something in return?'

'Of course.'

'What was his reaction?'

'I believe he's ready to help us, in the way we want.'

'That really is excellent news!'

Mehy put down the mirror and combed his black hair, which he was very proud of. Seeing that his powerful protector was satisfied, Abry began to relax.

'I shall make discreet preparations for this appointment,' announced Mehy. 'When it is made, you must question Sobek, who will tell us everything he knows about the Place of Truth and the measures taken to protect it. But don't forget that I gave you a second mission.'

'I haven't forgotten it, I assure you. But it is a long time since any craftsman stayed outside the village for any length of time.'

Mehy's eyes took on a fierce glint. 'That's very hard to believe. I think you failed to set up a network of watchers, and that the craftsmen have been moving about perfectly freely.'

'The men I hired weren't very alert, I admit, but it's a very delicate task.'

'My patience has run out, Abry. I want results.'

# 57

Since Neb had instructed Nefer to prepare the new shrine for the *ka* of Ramses the Great, Ubekhet had shared only rare moments of intimacy with her husband. After his initiation into the secrets of the shipyard, Nefer the Silent had climbed several more steps in the builders' fraternity, by dint of a thoroughness which found favour with everyone.

The other adepts believed that the young man assimilated new skills with great ease and that he had to make only a slight effort to prove his growing mastery; only his wife knew that this was not the case and that he owed his achievements to hard work. But this did not weigh heavily upon him, for Nefer was evolving in a world which was in perfect harmony with his being. He had been born for the Place of Truth; the gods had fashioned him so that he might become accomplished and serve it.

Despite the scope of the work and the demands of daily life, the years had flowed by with the sweetness of honey. While Nefer was training with the stone-cutters and sculptors, Ubekhet was receiving instruction from the priestesses of Hathor and the wise woman. The first offered her the dimension of rites and symbols, the second that of traditional knowledge and the understanding of invisible forces.

Ubekhet looked down on the craftsmen's village from the terrace of her home, as she did every morning. It lay huddled at the bottom of its valley, overlooked by a rocky spur considered to be the base of the sacred mountain. All along it little shrines had been built, dedicated to the gods and goddesses and to the memory of departed pharaohs who had protected the Place of Truth, notably Amenhotep I, Tuthmosis III and Seti, Ramses' father. These shrines ran in a winding line along the lower part of the cliff, and each of their innermost shrines backed on to the Peak of the West where, each night, the mystery of resurrection was acted out, away from human sight.

Not for one moment did Ubekhet regret leaving the east bank and the mundane life her upbringing had prepared her for. As with Nefer, her real homeland today was this modest but unique village. Here, she had learnt that a community's happiness rested on the exchange of offerings, and upon the quality of what was offered. By giving instead of receiving, a solidarity was established, which could overcome differences of opinion, enmities and selfishness. And it was the priestesses who ensured this permanent atmosphere of giving, and battled against the natural tendency towards greed.

Ubekhet loved the dynamic energy of the first moments of the day, and the way the light sprang forth from the Peak of the East; she had the feeling that life was being created afresh and that, with each dawn, creation soared up on new wings, the bearer of unhoped-for marvels.

Suddenly a silhouetted figure caught her eye.

The wise woman was moving stiffly along the main street of the village, the breeze stirring her magnificent white hair. Although she was having more and more difficulty in walking, she did not yet use a stick. As soon as she saw her, Ubekhet went down to open the door and wait for her on the doorstep.

The wise woman got there before her. How had she managed to cover the distance in such a short time?

'Are you ready, Ubekhet?'

'I was going to fetch the flowers from the main gate.'

'Someone else will do that. You are to follow me.'

Sensing that the wise woman would not answer her, Ubekhet asked no more questions and was content to follow in her footsteps. Her guide seemed to have rediscovered her former vigour as she crossed the village and set off along the path to the Valley of the Queens.

The wise woman stopped in front of seven grottoes hollowed out of the rock and arranged in an arc facing north. She said, 'Here reign Meretseger, goddess of silence, and Ptah, god of builders. Choose one of the seven grottoes. You will remain there in meditation until someone comes to find you.'

Ubekhet entered the first cave on her left. It had been made into a little shrine where a stele had been erected to Ptah, who had fashioned the universe with the Word. Ubekhet sat down in the position of a scribe and savoured the coolness and silence of the place.

In the middle of the morning, a priestess led her into the second cave which was ruled over by the goddess of the Peak of the West, in the form of a beneficent cobra. At noon, in the third cave, Ubekhet drank milk as she faced a carved panel showing the pharaoh being suckled by the Great Mother. In the fourth, she worshipped the creative power of Hathor, goddess of the stars; in the fifth, her *ba*, Hathor's capacity for sublimation which carried the thoughts of her faithful worshippers to the heavens. Evening was falling when, in the sixth cave, Ubekhet discovered a representation of the pharaoh offering flowers to Hathor; in the seventh, by the light of a torch, she saw King Amenhotep I and his wife Ahmes-Nefertari – whose skin was black to symbolise rebirth at the time of death – welcoming a new adept. The paintings were so expressive that they brought to life the royal couple, benefactors of the Place of Truth.

In the silvery light of the night-sun, Ubekhet was invited to emerge on to the lotus-strewn forecourt. A priestess handed her bread and wine.

As though she had sprung from the rock, the wise woman appeared before her.

'You are between the two lions, Ubekhet, between yesterday and tomorrow, between West and East. Up to now, you have been receiving my teaching; the time has come to create your own path, to commune with the beings of light who are present in the invisible world and to be born to your own true nature. Do you wish it?'

'If that is the right way to serve the Place of Truth, so be it.'

'As you drink this wine and eat this bread, think that each thing you do, even the most modest gesture, must be conscious. If not, your life will be no more than a shadowplay. Osiris was killed by the forces of darkness, but Isis brought him back to life. His blood became wine, his body bread. A human being is not God, but he can participate in the divine if he can step through the gates of mystery. If you have the courage to do so, follow me.'

Ubekhet did not hesitate.

The wise woman climbed a path which was so steep that her disciple had difficulty in following her. Suddenly, the night became very black, as if the moon was refusing to shine. But a strange halo of light surrounded the wise woman's hair and enabled Ubekhet to keep her in sight.

The climb seemed endless and more and more difficult, but she did not give up. Her guide was following a path on the edge of nothingness; not once did she turn round. At last, the wise woman halted at the summit of a rocky crest, and Ubekhet climbed up to join her.

'The village sleeps, dreams pass through bodies and the gods and goddesses continue to create, tirelessly. It is their work that you must see, not men's, which time will destroy. Listen, Ubekhet. Listen to the words of the sacred mountain.'

The silence was total. No jackal howled, no night-bird sang; it was as if the whole of nature had made a pact. For the first time, Ubekhet saw the sky. Not the visible sky with its constellations, but its secret form, the form of an immense woman forming a curving vault inside which sparkled the stars, the gates of light. The hands and feet of Nut, the sky-goddess, touched the edges of the universe. All the knowledge Ubekhet had gleaned since her admission to the Place of Truth took on a new dimension, in harmony with the feminine cosmos where life caused itself to be ceaselessly reborn.

'Come to meet your allies,' urged the wise woman.

She left the promontory and walked down into a very narrow valley surrounded by cliffs, where she sat down on a round stone shaped by wind and storms. The darkness was becoming less intense and the moon seemed to concentrate its brightness on this desert place. It was because of its light that Ubekhet saw them.

Snakes. Dozens of snakes of all different sizes and colours.

A red one with a white belly, another red one with yellow eyes, a white one with a thick tail, a white one whose back was spotted with red, a black one with a pale belly, a hissing viper, another which seemed to have a lotus-stem drawn on its head, a horned viper, and cobras poised to strike.

Although scared half to death, Ubekhet did not run away. If the wise woman had brought her here, it was not to harm her.

Ubekhet stared at the reptiles one after the other, while they formed a rough circle round her. She detected no hostility in their small, watchful eyes.

The wise woman's white hair shone in the darkness. When she stretched out her arms to the ground, in a gesture of peace, the snakes slid under the round stone.

'You will have no better allies,' she told Ubekhet. 'They do not lie, do not deceive and carry within them venom which you can use to prepare remedies for sicknesses. With me, in the mountain, you will learn to speak to them and to call them when you need to. Snakes are the sons of the earth-god. They know the forces that run through the earth, for they were present when the primeval gods fashioned it. They will make you understand that fear is a necessary step and that evil can be transformed into good. Do you accept the gift of the snakes?'

Ubekhet took the stick the wise woman held out to her: it changed into a long golden serpent whose mouth seemed to smile. The young woman did not loosen her grip.

# 58

The open tavern near the main market in Thebes welcomed Egyptian and foreign traders who came there to refresh themselves and talk. The atmosphere was cheerful: everyone was talking about negotiations and profits. With his plump figure and beard, Daktair could pass for a Syrian merchant in search of lucrative deals. Here, he ran no risk of encountering someone from the central workshop or a senior official, which was why he had chosen it for his meeting with a laundryman from the Place of Truth.

A round-shouldered man sat down opposite Daktair. It was rowdy enough for nobody to be able to hear them.

'I've ordered the best beer,' said Daktair.

'Have you got my cleansing powder?'

'There's a whole sack on the back of the donkey waiting for you outside. I have improved its effectiveness even further.'

'Good,' said the laundryman gratefully. 'If you knew how terribly difficult my work is . . . The worst things are the linens soiled by menstruating women. They are very demanding and refuse to accept them from me if they aren't dazzling white. You can see they never have to wash them themselves. Thanks to your powder, I save time and I can tend my vegetable garden.'

'It's our little secret.'

'Whatever you do, don't say a word to my superiors. They must go on thinking I work like my colleagues but that I'm the best.'

'Very well,' said Daktair, 'but you must do me a small service.'

'What service?' asked the laundryman, suddenly anxious. 'I'm a poor man and I can't pay you lots of money.'

'All I want is a little information.'

The laundryman lowered his gaze. 'It depends what . . . I don't know much.'

'Have you ever been in the village?'

'I'm not allowed to.'

'Have any other workers managed it?'

'No, the gatekeepers never bend the rules. Sobek has already strengthened the security measures, so no outsider would risk trying to force a way in. The villagers all know each other. An intruder would be spotted immediately, thrown out and condemned to death.'

'Doesn't curiosity get the better of people?'

'Certainly not. Everyone should keep to his own place. We lay workers are content with ours.'

'From the amount of laundry you and your colleagues wash, you must have a good idea of how many people there are in the village, and the proportion of men to women.'

The laundryman stared at him. 'Possibly. But we are warned to keep our mouths shut.'

'How much do you want?'

'Three free sacks of your powder.'

'That's very expensive.'

'The information you want is confidential. I'm taking a big risk – if people found out I'd talked, I'd lose my job. All things considered, it had better be four sacks.'

'I won't go higher.'

'That will do.'

The two men shook hands, like honest traders.

'By my reckoning,' said the laundryman, 'there are about thirty artisans. A few of them are unmarried, so there must be between twenty and twenty-five women.'

'Many children?'

'From what people say, most couples have two; but some of the priestesses of Hathor don't want any.'

A very small community, thought Daktair. It shouldn't be difficult to destroy it.

All the house-fronts had been restored, and their whiteness sparkled in the sunshine. Paneb was proud that he had mastered the art of plastering, but he was profoundly bored. Everything he was doing now was repetitive, passionless and soulless, because he had no more to learn about plastering.

The young giant had got used to Uabet being around. She did the housework and the cooking to perfection and never scolded him for the amorous hours he spent with Turquoise. Paneb's official wife was discretion itself and she knew not to bother her husband. When she talked to the other women, she never uttered a word of criticism against her young husband, but said she wished all of them could be as happy as she was.

Tomorrow, Paneb would confront the artists, and even Neb if need be. Having passed the test he had been set, he would set forth his demands and would not accept vague words. A good meal would strengthen his conviction.

But a new surprise awaited him. Standing on the threshold was Uabet, dressed in a white gown, with a collar of cornelians about her neck and a floral circlet around her forehead. She no longer looked like a modest housewife.

'Come in but don't say a word,' she urged him.

Irritated, Paneb pushed open the door and found Ubekhet and Nefer meditating before two limestone busts which had been set up in a niche hollowed into the wall of the living-room. One was of Ptah, the other of Hathor. The busts of the ancestors were cut horizontally just under the thorax, and were armless, with their chests covered by a broad pectoral collar. They looked out through eyes that were serious and deep.

Ubekhet burnt pastilles of incense on a little portable brazier which she held out to Paneb.

'Honour our ancestors with fire,' she told him. 'Thanks to their presence in each of our houses, the gods can manifest themselves. It is up to you to live with their power and not in dependence upon them. They show themselves in a thousand and one ways, they can make us blind or open our eyes. May the flame which burns within you destroy nothing.'

While Paneb was burning incense to the ancestors, Ubekhet poured a little water on the flowers and fruit she had arranged on an altar.

'It was time we sanctified this home,' commented Nefer. 'Come into the second room. I have placed a gift in there.'

The silent one had set a small limestone stele into the wall. It was rectangular with a rounded top, and it depicted an ancestor who bore the name of 'Effective, Luminous Spirit of Ra'. Beyond death, he was sailing for all eternity in the ship of the sun, identifying with it and shining upon the village.

'Did you carve it?' asked Paneb.

'Do you like it?'

'It's wonderful! The ancestor is holding the sign of life in his right hand, isn't he?'

'He will pass it on to us if we know how to hear his voice. "Listening is the best thing of all," said Ptah-hotep, and it is the heart that enables us to listen. If we follow its commands, it will make us upright beings. And if we don't separate our hearts from our tongues, all that we set out to do will be done.'

'Everything I set out to do, too?'

'It is thanks to the heart that all knowledge exists and thanks to it that we glimpse the light of our ancestors and the lotus perfume they breathe: that's what Neb taught me. This stele is one of the many points of contact between the other world and the village, between the gods and the living. The face of an ancestor is the ray of sunshine which lights up our day in the midst of the worst difficulties.'

'But the heart must also obey us and not be hostile towards us,' objected Paneb, impressed by the solemnity of Nefer's words. 'Mine has a tendency to leap, and I'm not sure I can control it.'

'Shall we eat?' suggested Uabet.

The two couples shared the food she had prepared. She was delighted to entertain her husband's friends. They laughed as they recalled the villagers' mistakes, without forgetting their own, then, at the end of the meal, Ubekhet arranged lamps in the four corners of the bedroom so that no demon would disturb the couple's sleep.

And so the sanctification of the house was complete.

Uabet the Pure's guests thanked her for her hospitality but, just as he was leaving, Nefer noticed that Paneb seemed annoyed.

'I have no intention of spending my whole life listening to other people,' he confessed. 'I want to draw, and people are going to have to listen to me!'

'Your back won't break if you bend it,' replied Nefer.

# 59

The wise woman woke Ubekhet and Nefer in the middle of the night. She looked exhausted.

'Ramose's wife is critically ill,' she said. 'There's no hope of saving her, but we can ease her pain.'

Ubekhet dressed quickly.

'Come with us, Nefer,' said the wise woman. 'Ramose wants to speak to you.'

The trio walked in silence to the most beautiful house in the village, whose interior was lit by oil-lamps. The wise woman and Ubekhet went into the bedroom, while Ramose asked Nefer to sit down opposite him.

'My wife is going to die,' he said, in a voice which was at once sad and serene. 'We have spent all our lives together and we have known happiness here. I shall not leave her to undertake the great journey alone; I shall not long outlive her. Old age is bad, Nefer; the heart sinks into torpor, speech becomes hesitant, the eyes dim, the ears are afflicted with deafness and the limbs lose their vigour. The memory falters, the bones are painful, breath is short. Whether you stand, sit or lie down, you are in discomfort, and you lose your taste for the marvels of life. Until today each new dawn brought me joy because I saw the sacred spirit kept alive in the Place of Truth. But without my wife, I shall not even have the strength to watch you leaving for work, you and your spiritual brothers. To be kept away from death is bad for men; it is a narrow passageway which leads us to the court of Osiris, and it is he who judges the quality of our hearts. Although you are still young, you should already be thinking of preparing your eternal home in the village cemetery, for the house of death is designed for life. There was one piece of work I had to do with Neb, a task in which he and I have decided to involve you: the recreation of the building dedicated to the royal *ka*. I would like Ramses to see it finished before he joins his predecessors in the Valley of the Kings. Promise me you will work on it unstintingly.'

'I promise.'

'True happiness is found in righteousness and the love of Ma'at, Nefer; Ma'at is what God and Pharaoh love, the justice of the creative act. Great is Ma'at, lasting and effective; she has not changed since the earliest times, and when everything has passed away she alone will live on. Pharaoh's principal duty is to replace disorder and injustice with Ma'at. Accomplish Ma'at, and she will unveil herself to you, she who is the honey-sweet food of the gods. The Divine Light lives through Ma'at, justice, thanks to which you will distinguish good from evil. Build your path with the light of the Place of Truth, Nefer, and do not forget the smile of Ma'at.'

Stern-faced, the wise woman and Ubekhet emerged from Ramose's wife's bedchamber.

'She is no longer in pain,' said the wise woman, 'and she is asking for her husband.'

Paneb walked determinedly towards the house of Ched the painter. He was the senior draughtsman, and it was him Paneb must convince that the gates of the profession should open at last. Since his entry into the brotherhood, Paneb had accepted stern tests and shown himself equal to them all. The years had gone by, and he had made no progress in the art that was so close to his heart. Still burning with the same passion, he could not bear any more waiting.

Suddenly, he stopped in his tracks.

Something was wrong. Ordinarily, with the first rays of sunshine the village came to life. People filled the water-tanks, ate their breakfast on the terraces . . . but this morning, life had stopped. Not a sound, not a single child's laugh, nobody in the main street.

Paneb ran to Nefer and Ubekhet's house, but they were not there. All the houses were empty.

He left the village by the little western gate and he saw the people standing together in front of one of the tombs in the cemetery.

'Here you are at last,' whispered Uabet.

'I got up later than usual – it's not an affair of state!'

'Be quiet. We're in mourning.'

'Who's died?'

'The Scribe of Ma'at, Ramose, and his wife. They were found side by side, hand in hand, peaceful.'

Kenhir, Ramose's successor and adoptive son, led the funeral rites. As soon as he had heard of the couple's death, the Scribe of the Tomb had sent a craftsman to find the embalmers who would transform the mortal remains into Osiran bodies.

In homage to Ramose and his wife, who were loved by all, the Place of Truth was in deep mourning. For one lunar month, the men would not shave and the women would not tend their hair. Each day, in the temple and the houses, the villagers would beg the ancestors to welcome the deceased into the celestial paradise where the ship of light sailed and where the banqueting-table was eternally laden.

The craftsmen halted all work to finish the Scribe of Ma'at's funerary furniture, and Ched the Saviour finished the papyrus of the 'Book of Going Forth by Day', which would be laid on the mummy to allow it to answer the gatekeepers of the other world and to speak the phrases of knowledge vital for resurrection.

Under the direction of Didia the carpenter, a tall man who moved slowly, Paneb put the finishing touches to the two funerary beds. He adjusted the four square wooden feet, held together with sturdy tie-beams, and the vertical supporting frame at the end of the foot of the bed, while Didia made the acacia rests on which the mummies' heads would lie.

'You all look deeply depressed,' remarked Paneb. 'Was Ramose such an important person?'

'Pharaoh gave him the title of "Scribe of Ma'at". Perhaps no other Scribe of the Tomb will ever have the right to bear it.'

'Don't you trust Kenhir the Ungracious?'

'Kenhir is Kenhir, and that's a great deal in itself.'

'That isn't a very informative answer.'

'Work as hard as you can, my boy, and light will dawn – if it wants to.'

On the day when the mummies were to be entombed, the craftsmen and their wives acted as priests and priestesses. Kenhir and the two overseers spoke the ritual words over the two mummies, which stood propped up, and whose mouths, ears and eyes they had opened.

Then the craftsmen placed the Osiran bodies in wooden sarcophagi decorated with figures of protecting gods and goddesses and with symbols like the key of life, the magic knot of Isis and the 'stability' pillar, the incarnation of the resuscitated Osiris.

Then began a slow procession of men and women bearing offerings which would furnish the house of eternity: canes, scribes' palettes, builders' tools, ritual clothing, beds, chairs, stools, chests containing jewels and balms, offertory tables and little wooden figurines of the 'answerers', who would continue to move around construction materials in the other world at the call of their reborn master.

The dead man's internal organs had been placed inside four vases decorated with effigies of the sons of Horus: a man who protected the liver, a falcon the intestines, a baboon the lungs and a jackal the stomach. On the other side of death, a body made of light would be reconstituted, and no part of it would be missing.

Nefer's emotion was perceptible. Ubekhet sensed that something was troubling him greatly.

'What are you afraid of?' she asked.

'Why were Ramose's last words addressed to me and not to his adopted son, Kenhir, or the overseer?'

'Ramose was goodness itself, but he fulfilled the office of Scribe of Ma'at and he did not act on whims. He knew the hour of his death, and he chose you and no other to deliver his last message.'

'I don't understand his decision.'

'Didn't he set you a special task?'

'I've already spoken to Neb about it.'

'How did he react?'

'As soon as the mourning period is over, I shall set to work unstintingly.'

Since the night she had spent on the mountain in the company of the wise woman, Ubekhet's eyes had begun to decipher fragments of the future. For her, Ramose's behaviour was not at all obscure.

The funeral ceremonies were ending. Although everyone was sure the court of Osiris would recognise the Scribe of Ma'at and his wife as just souls, the sadness weighed heavy. Not to be able to speak to them again, ask their advice, or have their wisdom as a guide, would be grave handicaps.

Only Paneb could not have cared less. The mourning period seemed interminable to him, particularly as Turquoise had refused to make love. Those who were dead were dead, and they would not come back from the kingdom of Osiris.

Life went on, and lamentations solved nothing.

He tapped Nefer on the shoulder. 'Are there any more ceremonies after this?'

'Each day, a priest and a priestess will honour the *ka*s of the departed.'

'So tomorrow life will get back to normal?'

'After a fashion.'

'Do you agree that I have legitimate demands to put forward?'

'What kind of demands?'

'To learn the secrets of drawing at last.'

'For the time being, you'll be working for me.'

'I'm not a stone-cutter,' protested Paneb.

'I have to finish an important job as quickly as possible, and I need all the help I can get.'

# 60

The day after Ramose's death, Kenhir had washed his hair three times; it was his favourite indulgence. As the Scribe of Ma'at's wife had also died, he had inherited all his protector's possessions and, notably, his fabulous library. This brought together the greatest authors like Imhotep, architect of the step pyramid at Saqqara; the sage Hordedef from the time of the great pyramids; the tjaty Ptah-hotep, whose teachings were copied out over and over again, the prophet Neferti; and learned Khety, who had written a *Satire of the Trades* boasting of the advantages of being a scribe.

When he moved into Ramose's beautiful home, Kenhir felt himself age with brutal suddenness. He had passed his fiftieth birthday without losing any of his vigour, but all at once he felt the weight of solitude. True, Ramose had delegated many responsibilities to him and he had full control in his capacity as Scribe of the Tomb; but Kenhir had frequently consulted his predecessor and, although he deplored Ramose's excessive kindness and tendency to understand human weaknesses too well, had derived great benefit from his opinions. From now on, he would be running the village alone, and discussions with the two overseers, who did not always see things his way, promised to be tough.

A fifteen-year-old girl, Niut the Strong, would do his housework and cooking. Kenhir had hoped to pay her the absolute minimum, but she had demanded a decent wage so forcefully that he had given in. At the beginning, he had thought of getting rid of the little pest, but she did the housework so well, never forgetting to dust his many papyrus scrolls, that in the end he chose to keep her.

Kenhir had no shortage of plans. First, he must give his authority an indisputable foundation by making the two overseers realise that he was indeed the Scribe of the Tomb, and that no decision could be taken without his agreement. Next, he would forbid a certain number of misdemeanours unworthy of the Place of Truth. Responsible to the tjaty for the quality of work produced by the brotherhood, each day Kenhir kept the 'Journal of the Tomb' in which he noted, in his ugly, almost illegible, handwriting, what everyone had done, reasons for absence, the nature and quantity of materials and tools delivered to the village. He alone really knew everything that happened and he would not be as tolerant as Ramose over petty offences. With him, discipline would be more than just a word.

Kenhir knew that most of the craftsmen thought him vain, abrupt, selfish and too full of his own powers, but nobody disputed his skills. Many did not know that he could be self-critical and recognise his own mistakes, as long as he was the only one to do so.

Kenhir greeted the two overseers in the reception hall of his new home. Sensing that they felt ill at ease, he immediately got to the point.

'This house belonged to Ramose, my predecessor. Today, with the consent of the brotherhood, it belongs to me. It is therefore here that our conversations and work meetings will take place. The fact that we revere the memory of the Scribe of Ma'at must not prevent us from carrying on the work of the Place of Truth.'

The two overseers conceded that this was true.

'As it must be, my first decision is to ask you to excavate

my own house of eternity, in the southern part of the cemetery. It should be large and elaborate, to celebrate the office I hold.'

'The port crew will have to do it,' said Neb. 'My stone-cutters are busy building the shrine for Ramses' *ka*.'

'Very well,' grumbled Kenhir, 'but I shall not tolerate any laziness. Being admitted to this village implies only duties, not preferential treatment. What work has been given to Paneb the Ardent, now that he has finished restoring the fronts of our houses?'

'Nefer the Silent has taken him on as an assistant.'

'Doesn't Paneb want to be an artist any more?'

'He has submitted to the demands of the moment.'

'Excellent! Long may he continue to do so.'

Kenhir was received by the tjaty, and assured him that Ramose's death would not change the rule of the Place of Truth in any way. Afterwards, Kenhir received warm congratulations from Abry, who invited him to lunch. They sat down in a shady arbour, where servants brought them red wine from the Delta, salad dressed with olive oil, and stuffed quails.

'We all miss dear Ramose,' declared Abry.

'With three tombs in the village cemetery,' Kenhir reminded him, 'he won't be forgotten.'

'But we must think of the future, and the future is you. For too long you have lived in Ramose's shadow, unable fully to express your own rich personality. Despite the pain his death causes you, you must admit that it opens up new prospects for you.'

Kenhir ate heartily. 'Which ones, precisely?'

'I don't doubt for a moment that you will be a great success, particularly since you have the support of the authorities. But life in that closed village cannot always be enjoyable.'

'You are absolutely right.'

Abry had difficulty hiding his astonishment. He had been expecting the Scribe of the Tomb to deny it with vigour and indignation.

'I would not wish my job on anyone,' Kenhir went on. 'No other scribe works as hard as I do for such small returns.'

The governor was delighted. Ramose the incorruptible would never have said such a thing1 With his corpulent body and clumsy gait, and the glint of cleverness in his eyes, Kenhir was undoubtedly a ruthlessly ambitious man who would be amenable to certain suggestions.

'This work,' said Abry. 'Can you talk about it?'

'I'm sworn to secrecy, but I can assure you that it holds very little interest. If you know any ambitious young scribes, advise them to avoid the Place of Truth.'

'Why did you accept the post?'

'An unfortunate chain of events,' explained Kenhir. 'I pursued long and difficult studies, and I hoped they would take me far, perhaps even as far as running a part of the domain of Karnak. When I met Ramose, I was won over by his intelligence and his knowledge, which he generously passed on to me; and, as he and his wife could not have a child, they adopted me on condition that I took on the office of Scribe of the Tomb. In the beginning, I was happy and flattered, but then I became disillusioned. And people say this job is one of the most coveted in Egypt!'

'If I can be of help to you . . .' said Abry delicately.

'I must resolve my problems alone, without talking about them to anyone, unless it is the tjaty.'

'Your secret is a weighty one. Shouldn't it be done away with?'

'This is a land of traditions, and it isn't easy to change them.'

Abry sensed that Kenhir was ready to make concessions, even confidences, but he must not rush him. Who better than Kenhir to reveal vital information about the Place of Truth? By befriending him, Abry would gain an unexpected advantage over Mehy and could begin to loosen the latter's grip.

'You're a very agreeable man,' he said, 'and I don't like seeing you having to deal with such troubles.'

'That's the law of the village. One problem after another – it never ends.'

'Problems? What sort of problems?'

'I'm not allowed to talk about them.'

'How alone you must feel!'

'I wouldn't mind a little more wine. You must have an excellent cellar.'

'Can I offer you a few jars of red wine from Athribis?'

'I'd be delighted. They'd make a pleasant change from my usual wine.'

'In the face of so many difficulties, what are your plans?'

Kenhir thought for a long time. 'As regards the Place of Truth, I cannot say. But I do have personal ambitions.'

The governor rejoiced inwardly. With Ramose's death, the craftsmen's village had lost its soul. And the Scribe of Ma'at had made a very bad choice of successor, an embittered, ill-tempered man who would not be difficult to corrupt.

'Are those ambitions secret, too?' asked Abry.

'More or less. Though I hope that one of them may even benefit from a certain notoriety.'

'Tell me about it, if you can.'

Kenhir stiffened. 'Do you promise me total discretion?'

'Of course.'

'I intend to write,' confessed Kenhir. 'The names of the great authors endure beyond their deaths, even though they haven't built pyramids. Their children are their texts, their wives are their palettes. The most solid of monuments crumbles, but people remember books. A good book builds a pyramid in the reader's heart; it is more lasting than a tomb in the West. What the great authors say is completed, what comes out of their books remains in the memory. They hide their magic power, but we benefit from it when we read them.' He stood up. 'I cannot stay any longer. Don't repeat these confidences to anyone,' he told a stunned Abry, 'and don't forget to deliver that red wine.'

# 61

At the main barracks in Thebes, where Mehy was trying out a new chariot with a reinforced shell, Abry told him of his conversation with Kenhir.

'I didn't manage to extract any information from him, but we mustn't give up.'

Mehy was irritable and in an abominable mood. 'Is he like Ramose?'

'Not at all. Don't worry.'

'But he still clings on to his secrets as a monkey clings to the trunk of a palm-tree.'

'It only seems that way. Kenhir complains constantly about the weight on his shoulders and the perpetual problems the villagers cause him.'

'What are his ambitions?'

Abry looked embarrassed 'He told me about only one of them.'

'What was it?'

'He wants to write books.'

Furious, Mehy dealt a black horse an infuriated punch on the flank, and it whinnied with pain.

'You're joking!'

'No, Commander! Kenhir extolled writers, whose work he believes is more lasting than stone buildings.'

'The man's completely mad.'

'Whether he is or not, we can exploit his dissatisfaction.'

'Let's hope this trail doesn't turn out to be as short as Sobek's.'

'What happened?' asked Abry.

'It was very simple. I suggested to the tjaty that Sobek should be transferred and promoted to assistant head of river security at Thebes. The first indiscretion of my career, because of your stupid idea! Only Pharaoh and the tjaty can decide on a change of posting for the commander of the guards of the Place of Truth, and they don't need any advice, particularly since Sobek is giving complete satisfaction. You made me blunder, Abry, and you won't wipe that out with Kenhir's ramblings. Try to make up for it, and quickly.'

'Over to you,' Nefer said to Paneb.

Just before the positioning of a large block which was to complete the upper base of the wall, Paneb used a plumb-line to check one last time that the work was straight. Then Nakht the Powerful and Karo the Impatient slid the block along on a layer of milk-fat, Fened the Nose used a finger-shaped piece of wood to smooth the joint and Casa the Rope, faithful to the method taught by Imhotep when he had built the first pyramid, passed a copper blade covered with an abrasive substance between the stones, in order to improve adhesion.

Since he had started work on the shrine of Ramses the Great under his friend's direction, Paneb's days were full of excitement. With his extraordinary stamina, he did wonders, and, as he knew hardly anything about the craft of building, he accepted the stone-cutters' orders without a murmur.

Paneb liked way Nefer organised the site. True to his nickname, he spoke little and never raised his voice, even when he was annoyed. He gave precise instructions according to the overseer's plan, then left the craftsmen great freedom to carry them out. Morning and evening, he assembled his colleagues and asked for their honest opinions on the quality of the work done. Open to criticism, Nefer refuted it calmly when he thought it unfounded, without sternness towards the man who had voiced it. He liked the little community to have time to think before acting, but, once the decision was taken, everyone used his own strengths and talents, without further discussion.

Neb the Accomplished inspected the site daily, sometimes accompanied by Kenhir. A meticulous man, he was sparing with his compliments and bluntly pointed out any imperfections, which had to be corrected immediately.

Paneb kept his eyes wide open: he observed the methods used by the artisans to remove the mistake and engraved them in his memory. Learning was the tastiest of dishes, and he thoroughly enjoyed being with these rough men, who never hesitated to criticise or to poke fun at him. The young man forgot his prickliness, the better to absorb their knowledge.

When Nefer first allowed him to use a plumb-line, which hung from a wooden frame, and whose stone end was shaped like a heart, Paneb had felt immense pride. People were putting real trust in him, the apprentice. And he contemplated the finished wall with the feeling that it included a part of his being.

Nefer put a hand on his friend's shoulder. 'You've worked well.'

'Feeling that plumb-line in my hand – it was marvellous!'

'Everything we do ought to be like the plumb-line, for incorrect conduct never produces good results. The man who has gone astray is not allowed on to the ferry to the land of the just, while the righteous man reaches the other side. Tools teach us the right way to behave; they are not interested in our weaknesses or our moods. Thanks to them, this shrine has been brought into existence.'

The main door led into a vestibule, which became a flagged passage leading to a hall with many-coloured pictures, depicting a vine with heavy bunches of grapes and hieroglyphic texts in blue. Ched the Saviour had created a masterpiece, his fine, graceful work crowned by a ritual scene showing Ramses offering perfumes to Hathor. This room opened into a vaulted hall, at the far end of which three steps led to a shrine. To the left of the steps were a hall of purification and altars where offerings would be laid. The pharaoh's private apartments comprised a bedroom, an office, conveniences and a terrace; they adjoined the sacred complex, and the little royal palace communicated with the courtyard of the temple of Hathor by a 'window of appearances' topped by a line of heads of Libyans, Nubians and other incarnations of the disorder and darkness which only Ma'at could overcome.

'We have finished,' said Paneb, 'but Ramses lives in his capital in the Delta and he'll never come here.'

'This building is called "*Khenu*", the "Interior", and that is precisely what we are: men of the interior, designed to protect the royal *ka* that gives us life. Whether or not Pharaoh is physically present, his *ka* shines out as long as the stones assembled are really alive. That is why the dedication ceremony is essential.'

'You do say strange things, Nefer. Anyone would think it was you who designed Ramses' dwelling.'

'All I've done is follow Ramose's directives and fulfil the plan dictated by Neb.'

'All the same,' said Paneb, 'you've supervised craftsmen who are more experienced than yourself.'

'The only person in charge is our overseer – you said so yourself.'

'Fened the Nose told me you've made a sculpture for the shrine of this palace.'

'Yes, I did.'

'Can I see it?'

Nefer took Paneb to the threshold of the shrine where, soon, the royal *ka* would be activated. Slowly, he took off a sheet of heavy cloth which covered a limestone lintel.

Opposite a large cartouche, the cosmic oval inside which his name was written, a tiny Ramses was protected by an enormous Hathor in cow form, emerging from a thicket of papyrus. The animal wore a collar of resurrection, whose energy protected the pharaoh.

'It's wonderful!' said Paneb. 'Did you choose the subject?'

'Of course not. The overseer gave me the working diagram, and I followed it to the letter.'

'The king is very small . . .'

'I asked Neb about that. He said that in this shrine the mother-goddess will cause the royal *ka* to be reborn each day; it will look like a child, while remaining an adult. Here the miracle of permanent regeneration will be accomplished, a miracle whose secret is known only to the gods and goddesses.'

'I'm not so sure,' said Paneb.

'What do you mean?'

'That light that can shine through a door – men saw it, here in this village, and they aren't gods. Look at this monument: you built it, but no one gave you the keys.'

'Each thing will come in its own due time, if we take the right path.'

'I don't share your fatalism, Nefer. I want to discover everything and know everything, uncover the mysteries of this village, understand why so few craftsmen are judged worthy of working here, know how a house of eternity is excavated, and see with my own eyes the moment of resurrection. And I'm convinced that the right path will lead me to that point.'

# 62

To celebrate the completion of Ramses' new shrine, the stone-cutters assembled in front of it. Not without difficulty, the overseer had obtained from Kenhir a jar of wine from Year Twenty-eight of the pharaoh's reign; it was an excellent vintage, and there was still a little left in the Scribe of the Tomb's cellar.

As an apprentice, Paneb had been instructed to clean the tools, put them into wooden boxes and give them to Kenhir. The scribe, according to his usual custom, had checked them minutely and at length before noting in the 'Journal of the Tomb' that everything was in order.

'You'd make a good stone-cutter,' Fened the Nose told Paneb.

'My path is drawing and painting.'

'You're a stubborn one, aren't you?'

'Never mind me. Tell me about yourself. Why are you called "the Nose"?'

'Don't you know that there's nothing more important than a good nose? When the masterbuilder judges an applicant, it's his nose he looks at first, because it is the body's secret shrine. To work in this brotherhood, my lad, you need a nose, plenty of nose, and even more breath. Not just the breath that passes into the noses of all living beings and enables them to breathe, but the breath of creation, which gives life to the pyramids, the temples, and the houses of eternity, which drives away mediocrity as the wind disperses the mist. You can read now, so you'll know that the word "joy" is written with a picture of the nose; and without joy, believe me, you cannot build anything lasting. The purest source of joy is practising your trade in the service of Ma'at.'

'Stop lecturing him,' said Nakht the Powerful. 'Can't you see he doesn't understand a word you're saying?'

'Is it compulsory for power to be associated with stupidity?' asked Paneb.

Nakht got to his feet, fists clenched. 'I'm going to make you take that back, youngster.'

Fened and Karo intervened. 'That's enough, you two! Don't spoil this good moment. Let's drink this excellent wine and prepare for the great feast of the new year.'

Nakht pointed a vengeful finger at Paneb. 'Just you wait!'

'As long as you like. You talk, but you never do anything.'

The stone-cutter smiled sarcastically. 'And you talk too soon.'

Festivals irritated Paneb, and this one irritated him more than the others. It was preventing him from taking the clan of artists to task and speaking with the overseer to obtain his rights. So, despite his wife's careful attention, he had been in a foul mood during dinner. Uabet had not reacted, and was content to fulfil the duties of a perfect housewife.

Angered by the idea that the village was going to abandon itself to celebrating the first day of the year while he was burning with impatience, Paneb had got up in the middle of the night, and left by the little western gate. He took the path to the pass overlooking the Valley of the Kings. Knowing he was being watched by Sobek's guards, he branched off into the scree where they could not see him, and sat down on a rock.

According to the specialists' predictions, this year's flood would be excellent and once again Hapy, the dynamic, fertilising god of the Nile, would bring prosperity to Egypt. But Paneb didn't give a damn about the silt, the fields and the country's wealth. He wanted to draw and paint. He'd been initiated into the brotherhood that held the secrets of his vocation, and still they persisted in closing the doors to him!

As for Nefer the Silent, he had taken giant steps forward. In a few years he had advanced several levels, and he already performed the role of the senior stone-cutter, even though he denied it. Paneb was neither jealous nor envious, but a little annoyed and, above all, frustrated. Every time he thought he was close to achieving a goal, an urgent task took him further from it again. True, he'd learnt a lot, but nothing he wanted to know!

Fine, gentle, perfumed hands were laid over his eyes. 'I was waiting for you.'

'Turquoise! How did you know I'd come here?'

'A priestess of Hathor has to be able to see further than most.'

With an imperious gesture, he caught her close against him.

'Don't forget you're married,' she said. 'Adultery is a serious transgression.'

Among all the marvels the gods had created, Turquoise was one of the most seductive. Paneb took off his kilt and her dress to lay them on the stones as a makeshift couch. He lay down on his back, forgetting the sharp pebbles as soon as Turquoise's light body melted into the sky.

Under the starry sky of the last day of the year, they made love until dawn.

When Paneb awoke, his mistress had disappeared. He closed his eyes for a few moments, reliving their delicious frolics in his mind, then set off back to the village.

As on the morning of the deaths of Ramose and his wife,

he was struck by the thick silence, which was even stranger on a festival day. There must have been another death, and so the celebrations had been cancelled. According to the dead person's position in the village, they were setting off on a briefer or longer period of mourning, which would force Paneb to keep silent and respect the community's sorrow.

No, he would not resign himself, even if it did mean breaking with custom. Nobody, not even an overseer, could oppose a legitimate demand. While the others lamented, he would work with one of the artists, gaining his help voluntarily or by force.

The little western gate, to which only the villagers had access, was closed. Intrigued, Paneb went to the main gate. All around was deserted, as the 'outsiders' were entitled to a day's holiday.

Squatting on his haunches, chewing a piece of sugary papyrus, the gatekeeper stared at him and nodded a greeting.

Paneb passed through the gate and closed it behind him. There was nobody in sight. The people were neither at the cemetery, nor in the village. They must be in the temple.

The young man walked down the main street and heard the sound of footsteps behind him. He turned round and saw Casa the Rope, Fened the Nose, Karo the Impatient and Nakht the Powerful standing in a line, armed with cudgels.

'Nice surprise, don't you think?' asked Nakht, amused. 'Come on, boy, we've been waiting for you.'

Userhat the Lion and Ipuy the Examiner joined the four stone-cutters. Six armed men, some of them pretty strong. It would be quite a fight, but Paneb was not afraid. Even if he took some punishment, he would hand out more.

'You can't run away,' Nakht warned him. 'Look in front of you.'

At the other end of the main street were Renupeh the Jovial, Ched the Saviour, Gau the Precise, Unesh the Jackal, Didia the Generous, Thuty the Learned and even Pai the

Good Bread, and they too were armed with cudgels and clearly determined to use them.

Only the overseer and Nefer were taking no part in the scramble for spoils.

The artists seemed less strong than the stone-cutters. Paneb would first break Pai the Good Bread's head, then seize his club and knock out his accomplices. And if he was eventually defeated by sheer weight of numbers, at least he would have fought back with all his stength.

All they had been thinking of was plotting to get rid of him! Sickened by such duplicity, Paneb felt rage increasing his strength tenfold, and he advanced menacingly towards the artists.

The group parted to allow the wise woman to pass. She was dressed in a fine dress of bright red, which set off her carefully combed white hair.

'Go no further, Paneb!' she commanded. 'For you, all is conflict and strife. You are right: that is indeed how we lead our existence. But life in the Place of Truth demands more from us than existence. It calls us towards fulfilment and serenity. Before that, we must vanquish our enemies, and above all the seething anger, intemperance and hatred that eat our hearts away. You have been chosen to embody these enemies, so that they may be prevented from doing harm, and a happy year for the brotherhood may be brought to birth.'

The starboard crew threw their cudgels into the air, shouted with joy and rushed at Paneb, who offered no resistance. With difficulty, they lifted him up and carried him to the Temple of Hathor. There, they tied him securely to a stake.

Everyone, from the youngest to the oldest, hurled insults at him, ordering him not to meddle in village life or he would be soundly beaten.

From his unenviable position, Paneb witnessed the banquet, during which the stone-cutters and certain wives drank a little too much wine. Turquoise did not even glance at him, Uabet threw him compassionate looks, Ubekhet and Nefer gave him friendly waves. It was also Nefer who several times brought him cool water, the only nourishment appropriate for boiling rage.

'You might have told me I'd been chosen,' said Paneb. 'I almost massacred half the crew. I don't suppose it was you who dreamt up this stupid idea, was it?'

Nefer did not reply. His expression was inscrutable.

Condemned to submit to his role as a scapegoat, Paneb took his punishment patiently, although hunger, sharpened by the sight of succulent dishes, gnawed at his stomach. Those who thought they could weaken him by imposing this new trial on him would get nothing for their pains.

When the star Sothis appeared, enabling the wise woman to proclaim the birth of the new year, marked by the tears of Isis which would unleash the flood, the overseer released Paneb from his bonds.

As the embodiment of seething anger was rubbing his wrists, Neb the Accomplished hit him hard on the back, between his shoulder-blades.

'The ear of your conscience is open, Paneb. Now the serious work begins.'

# 63

Sobek's inability to find out who had murdered the guard had cost him many hours' sleep. The potions prescribed by the wise woman calmed his nerves, but none of them could suppress his obsession. A man under his command had met a horrible death and the criminal remained at liberty, certain to escape justice.

Sobek could no longer meet a craftsman without suspecting him of being guilty, and this constant suspicion was poisoning his life, all the more so because not one shred of proof had come to light to support his hypothesis. And why had this murder been committed?

An unexpected event had made him consider a lead so improbable that he had to consult the Scribe of the Tomb.

Seated in his office in the fifth fort, Kenhir was writing his daily report in a hand which was becoming more and more illegible. He cursed the demands of an over-bureaucratic government which insisted on knowing the precise number of copper chisels used by the craftsmen of the Place of Truth. Of course, it was he who had to check them and call to order those who forgot to return them to him after work.

'You have chosen a bad moment, Sobek.'

With him, thought the Nubian, it's always a bad moment. He is exactly the opposite of Ramose.

'I know what you're going to complain about: the support

workers are demanding a change of work roster for the hot season. I can understand their point of view, but I must ensure the well-being of the village. Also, this kind of problem does not come within your jurisdiction.'

'I know that. I've come to consult you about something much more serious.'

The Scribe of the Tomb was intrigued. 'Sit down.'

Sobek lowered himself on to a stool. 'You know I'm still investigating the murder of one of my men.'

'A very difficult business,' said Kenhir. 'It was thought to be an accident, then someone raised the possibility of a crime, and since then the investigations have been forgotten.'

'Mine have not.'

'You have a lead?'

'Destiny may have granted me one, but I need your advice.'

'I'm not a security guard!'

'If I'm right, the very future of the brotherhood could hang in the balance.'

'Aren't you exaggerating a little?'

'Let us hope so.'

Kenhir grumbled, but Sobek was not in the habit of peddling rumours or getting carried away with mad ideas, so the scribe decided to waste a little time and listen to him.

'Whom do you suspect?'

Sobek gazed straight ahead of him, as if conversing with an invisible person. 'Abry, governor of the west bank, suggested that I should change my job and take charge of river security in Thebes.'

'A promotion worth having.'

'There are many better-qualified candidates for that post, and Abry implied that there would be a price to pay.'

Kenhir's curiosity was aroused. 'Was he trying to bribe you?'

'Yes, I think so. In exchange for the service Abry would do

me, I was to tell him everything I knew about the Place of Truth.'

The Scribe of the Tomb chewed a few watermelon seeds, recalling his own conversation with Abry. In the light of Sobek's revelations, it took on a rather worrying significance.

He asked, 'What did you do?'

'I pretended to be interested, and I think Abry took the bait. He was intelligent enough not to press the point, but he'll no doubt return to the attack.'

'He was lying to you.'

'How can you be so sure?'

'Because I know the tjaty is completely satisfied with you – as is the pharaoh himself. If Abry put your name forward for a new post, he would meet with a cut and dried refusal. By rights, I ought not to have told you – this is confidential information – but in the circumstances . . .'

'I am a guard officer and I like my profession,' said Sobek solemnly. 'Ensuring the safety of the Place of Truth is not a burden but an honour, and you mustn't think that Abry's suggestion struck the slightest chord in me.'

Sensing that the Nubian was becoming annoyed, Kenhir hastened to reassure him. 'The village has never been protected better, Commander Sobek, and you have my complete trust. But why do you link Abry's attempt at bribery with the murder of your man?'

'Because such a senior figure has no reason to be interested in me, except in my capacity as head of security for the Place of Truth. If he wanted me transferred, it may have been so that I'd have to drop the case, and it would be forgotten for good.'

Sobek's reasoning troubled Kenhir. 'I cannot quite see Abry sneaking up the mountain in the middle of the night and murdering a guard.'

'Nor can I, but perhaps he was complicit in the crime.'

'But why?'

'To infiltrate someone whose mission was to draw a plan of the area.'

'Are you thinking of an attempt to pillage the royal tombs?'

'That danger lies in wait at all times. Many think that they contain fantastic riches and dream of gaining possession of them. As long as their protection is ensured, the risks will be minimal. But suppose the villagers were under suspicion and discredited? Suppose an end was put to the village's activities?'

'That is impossible,' said Kenhir.

'I'd like to believe so, but shouldn't we imagine the worst?'

Pessimistic by nature, Kenhir was receptive to Sobek's arguments. He said, 'So you think a dangerous plot is being hatched against the Place of Truth and that Abry is one of its leaders.'

'I see no other reason for his attempt to bribe me.'

Kenhir regretted Ramose's death. The Scribe of Ma'at would have known how to defend the brotherhood.

After a short pause, Paneb the Ardent had been allowed to enjoy the festival meal, and then a long and delicious massage by Uabet, who was anxious about her husband's sore muscles.

At last, the overseer's words had opened the way for him! He would not set out for the fight without weapons. He would be properly equipped with the authorisation of Neb the Accomplished.

Cautious to a degree which surprised himself, the young man had asked Nefer for advice. He had given it unambiguously: the blow on Paneb's back signified that he was authorised to enter the company of artists.

Such long, hard years to get there – and this was only the beginning of the path! Paneb's enthusiasm had not diminished. On the contrary, the chance to prove his worth increased it tenfold.

His heart racing, he headed for the drawing-office, the workplace of Ched the Saviour, head of the artists.

With his fine hair, his neatly clipped little moustache and light grey eyes that were both disdainful and penetrating, Ched struck the young man as a formidable adversary. The painter was preparing colours, and several uncomfortable minutes went by before he deigned to notice Paneb's presence.

'What are you doing here? I thought you belonged to the stone-cutters' crew.'

'That was only temporary. Now it's finished, and I have come to place myself at your disposal.'

'I don't need anyone, my boy. Haven't I told you that already?'

'The overseer hit me on the back to let me know that I was ready.'

'That's surprising. Was it Neb the Accomplished himself?'

'Yes.'

'What exactly can you do?'

'I can prepare a surface by plastering it.'

'Good, good. Why don't you continue in that line of work? A good plasterer has a future in this village.'

'I want to go further.'

'Are you capable of it?'

'You'll see that I am.'

'No one can disobey the overseer's orders,' conceded Ched, 'and I should therefore place you in the hands of the artists so that they can teach you the rudiments of their skills and you can realise, like so many before you, that you have no aptitude for this profession. But that's not possible.'

Paneb growled, 'Why not?'

'Events beyond my control. In a few days, the village will be the setting for a special event, and we are required to finish certain projects. So we have no time to bother with teaching an apprentice.'

Paneb was sure that the painter was mocking him. 'What is this event?'

'Ramses the Great is coming here, to dedicate his shrine.'

# 64

What if the old king were to have a fatal accident? This seductive thought had haunted Mehy since he and the other Theban dignitaries were informed of the pharaoh's visit. It was Ramses alone who kept Sobek in his post, watching over the Place of Truth with never-failing vigilance. Once Ramses was dead, the village would lose its principal protector.

The guards protecting the monarch would not be fooled easily, and Mehy could not find any madmen willing to attempt to kill Ramses, who had become a living legend, not only in his own country but overseas.

While the former chariot officer was half-listening to his smiling, submissive wife babbling away, an idea came to him.

With a little luck, the king would not stand in his way for much longer.

Ramses' visit had aroused enormous excitement on the west bank of Thebes. Everyone was eager to see the king who had both established lasting peace and brought wealth to the Two Lands.

Elite guards watched over him, but who would have dreamt of attacking him? Accompanied by his faithful scribe Ahmeni, who was almost as old as himself, Ramses stood in a chariot driven by an experienced officer and pulled by two powerful but docile horses. A canopy shaded the illustrious traveller, who gazed with deep emotion at the Peak of the West and the Temple of a Million Years.

Leaving behind the farming area, the king's chariot rolled past the immense shrine of Amenhotep III; its style was reminiscent of the temple at Luxor, to which Ramses had added an extra courtyard lined with huge statues, a pillared gateway and two obelisks. The pharaoh drank in the air of the desert, a place where he had often drawn the strength necessary to fulfil his onerous office.

Sobek's guards were dressed in ceremonial uniform. They stood in two rows, forming a guard of honour as the monarch passed through the five forts, followed by a procession of dignitaries including the mayor of Thebes, Abry and Mehy.

All were astonished when Sobek stepped forward and forced them to stop at the fifth fort.

Abry jumped down from his chariot in a fury. 'What are you thinking of? We are the official procession!'

'Pharaoh's orders: no one goes any further.'

'That's ridiculous! We are to take part in a ceremony, and—'

'The dedication of the shrine is taking place within the sacred enclosure of the Place of Truth, and you are not authorised to enter.'

The protests died down quickly. Though outwardly calm, Mehy felt deeply insulted by this accursed brotherhood. Once again he had come up against their locked doors, but this affront would not endure for ever.

All the villagers, headed by Kenhir and the two overseers, had donned their ceremonial clothes of finest-quality royal linen, and they wore wigs and jewellery made by the community's goldsmith.

When Ramses set foot in the main street, men, women and children flung themselves to the ground before him. Even

Paneb was astonished by the power that emanated from the great old man.

Laughing nervously, a delightful little girl in a fringed blue dress ran up to the king, to present him with a bouquet of white lotus-flowers.

'For your *ka*, Majesty,' she said without hesitation, having rehearsed the phrase at least a thousand times.

Ramses kissed her with all the tenderness of a father and grandfather who had suffered many bereavements and saw the future of the village in this child.

Pink-cheeked, the little girl ran to hide in the arms of her mother, the wife of a young stone-cutter from the port crew. The incredible favour Ramses had just bestowed upon her would extend to touch all the families, who would thus be protected by the king's love.

Neb the Accomplished and his colleague Kaha accompanied the pharaoh to the recently completed shrine. The king walked slowly, leaning on a stick, but he did not hesitate over which path to follow. He knew everything about the Place of Truth, the secret soul of Egypt, the place where light was created to bring matter to life, whatever its nature and form might be.

Officiating as the High Priestess of Hathor, the wise woman welcomed the king at the threshold of the building.

'The doors of this temple are open,' she said. 'The smoke from the incense reaches the heavens. A thousand loaves of bread, a thousand jugs of beer and all those things which God loves are offered to him. May God protect Pharaoh and may Pharaoh give life to this shrine.'

Ramses turned to face the brotherhood. Far from being that of a sick old man, his voice was imbued with an authority which rooted Paneb to the spot.

'I know your worth and the skill of your hands, which work the hardest stone as though it were the finest gold. Your work is demanding and hard, but you know how to commune with the materials whose hidden beauty you reveal. The work you do is essential for the happiness of the country, and you derive intense joy from it, a joy which is not of this world. Continue to respect the rule of Ma'at, to be firm and effective, act according to the masterbuilder's plan, and Pharaoh's support will not fail you. I am the protector of your trades, and you will lack for nothing you require to practise them. Your food shall be as abundant as the tides of the Nile flood, and the lay workers will serve you zealously. If your hearts are full of love for your work, no misfortune will break your arm. And my heart shall be as one with yours as you work, for you are my sons and my temple companions.'

Kenhir, who had received the delivery note detailing the royal gifts, knew that Ramses was not boasting in speaking of a tide that would flood the village in the next few days: thirty-one thousand baked loaves in pots, thirty-two thousand dried fish, sixty blocks of dried, marinated meat, thirty-three beasts for slaughter, two hundred pieces of filleted meat, forty-three thousand boxes of vegetables, two hundred and fifty sacks of beans, a hundred and thirty-two sacks of various grains, high-quality beer and wine. The celebrations promised to be sumptuous, as befitted Ramses' *ka*.

Using a large gilded wooden adze, the two overseers performed the rituals of opening the mouth, eyes and ears of the temple, which Ramses had named *Khenu*, the 'Interior'. And in the vaulted hall where the craftsmen and priestesses of Hathor were gathered, the king saw the statue of his *ka*, his stone double, crafted by Neb the Accomplished.

'Pharaoh is born with his *ka*, his creative power,' said Ramses. 'He grows with it and it ceaselessly recreates the world and links us to the gods and the ancestors. A human being does not become real until he is united with his *ka* which is nourished by Ma'at, and it is here, in the Place of Truth, that the royal *ka* is invigorated.'

Paneb was overwhelmed. In those few words, Ramses had revealed the nature of the fire that burnt within him.

Brought to life by the word of Pharaoh, the statue of the *ka* was installed in the shrine where, from now on, it would lead an autonomous existence. The stone-cutters would erect a wall with a narrow slit in it, through which the statue's eyes would watch the world of humanity and cause its energy to radiate out into it.

'When a monument has been brought into the world,' concluded Ramses, 'power is maintained within it for ever.'

Paneb would have liked to ask the true master of the brotherhood at least a thousand questions, for each word was engraved in his consciousness. And he was convinced that his future plans would have no meaning unless they, too, were enlivened by the mysterious energy whose secret was known to the brotherhood.

On an order from Neb the Accomplished, the craftsmen positioned the shrine's last stone, the door lintel carved by Nefer the Silent and decorated in glowing colours by Ched the Saviour.

'Who is the creator of this work?' asked the king.

'Nefer, Majesty,' replied the overseer.

Nefer bowed. 'All I did was carry it out, Majesty. It was Ramose who specified the theme and composition, and it was Ched the painter who—'

'I know.'

For once, thought Paneb, Silent has talked too much.

'Do you know what the term "*hem*" means, Nefer?'

'"To serve" and "Majesty".'

'We are all servants of the Great Work being done in the Place of Truth, and we must devote ourselves to it. But serving does not exclude leading, and without good leadership, there is no true service. Now, leave me to gather my thoughts in this temple.'

Pai the Good Bread pulled Paneb's sleeve, forcing him to leave with the others. Fascinated by Ramses, the young giant would have loved to hear his conversation with the *ka*.

# 65

Ramses was preparing to leave for the Valley of the Kings in order to inspect his house of eternity, to which Ched the Saviour and his assistant had put the finishing touches before the king's arrival.

Paneb was instructed to carry fresh water to the pharaoh's horses, which had been placed in the shade of a canopy, guarded by their driver. As he approached the chariot, the young man glanced at the wheels. The work was magnificent, solid enough to pass any test, and the ex-carpenter marvelled at it.

The horses drank peacefully, and Paneb was about to leave when he noticed something odd. The spokes of the wheels were painted yellow-gold, but one spoke was brighter than all the others.

'Has this been repaired recently?' he asked the charioteer.

'I don't know anything about that. It's not my job.'

'Where did this chariot come from?'

'The main barracks in Thebes, where the specialists checked it.'

'It ought to be checked again.'

'Why don't you just mind your own business, boy?'

Paneb could easily have knocked out the soldier and then examined the wheel, but he felt it was better to follow protocol. He alerted the overseer, who immediately summoned Didia the carpenter.

Didia was unequivocal: one of the spokes had been replaced and hastily painted. Besides this negligent repair, the wheel itself had not been replaced properly, which would make it gradually distort and eventually break. The vehicle would have overturned and, even at moderate speed, the old king might have been fatally injured.

Another chariot, duly checked by Didia, was allocated to Ramses, who left with the two overseers, Ched the Saviour and a few craftsmen, including Nefer the Silent.

Paneb realised that his friend had climbed another step on the ladder and that he was going to have the immense good fortune to enter the royal tomb. But he never imagined that his vigilance had just saved both the pharaoh of Egypt and the Place of Truth.

Closeted in the office at his sumptuous house, Mehy was tearing old papyrus into shreds. This time there could be no doubt: supernatural luck protected Ramses. And yet the sabotage had been carried out with great care by a good, extremely well paid specialist, who, of course, had no idea why he had carried out this task. Then the wheel had been delivered to the barracks where it had been put on by a soldier who – as Mehy had hoped – had noticed nothing abnormal.

The accident would inevitably have occurred if one of the craftsmen from the Place of Truth had not been too curious. The commanding officer of the barracks would be blamed and his specialists punished. Mehy must act quickly to cut the thread that might enable people to follow it back to him.

At last, evening was falling.

'Are you going out at this hour?' asked his astonished wife.

'I am going to fetch a document from my office.'

'Can't you wait until tomorrow morning?'

'Busy yourself with dinner, Serketa. And make sure the cook does better than yesterday.'

If Ramses had died in an accident, the whole of Egypt would

have been content with ritual mourning, and nobody would have bothered about the chariot wheel. But since the anomaly had been noted, an inquiry was bound to be conducted.

The treasurer jumped on to his horse and galloped to a thicket of tamarisks, where he tethered it. Then he walked nervously towards the workshop belonging to the carpenter, a widower who, by a stroke of luck, had just lost his dog.

The man was alone and eating hot beans.

Mehy approached him silently, from behind. With a movement as sudden as it was precise, he covered his victim's head with a thick cloth bag; he held it in place until the carpenter had breathed his last.

It would be assumed to be a heart attack, and Mehy need not fear any idle chatter.

As treasurer of Thebes, Mehy received Daktair in an official capacity, in order to examine the provisional budget for his research department. They no longer had to hide themselves away.

The little fat man was very agitated, and kept plucking at his beard.

'My situation is becoming untenable,' he complained. 'Two years I've been working flat out to perfect a water-powered machine that will replace the *shaduf*s and all the other archaic devices, and at last I have succeeded.'

'Then you should be pleased,' said Mehy, astonished.

'I am, but my superior has ordered me to forget this superb invention!'

'Why?'

'It would be too effective and increase irrigation to an extent he considers disastrous. For him, only natural rhythms and respect for traditions count. In these conditions, it is impossible to make any progress. There is only one way: make nature submit to man. As long as this country fails to understand that, it will be backward.'

'Don't despair, Daktair. Let me settle into my job. I promised that you would one day be free to act as you wish, and I always keep my promises.'

'The sooner the better – particularly as I have uncovered two interesting leads.'

'Relating to the Place of Truth?'

'My superior is particularly vigilant about certain files. By trickery, I have obtained a few pieces of reliable information. Apparently expeditions are organised, with extreme secrecy, in order to obtain two materials: galenite and bitumen.'

'What are they used for?'

'Officially, they are simply for domestic or ritual use. If that's true, why take so many precautions? And why have craftsmen from the Place of Truth gone several times to the sites where they are extracted?'

'Can you find out more?'

'Not without taking ill-advised risks, no. I am only the director's assistant, and he is growing less and less fond of me. And yet I am convinced we are getting close to our goal. Galenite and bitumen must be delivered secretly to the craftsmen. If we knew where they are obtained, I could work out their exact nature and possible uses.'

Mehy dreamt of manufacturing new weapons, and Daktair had perhaps just found a decisive direction. It was time to get rid of the old priest of Amon who ran the workshop, put Daktair in his place, and get him involved in the expeditions.

Mehy was disenchanted.

The director of the workshop was a priest from Karnak, belonging to an extremely ancient body headed by the High Priest of Amon, appointed with the assent of the pharaoh and placed in charge of a fabulously wealthy domain. Neither the mayor of Thebes nor any other secular leader could demand his transfer.

Mehy did not give up, but gathered as much information as

possible about this inconvenient priest. He was seventy years old, married, the father of two daughters and had no material worries or any known vices. Trained in the temple school, he was an experienced and wise scholar whose opinions carried much influence.

That meant that one of Mehy's favourite weapons, calumny, was unlikely to work. No one would believe that the priest, with his intransigent morality and righteous career, kept mistresses or took bribes. He was too honest to attack that way.

Mehy considered another murder, but the priest led a very regular life and went to only three places: his home, the temple and the workshop. Killing him would not be easy, and a suspicious death would lead to a thorough inquiry.

The only thing left was to criticise his managerial abilities, by showing that his workshiop was in debt and cost the temple and the town too much money; but that argument might rebound on to the future director, whose funding would be restricted.

Mehy was despairing of finding a solution when luck smiled at him in several ways. First, the old priest died a natural death; next, the Karnak priesthood, preoccupied with internal problems, did not put forward a successor; finally, Mehy and Daktair had time to falsify his file, so that the dead man warmly recommended his assistant as his successor.

Judged competent and perfectly integrated into Theban society, Daktair obtained the post he had coveted for so long. On Mehy's advice, he showed only discreet satisfaction and, when he appeared before the tjaty, stressed the difficulties of his task and his willingness to walk in the footsteps of his wise predecessor.

Carried away by success, Mehy contrived a master-stroke: the workshop's transfer to new premises close to the Temple of a Million Years, under the pretext of easing congestion in the Theban government and saving money.

In this way, Daktair would be working very close to the Place of Truth and under the theoretical control of Abry, Mehy's faithful ally. The proximity of his enemy, and the prospect of the treasures to be plundered, would stimulate the scholar's all-conquering ardour and his thirst for discovery.

Mehy knew that, to develop strong power, he needed the unconditional support of people with knowledge and special skills. In his irreversible process of conquest, he had just taken a decisive step forward.

# 66

Paneb paced round his house like a caged lion.

'You should sit down and eat,' urged Uabet. 'The flatcakes will go cold.'

'I'm not hungry.'

'Why are you tormenting yourself like this?'

'Ramses the Great has gone, so has the overseer, and I can't find the painter or the illustrators. And Nefer has disappeared again.'

'Of course he hasn't.'

Paneb shrugged. 'Maybe you know where he's hiding.'

'He isn't hiding. He has just been admitted into the House of Gold.'

Paneb's eyes opened wide in surprise. 'The House of Gold? What's that?'

'The most secret part of the village.'

'What happens there?'

'I don't know.'

'How did you find out that Nefer has been admitted?'

'You are forgetting that I'm a priestess of Hathor. She is a benevolent goddess who confides in those who are faithful to her.'

Paneb lifted Uabet off the ground as if she weighed no more than a feather and pressed his face against hers. 'Tell me everything you know.'

'I'm a good wife and I don't hide things from my husband.'

Bare-breasted, Uabet wore nothing but a coarse linen kilt, which she unfastened, letting it slide down her legs. Pressing against her husband, she offered him the warmth of her slender body. Paneb more or less promised himself to resist, but he had not realised she was so pretty.

When Uabet felt her husband's desire begin to swell, she wrapped her legs round his waist and savoured the intense pleasure of becoming truly his wife at last.

A loud banging on the door awakened Uabet. Still deep in the delights of the conjugal bed, she covered herself with a light cape and went to open the door.

Gau the Precise, Unesh the Jackal and Pai the Good Bread stood there. Their faces were closed and stern.

'We've come to fetch Paneb,' said Gau drily.

'What do you want with him?'

'Overseer's orders. Tell him to hurry up.'

Paneb was on his feet instantly. He had already forgotten the eyes of love and turned his gaze on the three men.

'Follow us,' said Gau, whose large, rather soft body ended in an austere, quite ugly face which was inappropriately decorated with an over-long nose.

'Where are we going?'

'You'll see.'

'What if I refuse?'

'Leave the Place of Truth. The gate is wide open for anyone who wants to go out. It's only difficult to get through when you want to come in.'

Paneb hoped for an encouraging look from Pai, but he was as stern as his companions.

'Very well, then, but I warn you: if need be, I know how to defend myself.'

Gau took the lead, followed by Paneb, who had Unesh and

Pai on either side of him. He walked at his own pace, with slow but regular strides, and headed for the meeting-place of the starboard crew.

On the threshold stood Didia the carpenter. 'What is your name?'

'Paneb the Ardent.'

'Do you wish to know the mysteries of the shipyard?'

'The shipyard' . . . Nefer had been there! So, it was another name for the brotherhood's meeting-place which Paneb already knew.

'I do.'

'The *ukher*, the shipyard, that we depict on the walls of certain houses of eternity,' said Didia, 'is in reality the workshop where we create carpenters, sculptors, draughtsmen and the works they themselves bring into the world. On our path, everything is about putting things together. The ship of this community is found in separate pieces in the shipyard, and it is up to the craftsmen of the Place of Truth to reassemble those scattered pieces and give them a coherent structure. Beware, Paneb: if you are an illogical person, this place holds only disillusionment for you. Do you wish to continue?'

'I do.'

Didia and the three artists took Paneb into the hall of purification, where Gau the Precise measured him with a rope.

'God created the world with numbers and according to proportions,' Gau said. 'Enter into this interplay of harmonic relationships.'

Pai the Good Bread made Paneb kneel down facing a cube-shaped stone on which he placed his hands, washed by purifying water poured from a jar in the shape of the ankh sign, 'life', which Unesh the Jackal was holding.

Paneb got to his feet. Pai poured ointment on to his hands then drew an eye on each palm.

'Through this ointment, your hands truly take up their

office; because of this eye, they can see.'

In a corner of the hall, a large rectangular sunken pool had been filled with water. Unesh the Jackal undressed Paneb and ordered him to immerse himself in it.

'Only the primeval water will free you from your bonds,' he said. 'May it purify you as it ceaselessly purifies the creative forces. May it enable you to see the original energy without which our hearts and hands would be lifeless.'

Paneb experienced strange sensations. It was only cool water, but it enveloped him like a protective garment and gave him an impression of lightness which was at once pleasant and worrying.

He was instructed to get out of the pool and, guided by the three draughtsmen, crossed the threshold of the meeting-hall.

Standing on either side of the door were Userhat the Lion, the head sculptor, and Ched the Saviour, the painter. Userhat wore a falcon mask to represent the god Horus, and held a feather in the manner of Ma'at. Ched wore an ibis mask to represent the god Thoth, and held an ankh.

Paneb knelt in a basin in the form of a basket, the hieroglyph that signified 'mastery', which had given him his name.

Neb the Accomplished emerged from the gloom and hung round Paneb's neck a pendant bearing a heart.

From the tip and base of the feather, the oval and the transverse bar of the looped cross, waves sprang forth, visible in the form of broken lines. When they touched Paneb's body, he felt a tremendous surge of power, but no pain. It was like a gentle, penetrating fire, like a ray of sunshine after a cold night.

The light illuminated the meeting-hall. Paneb saw that all the members of the crew, including Nefer, were present.

Neb sat down on his chair.

'Our brotherhood is a ship, and this one's task is to sail across the celestial waters and commune with the stars. You have been called into this ship and you have seen the light in its shrine. May the ability to travel be given to you. May you seize the bow-rope in the ship of night and the stern-rope in the ship of day. May you be given light in the heavens, creative power on earth and a just voice in the kingdom of the other world.'

As Paneb looked on attentively, Nefer the Silent, Casa the Rope and Didia the Generous slowly assembled the parts of a model of a wooden boat equipped with a cabin in the form of a shrine.

'Engrave this mystery in your spirit, Paneb. Further along your path, you may perhaps understand its significance.'

High on Ardent's right shoulder, Gau the Precise drew a vase symbolising the heart's conscience, Unesh the Jackal drew the 'power' sceptre, and Pai the Good Bread drew the offertory bread, meaning 'to give'.

'In my capacity as overseer and head of the crew,' declared Neb, 'I know the secret of the divine words. Here is acquired the mastery of the magical incantations which enable the craftsmen of the Place of Truth to excel in their art, to know how to use the correct proportions, and render in sculpture and painting the gait of a man, the grace of a woman, the flight of a bird, the leap of a lion, the expressions of fear or joy. In order for you to attain these things in your turn, Paneb, you must work ceaselessly, learn to make pigments which melt without fire burning them, and which neither dissolve in water nor decay in the air. These are craft secrets which have never been revealed to any outsider. Do you swear to safeguard them, whatever may happen?'

'On the life of Pharaoh and that of the brotherhood, I take my oath.'

'Ched the Saviour and the artists of the starboard crew have agreed to teach you. From this day, you shall belong to their clan and you will carry out the tasks they entrust to you.'

# 67

After Paneb's initiation at the shipyard and the banquet that followed, Gau would have liked to take a nap. He often felt tired, especially after festivities, and the wise woman had already saved him twice from congestion of the liver, whose vessels were blocked.

But Paneb knocked on the workshop door first thing the next morning, determined not to lose a minute, and Pai, woken by his calls, had been obliged to go and find Gau.

'I'm ready,' said Paneb. 'Where do I start?'

'Our secrets are only passed on within our clan of artists. If your behaviour is unworthy, or if you turn out not to have sufficient aptitude, we will expel you, and the decision will be final. Before you arrived among us, several young men failed, for our work is very arduous. It demands knowledge of hieroglyphs, the words of the gods, of the art of the Line and the lore of Thoth. If you were thinking of doing exactly as you please, leave this workshop right now.'

'Show me the materials I'll use.'

As if Paneb's request was a great inconvenience, Gau slowly opened a rectangular basket, out of which he took a scribe's palette, mortars, pestles, brushes of different types and a knife.

'This palette is yours now. Don't lend it to anyone. In the round or square hollows, you will place the pigments you need.'

'How are they prepared?'

'We shall see that much later. For the moment, you will make do with blocks of colour we'll give you. You will dilute them using the water-pot and break them down with the pestles and mortars. Let's try that now.'

Gau was sure Paneb would ruin several blocks before getting satisfactory results. But Paneb did not rush; he checked the amount of water in the pot, felt the cake of red colour to check that it was indeed crumbly, diluted it with just the right amount of water and handled the pestle with the correct amount of force.

Gau was careful not to show his surprise, and he carried on talking in the same icy voice.

'You will provide yourself with shards or shells to prepare the tints or mix them, and you will apply your colours uniformly, with no shadows. Brushes are not easy to handle, and most apprentices lose heart.'

The variety on offer stunned Paneb. There were very fine reeds whose tips had been stripped and split, other thicker ones, a large brush made from palm-fibres folded and bound into place, one made from palm-ribs crushed at one end and with the fibres separated to form quite long hairs, one which was very elongated and narrow, another wider one, spatulas . . . With so many different diameters and points, it ought to be possible to draw the whole universe and its secrets!

This time, it wasn't a dream. Paneb had before him the tools he had hoped for and he handled them one after the other, lovingly and with respect. He experienced a happiness whose intensity he had already imagined, and which brought him close to tears.

Gau's rasping voice jolted him out of his ecstatic reverie. 'Pick up your materials and follow Pai the Good Bread. He'll take you to your first workplace.'

Still in a state of shock, Paneb followed the artist, who was only half-awake.

'I had a bit too much of Pharaoh's beer,' admitted Pai.

'Where are we going?'

'Your first efforts are bound to be poor, and Gau hates seeing a well-prepared surface ruined, so he's chosen a training-ground which will penalise no one but yourself: your own house.'

It was with some pride that Paneb laid out his different brushes on a low table, in the living-room in his house, watched anxiously by Uabet.

'Is it really necessary to dream up goodness knows what designs?' she asked. 'This austerity suits me, and—'

Paneb cut her short. 'I'm learning my trade.'

'Which colours do you want?' asked Pai.

'Red, yellow and green. I'm going to apply them in long horizontal stripes, one on top of the other.'

'Are you sure your wall has been well prepared?'

'Of course it has – I did it myself. I filled the holes with clay, which I made waterproof by mixing it with cut straw, then I covered it with chalk-based plaster.'

Pai seemed sceptical. 'As this is only a house, your mistake isn't serious, but it would be in a temple or a house of eternity.'

'What mistake?'

'Your surface is dead.'

'Dead? What do you mean?'

'It's too smooth, so it's lifeless. Every wall must be slightly undulated to illustrate and register the vibrations which pass constantly through space. Absolute symmetry and rigidity are other forms of death which your hand must overcome.'

Paneb contemplated the wall, seeing it in a completely new light. He suspected that he had a thousand things to learn, but his initiation at the shipyard had truly opened the gates to another world where everything had meaning.

He prepared his colours and, instinctively, drew broad bands across the base of the wall with a confident precision that amazed Pai, though he was careful not to betray his surprise. The young artist had chosen the correct brush, and his horizontal line was almost perfectly straight. Even Uabet was fascinated and she watched her husband working, using the tip of the fibres to take the exact quantity of paint necessary and bring forth a song from a wall which had been inert. Then he used a different brush to finish a green stripe and stopped when a third of the surface had been decorated.

'Any more,' he judged, 'and it would be overloaded. What do you think, Pai?'

'There is a special method for drawing stripes.'

'Why haven't you taught it to me?'

'I wanted to be sure you could take it in.'

'And can I?'

'Maybe. But you'll have to practise.'

Paneb realised his path would be littered with traps and illusions, but he cared little and would continue marching straight ahead. He'd been given tools, so he was no longer weaponless; with such allies, he feared no one.

'Do you want to try a few geometric shapes?' suggested Pai.

'Show me.'

Pai climbed on to a sturdy three-legged stool and, with a very fine brush, sketched a clump of reeds at the top of the wall. 'This sign ensures the magical protection of the wall, but it needs to be done in a band along the top of the wall, and that isn't easy to do.'

Paneb immediately tried to copy the example, and his attempt was not unskilful. There were a few imperfections in the tracing of the curves, which Pai corrected without a word. Paneb watched him and did not repeat his mistakes.

'What designs are suitable for a house?' he asked.

'Flowers and line-patterns,' said Pai, 'which evoke the

quiet joy of a home and the good orderliness of daily life.'

A thousand shapes jostled in Paneb's mind. He had already traced them in the sand or on fragments of limestone, but they had not really come to life.

'Will you do me a favour, Pai?'

The artist seemed reticent. 'That depends.'

'Could my wife stay at your house until tomorrow morning? I must try to decorate this house and I need to be alone.'

'But it will take you several weeks!'

'I'd like to prepare a plan for the whole project and then ask your advice.'

'As you wish. Very well, then: until tomorrow.'

Uabet was not happy about being sent out of her own home, even for a brief period and even though she was warmly welcomed by Pai's wife. As soon as the sun rose, she was determined to go back home.

When Uabet and Pai entered the house, they were dazzled.

Paneb had painted the band of protective reeds along the top of all the walls with surprising precision and regularity, but he had not stopped there. Each room had been given an enchanting decorative scheme, made up of rosettes, stylised lotus flowers, bunches of grapes, vine leaves, yellow persea flowers, red-brown poppies, diamonds and patterns of squares in contrasting colours.

Uabet closed her eyes, afraid she was seeing things. When she reopened them, the wonders were still there.

'I have the most beautiful house in the village,' she said. 'But where's Paneb?' She ran to the bedroom and threw herself on top of her husband, who had just lain down after his night's work. 'It's splendid, darling, splendid! Thanks to you, we're going to live in a real palace!'

Dumbstruck, Pai searched in vain for something major to criticise. Before he had even had access to the secret knowledge of the artists and painters, Paneb had created a masterpiece. He had an instinctive feel for proportions and colours. If fate or vanity did not wither his talent away, Paneb the Ardent would be one of the most dazzling servants of the Place of Truth.

# 68

Since becoming director of the central workshop, Daktair had his beard smoothed and perfumed every morning. As promised, he had announced to the team of researchers that he would continue the very traditional research pursued by his deceased predecessor, who had wisely fixed the limits of knowledge. He, the mere foreigner who was henceforth to be recognised as a dignitary, had decided to allow himself a breathing-space in which to enjoy his official residence, his servants and the respect that was at last accorded him.

This sweet comfort had almost lulled him to sleep, but his restless intellect had gained the upper hand once more, and he had renewed his interest in galenite and bitumen, which were not referred to in the files at his disposal.

There was, however, one precious piece of information: about once every two years, an expedition set off to obtain these materials for delivery to the Place of Truth. As director, Daktair would be responsible for organising it. Another six months' patience, at least, before the next one . . . Despite his exasperation, he must not depart from his usual routine. Soon, he would uncover one of the secrets of the brotherhood.

The close proximity of the village had allowed him to engage the 'outsider' whom he supplied with washing-powder as his personal laundryman.

This particular evening, his informant wore a satisfied

smile. 'I think I have something new. The village receives its letters from an official messenger, Uputy, and they hand him their letters to people in the outside world. Uputy is conscientious but sometimes he cannot keep his mouth shut, and he loves to talk. He's an observant fellow, and he's noticed that one of the craftsmen has written a lot of letters recently.'

'Who were they to?'

'Uputy cannot reveal secrets like that. But I also know that this craftsman has gone to the west bank on each of his rest days in the last two months. That's rather unusual. Perhaps he's simply visiting a customer, but it doesn't usually happen like that, it's just a question of order and delivery.'

'Of course, you know the name of this craftsman?'

'I have that good fortune.'

'How much?' asked Daktair drily.

'The washing-powder won't be enough. I need bars of copper.'

'You're becoming very expensive, my friend.'

'Information like this has its price.'

'The other lay workers probably know all this, too.'

'No, I'm the only one. Uputy greatly regretted letting slip this name, and he won't do it again. If you want to know it, pay me.'

Daktair pulled a face. 'Two ingots.'

'Four.'

'Three.'

'Four. This may be the biggest piece of luck I ever get, and I'm not throwing it away.'

'Three tomorrow, then a fourth in a week's time if the information proves useful.'

'In that case, three then two.'

'Done.'

The laundryman gave Daktair the name and description of the craftsman, a man who belonged to the starboard crew.

*

Mehy and Serketa were hosting a reception in honour of the mayor, who had been confirmed in his office by the tjaty, and Daktair had to wait until the end to pass on the information he had just obtained. At once, Mehy sensed that he had been handed an extremely interesting lead. He might not be able to obtain direct information about the craftsmen's secret activities, but perhaps he could acquire something even better: a spy in the Place of Truth.

'How am I to proceed with the laundryman?' asked Daktair.

'Tell him the copper will be given to him tomorrow evening, one hour after sunset, in the palm-grove to the north of Thebes, close to the abandoned well.'

'Where are we going to get it?'

'Don't worry, I'll take care of everything. If the guards question you about him, tell them he came to you for a job and you considered his rates reasonable. That was your only conversation, and you don't know any more about him.'

'And the craftsman . . . ?'

'I'll see to him, too. The less you're involved, the better. Concern yourself with the practical details of the expedition to obtain galenite and bitumen.'

The laundryman's legs trembled at the thought of becoming rich. True, he was breaking the oaths he had taken when he was engaged as a lay worker, but how could he pass up an opportunity like this? Once he'd made his fortune, he would leave a trade he despised. He would buy a farm in Middle Egypt, where the land was easier to work than in Thebes, and live out his days in peace.

Daktair had found the information useful, and had agreed to obtain the five copper bars without further ado. The laundryman regretted not asking for more. As soon as he had his due, he would vanish, never to return to Thebes.

'At the foot of the tallest palm tree, opposite the abandoned well,' Daktair had said, 'you will find the ingots in a sack, buried in a shallow pit.'

The laundryman checked that this part of the palm-grove was deserted. No one ever came to this spot at night, and no prying eyes would see him digging up his booty. Daktair had not lied. The sack was indeed at the foot of a majestic palm tree, and it took little effort to uncover it.

He was just about to untie the cord that bound it when a stern voice froze his blood.

'You there! Stand up, with your back to the palm tree, and don't try anything foolish. You are surrounded by guards.'

In panic, the laundryman clutched his treasure to his chest and made a dash for freedom.

'Stop!'

His only chance was to run very quickly and escape from his pursuers. But he ran straight into a guard who was brandishing a cudgel. The laundryman tried to knock him out with the sack, but the guard smashed his skull at the very moment when an arrow buried itself in his neck. His dead body fell to the ground.

The dozen or so guards who had laid the ambush gathered round the corpse. Their leader examined it. 'That's odd,' he said. 'We were told this man was a dangerous, well-armed thief.'

'What's in the sack?'

The leader opened it and emptied the contents on to the ground. 'Stones. Nothing but stones.'

'In the right hands, a sack as heavy as that one is a formidable weapon. We did the right thing in defending ourselves.'

Without appearing to attach the least importance to the news, Mehy learnt that a miscreant had been killed in the palm-grove. The guards had challenged him perfectly legally, but the man was so aggressive that they had had to kill him in self-defence.

The inquiry identified the dead man as one of the laundrymen who worked for the Place of Truth. His colleagues did not like him much, and no one spoke of him in glowing terms. He was even suspected of petty thefts, and the other laundrymen stressed his arrogance and aggressive nature.

Sobek confirmed their testimony. Since the affair had ended both tragically and conclusively, there was nothing to do but consign it to the files.

Mehy was no longer surprised by the good luck that served him so consistently. It was because he did the right thing at the right time that all his efforts were crowned with success and strengthened his position. He had been sure the laundryman would react like an imbecile and sign his own death warrant. Now that the man was out of the way, Daktair was safe from suspicion, and Mehy could exploit the information in perfect peace.

All the same, he must still not make any foolish mistakes: this time he could not use the guards. So he went to his wife, Serketa.

'I'm going to describe a man to you,' he told her, 'and you must try to pick him out when he disembarks from the ferry from the west bank. Then you must follow him and note where he goes.'

'But there are many ferries every day!' she protested.

'Watch just the early-morning ones.'

'I hate getting up early, darling.'

'Surely you won't refuse to do me this small service?'

'And what if this dreary chore goes on for months?'

'It's important, my dove, and I can't trust anyone else to do it.'

'What will you give me?'

'Do you want some new jewellery?'

'I wouldn't say no – I'm beginning to get tired of the old pieces. I've heard there's a goldsmith in Memphis who creates wonderful necklets of turquoises, but unfortunately he is overwhelmed with work.'

'Don't worry. For you, he won't be.'

On the eighteenth day of her watch, Serketa spotted the craftsman; he had taken the second ferry of the morning. She had no difficulty following him, and she saw him enter a warehouse where furniture of differing qualities was stacked up. Pleased with herself, Serketa stroked a finger across her throat, which would soon be decorated with a truly wondrous necklet of turquoises.

# 69

When Paneb entered the workshop of the Line, near the starboard crew's meeting-hall, he was surprised to find Nefer and Gau there. They were studying a papyrus entitled 'A sample calculation to probe reality and to find out that which is obscure'. It was covered with mathematical signs the young man had never seen before.

'Does this papyrus concern me?' he asked.

'The architect of worlds arranged the elements of life according to proportion and measurement,' replied Gau, 'and our world can be considered an interplay of numbers. Consider these as sources of energy and your thinking will never cease to progress. In our tradition, geometric thought governs mathematical expression. It is founded on the One which develops, multiplies and comes back to itself. The art of the Line is to reveal the presence of unity in all living forms.'

'Your own body exists because it is a collection of proportions,' commented Nefer, 'and you will need this knowledge to make your hand intelligent. But do not practise geometry for geometry's sake, or mathematics for the sake of mathematics; those who have been sidetracked in this way have been caught in the trap of sterile knowledge.'

'Draw a triangle,' ordered Gau.

Paneb picked up a very fine brush and did so.

'This is one of the simplest ways of representing the sun's light in an abstract way,' said his teacher, 'and we shall place your apprenticeship to the Line under its protection. The ancients say it allows a man to perceive the secrets of the sky, earth and waters, to understand the language of birds and fish, and to take on any form he desires.'

'Then let's get to work!'

Nefer saw that his friend had an unquenchable thirst for learning and that he had done the right thing in offering to help Gau, who was not strong enough to teach for hours on end.

Paneb swiftly carried out the four basic operations, discovered powers and roots, solved equations without difficulty and without ever being diverted from a practical application, such as the manufacture of a pair of sandals or the sail for a boat. In this way he became aware that none of the works produced by the craftsmen of the Place of Truth left any room for chance.

Whether it was a matter of division, multiplication or finding roots, Ardent was invited to relate them back to the first process of addition. In the decimal system, he used unitary fractions, with a numerator equal to the unit with the exception of ⅔, and he succeeded with the aid of tables given to him to check the results of his exercises.

'The hieroglyph of the mouth symbolises the original fraction,' said Gau, 'for all forms and shapes came forth from the mouth of our protector, Ptah, who created the world by the Word. Now, draw a circle.'

Paneb's hand was rock-steady.

'This is how to calculate the surface area of this circle: from its diameter, take away one ninth; square the rest and you will then determine the surface area,* which is vital in

*Egypt knew the number π. By comparing the circle to the square, whose sides would therefore represent eight-ninths of its diameter, π has a value of 3.16.

order to work out, for example, the volume of a cylindrical wheat store. All this will be useful to you when you are confronted with a wall, for you will have to organise the space in accordance with the laws of harmony.'

Nefer unrolled another papyrus, which left Paneb dumbstruck with astonishment. On it was drawn a grid of squares in red ink, containing the figure of a standing man, drawn in black. Each part of his body corresponded to a precise number of squares.

'This representation,' said Nefer, 'is founded on the basis of eighteen unities: six squares from the sole of the foot to the knees, nine to the buttocks, twelve to the elbows, fourteen and a half to the armpits, sixteen to the neck, eighteen to the hair. In this way the harmony of the human body is deciphered, in this way you can draw it without betraying it. But this is only an example, not a fixed system; the master craftsman has the ability to adopt other grids, which reveal other interplays of proportions.'

Paneb and Nefer sat side by side, beneath the sky's starry vault.

'I didn't know that it would be so extraordinary,' said Paneb. 'Or rather I did – my instinct always knew it, and I was right to listen to it. Why did I waste so much time?'

'Set your mind at ease,' said Nefer. 'You didn't waste a single second. The trials prepared you to live moments like that one intensely and to learn with your usual lightning speed. But this is only a beginning. As soon as possible, you'll go to study the pyramids. That will be a new stage on your path.'

'Will you come with me?'

'If the overseer authorises it.'

'You've been admitted to the House of Gold, haven't you?'

Nefer hesitated.

'Uabet told me,' said Paneb.

'She told the truth.'

'I know you're sworn to silence, but at least tell me if you've seen that light again, the one that passes through matter.'

'It exists, Paneb. You'll discover it too, if you become expert in your chosen discipline.'

'When a door opens in this village, there are another ten behind it – but I like that. Have you been into Ramses' house of eternity?'

'The Valley of the Kings won't disappoint you.'

'Will I work there, too?' asked Paneb.

'That is the destiny of an artist from the Place of Truth.'

'I'm ready.'

'No, not yet. You haven't pacified the eye.'

'I don't understand.'

'The universe is a gigantic eye, whose parts are dispersed by our own eyes. That eye guides our hands and inspires our work. We have a duty to reconstitute it, but before we do so we must pacify it so that it does not move away from us.'

Paneb still did not understand, but he sensed that his friend had just opened a new door for him. As he gazed up at the starry sky, he felt the presence of the complete eye which, one day, he would know how to reassemble through drawing.

Tran-Bel enjoyed eating and drinking. He was a stocky man, with black hair plastered to his round skull, a broad chest, and fingers and toes as plump as a new-born baby's. Libyan by birth, he had failed to make his fortune in his native land and had set himself up in Thebes, where luck had smiled on him. He was a trader through and through, lacking any moral code; his only love was acquiring more and yet more wealth, even if his methods were sometimes dubious. Cautious and cunning, Tran-Bel had not aroused the authorities' suspicions and even enjoyed a good reputation.

'Someone is asking for you, sir,' one of his workers informed him.

'I'm busy.'

'But you should go and see – he looks important.'

Another pathetic salesman, thought Tran-Bel. He'd get rid of the intruder with a few well-chosen words.

He got a big surprise. The man standing on the threshold of the warehouse looked very much like him: not a double, but with enough features in common to suggest he might be a brother.

'What have you to offer me, friend?' asked the trader.

'Are you Tran-Bel?'

'I'm in charge here, and I'm very busy.'

'Let's talk somewhere quiet.'

'Are you presuming to give me orders?'

'I'm sure I can do so in my capacity as treasurer of Thebes and commander of its armed forces.'

Tran-Bel swallowed hard. Like many, he had heard stories about this Mehy, whom people described as a ruthless administrator whom it was not a good idea to cross. But why would such a senior official be interested in him?

'Come this way,' he said. 'I have a quiet corner where I keep my records.'

Tran-Bel sensed that the wind had just changed direction. What mistake had he made to unleash an appearance by this formidable character?

The small room was dark, stuffed full of tablets covered in writing, and well away from the bustle of the workshop.

'I suppose you want to see my accounts,' said Tran-Bel.

'The fact that you're a petty crook who steals from his customers and cheats on his taxes does not interest me, but the fact that you make illegal use of the services of a craftsman from the Place of Truth is a serious offence, which carries a heavy penalty.'

Terrified, Tran-Bel did not even think of denying it. 'I

didn't realise . . . We met in the market. He criticised one of my stools and said it wasn't solid enough, we chatted, he offered to make me some much better ones, on condition that we shared the profits. Ever since, he's been coming here and producing very fine pieces.'

'And you sell them for very high prices, without declaring them to the government.'

'A simple slip of memory, which I promise to make good.'

'Oh no you won't,' said Mehy.

Tran-Bel could not believe his ears.

'It was probably you who made dishonest propositions to this craftsman, but only the result matters. I'll overlook your illegal trade on condition that you tell me about your accomplice's comings and goings, the nature of the work he does for you, and the amount of his secret earnings.'

'I am at your service,' said the Libyan, more relaxed now. 'Would you also like . . . a small commission on my profits?'

Mehy's icy stare filled him with terror.

'When I take,' said Mehy, 'I take everything. Try not to forget that and make sure that the information you give me is absolutely accurate. Also, you will keep absolute silence about our pact. One false move, and you will be killed.'

# 70

Uabet the Pure yielded not one cubit of ground to her sworn enemy, dust. Each day she cleaned the house from top to bottom, not missing a single nook or cranny; and she fumigated the whole house once a week. Like every good housewife, the young woman knew that strict cleanliness was the basis of good health. To that, she added an acute sense of tidiness; Paneb thought it excessive, but he had given up protesting.

So he was surprised, when he came back from the workshop of the Line, where he had been improving his geometry, to discover that a chair was not in its usual place and that one of his wife's dresses lay discarded on a stool. It looked as though something extremely urgent had thrown Uabet into turmoil.

'Are you there?' he called.

'In the bedroom,' replied a thin voice.

Paneb found his wife lying on her back, a cushion under her head.

'Are you ill?'

'Did you know that channels run from the heart to all the organs? Ubekhet told me when I went to consult her. In the heart the vital seeds are formed, including the sperm; and she also taught me that procreation is the meeting of two hearts.'

'Are you trying to tell me that . . . ?'

'Yes, I'm expecting your child, Paneb. Turquoise uses potions to prevent pregnancy. I don't.'

Paneb was thunderstruck. This was one trial he had not foreseen.

'Don't worry,' Uabet went on. 'I'll take care of it just as well as I take care of the house. Don't you want to know if it'll look like you?'

Paneb smiled and took his wife's hands gently between his own. 'I must admit I am a bit curious. But you're going to have to rest.'

'When the tiredness becomes too much, I'll ask one or two priestesses of Hathor for help. We're colleagues, we're used to helping each other.'

Uabet had feared Paneb would be angry, but the future father seemed in a state of shock. She would soon find ways to cure him of that slight sickness.

Mehy detested Egyptian law. In almost all other countries, he could easily have cast off a wife who bore nothing but girls; in the land of the pharaohs, it was impossible. Moreover, despite his little judicial schemes, which teetered on the extreme limits of legality, he had not managed to strip Serketa of her fortune. As Mehy could not bear to be deprived of the smallest part of what he had acquired, he would have to support his wife until her death. A divorce would mean financial disaster, but, on the other hand, her sudden death would look suspicious and would both attract annoying irritations and harm his reputation.

Moreover, Serketa was a party to weighty secrets and, in a moment of madness, she might have the annoying idea of talking. So Mehy was left with only one solution: he must turn her into the ideal accomplice.

After giving her the expensive necklace she had been dreaming of, he invited her to take a long, romantic sail on the Nile. Pastries and fruit juices were served to them by a little

Nubian serving-girl, who was delighted to have been taken on by such powerful people.

'It's a long time since you took such care of me,' Serketa said.

'Do you like the necklace?'

'It's not bad. What have you got in mind?'

'That we work together.'

'As equals?'

'I am a man, you are a woman: I shall lead. But I need a very active associate.'

Serketa's face showed her interest. At last she would escape from the boredom that was beginning to suffocate her. And her charming husband would never know the danger from which he had just escaped. After fearing him, Serketa had decided to rid herself of him. While she was looking for the best way to do it, he had offered her an alliance which promised to be exciting.

'Why not,' she said, 'as long as you keep nothing from me.'

'That goes without saying, my darling.'

'Let's begin with the evening when you went out to consult a file.'

'What was strange about that?'

'You came back without it.'

'You're very observant,' said Mehy.

'Where did you go that evening?'

'Do you really want to know everything?'

'Everything.'

'Be careful, my dove. You'll be not only my ally but my accomplice, and I won't tolerate the least indiscretion.'

At the thought of leading a dangerous life, Serketa felt deliciously excited. 'I accept the rules of the game.'

Mehy talked for a long time and omitted not a single detail. He saw wonder and desire sparkling in his wife's eyes.

'At first we must act in secret,' she decided, 'but

afterwards our success will be dazzling. Do you think you can really trust this Daktair?'

'He is spineless, deceitful, competent, greedy for wealth and power – useful qualities. Abry seems less dependable, but he's only a stopgap. Are you ready to carry out your first mission?'

Serketa flung her arms round Mehy's neck. 'Tell me quickly!'

'I warn you, it's very important.'

'All the better. I won't disappoint you.'

Mehy explained to Serketa what he expected of her, then they withdrew into the boat's central cabin, where he possessed her with his usual violence.

After the morning rituals, Ubekhet assisted the wise woman as she received the villagers and treated their bodies and minds. Ubekhet had learnt to listen to the patients, to calm the weeping children, to drive away worries and to give back hope to those who lacked it.

Endowed with a powerful magnetic force, the wise woman laid her hands on pain and made it go away. Ubekhet made sure that the hospital was well supplied with remedies, most of which she made herself, the rest being provided by the Health secretariat, to which the pharaohs had always attached great importance.

The wise woman spoke little but, each day, she allowed Ubekhet to make progress by passing on her experience and dwelling more on her failures than her successes, so that Ubekhet would draw lessons for the future.

Since he had been admitted to the House of Gold, Nefer had been working uninterruptedly at his task, and he was even more silent than usual. Ubekhet sensed every vibration of his soul, and contented herself with a look of solidarity to let him know that she was joining her strength to his own.

The day had been exhausting. No serious illnesses to take

care of, but an uninterrupted series of little problems and a heavier than usual daily routine. Ubekhet was in a hurry to go home and sleep.

'Come with me,' commanded the wise woman.

Ubekhet called up her last reserves of energy to follow her guide, who left the village and took the path up to the summit, as the sun was setting. This was the time when the snakes and scorpions came out of their hiding-places, but the two women did not fear them.

Each time she climbed the winding mountain paths, the wise woman seemed to rediscover her lost youth. Despite her tiredness, Ubekhet had less difficulty than usual in following her. Her beautiful white hair shone like a sun and lit up the ever-steeper slope, which led to a shrine hollowed out of the rock.

From this promontory, they could look down over the land belonging to the Place of Truth, the secret valleys where the pharaohs and their wives were reborn and the temples where their *ka*s lived for all eternity.

The wise woman faced the shrine and raised her hands in prayer. 'Men are the tears of God,' she said, 'and only the gods are born of his smile. Yet men are well provided for, the flock of God, for he created the sky and the earth for their hearts, and breath for their nostrils. For them, who are made in his image, he also created all foods. But they rebelled against him and preferred disorder to harmony. When the human race is snuffed out, the tumult will end and silence will come once more upon this land. And you, its goddess, will recreate the beauty of the first time.'

Out of the shrine came an enormous royal cobra, its head proudly erect. Its eyes were red and fire seemed to dart from them.

'Worship Meretseger, She who Loves Silence, goddess of the peak and protector of the Place of Truth,' the wise woman told Ubekhet. 'When I have returned to the West, may she become your guide and your eyes.'

# 71

What Nefer had seen in the House of Gold, he must translate into words. He had experienced the most secret ritual of the Place of Truth and discovered the essential mysteries which he was duty bound to pass on, but was he truly worthy?

To determine this, the brotherhood demanded that he must create a work which would show both his skill and the extent of his sensitivity. No recommendations had been made to him, no criteria imposed. It was up to Nefer to weigh up the years he had spent in the village, to draw from them the most important teachings and to fashion an object which would meet with the approval of the overseers and other high-ranking initiates.

In accordance with his usual custom, he had spent a great deal of time thinking. Several projects jostled for position in his head, but it was his heart which had chosen. After obtaining Ubekhet's positive opinion, he went to Neb the Accomplished, who, that very evening, took him to the Temple of Hathor built by the pharaoh Seti.

Nefer climbed the staircase leading to the entrance gateway, crossed the threshold, walked through an open-air courtyard then followed a paved path which led to a second courtyard. There, he was purified, and meditated before an offering-table.

Then he was taken to a covered hall with a flat ceiling held up by two columns, and a paved floor. Along the walls were stone benches on which the judges sat. At the far end of the hall was a door flanked by stelae showing the pharaoh before Hathor; it led to the shrine where the divinity shone out in secrecy.

Nefer knew this court would not be indulgent and he feared its verdict. If he was wrong, he would destroy all he had achieved since his admission.

'What have the gods taught you?' demanded the overseer of the port crew.

'I have tried to perceive the shining light of Ra, the creation of Ptah and the love of Hathor.'

'What qualities are needed to bring a work to fruition?' asked the overseer of the starboard crew.

'An awareness of life in all its forms, generosity of heart, coherence of being, the capacity for mastery and the power to turn an idea into reality. But they have no value unless they lead to bliss and peace, and no craftsman has ever attained the limits of the art.'

'Show us your work.'

Nefer drew away the veil that covered a statuette made of gilded wood. It was a cubit high and represented Ma'at, seated and holding the sign of life.

Unesh the Jackal certainly deserved his name. His long, narrow face was reminiscent of his protector animal, and he moved with the suppleness and speed of the jackal, one of whose major tasks was to rid the desert of corpses. By nature reserved, perpetually on the alert, with an inquisitive eye, Unesh seemed the bearer of a violence which was difficult to contain.

Paneb did not like him very much and was not expecting anything good from him. So when he found him standing with arms folded before the closed door of the workshop of the Line, he prepared for trouble.

'Are you barring my way,' he asked.

'Do you think I couldn't do it?'

'I am one of your clan now. You must let me in.'

'Don't you want to know more about the secrets of the trade?'

Paneb looked at Unesh with interest and suspicion.

Unesh grinned. 'Some learn the trade in the workshops, but I prefer more dangerous places. Follow me – if you dare.'

Paneb did not hesitate. Although he did not run, Unesh moved with astonishing speed. He crossed the desert wastes, entered a wheatfield and plunged into a thicket of reeds, beside a water-channel.

'Flat on your belly,' he ordered.

As protection against the mosquitoes, Paneb covered himself in mud. Lying on the artist's right, he saw a water-snake pass by.

'Watch carefully,' advised Unesh.

Paneb looked admiringly at an ibis which was moving elegantly, as if executing a perfectly created dance.

'What do you see?'

'The regularity of its gait – its stride is always the same.'

'The stride of an ibis is equivalent to one cubit. The ibis, the incarnation of Thoth, reveals this fundamental measurement to us, and it is also written on the god's forearm. The name of the cubit, "*meh*", also means the important terms "think", "meditate", "finish", "be complete, filled", for knowledge of the cubit will allow you to perceive the rule of the universe. Now you can go back to the workshop.'

For Paneb the discovery of the cubit, which Thoth had used to measure the earth, was an unforgettable moment. He quickly grasped the fact that it was divided into seven palm leaves and twenty-eight fingers and, when the overseer gave him a little folding measuring-stick to use in his work, Paneb had the feeling that he had become the repository of a priceless treasure.

So, one of the essential secrets of the work was present in the body of the ibis which the young man had so often looked at without seeing it. He realised that the gods ceaselessly expressed themselves through nature and that he must open his eyes and ears wider to see and hear their message.

The artists' attitude had changed. Gau taught with a little less coldness, Pai willingly guided his new colleague's hand, Unesh stressed the interplay of colours. Guided by these three experienced craftsmen, Paneb easily assimilated the essential skills which his hasty nature would happily have rejected.

Every evening he cleaned the workshop, without being told to. Before going home, he drew chariots, dogs or a walking man on fragments of limestone, then broke his attempts into a thousand pieces. One day, he was convinced, his hand would know how to create figures without the slightest flaw.

One night, as he left the workshop he bumped into Sobek.

'You're becoming a true professional,' said the commander.

'Does that annoy you?'

'You're still just as aggressive as ever, my boy. That attitude will play bad tricks on you.'

'What does the head of security want with me?'

Paneb turned to face the Nubian. A confrontation seemed inevitable.

'We don't much like each other,' observed Sobek, 'but I'm sure you aren't a liar.'

'If you accuse me of lying, you'll regret it.'

'Then tell me the truth. Did you murder one of my men up in the mountains?'

'You've gone mad!'

'So you say you're innocent?'

'Of course I do!'

'I suspected you, but I'm inclined to believe you.'

'You dared suspect me? *Me?* I'm going to split your head open,' said Paneb hotly.

'You'd be arrested and put to death. Better just keep on working hard.'

It's not him, thought Sobek as he walked away. He didn't regret what he'd done. It had given him a clearer view of Paneb and brought him back to the lead he had tried to forget: the one involving Abry. If he tried to follow up that lead, he might see his career destroyed. But his conscience forbade him to act like a coward.

Nefer and Ubekhet remained entwined on the terrace of their house until the sun's burning heat became unbearable. After making love, they had fallen asleep in each other's arms, dreaming of that memorable evening when he had learnt from the mouth of the master craftsman himself that his statuette of Ma'at had been recognised as being 'of just voice' by the court of the Place of Truth. Because of the quality of the craftsmanship, it would enter the temple treasury.

As a master-sculptor in the House of Gold, Nefer would henceforth devote himself to fashioning statues which would serve as receptacles for the creative power spread throughout the universe. By bringing the stone to life, he would be applying the teachings he had received and would thus participate in transmitting the mysterious light which no matter could stop. He would begin by creating a statue of Ramose, seated as if writing, which would serve as a model to the schoolchildren who were learning hieroglyphs.

The wise woman was sitting in front of her house, in the full light of the sun. This unusual posture worried Ubekhet, who was afraid she might be ill. But the wise woman spoke to her in a calm voice.

'I shall not treat anyone today. Are you ready to replace me?'

'I'll do my best. Are you ill?'

'I must spend the day in the temple to try and appease Sekhmet, the implacable lion-goddess.'

'Is the village threatened by danger?'

'Yes, Ubekhet. Great danger.'

# 72

Nefer was troubled. '"Great danger" . . . The wise woman said nothing else?'

'No,' replied Ubekhet. 'And now she has gone to the temple.'

'She never speaks lightly. If she has invoked Sekhmet, the threat is extremely serious.'

'What do you think it is?'

'I can't imagine – I really can't imagine. The village is under Ramses' protection, and no one would dare contest his authority.'

Ubekhet had no suggestions to offer, but she knew the wise woman was a true seer. Her prediction should not be taken lightly, but how could you struggle against a danger when you did not know what it was?

Karo the Impatient knocked at the door. 'The overseer wants to see Nefer. It's very urgent.'

Several members of the starboard crew had gathered in front of Neb's house. When Nefer entered, the wise woman was emerging from the master-craftsman's bedroom.

'He has only a few moments left,' she said. 'Hurry.'

The reality facing the crew hit Nefer full in the face: Neb was an elderly man, and old age had suddenly struck him down. His robust good health had seemed inexhaustible, but all his defences had given way at once, to the point of rendering him almost unrecognisable.

Neb was sitting in a chair whose legs were shaped like lion's paws. He wore a ceremonial robe which emphasised his dignity. His breath was short, his eyes filled with exhaustion.

'My years have passed by in the joy of the heart,' he told Nefer. 'I have not acted against the rule of our brotherhood and I have not strayed from the path of righteousness. You have become an accomplished sculptor, liked by all, but you must learn to lead. Seek out every opportunity to be effective so that your way of governing men is beyond reproach. Make others respect you because of your skills and calm speech; do not give orders except when circumstances demand it. Do not let a second-rate man take instructions or hand out tasks, for he will spoil the work and sow discord. Remember that great is he whose greatnesses are great, and venerable is he who surrounds himself with those who are noble of spirit. Your task will not be easy, but I die with a tranquil heart, for I know that no weight will be too heavy for your shoulders.'

Neb the Accomplished's head sank slowly forward, as though he were saluting his successor.

'I refuse,' Nefer told Kenhir. 'Neb the Accomplished was a master and an example to me, and I refuse to succeed him. My only goal is to serve the brotherhood and the starboard crew, not to lead it. Neb's trust touches the deepest part of me, but he overestimated my abilities.'

'It is not for you to judge yourself,' retorted Kenhir. 'And Neb, who had the strength of experience and clear-headedness, was only ratifying a decision taken by Ramose. It was the Scribe of Ma'at who recognised you as a future leader of the starboard crew and Master of the brotherhood. The Place of Truth passed on its knowledge to you, and you have seen the light in the House of Gold. If you wish to remain faithful to the word you gave, and to respect Ma'at, take up the office for which you are destined.'

Nefer searched for arguments which would persuade Kenhir to change his mind. But how could he oppose Ramose, who had been raised to the rank of Ancestor whose Spirit is Powerful and Filled with Light? There was, however, one last way out.

'Doesn't my appointment have to be approved unanimously by the starboard crew?'

'That is vital, indeed, for no one can lead without being loved and accepted by those he leads. They will be consulted this very day.'

Paneb loathed funeral rites. Turquoise always refused to make love, Uabet spent long hours at the temple with the priestesses of Hathor, work was interrupted, the workshops closed. And as it was the death of a crew-leader, the rites would be elaborate and the period of mourning interminable. He passed the time drawing caricatures of various people, so that he could continue to exercise his hand, which was beginning to assimilate the Line and its proportions.

To Paneb, Neb had remained a mysterious, distant man with whom he had had little contact; so he did not lavish hypocritical lamentations upon him. And yet he had felt a real respect for the dead craftsman, who, after heaping trials upon him, had opened the door and admitted him to the clan of artists.

Paneb was nibbling dried fish when Nefer entered his house, clearly in the grip of great anxiety.

'Sit down and have a drink,' said Paneb. 'You look as though you need one.'

'I consider you my friend, and I hope the feeling is mutual.'

'Tell me what's worrying you, and I'll sort it out within the hour.'

'You've already saved my life once,' said Nefer. 'Would you be willing to do it again?'

'By all the demons in the desert, what's happened?'

Nefer sat down on a mat. 'Ramose, Neb and Kenhir have chosen me as the new Master of the brotherhood.'

A broad smile lit up Paneb's face. 'It was bound to happen and it won't surprise anyone. It's splendid news! Look, with your natural rigour and your taste for perfect work, we won't have fun every day. But, on reflection, that's not what we're here for. Get up and let me embrace you!'

'You must vote against me,' said Nefer.

'What are you talking about?'

'I don't want to take on this office. The last hurdle to cross is unanimous approval by the members of the crew. If you really are my friend—'

'I'll vote for you not once but ten times over! And if anyone makes the mistake of opposing your appointment, there'll be a brief but heated discussion. You were born to live in the Place of Truth, Nefer; it has given you everything, and now you're going to show your gratitude by running it.'

In different words, Ubekhet said the same thing as Paneb. She added that Ramose had consulted the wise woman, whose vision was the same as his.

Nefer found no comfort, not even from his wife. He hoped that the oldest members of the starboard crew would speak against him, criticise his inexperience or his character, and start a debate which would force Kenhir to put forward another name.

But no one contested the appointment of Nefer the Silent as Neb the Accomplished's successor; on the contrary, they all rejoiced at it. The new Master had risen through all the ranks of the brotherhood without ever boasting of his advancement; he showed no penchant for authoritarianism, and had all the qualities necessary to get the work done.

In less than an hour the initiation ceremony would take place, and Nefer had no chance of escaping it, unless he fled and left the village for ever.

Ubekhet laid her head tenderly on her husband's shoulder. 'Insane ideas sometimes pass through our minds, but they're only mirages. Some struggles are in vain; they aren't worth the waste of energy. Take up the real fight you must wage, the preservation and passing on of our treasures.'

'All I wanted was to live in peace with you, in this village.'

'One day, you heard the call and you answered it. Did you think it would never come again? You are asked no longer simply to be yourself, but to carry out an office in the service of others and in the spirit of the brotherhood. That is how it is, and it should not be any other way.'

At the end of the mourning period, during which Neb was judged righteous in the eyes of earth and heaven, Nefer was raised to the high office of leader of the starboard crew of the Place of Truth, in the secrecy of the temple dedicated to Ma'at and Hathor.

At the age of thirty-six, he must become successor to the master craftsmen who had created houses of eternity for illustrious pharaohs in the Valley of the Kings, and conceived many other masterpieces which they created through the brotherhood's many talents.

When he appeared on the threshold of the temple, Nefer the Silent was acclaimed three times by all the villagers.

Moved to tears, he saw the full extent of his responsibilities and longed for the magical time of his apprenticeship, when it had always been possible to ask for help from a better-qualified craftsman. From now on, he would be the one whom people would consult, and it would be up to him to issue directions, and avoid mistakes which might have serious consequences.

Kenhir, Scribe of the Tomb, handed Nefer the golden cubit which passed from one crew-leader to the next. Each of its twenty-eight divisions contained the name of a divinity and that of the province which he or she protected, and the hieroglyphic inscription read: 'Cubit which can be used to become a being of light, powerful, of just voice, marked with the seal of life and of stability.' In accordance with the word of Ra, the all-creating Light, the Master's cubit embodied the universal rule to which it must conform.

Ubekhet was the first to embrace the new overseer, and he held her very close for a long time.

# 73

When the craftsman from the Place of Truth arrived at Tran-Bel's warehouse, he thought life was being rather good to him. In the village, he had received an exceptional education and acquired knowledge which would now enable him to sell his talent to the highest bidder. Since he had met the merchant, he had started to fulfil his secret dream: to become rich. And it was his right to use his free time as he wished.

During the period of mourning after Neb's death, he had remained in the village and he had written to Tran-Bel to arrange a meeting. Tran-Bel had to wait impatiently for new luxury objects destined for a clientele made up of connoisseurs and good payers.

'I have come to see your master,' said the craftsman to a workman.

'He's in his office.'

The craftsman crossed the warehouse and reached the isolated, quiet room where Tran-Bel kept his files. He pushed open the door and froze as he came face-to-face with a woman arrayed in a heavy black wig and thick eye make-up.

'Forgive me,' he said. 'I must have the wrong room.'

'You're in the right place,' said Serketa. 'I know who you are and why you're here. Close the door and let us talk.'

'I don't know you, I—'

'Your dealings with Tran-Bel are hardly honest. They

make you an accomplice in fraud, and you're liable to a heavy penalty and expulsion from the Place of Truth.'

The craftsman paled. 'You know that—'

'I know everything. Either you obey me, or your career is finished.'

The man shrank into a corner of the tiny room. Serketa slammed the door shut.

'What . . . what do you want?' he asked.

'I'll keep silent about your shady deals, which you can continue at your leisure, but on one condition: I want to know everything that happens in the village.'

'That's impossible. I'm sworn to secrecy.'

'Then so much the worse for you. First thing tomorrow, you will be denounced to the tjaty.'

'Don't do that, I beg of you!'

'If you want to avoid serious trouble, you have only one solution: talk.'

To obey this evil woman would mean betraying the brotherhood's rule, breaking an oath and losing his soul . . .

'Who are you?' he asked.

Serketa's smile was ferocious. 'It is not for you to ask questions, but nevertheless I'll answer, to show you that you have no choice. I'm the wife of an important man whose influence is growing all the time, and who will be sure to reward those who help him during his rise to power.'

For the craftsman, this detail was of no little importance. It was he, not Nefer, who should have been appointed head of the crew. By serving a master with extensive powers, he could obtain at once wealth and the post he coveted.

'Will you give me time to think?'

'No. I require your answer here and now.'

The craftsman had served Ma'at, the Place of Truth and the brotherhood for very little reward. This might be an opportunity to serve his own cause at last, by hedging all his bets.

*

Mehy was practising with his bow in the garden of his luxurious home. He fired arrow after arrow into the trunk of a palm tree, but did not manage to quell his anxiety.

Why was Serketa taking so long? Perhaps the craftsman had not kept his appointment with Tran-Bel. Worse still, perhaps Serketa had failed and dared not appear before her husband for fear of being beaten.

Mehy fired another arrow and missed his target. In rage, he trampled the bow underfoot.

'That bow wasn't worthy of you,' purred a honey-sweet voice. 'You shall buy a better one.'

'Serketa! What happened?'

She knelt to embrace her lord and master's legs. 'A total success.'

'He agreed to collaborate?'

'We're very lucky. He is an embittered man, greedy, sly and hypocritical. We could not have found ourselves a better ally. Are you pleased with me?'

Mehy pulled Serketa roughly to her feet, tore off her wig and placed his hands on her cheeks. 'You and I, my pet, are going to win great victories. How many craftsmen are there in that accursed village?'

'About thirty. The conditions of admission are very rigorous, and they must respect the rule of Ma'at.'

She outlined the main aspects of it, which the craftsman had divulged.

'Of no interest,' opined Mehy. 'Old principles which will soon fall out of use. Who heads the brotherhood?'

'The supreme leader is Pharaoh, who watches over the village's prosperity and ensures its safety.'

'I know, I know. But Ramses doesn't live in the village.'

'Three people share the power: the Scribe of the Tomb and the overseers of the starboard and port crews. The craftsmen liken their brotherhood to a ship, hence their division into port and starboard. The Scribe of the Tomb, Kenhir, is the representative of central power and is in charge of running the village; he is much less popular than his predecessor, Ramose, because he has a difficult, sour nature.'

'How old is he?'

'Sixty-two.'

'So he's nearing the end of his career. He'll soon be dead or replaced. Is he corruptible?'

'According to our informant, probably. But it is not certain that Kenhir knows all the secrets of the Place of Truth.'

'But the leaders of the crews must know them.'

'Yes, because they have been admitted to the House of Gold.'

Mehy's excitement was growing apace. 'What happens there?'

'Our informant doesn't know.'

'He's lying!'

'I don't think so,' said Serketa, taking a step back in case Mehy felt like slapping her. 'Seniority isn't sufficient reason to be admitted, and he hasn't yet found a way to force open the door to this mysterious place. But we mustn't lose hope.'

'What did he say about the crew-leaders?'

'Kaha, the leader of the port crew, is an old man, very austere, a specialist in excavating rock and cutting stone. He never leaves the Place of Truth and seems beyond reach. The leader of the starboard crew, Neb the Accomplished, has just died, and has been replaced by Nefer the Silent, a young, inexperienced man.'

'Why was he chosen?'

'Ramose chose him, and the senior members of the brotherhood approved the decision.'

'An old man's whim,' said Mehy scornfully. 'What does our informant think of this Nefer?'

'He's a good sculptor, a craftsman much taken with spirituality, very attached to the Place of Truth, where he was brought up. But he'll have the greatest difficulties in his new office. He'll have no idea how to lead or give orders, and he'll no doubt be demoted again.'

'Disappointment might make him less devoted, fill him with a thirst for revenge. Did you get an accurate list of the craftsmen?'

'Here it is.'

Serketa proudly displayed a scrap of papyrus. She and her husband were now in possession of a state secret.

Mehy read it quickly, only pausing when he came to a particular name, as the others were unknown to him. 'Paneb the Ardent . . .'

'Our informant thinks Paneb will never be integrated into the brotherhood and will be expelled for indiscipline.'

'He too shall fall into our hands. Thanks to you, my love, we've taken a big step forward. And this is only your first mission.'

Serketa purred. Greed and the desire to do harm had completely banished her dissatisfaction with life.

# 74

Although it was nearly the end of the dry season and the start of the Nile flood, the heat was less intense than usual, and the skies had been stormy for more than a week. The wise woman had suspended her consultations, leaving Ubekhet with the responsibility of replacing her.

In agreement with the Scribe of the Tomb, Nefer had given several rest days to the craftsmen, who had joyfully celebrated his appointment. The period of festivities was coming to an end, and he was preparing to embark on restoring the oldest tombs in the village when one day, just after dawn, Nakht the Powerful arrived with a message.

'A messenger from the tjaty is at the main gate. He demands to see someone in authority as soon as possible.'

Kenhir was still asleep and Kaha was ill. Anxiously, Nefer hurried on his way. Nakht opened the gate. Outside it stood the messenger, held back by the gatekeeper.

'Are you the Master?'

'I lead the starboard crew.'

'Here is a message which you are to give to the villagers: "The falcon has flown away to heaven. Another is raised up in his place, on the throne of Divine Light."'

The man leapt on to his horse and galloped away.

Nefer paled. Suddenly, he felt ill.

'What is it?' asked Nakht.

'Wake the villagers, from the youngest to the oldest, help the sick to get up and walk. Gather them all in the temple forecourt.'

Nefer went to find his wife, who was preparing to go out. 'The wise woman was right,' he said. 'Our protector has just died, and we are in great danger.'

In a few minutes, the little community was gathered together. His eyes swollen with sleep, Kenhir was ready to take stern measures if he had been woken up for nothing.

Nefer waved his hand and silence fell. 'After a reign of sixty-seven years,' he announced in a voice cracking with emotion, 'Ramses has left this earth to return to the sun from which he came.'

The villagers were astounded and bewildered. Ramses could not die. He had lived so long that death had forgotten him; it could not take him away from the love of an entire people who would feel abandoned and lost without him.

Kenhir drew Nefer aside. 'During the seventy-day mummification period, you and the artists will work in Ramses' house of eternity, so that you may progress to the final stages of the work. These shall be carried out in accordance with the monarch's wishes, contained in a sealed papyrus which I shall give you and which you alone may read.'

'Won't Kaha be accompanying me?'

'His health doesn't permit it, so you will have to take on his duties as well as your own. You are Master of the brotherhood, Nefer; since you know the secret of the House of Gold, you can transform a tomb into a house of resurrection.'

Nefer had never imagined that he would be burdened with such a responsibility, the heaviest that could weigh upon a craftsman's shoulders. Such was the terrifying anguish which twisted his belly and tightened his throat. It was he, and he alone, who must position the final stone of the structure destined to make Ramses the Great immortal.

*

The majority of the senior Theban dignitaries had assembled at the home of Mehy, who had invited them to share a light meal while they awaited the latest official news from the capital, Pi-Ramses.

At last, he appeared. 'Our new pharaoh is Meneptah, "Beloved of Ptah",' he announced. 'He has ascended the throne of the living and has been recognised and acclaimed as Lord of the Two Lands. He will officiate as priest at the funeral rites for Ramses, after which he will assume supreme power.'

'Long life to our new pharaoh!' cried Abry, and the others followed suit.

Given that Meneptah is sixty-five years old, thought Mehy, his reign will be a short one.

Mehy had gathered as much information as possible about him. He was said to be authoritarian and demanding, with a difficult manner, intransigent on the spiritual principles on which Egypt was built, hostile to innovation, solitary by nature, indifferent to the blandishments of courtiers. In short, exactly the opposite of the sort of ruler Mehy had hoped for.

But this portrait was of someone who had lived in the shadow of Ramses. The exercise of power would change him, and chinks would appear in his armour. The most annoying thing was his devotion to Ptah, the god of builders and of the Place of Truth. Would Meneptah continue Ramses' policy with regard to the village? If he did, the struggle promised to be lively. But Mehy felt stronger than ever, for he had powerful allies and a spy in the enemy camp. Moreover, Meneptah was far from being as popular as Ramses. It might not be impossible to foment a plot against him.

After a reign as long and intense as that of Ramses, Egypt would undergo a form of depression, and Meneptah would not have the necessary vigour to remedy it. Weighed down by cares of state, obliged to parry blows from all directions, the new sovereign would spend most of his time at Pi-Ramses, in the Delta, far from the Place of Truth, which he would more or less gradually abandon to its fate. And why should the pharaoh not place his trust in the Theban authorities, unaware that they were under Mehy's control?

Ramses had built his capital in the north, the better to defend Egypt against invaders. Mehy was convinced that his conquest of the country must begin by seizing Thebes and obtaining the well-guarded secrets of the Place of Truth. The craftsmen were not expecting to find themselves up against a powerful, determined enemy, and they were not even ready to fight.

Mehy's moment was approaching.

'I'm not sure that this is such a good decision,' said Ched the Saviour with contained irritation. 'To work swiftly and effectively in Ramses' house of eternity, we need experienced illustrators, and Paneb is hardly one of them.'

'According to his teachers,' objected Nefer, 'he's ready to assist them.'

'I don't want to insult you, but you mustn't let your friendship with him cloud your mind.'

Nefer's face took on an expression so stern that the painter scarcely recognised him.

'My role as overseer forbids me any personal bias, and none of my decisions will be taken in the light of friendship or animosity. If I believed Paneb wasn't competent, I'd keep him away from this site. And it is my opinion that no one among us can take his position for granted.'

Ched smiled enigmatically. 'Contrary to what some believed, you do seem to have a leader's temperament – all the better for the brotherhood. Since you command me, I shall obey. Paneb will assist us.'

'Tell him so. We shall leave for the Valley of the Kings this very evening, with the necessary equipment.'

'I'll see that we have everything we need.' Ched walked off, in his usual haughty way.

Suddenly, Nefer realised that he no longer saw the painter in the same way. And this change applied not only to Ched but to all the other craftsmen. Yesterday, he had been their colleague; today, he must direct their work and show that he could resolve the thousand and one problems which were certain to arise.

The villagers were in a state of great anxiety, for they had just learnt that Meneptah was the new pharaoh. Some thought that he would have no less of an iron grip than Ramses, others that he would necessarily adopt a different policy, and there were some who thought an economic crisis and social disturbances were inevitable. But Nefer had restored calm by announcing that for the brotherhood nothing had changed, and that, as was the custom, it would prepare the sovereign's last dwelling for the funeral ceremonies.

But he did not know what would happen in the alarming period between the death and burial of Ramses and the new king's assumption of power. It was up to Nefer to overcome his fears and ensure that the vital task entrusted to him was brought to a conclusion, whilst at the same time reassuring the village.

Before leaving for the Valley of the Kings, Nefer went to see the wise woman.

'The death of Ramses leaves us bereft,' he said, 'but I shall try to maintain our unity.'

'The danger has not disappeared. Quite the contrary.'

'People are going to try and attack us, perhaps even destroy us, aren't they?'

'You, too, are beginning to see things clearly, Nefer. Demons are on the prowl, and you will need much courage and sound judgement to overcome them. Never forget that the only way the Place of Truth can survive is by following one single path: the path of the Light.'